E. H. Carr: A Critica

Also by Michael Cox

FAREWELL TO ARMS? From Long War to Long Peace in Northern Ireland
(*editor, with Adrian Guelke and Fiona Stephen*)

SUPERPOWERS AT THE CROSSROADS: US–Soviet Relations after the Cold War

THE EIGHTY YEARS' CRISIS: International Relations, 1919–1999
(*with Tim Dunne and Ken Booth*)

THE IDEAS OF LEON TROTSKY (*with Hillel Ticktin*)

THE INTERREGNUM: Controversies in World Politics, 1989–1999
(*with Ken Booth and Tim Dunne*)

AMERICAN DEMOCRACY PROMOTION IN THE TWENTIETH CENTURY
(*with John Ikenberry and Takashi Inoguchi*)

US FOREIGN POLICY AFTER THE COLD WAR: Superpower without a Mission?

E.H. CARR: THE TWENTY YEARS CRISIS (*editor*)

E. H. Carr

A Critical Appraisal

Edited by

Michael Cox
Professor of International Relations
London School of Economics and Political Science

Foreword by John Carr

First published in hardback 2000

First published in paperback 2004 by
PALGRAVE MACMILLAN
Houndmills, Basingstoke, Hampshire RG21 6XS and
175 Fifth Avenue, New York, N. Y. 10010
Companies and representatives throughout the world

PALGRAVE MACMILLAN is the global academic imprint of the Palgrave
Macmillan division of St. Martin's Press, LLC and of Palgrave Macmillan Ltd.
Macmillan® is a registered trademark in the United States, United Kingdom
and other countries. Palgrave is a registered trademark in the European
Union and other countries.

ISBN 0–333–72066–0 hardback
ISBN 1–4039–3904–7 paperback

This book is printed on paper suitable for recycling and made from fully
managed and sustained forest sources.

A catalogue record for this book is available from the British Library.

Library of Congress Cataloging-in-Publication Data
E.H. Carr : a critical appraisal / edited by Michael Cox ; foreword by John Carr.
    p. cm.
    Includes bibliographical references and index.
    ISBN 0–333–72066–0
    ISBN 1–4039–3904–7 (pbk)
    1. Carr, Edward Hallett, 1892–1982. 2. Historians—Great Britain—
—Biography. 3. History—Philosophy. 4. World politics—20th century.
5. Nationalism—Europe—History—20th century. I. Cox, Michael, 1947–

D15.C375 E3 2000
941'.007'202—dc21

                                                        00–055677

10   9   8   7   6   5   4   3   2   1
13 12 11 10 09 08 07 06 05 04

Printed and bound in Great Britain by
Antony Rowe Ltd, Chippenham and Eastbourne

Contents

Acknowledgements   vii

Foreword   ix
John Carr

Notes on the Contributors   x

An Autobiography   xiii
E.H. Carr

Introduction: E.H. Carr – a Critical Appraisal   1
Michael Cox

I   Life and Times

1. E.H. Carr's Search for Meaning, 1892–1982   21
   Jonathan Haslam

2. E.H. Carr – the Aberystwyth Years, 1936–47   36
   Brian Porter

3. 'An Active Danger': E.H. Carr at *The Times*,
   1940–46   68
   Charles Jones

II   The Russian Question

4. Carr's Changing Views of the Soviet Union   91
   R.W. Davies

5. The Soviet Carr   109
   Stephen White

6. E.H. Carr and Isaac Deutscher: A Very
   'Special Relationship'   125
   Michael Cox

7. E.H. Carr, the Cold War and the Soviet Union   145
   Hillel Ticktin

III   International Relations

8. Carr and his Early Critics: Responses to
   The Twenty Years' Crisis, 1939–46   165
   Peter Wilson

9. E.H. Carr and the Quest for Moral
   Revolution in International Relations   198
   Paul Rich

10. Theories as Weapons: E.H. Carr and International
    Relations   217
    Tim Dunne

11. E.H. Carr, Nationalism and the Future of the
    Sovereign State   234
    Andrew Linklater

12. Reason and Romance: the Place of Revolution
    in the Works of E.H. Carr   258
    Fred Halliday

IV   What is History?

13. The Lessons of *What is History?*   283
    Anders Stephanson

14. An English Myth? Rethinking the Contemporary
    Value of E.H. Carr's *What is History?*   304
    Keith Jenkins

15. E.H. Carr and the Historical Mode of Thought   322
    Randall Germain

Appendices

1. *E.H. Carr: Chronology of His Life and Work, 1892–1982*   339

2. *Papers of E.H. Carr, 1892–1982*   344

Index   347

Acknowledgements

This volume began life as an international conference on E.H. Carr held in July 1997 at the University of Wales conference centre at Gregynog – the splendid house and grounds bequeathed to that fine federal institution by Lord David Davies of Llandinam, a Liberal to his core, and not surprisingly one of Carr's sworn enemies when Carr held the Woodrow Wilson Chair at Aberystwyth between 1936 and 1947. The first people I have to thank therefore are those who helped support the conference – especially Professor Steve Smith and Guto Thomas, Professor Brean Hammond – who opened it – those who spoke at it, and those who also sang on what turned out to be a splendid occasion, notably Charles Jones, who apart from his musical talents, happens to be the author of a very distinguished study of Carr's views on international relations. Many thanks are also extended to the librarians and archivists in the University of Birmingham (where the Carr papers are held) and at the International Institute of Social History in Amsterdam where the Deutscher papers are housed. In particular, I would like to extend a word of gratitude to Phillippa Bassett, Mieke Ijzermans and Marcel van der Linden. Carr's collaborator, Bob Davies, Professor Emeritus at the University of Birmingham, was extremely helpful in sorting out some of the bibliographical questions, and he was especially generous in allowing me to look at his wonderfully revealing correspondence with Carr. The many letters not only tell us much about Carr, but a good deal about his warm relations with Bob. Tim Farmiloe, former Publishing Director, of Macmillan, also deserves a mention. For years he was Carr's publisher at Macmillan, and no doubt because of this encouraged me in this project; and what Tim began was then skilfully steered home to port by Aruna Vasudevan, Peter Dent, Ruth Willats and Maike Bohn. I should also like to thank Justin Rosenberg of the Isaac and Tamara Deutscher Committee; it was he who suggested that I give the 1999 Isaac Deutscher Memorial lecture, some part of the research for which can be found in my chapter and introduction. Ken Booth, the first named E.H. Carr Professor in a British university, has to be mentioned too for rescuing the name of Carr from the realists in international relations. Jonathan Haslam deserves all our gratitude as well for having written such a fine biography of Carr. To a large degree we all stand on his shoulders when it comes to Carr. Finally, a very personal vote of thanks: first to Carr's children, John Carr and Rachel Kelly, for being so encouraging and helpful; to Caroline Soper – the editor of *International Affairs* – for publishing my 'think piece' on Carr in the July 1999 issue of the journal; to Christiane Seitz for helping me pull the original manuscript into shape; and to my wife Fiona and four children, Annaliese, Ben, Dan and Nell for always being there. To them I dedicate this work in love and deep appreciation.

Professor Michael Cox
University of Wales,
Aberystwyth

Foreword

John Carr

It is most gratifying that so many years after my father's death in 1982 his ideas are still being so widely studied – and used for discussion and debate.

In this book Professor Michael Cox has brought together a number of eminent authors in the various fields in which my father promoted learning, and often another point of view for thought. This study does not digress into the nooks and crannies of his personal family life, as these are irrelevant to the subject of history and the study of international relations.

The lengths to which a few opponents have gone to vilify the name of E.H. Carr are quite extraordinary. The stories are often so exaggerated and wild as to be untrue, and in no way address those arguments with which they happen to disagree.

Personally, I have happy memories of our family life when my father would choose to sit in the main sitting-room with us around following our own pursuits, while he wrote his profound thoughts on pieces of paper accumulated around his chair. As a man dedicated to his work he had little time to help with the normal family problems dealt with by most fathers. Nor was he able to respond to changes affecting the women in his life, and was thus bewildered when this resulted in the acrimonious breakdown of his relationships.

However, the dedication in 1999 of the E.H. Carr Chair in the Department of International Politics in the University of Wales, Aberystwyth will, I hope, stimulate further study and understanding of the future way forward in the world.

Notes on the Contributors

Michael Cox is Professor in the Department of International Politics in the University of Wales, Aberystwyth. His most recent books include *US Foreign Policy after the Cold War* (1995), (with Hillel Ticktin) *The Ideas of Leon Trotsky* (1996), *Rethinking the Soviet Collapse* (1998) and (with Tim Dunne and Ken Booth) *The Eighty Years Crisis* (1998) and *Controversies in World Politics, 1989–1999* (1999). He is editor of the *Review of International Studies* and has been a Research Associate at Chatham House since 1994.

R.W. Davies is Professor Emeritus at the University of Birmingham and formerly Director of the Centre for Russian and East European Studies at Birmingham. The author of many books on the history of the Soviet economy, he worked closely with E.H. Carr and co-authored with him *Foundations of a Planned Economy, 1926–1929* first published by Macmillan in 1969. His latest book published by Macmillan in 1997 is *Soviet History in the Yeltsin Era*.

Tim Dunne is Senior Lecturer in the Department of International Politics in the University of Wales, Aberystwyth. An associate editor of the *Review of International Studies* since 1997, he is the author of *Inventing International Society: A History of the English School* (Macmillan, 1998) and with Nick Wheeler, editor of *Human Rights in Global Politics* (1998).

Randall Germain was Senior Lecturer in Politics at the University of Newcastle before joining the Department of International Politics in Aberystwyth. He is author of the *International Organization of Credit* (1997) and editor of *Globalization and its Critics* (Macmillan, 2000).

Fred Halliday is Professor of International Relations at the London School of Economics. The author of over ten books on world politics including *The Making of the Second Cold War* (1983) and *Islam and the Myth of Confrontation* (1996), his most recent study is *Revolution and World Politics* published by Macmillan in 1999.

Jonathan Haslam is Fellow and Director of Studies in History at Corpus Christi College, Cambridge. The author of a three-volume study on the history of Soviet foreign policy in the 1930s including *The Soviet Union and the Threat from the East, 1933–1941*, he was a student of Carr and in 1999 published the biography, *The Vices of Integrity: E.H. Carr, 1892–1982*.

Keith Jenkins teaches at the Chichester Institute of Higher Education and is author of *Rethinking History* (1991) and *On 'What is History?' From Carr and Elton to Rorty and White* (1995).

Charles Jones is Assistant Director of the Centre of International Studies at the University of Cambridge and the author of *International Business in the Nineteenth Century* (1987), (with Barry Buzan and Richard Little) *The Logic of Anarchy* (1993) and *E.H. Carr and International Relations: the Duty to Lie* (1998).

Andrew Linklater was appointed Woodrow Wilson Professor in the Department of International Politics at Aberystwyth in 1999. The author of many studies on international relations, his most recent books include *Beyond Realism and Marxism* (1991), (editor with John Macmillan) *Boundaries in Question* (1995), (editor with Scott Burchill) *Theories of International Relations* (1996) and *The Transformation of Political Community* (1998).

Brian Porter joined the Department of International Politics in the University of Wales, Aberystwyth in 1965. The author of several volumes on international relations, he is the editor of the acclaimed *The Aberystwyth Papers: International Politics, 1919–1969* published in 1972.

Paul Rich has taught at the University of Warwick and Luton and is the author of nearly a dozen books on world politics, including studies on the history of international relations, Southern Africa, Europe and Islam.

Anders Stephanson is a regular contributor to *Diplomatic History*, Assistant Professor at Columbia University, and author of *Kennan and the Art of Foreign Policy* (1986) and *Manifest Destiny* (1995).

Hillel Ticktin was born in South Africa and lived in the USSR before taking up an appointment in the Institute of Soviet and East European Studies in Glasgow in 1965. A founding editor of the journal *Critique* in

1973, he is the author of many studies on the nature of capitalism, South Africa and the former Soviet Union. His most important and influential book is *Origins of the Crisis in the USSR: Essays on the Political Economy of a Disintegrating System* (1992).

Stephen White is Professor of Politics at the University of Glasgow and formerly President of the British Association for Slavonic and East European Studies. The author and editor of nearly twenty books on Soviet and post-Soviet politics, his most recent work includes *After Gorbachev* (1994), *Russia Goes Dry: Alcohol, State and Society* (1995), *How Russia Votes* (1997) and (with Evan Mawdsley) *The Soviet Political Elite from Lenin to Gorbachev* (2000).

Peter Wilson is lecturer in the Department of International Relations at the London School of Economics. He is the editor (with David Long) of *Thinkers of the Twenty Years' Crisis: Inter-War Idealism Reassessed* (1995).

An Autobiography*

E.H. Carr

'Security' is the first word which occurs to me if I look back on my youth – security not only in family relations, but in a sense scarcely imaginable since 1914.

My father was a member of a small family firm. His part of the business was never very prosperous, he was not ambitious and was less wealthy than most of his brothers. But it never for a moment occurred to any of us that we should not have plenty to satisfy our fairly modest needs. The world was solid and stable. Prices did not change. Incomes, if they changed, went up – thanks to prudent management.

The world at large was like that. It was a good place and was getting better. This country was leading it in the right direction. There were, no doubt, abuses, but they were being, or would be, dealt with. Changes were needed, but change was automatically change for the better. Decadence was a puzzling and paradoxical concept.

Perhaps my personal sense of security was helped by the fact that I was a clever boy at school. Invariably I came out top of the class, and never doubted my ability to do so in any subject except science, which any-how played no significant part in the curriculum. I had a first-rate narrow classical education, but I was encouraged also to read pretty thoroughly the classics of English literature. For a year or more (aged 16–17) I also became an omnivorous reader of current popular novels, whose names are now quite forgotten.

I did not worry about my future. I knew I didn't want to go into 'business'; I wasn't specially attracted to any of the professions. Top classical scholars went into the top ranks of the civil service. That was probably – in so far as I thought at all – my destination. But I certainly never thought of the Foreign Office. My world was wholly insular, and uninterested in foreign countries. As a boy, I was once taken on a holiday trip to Boulogne.

Boys who always come out top of the class aren't very popular with their schoolmates. This may have been one of the causes of a certain sense of 'isolation' – a second word which, with some reservations,

---

* Carr wrote this on request for Tamara Deutscher, in 1980. It appears here with the permission of the Carr family.

comes into the pictures of my youth. I think I have never lost the sense of not fitting easily into my environment. But my first experience as a dissident came quite naturally. My father had voted Conservative in 1895 and 1900. But he was an impassioned free-trader: his logical exposition of the merits of free trade and demolition of the fallacies of the 'tariff reformers' was my first insight into the processes of rational argument. He went over to the Liberals, and was triumphant over the 1906 election – my first political memory.

More surprisingly he stuck firmly with the Liberals throughout the Lloyd George period – social and budgetary reform, attack on the House of Lords, etc. I followed him with enthusiasm. But at least 95 per cent of my schoolfellows came from orthodox Conservative homes and re-garded Lloyd George as an incarnation of the devil. We Liberals were a tiny despised minority. One of us was the son of a Liberal MP which was some excuse. The rest of us were just freaks. This must have con-tributed to my feeling of myself as an odd man out.

At Cambridge I wasn't much interested in politics. The period of the great controversies was over. I had a friend who was reading philosophy. We discussed the meaning of life, and I first heard the name of Hegel, on whose behalf McTaggart was conducting a popular rear-guard action against Russell and Moore. But this was dwarfed by another influence. I encountered the most powerful intellectual machine I've ever seen in action, A.E. Housman, whose effortless handling of obscure classical texts I enormously admired and should have liked to emulate. Nothing of this has remained with me (the context was too limited) except perhaps a rather pedantic addiction to the minutiae of accuracy and precision. But I should like to think that I had learned something of his flair for cutting through a load of nonsense and getting straight to the point.

At this time I had no interest in history. English history as taught at school was contemptible, and nobody took it seriously. At Cambridge I studied Greek and Roman history; and a rather undistinguished classics don, who specialized in the Persian Wars, taught me that Herodotus' account of them not only contained a lot of pure mythology, but was shaped and moulded by his attitude to the Peloponnesian War, which was going on at the time he wrote. This was a fascinating revelation, and gave me my first understanding of what history was about. Probably the war also quickened my interest in history. Clearly changes were hap-pening in the world which would pass into history. The impact of the First World War in this country seems, in retrospect, paradoxical. The lives of millions of people were disrupted, often with the loss of near relatives. Yet few people thought of it as the end of an epoch, the death of a civilization. It was like an unpredictable natural calamity – a tornado or an earthquake. Once it was over and the damage had been repaired, life would go on as before. Perhaps we had even learnt something from it, such as the wickedness and futility of war.

But it was the Russian revolution which decisively gave me a sense of history which I have never lost, and which turned me – long, long afterwards – into a historian. There was a lot of chance about this. I worked in the F.O. in the Contraband (i.e. Blockade) Department; and one of the subjects I handled – of course, as a junior – was the transit of goods to Russia via Sweden under guarantee that they would not get diverted to Germany. At the moment of the revolution, a Russian trade delegation was visiting London, accompanied by a commercial attaché to the British Embassy in Petrograd, Peters, with whom I had several talks in the first few days of the revolution. Peters like everyone else, believed that this was all a flash in the pan, and that the Bolsheviks could not last for more than a week or so – till reinforcements arrived. From the first, owing to some *esprit de contradiction*, I refused to believe this. I studied eagerly every bit of news, and the longer the Bolsheviks held out, the more convinced I became that they had come to stay. It was a lucky hunch. I'm not sure how far I saw this at the time as a challenge to western society. But I certainly regarded the western reaction to it as narrow, blind and stupid. I had some vague impression of the revolutionary views of Lenin and Trotsky, but knew nothing of Marxism: I'd probably never heard of Marx.

A few weeks later the F.O. set up a new three-man section to deal with the Russian problem and sent me as the junior to it; the other two were regular F.O. officials. Then I was appointed to the British delegation to the Paris peace conference. But the F.O. people in Paris remained still very much on the fringe (Lloyd George had no use for them), and nothing that I did or wrote had any importance at all. I warmly approved Lloyd George's resistance to Churchill's schemes, and was disappointed when he gave way (in part) on the Russian question in order to buy French consent to concessions to Germany on Upper Silesia, Danzig and reparations. I remember spending a weekend writing a memorandum on the inadvisability of recognizing Kolchak, only to learn on the Monday that the Big Four had decided to offer him recognition on certain conditions. Fortunately he havered over the conditions, and the Bolsheviks defeated him before the plan got any further. I also remember that I came out in favour of recognizing the then small Baltic states, and was indignant when some War Office General argued that this would be futile, since 'sooner or later either Russia or Germany will gobble them up'. My Liberal principles were still intact. Also, like many members of the British delegation (not only the Liberals), I was outraged by French intransigence and by our unfairness to the Germans, whom we cheated over the 'Fourteen Points' and subjected to every petty humiliation – the mood in which Keynes wrote his famous book. This became important later.

From the end of the peace conference till I went to Riga in 1925 I was not concerned with the Russian revolution, and don't remember how much thought I gave to it. I do recall that during the Zinoviev letter affair of 1924, when I was working in the F.O., though not in the Russian department, I was again struck by the blind prejudice and smugness of the officials who dealt with it. I lived in Riga from January 1925 till the summer of 1929, a period of rising prosperity and optimism in most parts of the world. Our legation officially dealt only with three Baltic republics. But proximity made Russia the constant topic of interest. Riga was on the route for travellers in and out of Russia; I visited Moscow for the first time in 1927. More important, Riga was the headquarters of the British Intelligence in eastern Europe. I knew the two top people concerned. Both were British ex-residents in Russia, who had lost their fortunes in the revolution; their narrowness and bigotry far exceeded that of the comparatively sophisticated people in the F.O. We were, of course, never allowed to see their reports.

The years in Riga were probably the easiest and most carefree of my life. In Europe they were years of recovery, of increasing prosperity and stability, and of faith in the future. But Riga was an intellectual desert. A bunch of rather second-rate diplomats and a few local notabilities engaged in party-giving and party-going and cultivated the social conventions, spiced with occasional bits of émigré gossip about Russia. It was excessively boring. Opera was the prestigious form of public entertainment, and I have hated opera ever since. Probably the main significance for me of my stay in Riga was that, having light official duties and time to spare, I began to read a lot of Russian nineteenth-century literature. The authors who influenced me most deeply were (in that order) Dostoevsky and Herzen. Chance may have played some part in this: I picked up collected editions of both in the bookshops. I now perceived for the first time that the liberal moralistic ideology in which I had been brought up was not, as I had always assumed, an Absolute taken for granted by the modern world, but was sharply and convincingly attacked by very intelligent people living outside the charmed circle, who looked at the world through very different eyes. In other words, the first challenge to the bourgeois capitalist society came, so far as I was concerned, not from Marx or from the Bolsheviks, but from Russian nineteenth-century intellectuals, who were not in any strict sense revolutionaries at all. This left me in a very confused state of mind: I reacted more and more sharply against the western ideology, but still from a point somehow within it. (Perhaps I've never quite escaped from this dilemma.) This confusion is very apparent in my first book, the biography of Dostoevsky. Mirsky wrote a preface which puzzled a lot of people, and was omitted from the later paperback edition, but which I now perfectly understand.

My progress during the next few years was haphazard, but always towards more sweeping criticism of western liberalism. At Geneva I followed some of the debates about the economic crisis, which seemed to spell the bankruptcy of capitalism. In particular I was struck by the fact that everyone professed to believe that tariff barriers were a major cause or aggravation of the crisis, but that practically every country was busy erecting them. I happened to hear a speech by some minor delegate (Yugoslav, I think), which for the first time in my experience put the issue clearly and cogently. Free trade was the doctrine of economically powerful states which flourished without protection, but would be fatal to weak states. This came as a revelation to me (like the revelation at Cambridge of the relativism of historiography), and was doubly significant because of the part played by free trade in my intellectual upbringing. If free trade went, the whole liberal outlook went with it.

After exhausting Dostoevsky and Herzen (i.e. writing books about them), I became fascinated by Bakunin, probably as the figure embodying the most total rejection of western society. At this time the urge to write was extremely strong; and being in the F.O. I could not of course write on contemporary themes. I think this must have played some part in keeping my interest fixed on the nineteenth century. I now wanted very badly to write a biography of Bakunin. I even wrote a novel of which the theme was the impact of an outrageous and flamboyant character modelled on Bakunin on a conventional English group. The idea was good, but the execution feeble; it never saw the light, and some years later I destroyed it.

By this time I was familiar with the name of Marx and, in a general way, with his career. But my first close acquaintance with him came through my study of Bakunin's quarrel with him over the First International – not an epic in which showed Marx at his best. This had unfortunate results. Neither *Dostoevsky* nor *The Romantic Exiles* had been a publishing success; and when I sounded several publishers about a biography of Bakunin I drew a blank everywhere, and began to get rather desperate. Finally, I got an introduction to a man in Dents. He was more friendly than the rest, but agreed with them that nobody wanted a book about Bakunin. He did, however, want a biography of Marx (there was some publicity at the time about the approaching fiftieth anniversary of his death), and if I would write one, he would give me a contract and publish it. I succumbed to the temptation, not reflecting that I knew nothing about what was really important in Marx. I read the first volume of *Capital*, not understanding it all, the *18ᵗʰ Brumaire* and the *Gotha Programme*, a life of Lassalle and a lot of subsidiary material, and set to work. It was a foolish enterprise, and produced a foolish book: I have refused all offers to reprint it as a paperback.

From now on, however, I recognized Marx as the key figure in the revolt against bourgeois capitalist society, and began to read much more widely. A book which influenced me was Mannheim's quasi-Marxist *Ideology and Utopia*, which showed how the opinions of political and economic groups reflected this status and their interests. I think it would be fair to say that I've always been more interested in Marxism as a method of revealing the hidden springs of thought and action, and debunking the logical and moralistic façade generally erected round them, than in the Marxist analysis of the decline of capitalism. Capitalism was clearly on the way out, and the precise mechanism of its downfall did not seem to me all that interesting. In any case, Lenin was more up-to-date than Marx.

After my return from Riga, the Russian revolution, the starting point of all this turbulence, rather receded from my view. I listened to Litvinov at Geneva, admired his exposure of western hypocrisy about disarmament, deplored the campaign against 'Soviet dumping', and was thoroughly pro-Soviet (a dissident view at the time). I was also impressed by the notion of the Five-Year Plan, which seemed to me the answer to the anarchy of capitalism, so clearly demonstrated by the economic oasis. But I didn't follow at all closely what was happening in the USSR. From about the beginning of 1935, however, ignorance or concealment were no longer possible. The whole period of the purges was one of disillusionment and revulsion, the intensity of which was, I suppose, accounted for by my previous enthusiasm. I became very hostile to the USSR, and was never in the least attracted by the flood of recruits from the Left into the CPGB. There seemed to be no pigeonhole into which I could fit.

One result of my preoccupation with the Russian horrors was a neglect of what was going on in Germany. Fascism in Germany, like Fascism in Italy, was deplorable, but somehow incidental and peripheral. But another factor was at work here. I had not forgotten my sense of indignation in 1919 at some of the terms of the Versailles treaty. In the 1930s I was still primarily interested in foreign affairs; and the aspect of Hitler's policy which struck me most forcibly was his revolt against Versailles; this I think seemed to mask or excuse other things. I remember clearly that I refused to be indignant about Hitler's re-occupation of the Rhineland in 1936 (which coincided with my exit from the F.O.). This was a rectification of an old injustice, and the Western Powers had asked for what they got. I don't think it was till 1938, after the occupation of Austria, that I began to think of Hitler as a serious danger. No doubt I was very blind.

I visited Russia in 1937, and on my return wrote a pair of articles for *The Times* (my first appearance in its columns). Here I more or less turned a blind eye to the purges, and discussed its economic progress and problems – so far as I remember, in rather ambivalent terms. But about this time I began to take notice of rumours of secret contacts between Moscow and Berlin, and to find them plausible. It seemed to me folly for the British Government to pursue a line which antagonised both. As I became less inclined to appease Hitler, I became more inclined to appease Stalin. I remember seeing the guarantee of 1 April 1939, to Poland as the final recipe for disaster. We could not possibly implement it except in alliance with Russia and it was given in such a way as to preclude any such agreement. On the other hand, I did during these years a lot of reading and thinking on Marxist lines. The result was *The 20 Years Crisis*, which I first planned in 1936–37 and finished early in 1939 – not exactly a Marxist work, but strongly impregnated with Marxist ways of thinking, applied to international affairs.

The war came as a shock which numbed the thinking process. One became suddenly occupied with day-to-day problems. I was plunged into the Ministry of Information, and then into *The Times*, was content to follow the official line, and for a time stopped thinking at all. Nothing seemed to make sense. Then, like a lot of other people, I took refuge in utopian visions of a new world after the war; after all, it was on the basis of such visions that a lot of real constructive work was done, and Churchill lost sympathy by being openly impatient of them. I began to be a bit ashamed of the harsh 'realism' of *The 20 Years Crisis* and in 1940–41 wrote the highly utopian *Conditions of Peace* – a sort of liberal Utopia, mixed with a little socialism but very little Marxism. It was my most popular book to date, because it caught the current mood. But it was pretty feeble. *Nationalism and After*, which I wrote towards the end of the war, was better, but still had utopian elements.

But of course the event which influenced me – and most other people at the time – enormously, was the entry of Russia into the war. In *The Times* I very quickly began to plug the Russian alliance; and, when this was vindicated by Russian endurance and the Russian victory, it revived my initial faith in the Russian revolution as a great achievement and a historical turning-point. It was obvious that the Russia of the Second World War was a very different place from the Russia of the First – in terms of people as well as of material resources. Looking back on the 1930s, I came to feel that my preoccupation with the purges and brutalities of Stalinism had distorted my perspective. The black spots were real enough, but looking exclusively at them destroyed one's vision of what was really happening. (I think this explains the irritation I now sometimes feel about [Soviet] dissidents: exclusive concentration on them by the media and by western propaganda hopelessly distorts the perspective.) I became intensely interested in what the Russians had done, and how far this had any lessons for western society; and this tied up with my interest in the Marxist critique of capitalism and the bourgeoisie.

The first outcome of these ideas – apart from anonymous articles in *The Times* – was a set of lectures delivered in Oxford, early in 1946, just before the Fulton speech unleased the Cold War, and published with the title *The Soviet Impact on the Western World*. It was hastily written, one-sided (it didn't profess to be anything else), and contained some exaggerations. But it made a lot of valid points.

It was at this time that I formed the plan of studying and writing as detailed a history as I could, not so much of the revolution itself, as of its achievements and results. I looked at the available sources, and concluded that they were good and plentiful enough down to 1929, though not beyond. I learned an enormous amount while I worked. The earlier volumes are thin in comparison with the later ones. The balance no doubt changed in some respects, but I think my overall view remained fairly constant. My dabblings in Marxism and my diplomatic experience both contributed. My aim throughout was to explain what happened and put it in the right perspective. The fact that I was working against a Cold War background of western political opinion (the qualified let-up between 1955 and 1970 released a few documents and permitted some mild criticism of Stalin in the USSR, but scarcely modified the hostility of the west) inevitably meant that my work was regarded by my critics as an apology for Soviet policies. This I took philosophically: the verdict 50 or 100 years hence, if my work is still read then, will be more interesting.

During those years I returned to a subject which had long fascinated me – the nature of history and the relation of the past to the present. I first touched on this in 1951 in *The New Society*, and brooded on it intermittently in the next ten years. In 1961 I produced *What is History?*. I would be the last to claim that it resolves the eternal tensions between Causation and Chance, Free Will and Determinism, the Individual and Society, Subjectivity and Objectivity. One can go on investigating the causes of causes of causes in pursuit of a Final Objective Cause. But of course one never reaches it. Perhaps the world is divided between cynics, who find no sense in anything, and Utopians, who make sense of things on the basis of some magnificent unverifiable assumption about the future. I prefer the latter. I have never renounced the optimistic conclusion of *What is History?*. I cannot indeed foresee for western society in anything like its present form any prospect but decline and decay, perhaps but not necessarily ending in dramatic collapse. But I believe that new forces and movements, whose shape we cannot yet guess, are germinating beneath the surface, here or elsewhere. That is my unverifiable Utopia.

Am I a Marxist? People sometimes ask, and – unlike jesting Pilate – stay for an answer which they do not get. I believe that Marx, Darwin and Freud were very great thinkers who had new and deep insights, and fundamentally altered for succeeding generations the way in which we look at the world. But this does not mean that every word written by them must be taken as gospel, or that they anticipated everything that has either been discovered or thought in their respective fields. Marx's analysis of the rise and fall of western bourgeois capitalism, and the insight which he achieved into the workings of the whole historical process, represent an enormous advance in knowledge, unparalleled in the modern world. He professed to dislike Utopias. Of course he had his Utopia – he could not do without one – the vision of a united western proletariat conquering and replacing the bourgeoisie as the bourgeoisie had once conquered and replaced the landed feudal aristocracy, and of a classless society which, since all oppression was class oppression, would be free from oppression and compulsion by capitalist employers or by the state. But I fear he nourished the illusion that this vision was scientifically verifiable. He had just a glimpse – no more of the potential emergence of Asia, but did not allow it to affect his picture. Lenin went a little further in this respect, but not much. We can now I think, go a bit further still. But this does not help me to define my Utopia. I suppose I should call it 'socialist', and am to this extent Marxist. But Marx did not define the content of socialism except in a few Utopian phrases; and nor can I. Whatever its content, however, I cannot see the western proletariat, the progency of western bourgeois capitalism, as the bearer of world revolution in its next stage, and in this respect I suppose I am not a Marxist.

Introduction: E.H. Carr – a Critical Appraisal

Michael Cox

When Edward Hallett Carr died in 1982 at the age of 90 there was a definite sense in Britain at least that somebody rather special had passed from the scene, for Carr had – in his own, idiosyncratic and very English way – become part of the intellectual furniture, a monument to scholarship recognized and admired even by those many people he had annoyed and upset over the years. Naturally, not everybody was his fan. Some indeed disliked his work enormously. But the overwhelming majority of commentators seemed to stand in awe of the great man. The distinguished historian James Joll was one such, and in a review written only a few months after Carr's death described Carr's work, and in particular his several volumes on the Soviet Union, as 'one of the great historiographical achievements of our time'.[1] This point was taken up by others, including his old ally in many a Cold War battle, A.J.P. Taylor. Taylor agreed: Carr was without peer. Though, in a typically impish article, Taylor went on to point out that while Carr was 'a very great historian' he sometimes took silly things – notably the Communist International – much too seriously. But there was no doubting his standing.[2] Even his old newspaper, *The Times*, conceded that Carr was a most 'eminent historian'. There was, it was true, something deeply 'enigmatic' about his character; and it hinted, darkly, that he seemed to be 'happier with documents than he was with people'. Yet he had achieved a great deal and left a 'strong mark on successive generations of historians and social thinkers'. He certainly appeared to have left a strong mark on the paper itself, who paid him the very great compliment of devoting not one, but three full columns to describing the life and times of their former employee![3]

Born and educated in a quite different world from the one he later sought to understand and reform, Carr thus died as he had lived:

1

very much in the public eye.[4] But what brought him to the attention of the public was not that which made him so well known later – his work on the Soviet Union – but his somewhat tough-minded views on the nature of international relations before the outbreak of the Second World War. Certainly for many scholars today, he is best remembered not for his analysis of the early years of the Russian revolution (a subject that has gone out of fashion since the fall of the USSR), but for having authored one of the key foundational texts of the inter-war period: *The Twenty Years' Crisis*. Published on the eve of the most terrible war in history, the study was seen at the time, and was certainly read by subsequent students of international relations, as a masterly defence of Machiavellian realism. The book however was far more subtle and complex. Written in an almost delphic form which at times obscured its deeper meaning, the study was less a simple celebration of power politics, than a materialist attempt to decode its character. (Carr later conceded his work was 'strongly impregnated with Marxist ways of thinking'.) Moreover, though it could be read at one level as a polemic against utopianism in general, its real purpose was not to celebrate the status quo so much as attack all those liberals who thought they could build a new international system after 1919 without changing the basis of world politics. With its focus on change and crisis, and advocacy of an economic revolution – Carr speaks at one point of the need for 'radical' measures – *The Twenty Years' Crisis* reads nothing like a standard post-war realist discussion of the international system. It is too dynamic, too concrete and far too readily blurs the line between the domestic and the international to be acceptable to later theoreticians of that particular genre. But this did not bother Carr apparently who, having made his mark, took no further direct part in the debate he had ignited. He also took no serious part in the emerging discipline of international relations. Like many of his erstwhile friends on the Left he viewed academic 'IR' as little more than an intellectual rationalization for Anglo-American hegemony. He was also clear in his own mind that it could never become a true 'science'. Thus having reissued *The Twenty Years' Crisis* in 1946, he left it, as Marx once left *The German Ideology* to the 'gnawing criticism of the mice', and in Carr's case to what he saw as the trivial ruminations of those who were not good or industrious enough to become proper historians![5]

If Carr's indifference to post-war international relations was one reason for him not returning to *The Twenty Years' Crisis*, another was his preoccupation with the writing of his *History of Soviet Russia*. Conceived in the midst of war, Carr's 14-volume study has variously been

described by supporters as 'Olympian'[6] and 'monumental',[7] and by
enemies as a subtle apologia for Stalin which ended too early for Carr to
deal seriously with the phenomenon of Stalinism.[8] Even a few supporters wondered why it concluded in 1929 and did not deal with the
Soviet system in its more mature form. Carr however was clear in his own
mind. There was, in his opinion, not enough original material to sustain
serious research on the 1930s.[9] Moreover, and more importantly, he felt
that the system in its essentials was already in place by 1929. Hence
there was no need to go further. Anyway, even if he had, one doubts this
would have changed Carr's mind about the historical significance of the
Soviet experiment. Even so, his *History* was an amazing construction:
almost pyramid-like (the less kind might argue Heath Robinson) in its
architectural audacity. The scale of the project certainly says something
about the sheer determination of the man who planned and wrote it.
Even Norman Stone in an earlier, less caustic phase of his career, conceded that it exhibited 'brilliant narrative skills'.[10] Others were more
effusive. Alec Nove for one extolled its virtues,[11] while Isaac Deutscher,
in possibly the best assessment ever written about Carr, concluded that
his *History* was 'definitive' and Carr himself 'the first genuine historian
of the Soviet regime'.[12]

In the middle of his labours Carr was then invited to give the Trevelyan lectures in Cambridge. He decided to use the occasion 'to deliver'
what he hoped would be 'a broadside on history in general and on some
of the nonsense' which he felt was then being talked about it 'by Popper
and others'.[13] The result was published under the deceptively modest
title *What is History?*. The study proved an instant success and soon
established itself as the point of intellectual reference around which a
good deal of the subsequent debate about the nature of history revolved.
The book certainly did very well (so far it has sold close to 250,000
copies).[14] It also had a rather tumultuous career. Criticized for both its
epistemological relativism – a charge levelled at the book by Geoffrey
Elton,[15] as well as its challenge to history as a distinct and separate
discipline (a point made by Herbert Butterfield),[16] it provoked a particularly robust response from Isaiah Berlin, then guardian of the liberal
keep in Britain. Berlin praised the man but denounced what he saw as
'Carr's entire view of history as the story of the big battalions and of
progress as being whatever those in power will achieve'.[17] Carr remained
unbowed and unmoved. But if he was too deterministic for Berlin (and if
truth be known far too influential as well) he was not orthodox enough
for some sections of the sectarian left. Indeed, the book was banned in
certain revolutionary circles in Iran in the 1970s for being a 'bourgeois

treatise' which the Iranian intelligentsia could well do without reading at that particular 'historical moment'![18] For such a small book, *What is History?* had quite a big impact. It is no surprise that Carr hoped to bring out a revised second edition before he died.[19]

Finally, Carr was an accomplished biographer, a fact that rather refutes the charge usually levelled against him that he underestimated the role of the individual in history. But not only did he seem to like the biographical genre – though always wondered whether good biography could ever be good history – but wrote four studies of his own in just under six years: *Dostoevsky: 1821–1881* (1931); *The Romantic Exiles* (1933); *Karl Marx: A Study in Fanaticism* (1934); and *Michael Bakunin* (1937). The first was certainly competent, though was less a work of literary criticism than psychological analysis. The second, a sympathetic study of Herzen in exile, was undoubtedly the best of the bunch. The third, according to Carr, was 'unfortunate'. The last was his favourite, rather a strange choice, one might have thought, for someone later identified as the scourge of all utopians. But all four were important in Carr's own intellectual development. As he later confessed, it was as a result of studying these exotic people, especially those wild Russians rather than the 'orderly German' Marx, that he came to question the West and 'western ideology'.[20] Thus at about the same time that Carr was leaving the Foreign Office to take up the Woodrow Wilson Chair in Aberystwyth – a position established on sound Welsh liberal principles by the redoubtable David Davies in 1919 – Carr was already in an advanced state of alienation from liberal ideas.[21] Little wonder his appointment there to what he later termed 'a fancy chair' turned out to be rather controversial'.[22]

Carr's range was thus immense. Fluent in several languages, immensely hard-working, with what one observer has called 'a gargantuan appetite for detailed research',[23] Carr was, in his own way, a modern Renaissance man whose contribution was remarkable by any measure. His close collaborator Bob Davies did not exaggerate when he called him a 'towering eminence among twentieth-century intellectuals'.[24] Yet Carr always provoked the strongest of passions. He still does.[25] Accused at various times of being an appeaser of Nazi Germany, a fellow traveller of the Soviet Union, an 'evil communist', a 'bourgeois with a vicarious taste for revolutionary violence', someone who always surrendered 'to the immanence of power', and one of the most dangerous scholars in Britain (the last comment apparently coming from Zbigniew Brzezinski in 1963),[26] Carr not only courted controversy, but also managed to generate a great deal himself. Never one to mince his words on important issues, he was nothing if not a bruiser when it came to debate. He took few intellectual prisoners and amongst his more famous 'scalps' were Arnold Toynbee and Alfred Zimmern who placed more faith in the League of Nations than he; the historians Moshe Lewin and Stephen Cohen who happened to think that Bukharin offered an alternative to Stalin; and more traditional philosophers of history such as Karl Popper, Isaiah Berlin and Herbert Butterfield. Carr was especially impatient with those who assumed the status quo was always preferable to change. Always the iconoclast, and increasingly so during the Cold War, he had very little time for those who, in his words, 'expressed the fashionable weariness' of the age. As he made clear in one scathing review of a study on *The Price of Revolution* by fellow historian, D.W. Brogan, the subject was an intriguing one but far too important to be left to a writer who took it for granted that 'the old' was always 'better than the new'.[27]

No natural born rebel, the younger Carr might have remained a minor though well-regarded diplomat if it had not been for one very large event: the Russian revolution. Though at the time expressing no great sympathy for the Bolshevik experiment, he even helped plan its blockade after 1917, Carr was gradually impelled by a series of events – the world depression, the successes as he saw them of Soviet planning and Soviet victory in the war – to come to terms with what he regarded as the great challenge to a failing western civilization. Carr's attitude towards the USSR however was complex, and was most acutely characterized once as being consistently and unfashionably 'positivist' in character.[28] Thus if the system existed, then, in Carr's view, the most important job of the historian was to understand why, not to moralize about it. And if Stalin happened to win the struggle for power in the 1920s, then again the task was to explain how this had happened, not to 'throw stones' at him. Naturally enough, what might be termed Carr's deep-seated fatalism with respect to the past, was not to everyone's taste. It was also used against him and in a celebrated attack written in *Encounter* (a magazine Carr despised), Hugh Trevor-Roper argued that Carr never showed the slightest concern with the victims of history, he always preferred the 'victorious cause'.[29] This was harsh. However, his attitude towards History with a big 'H' infuriated people, even more sympathetic admirers who frequently criticized him for always assuming that just because things happened, they had to happen.[30] Carr, however, would not budge. The purpose of the historian, as he saw it, was to understand history, not to rewrite it. To ask what might have been, or what might have happened, struck him as being faintly absurd. As has been noted by others, Carr was always an impatient critic of retrospective day-dreaming, of counterfactual history.

But if Carr can justly be accused of a certain uncritical acceptance of the historical fact, this did not make him into a deferential worshipper of all that existed. Oddly enough, for such a tough-minded historian, he had a great deal of time for some of history's more celebrated utopians and losers. Thus he had a soft spot for the Russian anarchist Bakunin, an even softer one for the gentle Russian radical Herzen, and though he was never soft on Marx, he always regarded Marx as a man of genius. More-over, though he was highly critical of Marxism – disputing the labour theory of value and rejecting what he saw as the childish notion of a classless society (Carr once wrote that a ruling class would always be necessary) – he always felt it was important to understand Marxism.[31] So close did he come to doing so in fact that many later accused him, quite incorrectly, of having become a Marxist himself. For one accused of being a subtle apologist for Stalin and Stalinism, Carr also had some fairly positive things to say about Leon Trotsky, another obvious drea-mer and visionary. This was not because he agreed with Trotsky. As he made clear, he viewed Trotsky's theory of world revolution as so much political eye-wash and Trotsky himself as tactically inept when it came to fighting Stalin in the 1920s. But he still recognized the man's great-ness, and once even thanked Stalin in print for having expelled Trotsky from the USSR and thus saving this man of letters for posterity![32] Carr certainly rated his *History of the Russian Revolution* very highly.[33] He also thought Trotsky's analysis of the contradictions of the New Economic Policy was acute.[34] It was Trotsky, not Bukharin who represented the only 'convincing' alternative to Stalin – if indeed there was an altern-ative.[35] And according to Carr, Trotsky's assessment of the situation in Germany in the early 1930s was particularly brilliant. It is not insig-nificant of course that he held Trotsky's biographer, Isaac Deutscher, in the highest regard.[36] There were differences: Deutscher after all was a Marxist and Carr was not. Yet the two struck up a powerful relation-ship which lasted until Deutscher's sudden death in 1967.

Carr, it has been acutely observed, was never really at home with the rebels of society or its masters. An establishment man who could never quite be trusted to toe the party line, Carr invariably managed to use his privileged position as respected academic, leader writer for *The Times*, broadcaster and public lecturer to say some pretty radical things. Though a meticulous scholar in the tradition of the Cambridge classicist A.E. Housman ('the most powerful intellectual machine I've ever seen in action,' he later wrote) Carr was also one of the great popularizers of his age, and achieved the rare distinction amongst academics of getting his views across to more than the usual handful of devotees. As Edward Acton once explained, Carr's background and 'range of experience in the Foreign Office and as Assistant Editor of *The Times* gave him a healthy grasp of the world outside the ivory tower'.[37] This was undoubtedly true, and during and just after the Second World War in particular, he managed to reach something close to a mass audience. Indeed, some of his more influential work on Britain's position in the world, the *Conditions of Peace* (1942) and *The New Society* (1951) in particular were broadcast first or published in the influential magazine *The Listener*, before appearing in book form. Nor did Carr have much trouble getting his work reviewed. One sometimes wonders that if his critics had kept quiet, Carr might have exercised far less influence than he did. But they could not keep quiet, apparently, and attacked him whenever and wherever they could. Norman Angell, Susan Stebbing, Leonard Woolf, Winston Churchill, Isaiah Berlin, Hedley Bull, Hans J. Morgenthau, Whittle Johnson, Hugh Trevor-Roper, Geoffrey Elton, Arthur Marwick, Leopold Labedz and many, many more – liberals and conservatives alike – all lined up to put Carr in his place at one time or another.

Yet what was it that upset them so, almost to the point of distraction? It is a critically important question. After all, while Carr may have 'imbibed more from historical materialism than most parts of the British establishment could stomach',[38] he still felt that Marxism could not explain the complex nature of modern capitalism. And while he had a good deal of sympathy for the 'New Left', he felt the new generation of younger Marxists in the 1960s were far too concerned with method and not enough with doing proper historical research. Yet in spite of this, he generated an enormous amount of political abuse – both when he was alive and after he died. The most infamous, or celebrated, example of this was that which appeared in *The London Review of Books* in 1983. In this, a one-time admirer, Norman Stone, tore into Carr with everything he had, accusing him, amongst other things, of being a bad teacher, of never saying quite 'what he meant' and writing a 'useless set of volumes' (his *History of Soviet Russia*) which only masqueraded 'as a classic' rather than being the real thing.[39] It was all very strong stuff, which provoked a howl of understandable outrage from Carr's many supporters. But Stone's broadside was neither the first, nor was it to be the last; and if we were to judge Carr's career by the quantity of his critics alone, we would have to conclude that it was one of the more successful in the twentieth century!

Clearly one of the reasons why Carr aroused such passion was his own very individual and combative style of debate. Once asked by a sympathetic interviewer why he generated so much controversy, he replied that perhaps one of the causes was that he had a 'slightly provocative way of saying things' himself![40] This was something of an understatement. As one reviewer put it, rather more forcefully, Carr 'had a sharp tongue' and an even 'sharper pen'.[41] The Stone case serves as a rather good example of this. Few would dispute the fact that Stone's attack was vicious and defamatory. We should not forget, however, that only a few years before, Carr had written a devastating review of Stone's own book, *The Eastern Front: 1914–1917*. In an understated but forceful way he literally destroyed Stone's edifice, suggesting, amongst other things, that his whole approach was just a 'muddle'. One can only begin to guess how the irascible and ambitious young Scot might have felt about that![42] Anybody familiar with even a small part of Carr's private correspondence can also attest to his uncompromising assessments of those he deemed to be intellectually inferior, second-rate, philosophically confused, or just politically wrong. Carr was never personal or abusive. However, he did not suffer fools gladly. And even those who were not fools he attacked forcefully. Hence, he did not rate Leonard Schapiro highly as an historian of the Communist Party of the Soviet Union. He could not really take his friend A.J.P. Taylor too seriously. And Hugh Seton-Watson he regarded as an 'emotional mountebank' because he took up with the Conservative Right after the war.

Like all serious people with a mission in life, Carr was also a passionate human being with strong views about the world around him. Deutscher once suggested that Carr wrote as if he was above it all, *au delà de la mêlée*. Nothing could have been further from the truth. In fact, when you examine many of his more important books, it soon becomes apparent that they are – in their own very different ways – great examples of the polemical form that inevitably end up attacking somebody or something else. His *The Twenty Years' Crisis*, for example, was an extended and powerful attack on what he saw as the illusions of those who made the peace at Versailles His study *Nationalism and After* was one of the more savage intellectual blows aimed at the idea of self-determination. His editorials in *The Times* during the war were directed very obviously against the political Right. His now unread, but then highly influential, *The New Society* was a broadside against *laissez-faire* capitalism. And in his *What is History?* he quite literally challenged the English historical establishment to an intellectual fight. Carr was no wallflower when it came to debate.

But it was Carr's ideas on world politics, not just the manner of his writing, that upset so many people. There was of course the rather important issue of his early views on Germany. Like many of his generation he felt that Germany had been dealt an appalling hand at Versailles in 1919. This was hardly controversial. Unfortunately, this led Carr to justify German foreign policy for the greater part of the 1930s and more or less accept that Germany had a right to dominate Eastern Europe. For the same set of pragmatic reasons he was also prepared to let Soviet Russia do the same after the war. A modernist in every respect, Carr also had little or no time for those who stood in the way of what he liked to term 'progress', whether they were peasants who held on to their own pathetic parcel of land or romantic nationalists who clung to the outmoded form of the nation-state. Small powers in particular not only failed to arouse his sympathy (earlier in his career he had been less hostile) but in his view constituted one of the main obstacles to peace and the creation of a more rational international order. On the other hand, he appeared to have all the time in the world for the big powers. In one of his more remarkable observations, made in one of his most pro-Soviet tracts in 1946, he even went so far as to suggest that sooner or later all small nations would be drawn into the orbit of one or other of the Great Powers.[43] In another equally memorable piece he compared Soviet hegemony in Eastern Europe after 1945 with British imperial power. According to Carr, there was really no difference in principle between the two Empires, except perhaps that the British had ruled slightly more efficiently and with slightly less international fuss and bother being made about it by other major powers.

But even Carr's controversial views about Germany before the war or attitude towards small nations – 'national self-determination', he once opined, had 'awkward implications both for bourgeois democracy and international accord'[44] – cannot completely explain the hostility displayed towards him in the post-war period. Some of his critics had been appeasers too before 1939 and quite a few shared his opinion about small nations. Their hostility was a function of something else, and that 'something' was the Cold War and the pervasive impact it had upon political and intellectual life in the West after 1947.

First, unlike those who thought the Cold War was a western response to Soviet aggression, Carr felt it was, in the end, the fault of the West. The Soviet Union he insisted was no revolutionary danger to the West and had not been one since the early 1920s; thus if the conflict persisted it did so not because of any Soviet threat to western capitalism but because capitalism in general – and the United States in particular – refused to come to terms with the reality of Soviet power.[45] Carr also did not think the Cold War was in Britain's best interest. A patriot at heart, he speculated endlessly during the war about how best to preserve British influence after the war.[46] The solution, he believed, required radical reform at home and the preservation of the war-time alliance abroad. Unfortunately, when peace came, not only did the alliance collapse, but Britain quickly established something to which he was vehemently opposed: a close but subordinate 'special relationship' with the United States. This not only offended Carr's sensibility – he was never especially fond of America – but in his opinion could only weaken Britain's leverage in the larger international system. It was also premised on what he regarded, like George Kennan, as an absurdly apocalyptic reading of Soviet intentions and capabilities.[47]

The Cold War, moreover, had its own particular logic which Carr simply could not go along with. Hence while the establishment was trying to talk up the totalitarian character of Soviet communism, Carr was trying to talk it down – to the point of almost denying the system's more obnoxious features. And while liberal and conservative intellectuals were doing their best to bury Marxism alive, Carr at least was prepared to defend its right to exist and to be taken seriously as an intellectual discourse. This annoyed an enormous number of people, especially the influential Isaiah Berlin. Carr he knew from his own personal experience was no revolutionary. However, he cast what Berlin rather perceptively called 'a protective mantle over extremists, however foolish or misguided he may think them to be'.[48] The same could never be said about Berlin, who as we know intervened to prevent Carr's ally, Isaac Deutscher, getting a senior position at Sussex. But Carr paid a price for his integrity; and like most dissidents in the West in this period found himself being pushed increasingly outside of the system. He was denied posts at London, Balliol, Oxford, and then King's College, Cambridge; and even when he finally did find a position at Trinity (his old college) he did so not because he was a radical looking for an intellectual home but simply because he was famous!

The Cold War also required a certain official line to be adopted on the Russian revolution: again Carr would not oblige. Nor could he given long-standing belief that 1917 was a legitimate protest against a failed system. He certainly did not regard the revolution as a tragedy, a view propagated by his old enemy, Richard Pipes. Nor did he see it as a mere *coup d'état*. In fact, whereas more orthodox historians had a marked tendency to see what happened as a conspiracy at worst and a minority affair at best, Carr like Trotsky interpreted it as a mass spontaneous event with large-scale support. The idea, popular in some quarters, that Lenin was a German agent and the Bolsheviks an unrepresentative clique, he found risible. Carr also refused to join in the general condemnation of Lenin. Indeed, while influential historians like the American Merle Fainsod and the British scholar Leonard Schapiro seemed to detest Lenin and assume that Stalinism was inherent in the whole revolutionary project, Carr both admired Lenin and showed that during the first few years of Soviet power – those with which he was most familiar – there was genuine discussion and debate, at least within the Communist Party. Again this was not something his opponents wished to hear, especially from somebody as formidable and credible as Carr.

Lastly, while Carr was no apologist for the Soviet system, and publicly attacked those who were, he could never quite bring himself to condemn what had been established after 1929. This was not because he was ignorant of the facts, or was unaware of the costs involved in building socialism in one country. As he put it in one memorable, but deeply ambivalent phrase, 'seldom in history had so monstrous a price been paid for so monumental an achievement.'[49] But still, it was an achievement, and to deny it would not only do an injustice to history but provide aid and comfort to those Cold War warriors who were always on the look-out for what he saw as dirt to throw at the Soviet Union. As he made clear in an interview for the *New Left Review* just four years before his death, people in the West who moaned most about the abuse of human rights in the USSR were only looking for scapegoats. Hysteria in the capitalist world about what went on in Soviet Russia was, in his view, yet another malign 'symptom of a sick society'.[50]

Carr thus lived just outside the political pale – almost in splendid isolation like some 'prophet outcast' from the inner sanctum of power and influence: annoying the establishment without necessarily threatening them, but annoying them just enough (and often enough) to make him quite unacceptable, and for quite a while unemployable as well. And all the time he pressed on, relentlessly and at great personal cost to finish his *History*. Then, having completed his task, he pushed on once more, with Tamara Deutscher's help, to complete yet two more volumes on Soviet external policy in the 1930s: one on what he called *The Twilight of the Comintern* covering the years between 1930 and 1935, and the other on the Soviet role in Spain during the civil war. The first was published just after his death in 1982; the other by Tamara Deutscher in 1983, six years before the end of the Cold War and only eight before the disintegration of his obsession: the Soviet Union.

Which raises the obvious question: how should we regard Carr now that the object of his life's work has imploded? His critics are in little doubt. Carr, they argue, was a man of his times; those times are gone;

thus there is little point viewing him as anything other than a curiosity, a mere footnote in British intellectual life who was routed by the very thing he claimed to understand most: History. One can understand this reaction. Carr's purpose after all was not just to study any old country, but to assess the historical significance of an experiment within the larger context of what he viewed as a more general transition to planning. And that experiment has failed. Furthermore, it failed in ways that Carr had not anticipated. Ever worried about making moral judgements, and also concerned not to hand 'the other side' ideological ammunition in the Cold War, he seemed to avoid looking too deeply into the murkier side of Soviet reality. To this extent he was a little too 'balanced', too 'fair-minded' and too 'positivist' for his own good.

Yet to dismiss Carr as a relic of past illusions would be absurd, and those of his former enemies like Stone and Pipes who have tried to do so are simply being politically spiteful. Carr undoubtedly got many things wrong; and he was woefully blinkered when it came to the Soviet Union – like so many people on the Left before 1989. But far less able and significant figures than he have suffered illusions, but we still continue to read them. People also continue to read Carr, whose influence in international relations has probably never been greater than it is now (though not as a realist but as a critical theorist), whose views on the nature of history continue to shape the debate – as the more recent contribution by Richard Evans shows only too clearly[51] – and whose work on the early USSR still remains the standard reference point. Not bad for a writer who has apparently failed the test of time. As his political enemy Winston Churchill might have put it, 'some writer, some failure'!

This collection is in large part driven by the belief that Carr was a central figure in the history of the twentieth century, one who is too important either to be left to those so hostile to him that they cannot see his virtues or so uncritical that they cannot see his faults. As the reader will quickly discover, not all the contributors here sing from the same political hymn sheet. Nor are they just interested in Carr the student of early Soviet affairs. Indeed, they come from a variety of backgrounds and disciplines from Soviet studies to history, international relations to political theory. But they have all been able to discover something in Carr. Even those who disagree with what he has to say – and many here disagree with Carr quite forcefully – still find him remarkably stimulating. Nor should this come as much surprise. Not only did he write extremely well on many issues, but he was at the heart of most of the key debates of his day. For this very obvious reason we are almost impelled to revisit Carr: for his many insights into the inter-war period, for an understanding of the discussions that went on at the highest level in Britain during the Second World War, for some feel for the bitter controversies that so divided intellectuals during the Cold War, and for some understanding of the dilemmas facing intellectuals in a world now dissolved where there were no easy choices and no facile solutions.

The volume is divided into four parts: the first deals with Carr's life and times. Chapter 1 is by his biographer Jonathan Haslam and plots Carr's evolution from pre-war liberal to inter-war outsider searching for meaning in a world turned upside down by war, revolution and western economic collapse. This is followed by Brian Porter's chapter on the 'Aberystwyth years', an odd interlude at one level, but still a critically important period in Carr's life during which he not only wrote *The Twenty Years' Crisis* and the highly influential *Conditions of Peace*, but became embroiled in a bruising battle with the redoubtable Welshman, Lord David Davies – staunch Liberal, sponsor of the Wilson Chair, devotee of The League of Nations and deeply opposed to nearly everything Carr stood for. Charles Jones then takes the story forward in Chapter 3 to the war-time years when Carr as leader writer for *The Times* found himself under fire again: not for his scepticism about the League of Nations or lukewarm attitude to Woodrow Wilson but advocacy of planning on the home front and permanent alliance with the Soviet Union. As Jones points out, these were turbulent days for Carr, which he began at the heart of the British political establishment and ended as virtual political exile in a world rapidly – and in Carr's view tragically and unnecessarily – moving towards Cold War confrontation.

The Cold War, of course, revolved around competing views about the Soviet Union, and the next part, logically enough, deals with Carr's analysis of the former Soviet regime. It begins, fittingly, with a chapter by his friend and collaborator, Bob Davies. Davies reveals the complexity of Carr's changing analysis of the Soviet Union from the 1930s until his death half a century later. As Davies makes clear, while Carr was favourably disposed towards the Soviet system, he was not the simple-minded fellow traveller he is often portrayed as being by his many enemies. Stephen White then continues the discussion with a careful dissection of the way in which Carr's work on the Soviet Union was received and reviewed in the Soviet Union itself. What White reveals is vitally important: that Carr, the so-called 'communist apologist', took far more than his fair share of criticism from Soviet writers. If Carr was an apologist this was not something that those within the former USSR seemed to detect at the time. None the less, he did retain some optimism about its future evolution, a view he shared with his close friend and intellectual mentor, Isaac Deutscher. The important relationship between the two men is explored by Michael Cox. According to Cox the relationship was a complicated one. Carr admired Deutscher and valued his support. But the differences between the two – in essence the difference between an English empiricist with an interest in radical thought and the most orthodox of continental Marxists – could never be overcome. This theme is further developed in the next chapter by Hillel Ticktin. However, rather than merely criticizing Carr, Ticktin seeks to place Carr within a larger historical context – something which Carr would no doubt have approved of – and argues that while Carr played an honourable intellectual role in the Cold War, the same Cold War also distorted his perspective and made him much less critical of the Soviet system than he might otherwise have been.

The following five chapters taken together present one of the most systematic attempts to date to retrieve Carr, warts and all, for the discipline of international relations. The discussion begins with a wide-ranging historical reconstruction by Peter Wilson of the reception afforded Carr's *The Twenty Years' Crisis*. Wilson himself views the much cited and much misunderstood book as a classic. Its insights he accepts are profound. But he is concerned that Carr's various 'idealist' critics have been too readily ignored by later writers, who have been more keen to exploit what they see as the 'realist' truths contained in Carr than to explore the alternatives put forward by his many opponents. Paul Rich raises equally critical questions in his contribution. Rich is more than willing to concede Carr his rightful place in British intellectual history. He wonders however about Carr's relevance for understanding a post-war world where the market, rather than planning, continued to shape relations between and within the major western states. This would not deny him his place in British political life before the onset of the post-war boom. But it would ask us to think of Carr not as some guru figure but as a product of a very specific moment in time when faith in the capitalist order had all but collapsed. Tim Dunne is equally keen to situate Carr in time and place. Indeed, his main point would seem to reinforce that made by Rich: that we should stop looking for some universal 'realist' or even 'Marxist' truths in Carr's work and rather be guided by what Carr himself suggested in *What is History?*. That there are no objective facts about the world 'out there' only a series of competing interpretations. Andrew Linklater approaches Carr somewhat differently. He does believe we can extract some key ideas from Carr. But we have to be careful which ones we select. Clearly, we can no longer accept his rather naïve faith in the possibilities of planning. However, once shorn of this particular idea (there are others) Carr's work, according to Linklater, can still be effectively deployed by those seeking to engage in a genuinely critical discourse about international relations as a discipline. Halliday agrees. Carr, he readily admits, got a number of things wrong. In particular, he failed to see the possibility of the film of 'progressive' history running backwards. On the other hand, he has many profound things to say about the dynamics of revolution and the impact that revolutions have had on the international system in the twentieth century, and for this reason – if no other – we can still read him to great purpose.

This brings us then to the last three chapters. These deal in very different ways with Carr's important contribution to history and historiography. The discussion opens with an elegantly composed exploration of the deeper meaning of *What is History?* by the American historian, Anders Stephanson. Stephanson is in little doubt about the central importance of Carr's work and the impact it has had on the study of history since it was first published in 1961. What he questions is the extent to which Carr ever managed to solve the many methodological problems he sets himself. Certainly, in our pessimistic, postmodern times Carr must seem somewhat *passé*: that at least is the starting-point of Keith Jenkins' powerful critique of Carr. And if Stephanson is at least sympathetic to the epistemological dilemmas faced by Carr in *What is History?*, Jenkins is most definitely not. The problem with Carr, according to Jenkins, is not that he arrived at the wrong answers but that his working assumptions were entirely false. Most erroneously he still believed in his good old-fashioned Victorian way that objectivity and historical truth were possible. This is why he cannot, indeed should not, be taken seriously today. This is not an issue that concerns Randall Germain in the last chapter; what intrigues Germain – and in his view makes Carr one of the more interesting thinkers of the twentieth century – is less Carr's method and more his enormous sensitivity to the historic process. This may or may not be enough for the postmodernists, but it does mean that Carr can still be used in a creative and critical way to explore some of the key forces shaping international politics today. Indeed, just by recognizing the present as history and history as an unending process, Carr makes it possible for us all to explore world realities in a more complete, dynamic fashion. We need not agree with him about the idea of progress, or accept his views about the decadence of capitalism. What we can share with him however is the belief that history has the uncanny knack of upsetting all cosy assumptions. His were most definitely upset by the collapse of what many viewed (though not Carr) as the socialist alternative in the Soviet Union. The point can hardly be disputed. But history still holds the capacity to shock and surprise, and if the past is anything to go by, the future will pose new questions to which old answers will clearly not be adequate. Carr, one suspects, would have relished the challenge.

Notes

1 See James Joll, 'Towards the Seventh World Congress', *The Times Higher Education Supplement*, 28 January 1983.
2 A.J.P. Taylor, 'The Comedy of Errors', *The Sunday Times*, 23 January 1983.
3 'Mr E.H. Carr: Eminent Historian of Soviet Russia', *The Times*, 5 November 1982.
4 For a short and insightful guide to Carr's life see his own 'autobiography' written for Tamara Deutscher in 1980, and published for the first time in full in this volume.
5 In a letter written to Stanley Hoffmann on 30 September 1977, Carr noted that there was no such 'science of international relations . . . no science of international relations exists. The study of international relations in the English speaking world is simply a study of the best way to run the world from positions of strength.' This letter can be found in the Carr Papers held in the Special Section of the University of Birmingham library.
6 'E.H. Carr is an Olympian among historians, a Goethe in range and spirit,' wrote his ally and friend, the British historian A.J.P. Taylor in 'Cold-blooded Historian', *The Observer Review*, 26 January 1969. See also his 'View from Olympus', *The Observer Review*, 1 February 1981.
7 Moshe Lewin, 'The Making of Stalinism', *The Guardian*, 2 December 1971.
8 See, for example, Leopold Labedz, 'E.H. Carr: Overtaken by history', *Survey*, March 1988, Volume 30, pp. 94–111.
9 This was the view Carr defended in 1978 in an interview. See his 'The Russian Revolution and the West', *The New Left Review*, Number 111, September–October 1978, p. 27
10 See Norman Stone, 'Building Time', *The Guardian*, 9 December 1976.
11 See Alec Nove, 'Executing the Marxist Testament', *Times Literary Supplement*, 11 January 1980.
12 Isaac Deutscher, 'Mr E.H. Carr as an historian of Soviet Russia', *Soviet Studies*, Vol. VI, No. 4, April 1955, p. 339.
13 Quote taken from private letter from Carr to Bob Davies, 9 December 1959. My thanks to Davies for permitting me to examine his personal correspondence with Carr.
14 Figure quoted in Jonathan Haslam, *The Vices of Integrity: E.H. Carr 1892–1982* (London, Verso, 1999), p. 217.
15 See Geoffrey Elton, *The Practice of History* (1967; Glasgow: Collins Fontana, 1975).
16 Herbert Butterfield, 'What is History?', *The Cambridge Review*, 2 December 1961.

17 Isaiah Berlin, 'Mr Carr's Big Batallions', *New Statesman*, 5 January 1962.

18 This story is told by Ali Gheissari in 'Truth and Method in Modern Iranian Historiography and Social Sciences', *Critique: Journal for Critical Studies of the Middle East*, No. 6, Spring 1995, pp. 48–9. I am indebted to Fred Halliday for passing on this tit-bit to me.

19 Bob Davies in the end brought out a second edition of *What is History?* in 1987 (Harmondsworth: Penguin) with a very useful guide to Carr's 'revised' thoughts. Carr's reading for the second edition can be gleaned from the Carr Papers.

20 'The first challenge to bourgeois capitalist society came, so far as I was concerned, not from Marx or the Bolsheviks, but from Russian nineteenth-century intellectuals, who were not in any strict sense revolutionaries at all.' Quote from Carr's 'Autobiography'.

21 David Davies later wrote to Gilbert Murray that he was deeply disappointed with the Carr appointment to a Woodrow Wilson Chair when Carr himself was so anti-Wilson. More to the point, Carr in his opinion was not doing his 'duty to the College, to the Chair and especially to the young generation who have been pitchforked into this war' (5 June 1942). This correspondence can be found in the College archives at the University of Wales, Aberystwyth. My thanks to Guto Thomas for passing this morsel of anti-Carr on to me.

22 Carr later used the term to describe the Woodrow Wilson Chair in an interview with Peter Scott, 'Revolution without the Passion', *The Times Higher Educational Supplement*, 7 July 1978, p. 7.

23 Edward Acton, 'Historical Bees Abuzz', *Sunday Times*, 13 February 1983.

24 See R.W. Davies, 'Edward Hallett Carr: 1892–1982', *Proceedings of the British Academy*, 1982, p. 473.

25 Among the more recent attacks on Carr – masquerading as reviews of the Haslam biography – see Norman Stone, 'Horrible History Man', *The Spectator*, 4 September 1999, and Richard Pipes, 'A Very Cold Fish', *Times Literary Supplement*, 10 September 1999.

26 These various assaults were launched, in order, by Andrew Roberts, 'How We Met', *Independent on Sunday*, 14 January 1996, the former Trotskyist Max Eastman in the *New York Times*, 27 August 1950, and Hans J. Morgenthau in his polemic, 'The Surrender to the Immanence of Power: E.H. Carr', in his *Dilemmas of Power* (Chicago: Chicago University Press, 1962), pp. 350–7.

27 See E.H. Carr in *The Listener*, 17 January 1952.

28 See James Joll, 'Towards the Seventh World Congress', *The Times Higher Education Supplement*, 28 January 1983.

29 Hugh Trevor-Roper, 'E.H. Carr's Success Story', *Encounter*, May 1962, Vol. XVIII, No. 5, pp. 69–77.

30 Nove, *ibid*.

31 Carr's not entirely hostile views on Marx are expressed in his 'Karl Marx: Fifty Years Later', *Fortnightly*, March 1933, pp. 311–21 under the assumed name of John Hallett.

32 Carr wrote that 'History and even literature owes a debt to Stalin, who so opportunely curbed Trotsky's ambition to go on making revolutions, and drove him, perforce, while still in the prime of life to the more rewarding alternative of writing about them.' See his 'Trotsky's History Of the Russian Revolution', *The Sunday Times*, 16 September 1934.

33   Carr did several reviews of Trotsky's *History of the Russian Revolution* in the 1930s. See however his 'Trotskyism and Bolshevism', *The Spectator*, 2 July 1932.

34   See his 'The Legacy of Stalin', *The Times Literary Supplement'*, 23 January 1976.

35   See his critical review of Stephen Cohen's biography of Bukharin 'The Legend of Bukharin', *The Times Literary Supplement*, 20 September 1974.

36   See his 'In Memoriam' to Isaac Deutscher in E.H. Carr, *1917: Before and After* (London, Macmillan, 1969), pp. 177–8.

37   Acton, 'Historical Bees Abuzz'.

38   *Ibid.*

39   Norman Stone, 'Grim Eminence', *The London Review of Books*, 20 January 1983.

40   See the interview with Richard Gott, 'E.H. Carr's Russia', *The Guardian*, 25 November 1978.

41   Acton, 'Historical Bees Abuzz'.

42   See E.H. Carr 'The War No One Won', *The New York Review of Books*, 29 April 1976.

43   See E.H. Carr, *Soviet Impact on the Western World* (London: Macmillan, 1946).

44   See his *From Napoleon to Stalin And Other Essays* (London: Macmillan, 1980), p. 7.

45   Significantly, William Appleman Williams – the inspirer of American Cold War revisionism – had extensive correspondence with Carr in 1952 sending him large amounts of his own research on the early years of the revolution and showing, of course, that the US was totally hostile to the USSR from the very start. The communications from Williams to Carr can be found in the Carr Papers.

46   See Charles Jones, *E.H. Carr and International Relations* (Cambridge: Cambridge University Press, 1998).

47   See Carr's sympathetic review of Kennan's classic on American diplomacy in *The Listener*, 17 January 1952.

48   On Carr's relationship with Berlin, see Michael Ignatieff, *Isaiah Berlin: A Life* (London: Chatto & Windus, 1998)

49   Quoted in *The Foundations of a Planned Economy*, 2 (Harmondsworth: Pelican Books, 1976), p. 477.

50   'The Russian Revolution and the West', *New Left Review*, p. 31.

51   Richard Evans, *In Defence of History* (London: Granta Books, 1997).

I
Life and Times

1

E.H. Carr's Search for Meaning, 1892–1982[1]

Jonathan Haslam

Born and educated in an age of certainty, Carr matured and died in an age of doubt. This bleak contrast in circumstance proved to be the catalyst which made Edward (Ted) Hallet-Carr, the promising young scholar and diplomat, into one of the most extraordinary and controversial historians of our time. The collapse of the world he knew and loved in 1914, and its remnants between 1929 and 1939, caused him to look elsewhere for the belief in progress that had so characterized the Victorian era to which he belonged. Under Lenin and his immediate successors, the Soviet regime lifted the Victorian spirit from the rotting corpse of imperial Britain and implanted it into the alien but receptive frame of Russia resurgent.

Carr was born in the summer of 1892, into a solid, suburban, Victorian middle-class household in north London, into a world of values that was aptly described by the economist John Maynard Keynes as his own:

> Europe was so organised socially and economically as to secure the maximum accumulation of capital. While there was some continuous improvement in the daily conditions of life of the mass of the population, Society was so framed as to throw a great part of the increased income into the control of the class least likely to consume it.... The immense accumulations of fixed capital which, to the great benefit of mankind, were built up during the half century before the war, could never have come about in a Society where wealth was divided equitably.

The working classes accepted or were compelled to take very little of the cake. Instead,

> the capitalist classes were allowed to call the best part of the cake theirs and were theoretically free to consume it, on the tacit

underlying condition that they consumed very little of it in practice... the virtue of the cake was that it was never to be consumed, neither by you nor by your children after you... Society was working not for the small pleasures of to-day but for the future security and improvement of the race, – in fact for 'progress'.[2]

This world, Carr recalled, 'was solid and stable. Prices did not change. Incomes, if they changed, went up.... It was a good place and was getting better. This country was leading it in the right direction. There were, no doubt, abuses, but they were being, or would be dealt with.'[3] His smooth progression via scholarships through Merchant Taylors' School and the Classics tripos at Trinity College, Cambridge, interrupted only by ill-health, undoubtedly reinforced a tendency to see life as a linear advance to the highest of achievements, whether one thought of the individual or society. Self-discipline, duty, order, sacrifice and self-perfection were part and parcel of his upbringing.

The old order crumbled under the artillery barrage of the new after the outbreak of war in August 1914: a catastrophe for which no one was prepared, a trauma from which no one and few ideas emerged unscathed. He escaped the battlefield because of a weak heart, damaged by illness; instead, he was drafted into the diplomatic service on graduating in 1916. The dreadful blood-sacrifice made by his generation none the less made itself felt. The sense of loss haunted him and his generation for the rest of their lives. Carr was no sentimentalist. Nostalgia was nevertheless unavoidable. On 9 August 1982, just three months before he died, Carr wrote to his close friend and collaborator, Tamara Deutscher, '80th anniversary of the Coronation of King Edward VII, postponed from June for the removal of his appendix. I was on a family holiday at Exmouth, and remember the decorations and fireworks. Why could we not go on living forever and ever in that innocent world?'[4]

Out of that morass, two new forms emerged: a revolution in distant Russia in 1917 and the birth of the League of Nations at Paris in 1919 – both of mixed and somewhat doubtful parentage: the revolution was Marxist in its conception, the League the ill-proportioned offspring of the liberal tradition in which Carr was reared. He came into immediate contact with both at the Foreign Office, first at the Contraband Department and later on the British delegation to the Paris Peace Conference. Up to the time of the revolution in November 1917 his job had been to get goods into Russia; after the revolution his purpose was to keep them out. And he did that job with a ruthless efficiency for which he became well known. As a result of Lenin's seizure of power, a three-man team was set up to deal with the Russia problem. Ted was taken on as 'junior bottle-washer'.[5] His sympathies were certainly not with the revolutionaries. 'I do not know much about our Russian policy,' he minuted, 'but I take it that while being outwardly polite to the Bolsheviks we should be only too glad to see them collapse. The thing most likely to cause their collapse is I take it hunger in Petrograd and Moscow, and if we supply food there, we shall be simply defeating our own ends.'[6] Instead, Carr identified heart and soul with the new League of Nations which emerged from the Paris Peace Conference, where he served as secretary of the New States Committee. There he pressed for the rights of suppressed nationalities such as the Balts and the Poles; also the Jews. Lloyd George was his hero, even though the Prime Minister all but ignored the advice of his officials. Carr's only reservation was the harsh treatment meted out to defeated Germany in the terms of the Versailles treaty concluded in June 1919, a concession to the French in a *quid pro quo* for the higher priority of further British imperial expansion.

The young Carr's liberalism was most evident in his sympathies for the new states of Eastern Europe. He had pressed for immediate recognition of the Paderewski Government 'supported by the vast majority of Poles'[7] and argued against a special status for Danzig that might deprive Poland of full sovereign rights over this key Baltic port. But the ugly struggle for power that ensued in Eastern Europe – not least the pogroms that so upset his colleague Lewis Namier – tested these liberal beliefs to breaking-point. In June 1920 a tour of Danzig, Warsaw and the 'Eastern Plebiscite Areas' took Carr to Teschen, a region disputed between the Poles and the Czechs. From there he reported that in spite of tragic incidents, the situation was farcical and a clear warning to those tempted to treat the successor states of Eastern Europe as serious entities. Disappointed, yes, but not entirely disillusioned – yet: at his new posting in Riga in the mid-1920s he steadfastly defended the right of the Latvians to sustain their national identity: 'It is scarcely decent for those who have comfortable seats inside to shout to those who are struggling in the doorway that these new languages are a nuisance,' he wrote in one despatch to London.[8] Much as he later became so clearly defined as a 'realist', he never really lost a deep sense of right and wrong in politics. The realism came to overshadow but never obliterated strongly held beliefs. As Tamara Deutscher used to observe (after Goethe), his were two hearts beating in the same breast.

For the time being, the loss of the golden age was seemingly compensated for by the new liberal vision of world order. At a time when the Bolsheviks themselves appeared on the retreat back to capitalism just as

Lloyd George had hoped, with the New Economic Policy in 1921, the 'visionary hopes' of post-war liberalism still stood untarnished. The revival of the international economy in the 1920s spelt an end to extravagant notions of world revolution which still hypnotised many in Moscow. In Riga, a boring backwater for an ambitious diplomat obliged to live there as the cheapest way of sustaining his newly acquired family, Carr occupied his many idle hours with Russian lessons taken with a priest and absorption in a culture that stood in stark antithesis to the complacent liberal rationalism in which he had been educated. In this connection it is striking that both Carr and his American counterpart, George Kennan, a little younger, should have undergone a similar experience and transformation, barely a few years distant, in Riga. For Carr, however, the metamorphosis went deeper, most probably because the contrast with his upbringing was all the more severe. In 'Notes from the Underground', Dostoevsky wrote: 'anything can be said about world history, things that might enter the head of only the most disordered imagination. The only thing that cannot be said is that it's rational.'[9] In *Crime and Punishment* the murderer Raskol'nikov defies morality. Although by temperament Carr was still recognizably a radical liberal, intellectually he had stepped out into a parallel universe. To what extent exposure to Russian culture added to what was already there in terms of ethics and morality, and to what extent it transformed what was in place, is difficult to measure. Certainly there were peculiarities of character, stemming from an unorthodox upbringing which estranged him emotionally from his parents, which the immersion in things Russian like Dostoevsky accentuated. 'I hate this conception of "ought", it's like "conscience",' he wrote many years later.[10] Raskol'nikov certainly felt similarly.

Always an outsider – even within the charmed and snobbish circle of the pre-war Foreign Office – Carr now acquired an outlook to match an instinctive heterodoxy. This outlook was not Bolshevik or Marxist – far from it. It was drawn from the exotic world of nineteenth-century Russian ideas. But it shared something with Bolshevism, itself a curious blend of old Russia and western Marxism, in its subversive effect on the Anglo-Saxon mind. For Bolshevism still held no attraction for the liberal. It was apparently incapable of remoulding the world it had inherited and, despite the enormity of the blood-sacrifice in its wake, it had yet to prove itself a self-sustaining force, let alone a model for others. None the less Carr's attachment to Russian culture chipped away at the foundations of his liberalism. The Great Depression threatened to undermine its bases entirely since the free market was its foundation and simultaneously swept an entire country – Germany – into an irrational barbarism under the charismatic charm of Adolf Hitler, a phenomenon the liberal mind was incapable of accurately assessing until it was too late. And Carr, not unlike many liberals and not a few conservatives of his disoriented but still self-confident generation, saw Hitler as a manifestation of German revival.

Quite apart from its devastating impact upon the economic life of the western world, the Great Depression sapped the spirit of progress so dear to the Victorian mind. Carr was profoundly disturbed. 'The prevailing state of mind in England to-day is one of defeatism or...scepticism, of disbelief in herself. England has ceased to have ideals or, if she has them, to believe in the possibility of their fulfilment. Alone among the Great Powers she has ceased to have a mission.' 'The government of the day,' he wrote in 1930, 'has so little faith in its capacity to tackle the major problems of our generation that it invites the other parties to assist with their advice (imagine Mr Gladstone invoking the assistance of Lord Beaconsfield!); and the principal opposition party, knowing full well there is no solution, declines the invitation and keeps its hands free to wash them of the consequences...We have no convictions beyond a vague sort of fatalism.' Yet Carr was at heart always the optimist: 'We shall begin once more to believe in ourselves, to find creeds worth defending, causes worth fighting for, missions worth fulfilling. The fashion of indifference and the cult of futility will pass away; and we shall cease to be defeatists. But in the meanwhile we need a faith – or at any rate a passable fetish,' he concluded, never able to resist an opportunity for a light touch of irony.[11]

Into this vacuum strode a brutal visionary, Stalin. Instead of succumbing feebly and indecisively to the apparently irresistible advances of world capitalism, the Russians launched themselves into a frantic programme of re-industrialization and the forced and therefore bloody collectivization of agriculture, designed to provide the material bases for the security of the regime and, so they desperately hoped, more than a modicum more. Still in the remote offices of Whitehall and supposedly busying himself with the duties of state, Carr was clearly intrigued:

They have discovered a new religion of the Kilowatt and the Machine, which may well be the creed for which modern civilisation is waiting...This new religion is growing up on the fringes of a Europe which has lost faith in herself. Contemporary Europe is aimlessly drifting, refusing to face unpalatable facts, and looking for external remedies for her difficulties. The important question for

Europe at the present time is . . . whether the steel production of the Soviet Union will overtake that of Great Britain and France . . . whether Europe can discover in herself a driving force, an intensity of faith, comparable to that now being generated in Russia.[12]

No sooner had the liberal economic order collapsed than its offspring, the international order, followed suit. The Japanese successfully invaded China with scarcely a squeal of protest from the West, all-absorbed in its own domestic disarray. The British navy mutinied. The Americans turned their backs contemptuously on the outer world. The French encouraged the Japanese against Moscow. Mussolini soon marched into helpless Abyssinia and the poison gas had barely dispersed when Hitler uprooted the Versailles settlement and began to drag the rest of Europe into barbarism.

In this baffling chaos many reached out for a new faith, fascism or communism. The examples come immediately to mind of Oswald Moseley, Harold Nicolson and even Aneurin Bevan's future wife, Jenny Lee (temporarily), groping towards activism of the Right, largely out of sheer frustration; Philby, Burgess, Maclean, Blunt and Cairncross, on the Left. Carr always recognized the importance of belief and commitment but was himself too much the outsider, his own Victorian individualism too deeply engrained, to surrender his identity, to join a new and fashionable tribe and submit to alien customs. Although vehemently critical of the age of scepticism and indeed contemptuous of the apparent nihilism of 'The Waste Land', his own earlier beliefs had been undermined almost entirely. Hereafter he was, as Isaac Deutscher later noted, *au-delà de la mêlée*. Willing to diagnose, perhaps even too eager to prescribe, he was never really prepared to join others in attempting to treat the patient, at least under anyone else's authority.

Carr's pro-German sentiment to some extent curtailed his career at the Foreign Office, not surprisingly given the Permanent Under-Secretary Robert Vansittart's rather different views. 'Germans enter Rhineland,' Carr wrote in his diary on 7 March 1936. 'Home to lunch.' A radio broadcast he gave a year later made clear that this was a considered, not an impetuous, reaction (much to the unease of the producer). In these last months at the Office he was even willing to advocate amputation of other countries to appease the German appetite. His newfound realism combined with his pro-Germanism to make him the foremost proponent of abandoning south-eastern Europe to Hitler's domination, a move which Prime Minister Neville Chamberlain later made, with disastrous consequences in March 1939 when Hitler's troops marched in and the British washed their hands like Pontius Pilate, though arguably with less dignity. It was amidst these momentous events in the international arena that Carr took up the Woodrow Wilson Chair in International Politics at the University of Wales in Aberystwyth, a position he used to proselytise for the appeasement of Nazi Germany. Carr was never anti-Semitic. On the contrary, his best-loved intellectual company was invariably Jewish – to name only the most prominent: the novelist Stefan Zweig, the historian Namier, the Deutschers, indeed his last wife, Betty Behrens. But he had a deep-seated respect for German culture typical of upper-middle class Victorians and a natural disdain characteristic of Liberal and Labour opinion (he was a *Manchester Guardian* reader) for the heavy-handed treatment meted out to Germany in 1919. It was therefore inevitable that when he embarked on the composition of a text on international politics, it should end up as part polemic for the German case and part abstract analysis of the nature of international relations.

The resulting work, *The Twenty Years' Crisis*, was the product of bitter disillusion with the liberal world order and all that went with it, including classical economics and the easy assumption originating with Florus the epitomist that trade forges the bonds that bind mankind together. The title was originally to read *Utopia and Reality*. Nothing that had come before quite prepared the reader for such a devastating and brutal assault on cherished values. Like Machiavelli's *The Prince*, the text drew both from personal experience of statecraft and from intensive reading. Carr was also greatly influenced by Niebuhr's *Moral Man and Immoral Society* which presented modern society in the spirit of Rousseau, with the same present pessimism and only distant optimism, and by the work of Karl Mannheim, who borrowed from the spirit of Marx. The sparks of illusion still remaining were all but extinguished when Stalin turned on the Soviet people with a savagery difficult even for the Fabian left to ignore; though some did so with alarming consistency (notably the Webbs, Sidney rather more than Beatrice). 'The liberal friends of the Soviet Union, who took at its face value the new "democratic" constitution announced for adoption ... next November [1936], and who persuaded themselves that the Soviet regime were really moving at last in the direction of liberty and toleration, cannot conceal their bewilderment,' Carr wrote, in large part expressing his own opinion, as well as that of many others.[13] The outbreak of war in 1939 thus found him rudderless in open sea.

Yet even while the shocks to his ideals were having their most forceful and degenerative impact from the Great Depression through to the outbreak of war, Carr spent a good deal of time researching and writing two works which highlight another side to his spirit. These were *The Romantic Exiles* and *Michael Bakunin*. Nothing seemed more odd to proprietorial intellectuals like the disgruntled American Edmund Wilson than for a pin-striped British bureaucrat to spend his idle hours collecting and dissecting exotic Russian revolutionaries of the nineteenth century. At New College, Oxford, the young and ambitious Isaiah Berlin saw Carr as a kind of whimsical butterfly collector who merely happened on an unusual variety from the human genus worth pinning stuffed under glass for posterity. Some critics, indeed, found it not merely odd but positively disgraceful, and castigated him severely for doing so. Yet these works still have an extraordinarily wide range of admirers, such as the retired American statesman Paul Nitze, not themselves noted for undue squeamishness; the kind that laughs at Chekhov rather than cries into their handkerchief.

'The war came as a shock which numbed the thinking process,' Carr recalled.[14] Yet he was least of all passive, even when undergoing a crisis, however serious. He began writing leaders and before long he was ensconced in the Assistant Editor's chair at *The Times*. Soon he became Churchill's *bête noire* with his advocacy of 'a sort of liberal Utopia, mixed with a little socialism'.[15] The Prime Minister, Carr wrote in July 1940, 'expressed the mood of the nation when he declared that our only present war aim is victory. Nevertheless the British will to victory is still bound up with the conviction that our war aims stand on a different plane from those of the enemy, and that victory for our aims will point the way to a new social and international order in Europe.' What he advocated was a sort of common market involving some kind of supranational planning; 'some measure of pooled resources and centralized control is necessary for the survival of European civilization,' he wrote. And the democracy he envisaged as the framework for this new order was not merely political, but also social democracy, including the 'right to work'. 'The new order cannot be based on the preservation of privilege, whether the privilege be that of a country, of a class, or of an individual,' he concluded.[16]

It was as a result of this socialist proselytism that *The Times* was disparagingly referred to in some quarters as the threepenny *Daily Worker*. Yet, however shocking to self-satisfied establishment opinion, these utopian excursions matched the mood of war-torn Britain, desperate for change and fed up with the assemblage of stuffy old men still running the country. Carr's book *Conditions of Peace*, which amplified this major theme, swiftly became a best-seller. People were yearning for something different, and the massive victory of the Labour Party at the polls in the summer of 1945 testified as much. But it was Russia's enforced entry into the war which struck the greatest resonance in Carr's own mind. He recalled:

> In *The Times* I very quickly began to plug the Russian alliance; and, when this was vindicated by Russian endurance and the Russian victory, it revived my initial faith in the Russian revolution as a great achievement and a historical turning-point. It was obvious that the Russia of the second world war was a very different place from the Russia of the first – in terms of people as well as of material resources. Looking back on the thirties, I came to feel that my preoccupation with the purges and brutalities of Stalinism had distorted my perspective. The black spots were real enough, but looking exclusively at them destroyed one's vision of what was really happening.[17]

Russia's outstanding performance in the war – despite unpreparedness at the time of invasion and the ghastly strategic mistakes precipitated by Stalin in 1941–42 – thus triggered in Carr the decision, reached in the autumn of 1944, to write a history of the 'political, social, and economic order' which emerged from the ashes of the October Revolution. 'I began to see that the Russian Revolution occupied the same place in the modern world as the French Revolution,' he later acknowledged, 'and that, in spite of its horrors and of the hostility it provoked among most civilized people, it had brought into the world a lot of new concepts and new ways of looking at, and organizing, society. I wanted to study this, and discover what these new ways were and how they worked.'[18]

Initially he hoped 'to go as far as the Stalin constitution [1936] . . . or perhaps to the beginning of the second world war, though this might mean more than a five-year plan for myself.'[19] And by then he was well into the writing of *The Bolshevik Revolution*, the first of what would finally amount to fourteen weighty tomes. His aim was 'to combine an imaginative understanding of the outlook and purpose of his *dramatis personae* with an overriding appreciation of the universal significance of the events' he intended to describe.[20] The task soon enveloped him, absorbing his tireless mind and providing a sense of mission and commitment in a life that had hitherto wanted in central purpose.

It is difficult to outline Carr's qualities as a historian without slipping into cliché, yet the picture would be sadly incomplete without some attention to them. First, there was his almost unfailing precision, imbued into him by his former classics tutor A.E. Housman, whose ruthless criticism of those unhappy enough to be caught in his line of fire was notorious: 'accuracy is a duty, not a virtue'.[21] It is, indeed, worth comparing Housman's ruthless reviews with Carr's sometimes caustic essays in the *Times Literary Supplement*. Second, his approach to sources was fastidious. He would tick off others in no uncertain terms for being too trusting of evidence merely because it was in print. 'It is a common illusion,' he used to say, mixing acid with his ink, 'that bad sources become reliable when no good source is available to refute them.' Third, the range of his research was vast. When hostile critics accused him of being 'encyclopaedic', as indeed did the Polish-American Richard Pipes, they were not wrong. Fourth, there was his treatment of sources. He would quickly pick them up, turn them upside down, shake them, look at them from every conceivable angle and, if he did not then discard them, he would squeeze them to the last drop. These sources were then framed within an overarching vision and brought to life through the exercise of an acute historical imagination. For Carr the historian was no mere chronicler. He like Collingwood deeply disparaged 'scissors-and-paste history'.[22] And his very method of composition, as described below, bears out his insistence on interpretation first:

> The commonest assumption appears to be that the historian divides his work into two sharply distinguishable phases or periods. First, he spends a long preliminary period reading his sources and filling his notebooks with facts: then, when this is over, he puts away his sources, takes out his notebooks, and writes his book from beginning to end. This is to me an unconvincing and unplausible picture. For myself, as soon as I have got going on a few of what I take to be the capital sources, the itch becomes too strong and I begin to write – not necessarily at the beginning, but anywhere. Thereafter, reading and writing go on simultaneously. The writing is added to, subtracted from, re-shaped, cancelled, as I go on reading. The reading is directed and made fruitful by the writing: the more I write, the more I know what I am looking for, the better I understand the significance and relevance of what I find.[23]

For Carr history was both art and science; science with respect to accuracy and analysis, art with respect to imaginative reconstruction. History, he insisted, could not be written unless the historian is able attain some kind of empathy with the mind of those about whom he is writing.[24] He himself had an amazing capacity for bringing long-dead characters to life after his reading a minimum of material. His penultimate volume, *The Twilight of Comintern*, bears eloquent witness to this. The vision was then speedily translated into organizational form. Unfortunately with respect to the magnum opus, the *History of Soviet Russia*, and to the bewilderment of the purchaser, the mansion under construction had a tendency to assume a life of its own, sprouting enormous east wings, west wings, attics, balconies, basements, seemingly redundant outhouses and garden follies, making the original plans a historical curiosity rather than a working outline. None the less, individual volumes – most notably *The Interregnum* – have an elegance of form and structure that only the envious critic would deny.

Lastly, the imposing framework encased a lucidity of exposition, which was the product of both a supremely confident mastery of the sources and casual fluency sustained by constant practice. Indeed, his only advice to a graduate student was to write and keep on writing. Drafts were farmed out to the informed for criticism – usually to those who had no idea anyone else was so privileged! On return they were then worked over repeatedly until the mosaic was at last complete. The final product, an imposing and intimidating edifice, aroused intense animosity as much as widespread acclaim. What some referred to as detached objectivity, others chose to damn as a bloodless quality – points of praise were easily inverted into evidence for the prosecution. One feature, though, which is generally accepted by both critics and supporters alike is Carr's tendency to see developments from the top of the pile. Just as his nostalgia for Edwardian England was peculiar to his station in life, so too did he instinctively identify with the views of Soviet leaders – as patrician as the Victorians – who were dragging their country into the twentieth century. Carr was also working against the prevailing dogma that the history of the Soviet Union should be written through the eyes of the *émigré*. Whereas he read and absorbed what they had to say, where possible he cited Soviet documentation, which became a point of irritation as much with the Deutschers as it did with the likes of Bertram Wolfe or Richard Pipes. Yet in basing the bulk of his interpretation on an analysis of Soviet official sources he was merely following standard Foreign Office practice – indeed, Quai d'Orsay or Farmesina practice – which continued to the end. Besides, Carr also made extensive use of foreign archives. He could read Russian, French and German with no difficulty at all. He relied on others for material in Polish, Italian, Spanish, Mongolian, Japanese and Chinese. This illustrates a related quality, that, despite accusations of arrogance, which were not entirely without foundation, he had the humility to work by

Cato's maxim: that a wise man learns even from fools, whereas a fool fails to learn even from the wise. Indeed, the queue of those – by no means fools – who contributed to his research, paid and unpaid, is longer than many might suspect.

Carr's death in 1982 prompted an unpleasant outburst of vituperative and personal criticism, not unconnected with the revival of the Right in Britain under Mrs Thatcher's premiership. The vultures were already gathering overhead as his life gave out. He took the view that the hostility aroused in the West by his work largely resulted from the fact that the political climate in which he was working had turned markedly anti-Soviet:

> When I first planned my work . . . it seemed natural (though no doubt foolish) to hope that the co-operation uneasily established during the war would be continued and further developed after the victory. When my first volume was published in 1950 disputes between east and west had reached a high pitch of exasperation; the 'people's democracies' had belied their name, and the seeds of McCarthyism were beginning to sprout.[25]

Indeed, no sooner had the great undertaking begun than Carr found himself almost alone in the wilderness. His outspoken pro-Sovietism exiled him from establishment circles. He was denied Chairs at London and Oxford. Even King's College, Cambridge, found him too controversial to absorb. Finally he found a tenuous position at Balliol for a couple of years where he was unhappily denied a Fellowship and then a firmer seat at his alma mater, Trinity College, Cambridge, which, typically, knew next to nothing of his work but took him in because they knew him to be famous. Consolation was also found throughout the ordeal in the company of fellow outcasts such as the Marxist Isaac Deutscher, a man even more unacceptable to polite society; given the thumbs down by Isaiah Berlin when considered for a Chair at Sussex University.[26] Britain, too, had its dose of McCarthyism, though, unlike the United States, tempered by a liberalism indigenous to the political culture. It was none the less sufficient to induce a debilitating self-censorship into the minds of a generation and block the vociferous dissentient from the highest seats of learning.

The isolation, imposed from without, nevertheless found an echo within. Carr suffered a perpetual sense of anomie, which inevitably increased his natural independence of mind. 'I am not prepared to submit to this kind of moral blackmail' was a phrase that came readily to his lips. At Trinity as an undergraduate he had studied Greek and Roman history under a classics don who taught him that Herodotus' account of the Persian Wars 'was shaped and moulded by his attitude to the Peloponnesian War, which was going on at the time he wrote'.[27] Carr found this 'a fascinating revelation', and he never forgot the lesson it imparted. Both in his history writing and in his political posturing, Carr consciously distanced himself from the dominant ideology, the prevailing intellectual fashion – at times to an almost perverse degree. This feature was particularly evident in his *History of Soviet Russia*. It was a quality reinforced by the extraordinary fatalism with which he accepted the enormous and traumatic changes that struck the world during his long lifetime. This sense of fatalism set him apart from those who found these changes unacceptable. It was also a vital precondition for a writer of contemporary history. It was second nature for him to reverse the telescope onto the recent past, and he had little time for those who squirmed at the idea that past events were anything other than inevitable:

> The trouble about contemporary history is that people remember the time when all the options were still open, and find it difficult to adopt the attitude of the historian for whom they have been closed by the *fait accompli*. This is a purely emotional and unhistorical reaction,[28]

he declared, swatting the mosquito with a decisive and fatal blow.

This is the thread that binds the cool and dispassionate survey of the history of Soviet Russia to the outspoken and emotionally charged condemnation of those in the west who attacked the USSR in his lifetime. He lived too long, witnessed too many twists and turns in fickle public consciousness to accept meekly what was in fashion as an essential truth. He loved to spit at orthodoxy, and one cannot but see his latter-day empathy with the New Left partly as the product of this still youthful spirit of rebellion and partly, but perhaps more importantly, as an extension of his life-long concern at the process of decay eating away at the vitals of British society since 1914. At least the New Left held dear some essentials of the society in which he was reared: a belief in progress, a combative spirit. a dynamism then sadly lacking within the amorphous lump that occupied the centre of the political arena in Britain. Here, perhaps, lay the seeds of a better time to come, the hidden link with the nineteenth century, the heirs to Marx and Victoria in one.

The Soviet Union collapsed in 1991 and with it the hopes of many left of centre and not merely Communists – J.K. Galbraith being one prominent example – who had expected a more humane version of Soviet socialism to survive and, indeed, prosper. But it was all too late. The tanks that crushed the Prague Spring in August 1968 had at Bratislava passed a milestone on the road to the system's self-destruction. Carr himself would have been crestfallen, deeply disturbed by the sudden collapse under Gorbachev. The new Russia took off in a direction few if any envisaged at the start of the Gorbachev era and Yeltsin's Russia came to resemble the comprador capitalism of early eighteenth-century Britain, with all the vigour and corruption characteristic of that time and place present in equal measure: 'All Trades and Places knew some Cheat/ No Calling was without Deceit.'[29]

Although Carr acquired an emotional attachment for the Soviet system, one should not ignore the fact that the attachment to Russia predates his interest in the system, and that he came into things Russian via literature not politics. Carr was invariably pro-Russian, regardless of the system. Even mild criticism of the Orthodox Church would upset him and produce a tart retort. So, though despairing at the loss of so many dreams, Carr would not have completely written off this very different future. He was ever the optimist, regardless of the odds; his life, having been shorn of its original roots, spent searching for a meaning that ultimately defied him. The precise meaning of 'progress' had eluded him, dissolved into a 'general advance'[30] that entailed the 'progressive development of human potentialities,'[31] a broad sweep that encompasses Mill as well as Marx. In the end it was the fact of movement that raised his spirits. It was this that always held him back from condemning out of hand any part of the historical process and that would have included what is happening in Russia today.

Notes

1   For a much fuller discussion of the issues raised here see the author's biography of Carr, *The Vices of Integrity: E.H. Carr, 1892–1982* (London, Verso, 1999). Meanwhile, let the author record here his gratitude to the late Tamara Deutscher, who opened a window onto Carr's life which no one else could have done.
2   J.M. Keynes, *The Economic Consequences of the Peace* (New York, 1920), pp. 18–21.
3   Carr's autobiographical note, written for Tamara Deutscher, in 1980. (See above, pp. xiii–xxii).
4   Carr to Tamara Deutscher, 9 August 1982.

5 Carr's autobiographical note.
6 Minute for Sir Eyre Crowe, 29 December 1917: *Foreign Office* (FO) 382/1421 (Public Record Office, Kew).
7 Minute, 10 February 1919: *FO* 608/61.
8 Carr to Austen Chamberlain, Foreign Secretary, 30 October 1926: *FO* 371/11736.
9 F. Dostoevsky, *Notes from the Underground and the Gambler* (Oxford, Oxford University Press, 1991) p. 31.
10 Carr to Tamara Deutscher, 23 June 1974.
11 'England Adrift', *The Fortnightly Review*, September 1930.
12 *Ibid.*, September 1931.
13 'The Twilight of the Bolsheviks', *The Spectator*, 28 August 1936. It is a striking testimony to the consistency of Carr's thinking and the pattern of his memory that when he came to choose a title for his penultimate work, he settled upon *The Twilight of Comintern* 1930–1935 (London, Macmillan, 1982).
14 Carr's autobiographical note.
15 *Ibid.*
16 'The New Europe', *The Times*, 1 July 1940. One has to be careful, however, in quoting the editorials entirely as Carr's opinions. The then Assistant Editor, later Editor, all too often – from Carr's point of view – toned down the more controversial expressions of opinion. Carr wrote a note to me to this effect in the summer of 1982.
17 Carr's autobiographical note.
18 Carr to Betty Behrens, 19 February 1966.
19 'Work in Progress: Problems of Writing Modern Russian History', *The Listener*, 7 October 1948.
20 *History of Soviet Russia: The Bolshevik Revolution*, Vol. 1 (London, Macmillan, 1950), p. v.
21 Quoted from M. Malunius, *Astronomicon: Liber Primus* (Cambridge, Cambridge University Press, 1937), p. 87, in Carr, *What Is History?* (New York, Macmillan, 1962), p. 8.
22 Carr, *What Is History*, p. 30.
23 *Ibid.*, pp. 32–3.
24 He was, however, very careful to distinguish empathy from 'sympathy': *ibid.*, pp. 26–7.
25 Carr's autobiographical note.
26 Berlin insisted to me, by way of exculpation, that he had said Deutscher would be worthy of a Chair of Marxism, but not a Chair of History.
27 *Ibid.*
28 Carr, *What Is History?*, p. 128.
29 B. Mandeville, *The Grumbling Hive: or Knaves turn'd Honest.*
30 *What Is History?*, p. 208.
31 *Ibid.*, p. 157.

2

E.H. Carr – the Aberystwyth Years, 1936–1947

Brian Porter

Edward Hallett Carr was appointed to the Woodrow Wilson Chair of International Politics at Aberystwyth in March 1936 at the age of 43. A Cambridge double-first in classics, he had joined the Foreign Office in 1916 as a career diplomat. Three years later, as one of the British delegation to the Paris Peace Conference, he saw high-level diplomacy at first hand. He later served in Latvia and Geneva, and back at the Foreign Office as adviser on League of Nations affairs. But he was also a scholar, with a particular interest in Russia and Russian literature. His years in Riga (1925–29), then a listening post for events in the Soviet Union, gave him the opportunity to develop this interest. Already on coming to Aberystwyth he had published works on Dostoevsky, Marx and Alexander Herzen and his circle, and he was now engaged on a life of the revolutionary anarchist, Michael Bakunin.

That Carr in his forties should have decided to enter academic life, and by applying for a post so far from the political heart of the country as Aberystwyth, may seem surprising, but the Woodrow Wilson Chair had unusual advantages. As few students took papers in the subject, which had then to be combined with either History or Economics, the tutoring demands were slight, and although the professor was required each year to give a number of public lectures at Aberystwyth, plenty of time was available for anyone wishing to travel or write. It was, in effect, a research chair. That it had been set up in the first place was owing to the idealism, enthusiasm and forceful personality of the President of the University College of Wales, Lord Davies of Llandinam, and the story of Carr's tenure of the Chair cannot be fully understood without first looking at the intentions and hopes of that extraordinary man, its founder.

David Davies was born in 1880, the grandson of a Welsh industrial pioneer who had made a fortune from the bulk export of coal from

South Wales. Like his grandfather he had entered politics as a Liberal and served as MP for Montgomeryshire from 1906 to 1929. The Davies family saw their great wealth as a debt which in one way or another had to be repaid to the people of Wales, and they did this both through public service and by supporting such causes as health, medicine, education and the arts. Towards the University College of Wales at Aberystwyth they had been outstanding benefactors, and now, at the conclusion of the Great War, came one of the most imaginative and innovative of their munificent gifts.

Having served on the Western Front, where he commanded a volunteer battalion of his own raising until recalled by Lloyd George to serve as his Parliamentary Private Secretary, Davies emerged from the war appalled by the waste and carnage he had witnessed. He thereupon resolved to do all in his power to ensure that such a catastrophe should never recur. To this end, and as a tribute to those of its students who had fallen in the war, he and his sisters, Gwendoline and Margaret Davies, subscribed £20,000 to found at the College a Chair for the systematic study of international politics with particular emphasis upon the promotion of peace. This was a brilliant academic innovation, and to Davies must go the credit for having founded a new university discipline which is now taught and studied the world over.

He was also much attracted by the whole conception of the League of Nations, and threw himself into the work of organizing the public support which he believed necessary for its success. Indeed, he soon saw the Chair as the ideal instrument for giving intellectual support to the League idea and in 1922 named it 'The Woodrow Wilson Chair' in honour of the League's principal founder and advocate.

The restless energy of David Davies found its outlet all through the inter-war years in the vigorous pursuit of idealistic schemes, mostly with world peace as the objective, and invariably reflecting his impatient, impulsive, authoritarian personality. No one could say that his ideas were not original and daring. One such, before the League had even begun, was that its headquarters should be sited on the outskirts of Constantinople, not only to serve as a bridge between East and West, between Islam and Christianity, but that, so placed, the world body could both over-awe the turbulent Balkans and protect neighbouring Armenia, then briefly enjoying independence. Geneva he ruled out. The League must be a 'doer' like himself and he had no time for the tradition of Swiss neutrality and hence for Geneva as a setting for the dynamic and potent body he deemed essential for preserving world order. But Geneva was chosen and in various other ways Davies became disenchanted with the institution in which he had placed so much hope. By the end of its first decade he had become convinced that the League as it stood could not prevent a war. Indeed, it seems to have been in his eyes little more than a 'Neighbourhood Watch' scheme in the world of Al Capone. What was wanted, he concluded, was an all-powerful international police force, using the latest in modern weaponry, and capable of crushing any aggressor with speed and determination. This idea, which was to become obsessive with him, was fully worked out in a large tome which he published in 1930: *The Problem of the Twentieth Century*.

It is worth, at this point, describing the Davies plan for world peace in a little detail for, although pacifism in one form or another seems to have made a greater public impact, it illustrates the type of thinking that was symptomatic of the 1930s. Indeed, Davies' book received respectful reviews from both *International Affairs* and *The Times Literary Supplement*, so indicating something of the prevalence of the thought-world with which Carr would later have to grapple. Under the Davies plan, the League Council was to be a businesslike body unhampered by the unanimity principle and the presence of minor states. It was to be more like the future UN Security Council, although without the veto. Whenever a dispute arose, it was to go to the International Court if it was justiciable, and to an Equity Tribunal consisting of impartial and disinterested experts if it was not. The role of the police force, made up of quotas of men and armaments drawn from the member states, was to enforce, if necessary, the decisions of these bodies, as well as to take instant retaliatory action should a clear case of aggression occur.

How the police force was to operate was spelt out in detail. It was to be under five Constables, each of which would be provided by one of five major powers in turn. They were to be, in the first instance: a High Constable (French), a Naval Constable (British), an Air Constable (Italian), an Artillery Constable (German) and a Chemical Constable, to take charge of poison gas (Japanese). Moreover, these five Constables were to command a monopoly of the world's most devastating weapons – bombers, tanks, heavy guns, submarines and poison gas – which were to be stored in what he saw, through its Christian associations over nearly 2,000 years, as the fountainhead of peace: Palestine. This was to be the freehold territory of the force which also, he suggested, should control Suez, the Bosphorus, Gibraltar and Panama, and have bases, in return for protection, in small states such as Haiti, Albania and Monaco. That the United States and the Soviet Union had hitherto not joined the League did not deter the plan's author; he had every hope that they would take part once they were persuaded of the incalculable benefits it would bring both to themselves, in the form of savings on the cost of armaments, and to the world at large.[1]

This idea, in its various elaborations, David Davies seized every opportunity to promote: through the League of Nations Union, of which he was a Vice-President; through a new body which he himself founded and financed called the New Commonwealth Society; and, after his elevation to the peerage in 1932, in the House of Lords. Indeed, whenever the subject of a debate allowed, he argued for an international force to ensure the peace of Europe, claiming that this could be done with the deployment of 1,000 aeroplanes, manned by volunteers.

To Lord Davies' surprise and vexation, none of the professors appointed to the Woodrow Wilson Chair had shown much enthusiasm for these ideas, even though the urgent need for the full implementation of them was to him self-evident. True, they were interested in the League, and gave proper consideration to it in their teachings; indeed, the second professor, Charles Webster, had, in co-operation with his junior colleague, Sydney Herbert, published in 1933 a book entitled *The League of Nations in Theory and Practice* and dedicated it 'To Baron Davies of Llandinam, A Fighter for Peace', but Webster's successor, the retired American banker, Jerome Greene, had expressed an unhelpful scepticism about the use of sanctions as a means of preserving world order. Lord Davies expected more from the Chair and Department which he had founded. The Principal, Ifor Evans, later recorded that in July 1934 Lord Davies had told him:

> he had been greatly disappointed to find that Professor Greene had expressed opinions on the proposed international police force which were diametrically opposed to those he himself advocated and felt that, as founder of the Chair, his views were entitled to some consideration when the new appointment was made. This remark caused me very considerable anxiety.[2]

This was the first intimation of a brewing storm which would later rage around Carr.

The chance that Lord Davies could secure for the Chair a candidate more of his way of thinking had come with the resignation of Greene in March 1934. In the first months of the vacancy a number of nominations were made and discussed, including those of David Mitrany, the Romanian-born pioneer of 'functionalism'; Sir Ronald Graham, former Ambassador to Rome; C.A. Macartney, historian, and currently employed in the Intelligence Department of the League of Nations Union;

D.W. Brogan, a lecturer at LSE, of whom Webster thought very highly; Vernon Bartlett, the writer on current affairs; and Professor Arnold Toynbee. There was also the suggestion that a German-Jewish refugee should be found and appointed, some 'Einstein' in the world of international politics.[3] (Curiously, the nearest approach to such a one, Hans J. Morgenthau, was shortly to look for employment, to be appointed, only months before the onset of the Spanish Civil War, to a lectureship in Madrid.)

An unusual candidate was W. Arnold-Forster, nominated by Sir Arthur Salter of All Souls. He was by profession a painter who had studied at the Slade, and had no academic background in either international politics or relevant subjects. But he had written on such topics as arbitration, security and disarmament, he supported the cause of the League with an evangelizing fervour, and he impressed his sponsor. Salter wrote of him to Davies: 'Arnold Forster [sic] is the best man. He has a quite extraordinary knowledge of the "international" history of the last two decades; he has had administrative experience in the blockade work of the Foreign Office and the Supreme Economic Council; he is a lucid and good speaker; and a quite exceptionally good writer of pamphlets. He is an extremely hard worker...'[4] At this stage Lord Davies replied that although these were strong arguments, 'I still have my doubts as to whether he is the right man for the Chair at Aberystwyth.'[5] Arnold-Forster also received backing from Gilbert Murray, who described him as 'our strongest card' and a 'live wire', as well as from Lord Robert Cecil: 'I certainly know no-one who would be more qualified to fill such an appointment as he.'[6]

The selectors, however, were prepared to take time to make the right choice, and for a while matters remained at a standstill until later in 1934 an approach was made to Kingsley Martin, the editor of the _New Statesman_, who was given six months in which to make up his mind.[7] His reply that he was not quite what was required must be accounted one of his sounder judgements. Still, like Denis Healey in 1950, he was certainly one of the more interesting of those who, it seems, could have had the Chair for the asking, but for whom, in the event, the pull of London proved too strong.

On 9 August 1935 the Joint Selection Committee decided to advertise for candidates by publishing the following notice:

There is at present a vacancy in the above Chair for which applications are invited. The Professor will normally be expected to lecture in Aberystwyth for two terms in each academic year. The salary of the

Chair is £1,000 a year, with superannuation under the federated superannuation scheme for Universities. Travelling expenses will be granted for the pursuance of approved schemes of research and travel. These will not normally be less than £200 nor more than £400 in any given year. The subject of 'International Politics' is defined, in the Trust Deed, as being 'political science in its application to international relations, with special reference to the best means for promoting peace between nations'. Applications, together with any references or testimonials, should be sent by 5th October, 1935, to the Principal, who will provide further details if desired.[8]

The provision made for travel was one of the attractions of the Chair. In 1919 during the early months of his tenure, Zimmern, the first professor, had visited Egypt before going on to Palestine to investigate the conditions for Jewish settlement; Jerome Greene had returned to the United States to enquire into the Depression; but the greatest traveller of all was the second professor, Charles Webster, who, in pursuance of Lord Davies' desire that the cause of the academic teaching of International Politics should be fostered throughout the world, did an enormous amount of journeying and lecturing abroad, usually taking off for the purpose two terms in every three, but whole years in 1927 and 1929–30.

The advertisement of the Chair brought in 37 applications additional to those of Arnold-Forster, Mitrany and Macartney, held over from the previous batch of nominations. Amongst the applicants this time were: Stanley Bailey, Senior Lecturer in International Relations at LSE and with a growing reputation in the subject; Geoffrey Barraclough, historian, of Merton College, Oxford; Herbert Butterfield, historian, of Peterhouse, Cambridge; E.H. Carr at the Foreign Office; Alfred Cobban, the future historian of modern France and of national self-determination; and Sydney Herbert.[9] The last had been involved in the Department at Aberystwyth from its very beginning in 1919. A young civil servant whose qualities had so impressed Zimmern that he persuaded the Trustees to appoint him as his assistant, he proved indispensable to the first two professors and took over the Departmental duties both during the year-long vacancy following Zimmern's departure in 1921, and throughout Webster's lengthy absences abroad. A formidable pacifist whose recreation was fencing, he transferred to the History Department in 1930.

At the end of 1935 the Woodrow Wilson Advisory Board, sitting as a selection committee, met to consider the applicants. The membership of the Board had been laid down by Lord Davies and the College in

1922. It consisted of the College Principal, chairman *ex officio*, and nominees of: the College Council and Senate, the Foreign Secretary, the League of Nations Union, the Royal Institute of International Affairs, and the two ancient universities alternately. On this occasion the members were: Ifor L. Evans (Principal), Lord Davies (Council), Professor E.A. Lewis (Senate), Lord Granville (Foreign Secretary's nominee), Professor Gilbert Murray (LNU), General Sir Neill Malcolm (RIIA), and W.G.S. Adams (Warden of All Souls, it being Oxford's turn).[10] Their first task was to reduce the 40 applicants to a short list, four being chosen: Arnold-Forster, Butterfield, Carr and Macartney (Mitrany was dropped through being 'out of England'). It was decided to interview them at the Great Western Royal Hotel, Paddington (the usual venue for Aberystwyth staffing business) on 24 January 1936.

Surprisingly, the selectors began by eliminating Butterfield, a prolific historian who was later to become a noted theorist in International Relations. (Forty years later, when a guest lecturer at Aberystwyth, the former Vice-Chancellor of Cambridge, Master of Peterhouse and Regius Professor, made an amusing reference to this 'hiccup' in his career.) This left three candidates and the committee voted on them by the preference method, the first preference being accorded one point, the second two and the third three. Whoever had the greatest number of points against him would therefore be eliminated. The voting was: Macartney (12), Carr (13) and Arnold-Forster (17). They then had to decide between Macartney and Carr, and the result was a tie, with three votes given to each, at which the Principal, as chairman, gave his casting vote in favour of Carr. At this, Lord Davies, incensed that his first choice, Arnold-Forster, was already out of the running, vehemently objected, describing the proceedings as 'a farce' and declaring that he would have to explain to the Council that there was no unanimity in the committee. The Principal in consequence withdrew his casting vote and it was agreed to send both names to the College Council for final decision.[11] Lord Davies supported this proposal but immediately regretted doing so. He later wrote:

> It was at this point I made a bloomer. I should have then pressed for my former motion that all three names be sent up. Unfortunately this did not occur to me in the heat of the moment and some members of the committee were anxious to catch their trains. Trains are always the bugbear of committees.[12]

On the way to the platform Gilbert Murray said, 'We have done the wrong thing, we should have appointed Arnold-Forster, we have made a great mistake,' and Lord Davies agreed. 'Can't you think of some way out of it?', asked Murray. Lord Davies said he would try. He considered that the only way to retrieve the situation was to draft a minority report, which he and Gilbert Murray would sign, stressing the right of the Council to make its choice from all three candidates:

> I sent this report to Murray who signed it, then, before the Council met, he ratted and signed the majority report, so that I was left high and dry.... In the meantime the Principal had whipped up all the academic members and had suggested that, because my sisters and I were the founders of the Chair, we were bringing undue pressure upon the Council and of course these gentlemen, under the impression that the lay members were usurping their rights, supported our youthful dictator.[13]

At the same time, Lord Davies was also whipping up support for his favoured candidate and elicited a very strong letter of recommendation for Arnold-Forster from Sir Arthur Salter. Another marked 'Very Private' came from Philip Noel-Baker, who wrote on the very eve of the Council meeting:

> I believe Arnold-Forster to be extraordinarily well qualified from the academic point of view for a Chair. He has greater knowledge, theoretical and practical, of present day international relations than any professor of International Relations in England or the United States. I say that with confidence, knowing, I think, all the existing professors. I would not like this statement to be quoted as from me, because it might make me enemies among the existing professors. But my view is unreserved and emphatic.[14]

Among 'the existing professors' were Sir Alfred Zimmern at Oxford and Charles Manning, who in 1930 had succeeded Noel-Baker in the Chair at LSE. But Noel-Baker had little time for Manning, whom he used to refer to as 'that South African', and indeed he was dismissive of anyone not wholly committed to his own cherished cause of disarmament.[15]

The College Council travelled to Paddington on 6 March and assembled in the Great Western Royal Hotel. It had before the majority report asking it to decide between Carr and Macartney, and the minority report requesting that it consider all three. As before, the meeting was long and acrimonious. Lord Davies, in what the Principal later described as a long and rambling speech, with much shuffling of papers and

embarrassing to witness, sought to justify the line he had taken throughout these proceedings, claiming that as founder of the Chair his views
were deserving of due regard. The Council, however, rejected his minority report and, having interviewed the two candidates, appointed Carr, at
which Lord Davies angrily walked out of the meeting and immediately
afterwards resigned from the Presidency of the College.[16]

The circumstances in which E.H. Carr was appointed to the Woodrow
Wilson Chair in 1936 have a significance far greater than the mere
filling of a post, for the all-important principle of academic freedom
was at issue. For Lord Davies the overriding consideration was the cause
of world peace as furthered by a strengthened League of Nations and he
had come to believe that Arnold-Forster would prove a vital asset in that
campaign. 'My whole object,' he wrote to him a week before the Council
met, 'is to serve the cause of international relationships by securing a
professor for the chair who is wholehearted in his devotion to the cause
of international co-operation', and, a month after Arnold-Forster had
finally been turned down: 'in a sense one is fighting for the cause against
people like the Principal, who has very little interest in the development
of the ideas which you and I have so much at heart.'[17] In his letter of
resignation Lord Davies spoke bitterly of 'academic intolerance and
dictation', of a Council that had 'shirked its duty' and thus 'lost the
services of an outstanding personality who for so many years had
devoted his life to the cause of justice and peace in international relationships'.[18]

Principal Evans, for his part, smelt a conspiracy to 'fix' the appointment. He later wrote:

> It was obvious that a good many wires were being pulled by people
> who were not members of the Committee and had no connection
> with the College but who happened to be actively interested in the
> League of Nations Union. The subsequent publication of private
> correspondence by Lord Davies showed that those primarily con-
> cerned in this very unprofessional activity were Mr. Philip Noel-
> Baker, Lord Cecil and Sir Arthur Salter. Whether the lead originally
> came from them or from Lord Davies, it is impossible to decide on the
> evidence before me.[19]

He firmly believed that experience, power of analysis and intellectual
range should count for most in an important academic appointment,
and these he considered Carr possessed to a degree which Arnold-Forster
simply could not match. And most of the selection committee, as well as

the academics on the College Council, agreed with him. He was dismissive of Arnold-Forster, later commenting:

> In such a field as this there was no place for a nervous eccentric person, with no academic qualifications whatsoever, simply because he had done much useful work for the League of Nations Union. By occupation a painter and by predilection a propagandist, W. Arnold-Forster was simply not in the running and his appointment to an academic Chair would have been ridiculous. This was the view of a majority of the Committee. It was not the view of Lord Davies, who alone gave Arnold-Forster his first preference, because he, influenced by his friends of the League of Nations Union, regarded the Chair he had helped to found as a focal point for the spread of a given body of doctrine and not as a foundation devoted to the objective study of international affairs.[20]

This somewhat harsh verdict on Arnold-Forster (it underrated him according to Professor C.A.W. Manning of LSE[21]) reflects the intense antipathy that the Principal and the President had, by the time of the Carr appointment, come to feel for each other. It threw its shadow into the future and was to affect Carr's position at Aberystwyth throughout most of the time he was to hold the Chair. In part, this antagonism may have been due to the clash of two strong personalities, but an added factor was the peculiar character of the University of Wales, and the University College at Aberystwyth in particular.

The College had been founded in 1872 not only to provide Wales with a centre of higher education, but to be the leading educational expression of the Welsh national identity. In consequence, influential lay figures of the sort who had founded and financed the College, including some who were prominent in Welsh public life, had always played a major part in its supervision and in the appointment of its principal officers. For the most part, the Principal, always a Welshman and usually an academic, worked in harmony with this lay element, but occasionally he did not, and resented its interference in academic matters. The tension was potentially always present, and at times it broke surface. This was one such occasion, perhaps the most fractious in the history of the College. Lord Davies, first as Treasurer then as Vice-President, and finally, from 1926, as President, had occupied a key place in the lay governance of the College ever since 1903. Ifor L. Evans was his fourth Principal, and a young one at that. The scene was set for the sort of Trollopian imbroglio which every now and then, to public amazement, erupts in some Cathedral chapter-house. In his retrospective comment on the affair, Lord Davies wrote:

> The Welsh Colleges have always been regarded as democratic institutions. They are not supposed to be controlled by the academic gentlemen who are responsible for their administration but not their control.[22]

And in reply to the Principal who, in his letter pointing out that Arnold-Forster's appointment would be 'a disaster', had described himself as the President's 'principal academic advisor', he declared:

> you are certainly mistaken if you imagine that on every occasion, and under all circumstances I, or any other official of the College or member of the Council, must necessarily accept the advice of what you describe as our 'principal academic advisor'. The poor President or Chairman of the Council surely must be allowed to form his own opinions occasionally, even upon academic questions, especially the qualifications and merits of candidates for Chairs, and other appointments. I don't think . . . that the Principal should necessarily assume, or that he should occupy the status of the Mayor of the Palace or of a shogun, with whose ruling everyone else is expected to agree.[23]

Finally, in a letter to Gilbert Murray he commented: 'There are lots of Mussolinis knocking around. The only way of dealing with them is to fight them in the open, not to knuckle under in the dark.'[24]

Lord Davies was so far from 'knuckling under in the dark' that in resigning from the Presidency, a post he had held for a decade, he saw that his bitterly expressed letter of resignation, already referred to, was made available to the press. The repercussions spread outside Wales. Several ardent supporters of the League of Nations besought Lord Davies to move the Wilson Chair elsewhere, perhaps to 'Oxford, Cambridge or Edinburgh, where it might be more appreciated'.[25] But the fact was, it was in Wales, and Wales remained very much at the heart of Lord Davies' concerns.

The relationship between Wales and the international world, or rather how that relationship was perceived by certain people, forms part of the back-cloth to the job that Carr was now taking up. That Wales, small though it was, should concern itself with the destinies of the world, and should be seen to do so, was a view taken by many public-spirited Welshmen at the time and not least by Lord Davies, and by his secretary, co-worker and namesake (although no relation), the Reverend Gwilym Davies, a Baptist minister. Partly this was a reaction to the Great Power-dominated system of the nineteenth century, which, it was widely believed, had inevitably led to the Great War; with the League of Nations small states and nations had come into their own, and would, it was hoped, have a moderating and civilizing influence over brute power. In 1926 an opportunity presented itself to Lord Davies to make the League of Nations and its supporters aware of Wales. On finding that the delegates of the International Federation of League of Nations Societies were being prevented for political reasons from holding their annual conference in Dresden, he took the astonishing step of inviting them – more than 122 countries – to Aberystwyth, paying all their expenses from the moment they boarded a special first-class train at Paddington. He enlisted staff from the College to act as interpreters, secretaries, translators and guides, and arranged not only for coaches to take the foreign visitors into the countryside, but for the women of each village to greet them in Welsh national dress. In such ways did he aim to put Wales on 'the world map' as a nation committed to internationalism and peace.

The Reverend Gwilym Davies was equally active and ingenious in promoting Wales in these endeavours. In 1924 he organized a petition, pleading the cause of the League of Nations, and for which 400,000 signatures were collected, from the women of Wales to the women of the United States. A delegation of Welsh women took the petition to Washington, where they were received by President Coolidge and met Mrs Eleanor Roosevelt.[26] Another of his schemes was the broadcasting each year of 'A Message of Peace from the Children of Wales to the Children of the World' in the languages of all the countries he could persuade to participate. Not all the children of Wales were as eirenic as their self-appointed spokesman, however, and young Desmond Enoch, a neighbour's son and later to become a Marine, habitually thrust his toy tommy-gun into the author of the Message of Peace, with a cry of 'Stick 'em up, Mr Davies!'[27]

Both the Davieses, in their different ways, saw public support for the League as the main hope for mankind, and it was as a fitting headquarters for the Welsh League of Nations Union that Lord Davies presented it, in Cardiff in 1938, with his imposing 'Temple of Peace', just as peace was coming to an end. And so enthusiastic was the Reverend Gwilym Davies for the League, and so often did he attend its sessions, that in Welsh circles he came to be known as 'Jenny Geneva'.

It was into this curious world of naïve and enthusiastic idealism, made up partly of nonconformist pacifism, and partly of Celtic knight-errantry, that Carr arrived in June 1936. The Department he had come to take over was younger than its youngest student. In common with its near-contemporary, the LSE Department (founded in 1924), and the recently established (1930) Chair at Oxford, occupied by Sir Alfred Zimmern, the first Professor at Aberystwyth, it reflected the prevailing view of the 1920s and early 1930s that a thorough understanding of international institutions and law, combined with a prescriptive approach to the world and its problems, were the essential foundations for the creation of a permanently peaceful international order. Hence there was much concentration, both in teaching and research, upon the League of Nations and especially upon the role of the Covenant as the great constitutional hope of the world. These were the lines along which Carr's predecessors had worked, and both Zimmern and Webster (the latter in collaboration with Sydney Herbert) had, by 1936, published notable books on the League. Carr, however, resolved to change the whole approach to International Politics, and thus the content of the syllabus. Closely involved with the League at the Foreign Office, he did not share the view of it just described, and certainly did not believe it should be the main focus of study. Instead, he concentrated upon the behaviour of the major states since the War and, in the realm of ideas, upon political thought from Machiavelli to contemporary democracy, communism and fascism.

At the same time there were changes in the teaching staff. Each professor since Zimmern had employed a lecturer to assist him and take over in his absence. On the departure of Sydney Herbert for the History Department in 1930, and his own impending absence abroad, Webster persuaded Lilian Friedländer, who had taught for him four years earlier, to return to the Department. As she had recently married Dr Jirí Vránek, a graduate of Prague, it was eventually agreed that they should both be taken on as part-time lecturers. In 1935, Dr Vránek resigned to take up in Paris a post with the Institute of Intellectual Co-operation – the forerunner of UNESCO. His wife, who in 1935–36 was left in sole charge, has the distinction of being the first woman in the world to teach International Politics or Relations in a university specifically offering that discipline. Born in London of a Königsberg-Jewish family, as a promising LSE graduate she had been awarded an Aberystwyth research fellowship in 1924 and the following year had been engaged by Webster as assistant lecturer for the year Sydney Herbert was in the USA. She was fully involved in the 1926 conference of foreign delegates described above. Her second engagement terminated in the summer of 1936, and so, when Carr first visited Aberystwyth in mid-March, it fell to her to introduce him to the Department. This involved showing him over the double-fronted late Georgian house, abutting the Old College and facing the sea, which until 1965 was where the Department was housed. It was, she later said, a 'melancholy' experience 'taking him round the cramped, shabby, ill-equipped quarters'.[28] She showed him the library – the Department had its own – occupying a room on the ground floor, and dominated by the sombre ranks of black-bound volumes of the complete proceedings of the Council, Assembly and agencies of the League of Nations, and she also introduced him to the formidable Miss Elizabeth ('Bessie') Morris who had acted as secretary and librarian to the Department since 1928.

With the beginning of the new academic year, Carr settled into his routine. It was a peculiar one. Lord Davies had expected the Wilson Professor to travel, but hardly in the sense that Carr travelled. He continued to live at 'Honeypots', his house in Woking, arriving at Aberystwyth by train each Tuesday and returning to London each Thursday. Staying at the Belle Vue Hotel, on the Front, only a few minutes' walk from the Department, he managed to get all his teaching done in those two days, during which time, it was said, he never shaved. For a senior academic in pre-war Wales, his appearance was also unusual in that he was much given to wearing sandals.[29] All this commuting between the Cambrian coast and the capital had one great advantage. In those days of steam – unlike the shuddering diesels which later made the long run between Shrewsbury and Aberystwyth so vibrant an experience – trains were steady enough to enable passengers not only to read but also to write. That he was able to publish so much in his first three years can in part be attributed to the ten hours of sedentary leisure provided him each week by the Great Western.

Lord Davies, still seething with indignation that the Principal's favoured candidate and not his own had obtained the Chair (he much regretted that he had not taken the fight to the Court of Governors) did not at this stage object to Carr because of his ideas. Indeed, as Carr had published nothing as yet on International Politics, he hardly knew what these ideas were, and in fact, when it had come to choosing between Carr and Macartney, had cast his vote for Carr.[30] But any uncertainty about the new professor's view of the world was at once dispelled by his Inaugural Lecture.

Carr was a brilliant speaker; a future head of the History Department rated him as 'the best lecturer I have ever heard'.[31] Owing to the terms of the endowment, half a dozen public lectures, usually on subjects of current interest, were to be delivered by the Wilson Professor each academic year. And if the professor was travelling abroad, as Webster often was, his observations on what was happening there were heard with keen attention upon his return. Thus, although they were frequently absent, the professors of International Politics came to be well known in the town, and years afterwards members of the interested Aberystwyth public could often recall their names. Thus an Inaugural Lecture by a newly appointed Wilson Professor, and at a time when the international scene, particularly in Europe, looked increasingly ominous, was something of an event. Indeed, all such Inaugural Lectures were quickly and separately published. Early in October 1936, therefore, notices were displayed that 'Professor E.H. Carr, CBE, MA' would deliver his Inaugural Lecture on Wednesday, 14 October, 1936 at 5.30 pm in the Examination Hall at the College, the subject being 'Public Opinion as a Safeguard of Peace'. The public were invited and admission was free.

Carr began with the disarming assertion that he was at one with the founders of the Chair that in an understanding of international politics lay the best means of promoting peace between nations. He then analysed the various panaceas commonly put forward to solve the problem of war: pacifism (much of which, he suggested, was a flight from responsibility), isolationism (the idea that the British Empire and navy ensured peace, which he condemned as an aristocratic creed assuming the right of control over the less favoured) and collectivism. The collectivists, he held, fell into two groups: those who believed that the world sufficiently approached the state of domestic society that peace-keeping could be entrusted to a super-national police force directed by a super-national executive, as advocated by the New Commonwealth Society; and those who believed that the international community was still in too primitive a stage for such a solution and that the best method was for sovereign states to combine against the aggressor, as provided for in Article 16 of the Covenant. He then made a plea for realism, taking things as they were rather than as one would wish them to be. Utopianism, he declared, was the intellectuals' pastime, and one of the besetting faults of intellectuals was in exaggerating the intellectuality of mankind. Instead of designing perfect schemes for the salvation of the world, they should, if they wished to have any influence over public opinion, keep in touch with it, with the political thinking of the man in the street. Moreover, the intellectual believed that the way to make the League more effective was to amend the Covenant, making its penal provisions more comprehensive and precise, whereas for the layman faith in the League was religious rather than political, rooted in emotion rather than the intellect, and 'reinforced by the ancient and instinctive British prejudice against written constitutions'. No democratic government could wage war without the backing of its people, and any scheme involving automatic military sanctions would be rejected by the great mass of British opinion.

Here Carr was stating in unambiguous terms how far he was from the whole school of League reformers represented by Lord Davies, Philip Noel-Baker and others of the League of Nations Union, although he mentioned no one by name. He then turned to the peace settlement of 1919.

British public opinion, he said, would never countenance collective security measures aimed to perpetuate Versailles. Treaties are in essence ephemeral for in the end the dynamic must always overcome the static. Furthermore, to tie democracy to the static would be to drive all the forces making for change towards Fascism, just as, following the peace of 1815, they were driven towards democracy. 'If European democracy,' he declared, 'binds its living body to the putrefying corpse of the 1919 settlement, it will merely be committing a particularly unpleasant form of suicide.'

This was probably the best intellectual justification of appeasement ever offered and put Carr firmly in the camp against its critics, represented by Lord Davies and the New Commonwealth Society, no less than by Winston Churchill, who had recently become president of the Society's British Section. Finally, with the caveat that it 'may be the ultimate ideal', he declared:

> I do not believe that the time is ripe...for the establishment of a super-national force to maintain order in the international community and I believe any scheme by which nations should bind themselves to go to war with other nations for the preservation of peace is not only impracticable, but retrograde.

And he added that it would be 'a crime' if any opportunity for Great Britain and France to negotiate bilaterally with Germany were rejected 'in the name of some grandiose scheme of world or European peace'.[32]

Such were the relations between the Principal – who would have introduced the lecturer – and Lord Davies – who at their first meeting following the Carr appointment pointedly ignored the Principal's outstretched hand[33] – that it is most improbable that the former President was in the audience. But he would soon have read the published version, whether as separately printed or as published in the November issue of *International Affairs*, and have concluded that his worst fears had been realised: the man appointed to the Chair he had founded, and whose salary was in part derived from the endowment he had provided, was totally dismissive of his own ideas for ensuring peace and order in the world.

The curious thing about these two men, apparently poles apart, is that unlike so many of their contemporaries, both were highly conscious of power. Carr saw it as a fact of international life which had its own imperatives and which had to be allowed for; Lord Davies viewed it as a potential threat to the status quo which had to be met, and if need be vanquished, by even greater power.

During the first three years of his tenure, and the last three of peace, Carr produced more significant books than, so far, any other Wilson Professor over a comparable period. In 1937 he published his *Michael Bakunin*, an account of the larger-than-life Russian revolutionary anarchist, Marx's contemporary and rival, which Carr liked almost the best of his books and which remained the only significant study for nearly half a century. Also that year came *International Relations since the Peace Treaties*, a lucidly written guide to the post-war years which was of sufficient public interest to appear, shortly after, in a Welsh translation: *Cydberthynas y Gwledydd wedi'r Cyfamodau Heddwch* (1938). At the same time Longmans decided to publish studies of the foreign policies of the major powers called the 'Ambassadors at Large' series, of which Carr was appointed General Editor, with each study being written by a national of the power concerned. Those on Italy and France appeared early in the summer of 1939, with a Preface to the series by Carr, but war broke out before the studies on Germany, the Soviet Union and Japan were ready. Carr himself was responsible for the British volume which, as *Britain: A Study of Foreign Policy from the Versailles Treaty to the Outbreak of War*, was in page-proof when war came. The Foreword by Viscount Halifax, then Foreign Secretary, in which he commends Carr for having distinguished himself at the Foreign Office 'not only by sound learning and political understanding, but also in administrative ability', is dated 3 August 1939. Another work, sent to the press in July, was published later in the year as *Nationalism: A Report by a Study Group of Members of the Royal Institute of International Affairs*. This comprehensive analysis was the outcome of long discussions, chaired by Carr, of a group of nine scholars who had met at Chatham House, for the most part monthly, since November 1936.

The third book about to appear as war broke is his masterpiece in the field of International Relations, *The Twenty Years' Crisis*, which he had originally planned in 1937. This brilliant if controversial work has been extensively discussed elsewhere in this volume. Although much of it is a critical dissection of the 'utopianism' so characteristic of the period, he makes only passing reference to the ideas of Lord Davies and his New Commonwealth Society. Quoting from Lord Davies' book, *Force* (1934), he examines the idea of an equity tribunal as an answer to the inadequacies of law and argues that it falls into the grave fallacy of forcing politics into a legal mould, for in politics 'power is an essential factor in every dispute'. An international tribunal, he says, going beyond international law and legal rights, and attempting to settle matters on the basis of common assumptions when these clearly do not exist, remains 'an array of wigs and gowns vociferating in emptiness', and he cites these words of Zimmern's as most appositely applicable to the equity tribunal advocated by the New Commonwealth Society.[34]

Before sending *The Twenty Years' Crisis* to the press, Carr asked Professor Manning and Dennis Routh, recently his colleague at Aberystwyth, to comment on the manuscript, and records his gratitude for their observations. Routh had succeeded Mrs Vránek as International Politics Lecturer in 1936, but now, after three years, he was awarded a Fellowship at All Souls. This left a vacancy which Carr had to fill. The post was advertised and amongst the applicants was Martin Wight, who after the War was to establish himself as one of the foremost thinkers in International Relations, a reputation established at LSE and more recently enhanced by several posthumous publications. The lectureship was awarded, however, to Hugh Seton-Watson, the elder son of R.W. Seton-Watson, champion of Czechoslovak independence. Perhaps, with his interest in Russia, Carr felt an affinity with this young and brilliant scholar, with his extensive knowledge of Eastern Europe and its languages.

The war brought Carr's active involvement with Aberystwyth virtually to an end, for although he was to remain Woodrow Wilson Professor for nearly eight more years, it was only for a few months in 1946–47 that he was to resume teaching. For the duration of the war, and some time after, he was employed in London, first in the Ministry of Information and then on *The Times*, although he continued to travel down to Aberystwyth to give his public lectures. On 14 September 1939, from the Locarno Room in the Foreign Office, he wrote to Ifor Evans, the Principal, that up to the last moment he really did not believe in the outbreak of war and was 'even more afraid of the peace than I am of the war'.

> I do not suppose [he added] you are expecting me in Aberystwyth in the near future! I take it that nobody will wish to study international politics for the present. Young Seton-Watson was here the other day,

running around to search for a job and will pretty certainly get one, if only on the strength of his exotic languages.[35]

In fact 'young Seton-Watson', after serving first in the Bucharest and Belgrade Legations, and then in the Army, returned to Oxford after the war as a Fellow of University College, and never visited Aberystwyth in his life. He achieved, however, the remarkable feat of writing and publishing, while in the Army, his *Eastern Europe between the Wars, 1918–1941*, and thus contributed to the Departmental list of publications. Carr continues:

> Meanwhile, I have had a rather foolish letter from Professor Keeton, who appears to combine international law at University College with the New Commonwealth, saying he would like to discuss co-operation between our departments. I should be delighted for him to use our Library, but I don't know what other form of co-operation is possible: he probably thinks international law is a good substitute for international politics – I don't! . . . . I'm sure Aberystwyth will appreciate the honour of having the New Commonwealth established on Marine Parade.[36]

(This is a reference to the evacuation of University College, London, to Aberystwyth.) Carr adds:

> Seriously, all I can do at the moment is to keep in touch with Miss Morris as regards the ordinary routine business, and see as far as possible that the Library is kept up-to-date.[37]

The Principal replied (on 16 September) that Carr would be on leave of absence: 'The arduous teaching duties of the Department will be postponed until you return.'[38]

On the outbreak of war Carr found employment in the Foreign Publicity Directorate, which was attached to the Ministry of Information, and of which he became head in December 1939. Here he hoped to make his influence felt in the formulation of British war aims as well as in the propaganda directed to foreign countries. But owing to the constraints of the civil service, the relative ineffectiveness of the Ministry, and differences and wrangling with the new Minister, Sir John Reith, Carr resigned from his post in March 1940.[39]

At first he was tempted to return to Aberystwyth, but concluded it would be 'a dirty trick' to resume teaching at this stage of the academic year. The Principal did not agree and commented: 'Yours is essentially a research Chair: indeed your appointment dates from 1 July and not from 1 October, as in every other case.'[40] Instead Carr proposed a visit to war-time Paris.[41] Already, in 1937, he had met the requirements of the Chair that the Professor should travel abroad, by visiting the Soviet Union and Nazi Germany, and on his return had declared to a Chatham House audience that Germany under Hitler was 'almost a free country as compared with Russia'[42] – which hardly bears out the later accusation of his being soft on Stalin's Russia. His visit to France was planned for May 1940, but on 10 May came the German offensive in the West, with the result that the Führer got to Paris before Carr.

From 1937 he had occasionally written pieces for *The Times*. As 'nothing else worth while' was offered him in government service, he was glad to take up the invitation to contribute, from May 1940, leading articles to a newspaper which, despite having a circulation of only 192,000, was regarded throughout the world as a semi-official mouthpiece of the British Government. Here Carr, who joined the editorial team and was appointed Assistant Editor only a year later, found he could exercise an influence far greater than was available to him at the Ministry of Information. Writing, in all, a total of over 350 leading articles, he played an important part in influencing domestic and foreign opinion although the line he took as the war approached its end diverged increasingly from government views and policy.[43]

This new role, however, produced an unexpected result. Lord Davies had given Carr no trouble since the row over his appointment, even though, in April 1937, he had resumed the Presidency of the College after threatening to stand against the innocuous young peer who was proposed in his place. He had, indeed, his own agenda as war threatened, not only in opposing the appeasement policies of the Chamberlain government, but in attempting, in 1938, to raise a private airforce to bomb the Japanese in China. Because of likely official opposition, and hence the impossibility of a public appeal, it was hoped that the scheme, which had the backing of Noel-Baker, Sir Arthur Salter and Lord Cecil, who had all been keen supporters of Arnold-Forster, could be covertly financed by the eccentric American aviator-tycoon, Howard Hughes. This plan, code-named 'The Quinine Proposition', collapsed when, despite a secret visit by Lord Davies to Los Angeles in an attempt to win him over, Hughes declined to become involved. The next year there came the Soviet attack upon Finland. Lord Davies at once organized a Finnish Aid Committee, urged aid for the Finns in Parliament, and in February 1940 travelled to Helsinki and the war zone with the intention of arranging for the arrival of a brigade of British troops. Already at war with Hitler's Germany, it seemed that we were about to take on Stalin's Russia as well. A big-game hunter in his early manhood, Lord Davies, one feels, regarded rampaging Great Powers as the biggest of all big game. This scheme, too, failed, with the collapse of Finland, and in the national emergency of 1940 Lord Davies, a colonel in the First War, joined the Llandinam Home Guard as a private in the Second.[44]

Freed at last from the demands of trying to prevent war and aggression, for war and aggression everywhere abounded, Lord Davies returned once more to the problem of Carr and the Chair, a subject which provided a focus for his energies, and an outlet for all the frustration he had accumulated over the continual thwarting of his schemes and public campaigns.

His irritation with Carr is already evident with the publication of *Conditions of Peace* in 1942. In a letter to R.B. McCallum, who had given it an adverse review in *The Oxford Magazine*, Lord Davies wrote (24 June 1942):

> I confess I have not yet had time to digest Carr's book, but I feel sure he deserves the chastisement which you have given him. Honestly I think you dealt very tenderly with him!

He then goes on:

> It so happens that my sisters and I founded the Wilson Chair at Aberystwyth at the end of the last war, in the hope that it might become a progressive centre of research in the sphere of international relationships. Especially we hoped that it might assist in discovering the weaknesses of the League, and suggest ways and means of improving that infant institution. Unfortunately, so it seems to me, just the opposite has happened, and whereas some of us, including myself, have worked hard during the last twenty years to equip the League with institutions for the settlement of all international disputes, i.e. an Equity Tribunal, and the scientific organisation of sanctions to maintain law and order, i.e. an International Police Force, our efforts have been hindered rather than helped by the holders of the Wilson Chair. I have therefore come to the conclusion that endowing Chairs is a very dangerous experiment. . . .[45]

Lord Davies had got the bit as firmly between his teeth as any of his hunters, and when, in October 1942, he attended his first College

Council since Carr's appointment over six and a half years earlier, the Principal thought it ominous. 'I realized,' he later wrote to the Master of St John's College, Cambridge, 'there was more trouble in store.'[46] The form this trouble took was a series of letters from the President requiring every sort of detail and statistic relating to the operation of the Chair and Department since their foundation. The Principal managed to piece together the detailed information Lord Davies demanded: the number of students each year, the time the Professors spent at Aberystwyth, the numbers of lectures delivered, the salaries paid and particulars on much else. Little in the answers seemed to satisfy him. He expressed himself as being wholly dissatisfied that before the war an average of only seven students a year had taken papers in the subject, and he was incensed to learn that Carr had continued to draw his professorial salary of just over £1,000 per annum while working for the *The Times*.[47] He had accepted Carr's employment in the Ministry of Information as being government war-work, but his taking a paid position at *The Times*, 'a private commercial enterprise' as he put it, when still in receipt of his Aberystwyth salary, he saw as a kind of 'moonlighting'.[48] On 20 February 1943, he wrote:

some people may say that I am raising this subject on account of my opposition to the appointment of the person who holds the Chair. I think, however, that the correspondence speaks for itself and discloses one of the most flagrant cases of war-profiteering I have yet come across.[49]

At the Council meeting summoned for 3 March, Lord Davies was determined to ask for an enquiry and wrote to many members soliciting support. Most replies were guarded, and it was clear that many of the Council were not going to turn up. Amongst those who did there was a general feeling that Carr was 'a great man' and was 'doing very good work'.[50]

In justice to Carr, he had felt uneasy about the financial arrangements during wartime and had put aside £1,000 of his salary, a sum later used in connection with the Chair when the war was over. Moreover, he had done nothing underhand because the Wilson Advisory Board and the Council had endorsed his proposed arrangements with *The Times*. These considerations did not, however, mollify Lord Davies and he expressed his viewpoint with growing bitterness and fury:

The central fact emerging from the correspondence is that the Professor is drawing two salaries, one from the College and another from the *Times* newspaper.... If this attitude of mind really represents the public majority in this country it isn't surprising that we should have landed ourselves in this unholy mess. I understand that Professor Carr spends a considerable amount of his time in writing up the Beveridge report and kindred subjects. What this has to do with International Relationships I don't know. Of course, he is a bosom friend of the Principal, and between them they have wangled the whole business and prostituted the Wilson Chair for their own purposes, and, in Carr's case, for increased emolument.[51]

And in a later outburst, he wrote:

Frankly, I am amused that the Council should thank Professor Carr for his generous gesture in refunding £1,000. I don't believe that he would have disgorged this amount had it not been for the discussion which took place at the Council on the correspondence between the Principal and myself....

Even before the war Professor Carr only spent two days a week lecturing to his students, and carrying on his department at the College. How he occupied himself the remaining five days I don't know. Possibly in writing a book, but this, of course, he could have done had he remained at Aberystwyth, as Professor Webster used to do during the whole term, instead of dashing backwards and forwards to London every week. Furthermore, if the Principal had been concerned with the true interests of the College, and the success of the department, he should never have allowed this state of affairs to happen.[52]

Gilbert Murray now came into the picture and put it to Carr that although he was 'a competent professor' and his writings had 'more popularity and influence than those of any other teacher of your subject', there was one justifiable criticism:

The Chair is a 'Wilson' Chair, and was certainly intended to be a Chair for the Exposition of the League of Nations idea, and the founder has a right to be rather upset when he finds his professor carrying on a sort of anti-Wilson and anti-League campaign. It is not as if you merely criticised the League and wanted it changed and developed; you consider it fundamentally wrong and Wilson's principles as self-contradictory.[53]

It would be rather like, he added, the holder of a Chair at a Homeopathic Hospital arguing that Homeopathy itself was a delusion. To this Carr responded:

> May I suggest a closer parallel than yours? Would a Newton Professor of Physics be precluded from arguing that Einstein had demonstrated the inadequacy and over-simplification of Newton's laws?[54]

On the same day he wrote to the Principal:

> I have had correspondence with Gilbert Murray of which I enclose copies. From the point of view of the fun we are going to have, the more red herrings the better. But seriously, this is becoming rather disquieting. I should have to resign if the issue of freedom of opinion were seriously raised.[55]

More was to come. On 12 June 1943 Carr wrote to the Principal:

> Your friend G.M. has put me badly in the cart, and made me for the first time seriously think of resigning the Chair.

In what Carr described as a 'monstrous letter' Murray had alleged to Lord Davies that Carr *was The Times*, and that its policy was *his* policy. This letter, with his own reply, Lord Davies had circulated to members of the College Council.[56] Carr continued:

> I have long been warning well-wishers how embarrassing it is to me to be credited with foisting a personal policy of my own on a supine and spineless Editor: nothing is more calculated to make my position difficult. What do we do next? If the letter is not withdrawn, I shall write a stiff letter to the Council expressing my dissent from its contents and my extreme surprise at the action of G.M. and D.D.: I should hope to make it clear without actually saying so that, unless they resigned, I should . . . .
> [I shall be with you] on the evening of June 30 – if indeed I am still Wilson Professor by that time.[57]

This particular squall blew over. Indeed from the start of this imbroglio powerful voices were raised against the line Lord Davies was taking and spoke out on Carr's behalf. The Principal was a firm ally. Both he and Carr were Cambridge men and shared much more of a cosmopolitan experience and outlook than most Aberystwyth academics. In answer to the President's complaints about him, he pointed out that Carr had continued to deliver his quota of public lectures as well as to publish works on International Politics. He also had in mind the fact that the Davies Endowment was equally matched with a Treasury grant, and that as Lord Davies had contributed only one-third of the former, he was really, for all the leverage he sought to exercise, the source of only one-sixth of the Professor's salary. Another considerable influence was Charles Webster, Wilson Professor for ten years and Carr's predecessor but one. He took great umbrage at Lord Davies' criticisms of the pre-war Chair and Department and sent him a resounding reply, which was widely circulated, of trenchant justification.[58] But perhaps the most telling support of all came from Thomas Jones, for many years in the Cabinet Secretariat, adviser to successive Prime Ministers, and one of the most influential of all Welshmen. He sent a telegram to the Principal which he asked him to read to the Council meeting of 3 March suggesting that the matter of Carr's salary be referred 'without discussion' to the Wilson Board, hoping that the President 'after many years absence from duty' would attend it, and concluding with the opinion that 'Professor Carr on *The Times* is worth several generals in the field and the brilliant strategist who put him there should be promoted Field-Marshal of the Home Guard'.[59] Later in the year, in a letter to Professor Fleure, he made the point with brutal precision: 'Should D.D. attempt to dislodge Carr he will be fought to the death.'[60]

Death, however, came to Lord Davies in a more natural way, and only a few months later (June 1944). Wrong-headed in many ways he may have been, yet he had great achievements to his credit, and nothing can take from him the distinction of creating in Wales a new university discipline and then pushing the cause of it throughout the world university scene. Yet ironically what was, perhaps, his greatest and most enduring legacy he had come to think of as an almost total disaster. His final verdict on it was best expressed in the closing paragraph of his letter to Burdon-Evans on 5 March 1943:

> I wish to God I had never initiated this proposal. Almost since the inception of this department it has worked consistently against the programme I have spent most of my time and money in advocating, namely, the development of the League into a real international Authority.

Then, warming to his theme, he seemed to equate Zimmern, Webster, Greene and Carr with the Four Horsemen of the Apocalypse:

All the professors from Zimmern onwards opposed these ideas with the result that we have been landed in another bloody war which is going to ruin most of us, and will inflict untold misery and impoverishment upon every country in the world. However, it is no use crying over spilt milk. One lives and learns![61]

Perhaps, had he lived to see the 1990s, the increasing part played in world order by the league's successor, and the use of 'Daviesian' methods against Iraq and Serbia, he would not have felt so despondent.

Carr remained at *The Times* not only for the rest of the war but – because the gradual demobilization meant that normal university working could not begin for some time – for one year afterwards, his resignation as Deputy Editor taking effect on 31 August 1946. From then on a normal complement of students was to be expected, and because Seton-Watson was not returning to claim his lectureship, a successor had to be appointed. Applying for the vacancy was Ieuan John, a young Welshman who had recently served as a lieutenant-commander in the Navy and who before the war had studied International Relations under Manning at LSE, and at the Geneva Summer Schools run by Zimmern. He had made Germany his particular field of interest. Warmly recommended by Manning and others, he was interviewed by Carr at Chatham House and appointed Assistant Lecturer. Nearly thirty years later he himself succeeded to the Woodrow Wilson Chair.

Resuming his full duties and salary as a Professor in September 1946 (at his own request he had received only a nominal sum of £10 per annum since 1943), Carr returned to Aberystwyth to teach the new intake. But he was also busy with his public lectures, which were drawing record audiences (with the worsening of relations, everyone wanted to hear his views on Soviet policy), and with a further spate of publications. He produced two slim but influential books – *Nationalism and After* in 1945, and *The Soviet Impact on the Western World* in 1946 – and issued a revised version of his pre-war diplomatic history as *International Relations between the Two World Wars, 1919–1939* in 1947. In the last winter of the war, Carr also began planning his *magnum opus*, a history of the Russian Revolution and its aftermath, which was not to achieve completion until a third of a century and 14 volumes later. Even though the conception of the work expanded as he wrote it, there was something heroic in a man's embarking upon so huge a project in his fifties. One is reminded of Carlyle's monumental *History of Friedrich II of Prussia, called Frederick the Great* and, indeed, these two works have several points in common. Both were the multi-volume labours of their authors' old age; both were written in justification of a theme (heroic kingship, a planned economy); and both have undoubtedly suffered in readership interest through the regimes whose origins they covered so exhaustively (the Prussian monarchy, the Soviet state) having been swept away not all that long a time after the deaths of their respective authors (37 years, nine years). Nevertheless, whatever the ultimate verdict on it, and *pace* its critics, it was intended as an account less of the country than of the Bolshevik 'experiment', *A History of Soviet Russia* remains a towering achievement of twentieth-century historiography.

After all the storms and controversy accompanying Carr's appointment and tenure, just as it seemed his academic career was entering calmer waters, a personal matter brought his connection with Aberystwyth to an end. At the first social gathering of College staff which Carr attended after his appointment, it was noticed that for an hour or more he was penned in a corner by Professor Daryll Forde, whose reputation as an anthropologist was somewhat offset by his tendency to glaze the eyes of those with whom he was conversing.[62] Within a year of the end of the War, Daryll Forde had left for the University of London, and Mrs Daryll Forde had left for Carr. Soon after, Carr confided his personal situation to the Principal and spoke of getting another job.[63] As Zimmern found a generation earlier, conjugal irregularity was utterly beyond the pale in the Aberystwyth of the time, and Carr's action, although perhaps chivalrous, was certainly imprudent. The upshot was that in December 1946 he resigned, this to take effect on the last day of June 1947, so completing eleven years in the Chair. But well before then, on 26 February, he gave his last lecture and said farewell to his students. A notable professorship was at an end.

Epilogue

God, it is said, moves in a mysterious way. And surely He did so, and with high empyrean humour, in the bringing to pass of *The Twenty Years' Crisis*. For this work, which may eventually take rank with *The Prince* and *The Leviathan* as a great political classic revealing to the world the world as it really is, required for its appearance the unlikely conjunction of three such disparate characters as Lord Davies, Principal Evans and E.H. Carr, two of whom heartily detested each other, with the third, to a degree, a victim of the 'fall-out'. Had not Lord Davies founded the Chair, it is unlikely that Carr would have turned his mind to International Politics, no other Chair in the subject being available for many years; and had not Ifor Evans been there to exercise his powerful advocacy on Carr's behalf, it is unlikely that he would have got it. By such strange currents is the human understanding sometimes advanced.

Carr's departure left a hiatus longer even than that which preceded him, and for three years no appointment was made, with Ieuan John carrying on the work alone. The reason given was the inadequacy of the original Endowment Fund, but it may also have been that Carr's tenure was too unusual, too disturbing, and that time was needed to rethink the whole conception of the Chair and make the right choice about who should fill it. In his memoirs, Denis Healey makes the interesting comment:

> I had been approached to take E.H. Carr's chair at Aberystwyth University as Professor of International Relations, but they wanted a full-time academic to replace Carr, who had spent too much of his time writing editorials for *The Times.* . . .[64]

If this was the prevailing academic view, did it tell against him? London failed to elect him to the Chair of Russian History, and Oxford, scandalously, to that of International Relations. In 1955, after two years of tutoring in Politics at Balliol, he was rescued by his old Cambridge College, Trinity, which elected him a Fellow, thus facilitating progress on his massive Soviet history.

Aberystwyth must have seemed very distant, but in 1969 he had two further contacts with it. In the spring of that year Dr. E.L. Ellis of the History Department visited Trinity in order to arrange for the Prince of Wales to continue his studies at Aberystwyth during the following term. Ellis, who met Carr at dinner, and who was preparing the official history of the College for its centenary year in 1972, asked Carr if he would read through those passages dealing with himself. This he was glad to do, and commended the fairness of what had been written, remarking only that he had not before realized the full depth of Lord Davies's hostility towards him.[65]

Then, in December 1969, he was invited, along with other eminent scholars, including Morgenthau, Manning and Butterfield, to a great celebratory conference at Gregynog Hall, Montgomeryshire, once the home of Lord Davies's sister, co-founders of the Chair. The conference, the theme of which was 'International Politics 1919–1969', was held to commemorate the founding of the Chair and Department in 1919. To the surprise and delight of all involved, he accepted, and one recalls this legendary figure, tall, spare and now soberly dressed, fulfilling with quiet efficiency his duties as chairman at the reading and discussion of

Butterfield's paper on 'The Changing Moral Framework'. Shortly after he arrived, a formal photograph was taken of the Department with its eminent former professor. In the foreground sat the Principal, Sir Goronwy Daniel, the President, Sir Ben Bowen Thomas, and E.H. Carr – with the then Wilson Professor, Trefor Evans, and the rest of the Department lined up behind. It looked rather like a parody of Yalta.

Three years later the book of the Conference, *The Aberystwyth Papers*: *International Politics 1919–1969*, was published, of which Carr was sent a copy with an illuminated tribute on the fly-leaf. But as 1972 was also the centenary year of the University College of Wales, it seemed to the present writer that an honorary doctorate for one who had lent such distinction to the Chair and the College would be fitting, particularly as no official recognition of his impressive scholarly achievements had been forthcoming either from Whitehall or – less surprisingly – from Moscow.[66] He therefore wrote to the President:

> Could not the College do something to honour this scholar of world reputation during the Centenary Year, even if it means drawing up a Supplementary list of honorary doctorates? The whole Department feels that to ignore him completely would look very bad.[67]

Sir Ben Bowen Thomas replied:

> I shall follow up your very good suggestion about E.H. Carr, – with the Principal in the first instance and I shall mention it informally to Professor Evans. . . . [68]

The Principal in due course wrote as follows:

> The President has passed to me your letter to him of the 14th November suggesting that Mr E.H. Carr ought to be considered for an honorary degree during our Centenary year. He was indeed considered by the relevant committee and came within an ace of being included in the list. Amongst the difficulties, however, were that another very distinguished old Professor with a strong claim for an honorary degree was Professor Daryll Forde and, no doubt, you appreciate the difficulty of distinguishing between these two men.[69]

Difficulty indeed! Apart from the posthumous steps of instituting an annual lecture, and later a Chair in his memory, there was, however, one last thing that could be done. On 28 June 1982, Carr reached the great age of 90. A large card was bought depicting, in watercolour, Tintern Abbey, and inside was inscribed:

> *To Edward Hallett Carr*
> *With best wishes for his ninetieth birthday*
> *and in token of the honour and esteem in*
> *which he is held by the Department of*
> *International Politics, Aberystwyth.*

All eleven members of the Department then signed their names. At Carr's Memorial Service held in the Chapel of Trinity College seven months later, the writer, who went to represent the University College of Wales, was told by one close to him how greatly moved Carr had been to receive this birthday tribute from his old Department. Relations with Aberystwyth had, after all, ended on a note of serenity.

Notes

1 D. Davies, *The Problem of the Twentieth Century* (London, E. Benn, 1938), ch. 12, *passim*.

2 I.L. Evans, *Lord Davies, the Wilson Chair, and the Presidency of the College*, February 1941, p. 6. University College of Wales Archives, International Politics (TS).

3 For the names of the candidates and the 'Einstein' suggestion, as well as for all future references to the Davies papers, I am indebted to Guto Thomas, formerly Deputy Warden at Pantycelyn, who worked on them for his unpublished paper, '"The Tiresome Aberystwyth" or "This Carr Business"' (July 1997). These nominations occur in correspondence with Lord Davies and other members of the Wilson Advisory Board, April–May 1934 (Llandinam MSS: National Library of Wales).

4 Letter, Sir Arthur Salter to Davies, 3 June 1934 (Llandinam MSS).

5 Letter, Davies to Salter, 4 June 1934 (Llandinam MSS).

6 Letters, Gilbert Murray to Davies, 8 June 1934; Lord Cecil to Davies, 27 March 1935 (Llandinam MSS).

7 C.H. Rolph, *Kingsley: The Life, Letters and Diaries of Kingsley Martin* (London, 1973), p. 205; E.L. Ellis, *The University College of Wales, Aberystwyth 1872–1972* (Cardiff, University of Wales Press, 1972) p. 245.

8 Minutes of a Meeting of the Wilson Chair of International Politics Joint Selection Committee, 9 August 1935 (University College of Wales Archives).

9 Minutes of a Meeting of the Wilson Chair of International Politics Joint Selection Committee, 11 December 1935.

10 Ellis, *The University College of Wales*, p. 246.

11 Minutes, Joint Selection Committee, 24 January 1936; Letter to Davies, 11 April 1936 (Llandinam MSS); Evans, *Lord Davies, the Wilson Chair, and the Presidency of the College*.

12   Letter, Davies to Edwards, 20 August 1942 (Llandinam MSS).
13   *Ibid.*
14   Letter, Noel-Baker to Davies, 5 March 1936 (Llandinam MSS).
15   Lorna Lloyd, former research assistant to Noel-Baker, to the author.
16   Ellis, *The University College of Wales*, pp. 246–7; Evans, *Lord Davies, The Wilson Chair, and the Presidency of the College.*
17   Letters, Davies to Arnold-Forster, 27 February and 9 April 1936 (Llandinam MSS).
18   Ellis, *The University College of Wales*, p. 247; *Welsh Gazette*, 30 April 1936, 4, col. 4.
19   Evans, *Lord Davies, the Wilson Chair, and the Presidency of the College*, p. 12.
20   *Ibid.*, pp. 28–9.
21   Letter, C.A.W. Manning to the Author, 15 November 1972: 'I was glad that a crusader like Arnold Forster missed the target: but I saw him as more formidable than you seem to me to suppose [referring to the Ifor Evans quotation]. His eloquence was as self-assured as Caradon's. And his zeal more selfless.'
22   Letter, Davies to Edwards, 20 August 1942 (Llandinam MSS).
23   Letter, Davies to I.L. Evans, 7 February 1936 (Llandinam MSS).
24   Letter, Davies to Gilbert Murray, 24 February 1936 (Llandinam MSS).
25   Ellis, *The University College of Wales*, pp. 247–8.
26   Mrs Gwilym Davies (as Miss Mary Ellis a member of the 1924 delegation) to the Author; Peter Lewis, *Biographical Sketch of David Davies (Topsawyer) 1818–1890 and his grandson David Davies (1ˢᵗ Baron Davies) 1880–1944* (Newtown n.d.), p. 33.
27   The Reverend Principal Ifor Enoch, father of the bellicose boy, to the author.
28   Letter, Mrs J. Vránek to the author, 10 December 1992.
29   Professor Fergus Johnston to the author.
30   Letter, Davies to Edwards, 20 August 1942 (Llandinam MSS).
31   Professor Fergus Johnston.
32   For the text of Carr's inaugural lecture, see *International Affairs*, Vol. 15, No. 6, November 1936.
33   Mrs Ruth Evans, widow of Principal I.L. Evans, to the author.
34   E.H. Carr, *The Twenty Years' Crisis*, 2nd edition (London, Macmillan, 1946), pp. 203–7.
35   Letter, Carr to I.L. Evans, 14 September 1939 (University College of Wales Archives).
36   *Ibid.*
37   *Ibid.*
38   Letter, I.L. Evans to Carr, 16 September 1939 (U.C.W. Archives).
39   C. Jones, *E.H. Carr and International Relations* (Cambridge, Cambridge University Press, 1998), pp. 24, 70–1.
40   Letter, I.L. Evans to Carr, 20 March 1940 (UCW Archives).
41   Letter, Carr to I.L. Evans, 4 May 1940 (UCW Archives).
42   R.W. Davies, 'Edward Hallett Carr 1892–1982', *Proceedings of the British Academy*, Vol. LXIX (Oxford, 1983), p. 483.
43   Letter, Carr to I.L. Evans, 22 March 1941 (UCW Archives); Jones, *E.H. Carr and International Relations*, pp. 72–3, 110–12; Davies, 'Edward Hallett Carr 1892–1982', pp. 487–9.

44 For these escapades of Lord Davies, with further references, see: B. Porter, 'David Davies and the Enforcement of Peace', D. Long and P. Wilson, eds, *Thinkers of the Twenty Years' Crisis* (Oxford, Oxford University Press, 1995); P. Lewis, *Biographical Sketch*, pp. 42–4.

45 Letter, Davies to McCallum, 24 June 1942 (Llandinam MSS).

46 Letter, I.L. Evans to the Master of St John's College, Cambridge (marked 'Personal'), 8 May 1943 (UCW Archives).

47 Davies-Evans correspondence of October–December 1942 and especially letter from Davies to I.L. Evans, 24 December 1942 (UCW Archives).

48 Ellis, *The University College of Wales*, p. 258.

49 Letter, Davies to Richard Hughes, 20 February 1943 (Llandinam MSS).

50 Ellis, *The University College of Wales*, p. 259.

51 Letter, Davies to Major W.G. Burdon-Evans, J.P. (Confidential), 5 March 1943 (Llandinam MSS).

52 Letter, Davies to Sir George Fossett-Roberts, 26 June 1943 (Llandinam MSS).

53 Letter, Gilbert Murray to Carr, 8 March 1943 (UCW Archives).

54 Letter, Carr to Murray, 11 March 1943 (UCW Archives).

55 Letter, Carr to I.L. Evans, 11 March 1943 (UCW Archives).

56 Letters, Murray to Davies, 31 May 1943; Davies to Murray, 5 June 1943 (UCW Archives). This exchange between Gilbert Murray, the champion of Ancient Greece, and Lord Davies, the champion of modern Wales, reveals that one of their objections to Carr was his lack of sympathy for small nations.

57 Letter, Carr to I.L. Evans, 12 June 1943 (UCW Archives).

58 Letter Webster to Davies, 20 February 1943 (UCW Archives).

59 Telegram, Thomas Jones to I.L. Evans, 3 March 1943 (UCW Archives).

60 Letter, T. Jones to H.J. Fleur, FRS, 4 November 1943 (Thomas Jones MSS).

61 See Note 51 above.

62 Professor Fergus Johnston, present at the occasion, to the author.

63 Letter, Carr to I.L. Evans, 3 June 1946 (UCW Archives).

64 D. Healey, *The Time of My Life* (London and Harmondsworth, 1990), p. 129.

65 E.L. Ellis to the author, including letter of 13 January 1999.

66 Carlyle received from Bismarck Prussia's highest award, the *Pour le Mérite*, for his Life of Frederick the Great; from the Soviet Authorities Carr, a 'bourgeois' historian, received no official honour for his great work, although they had it translated and printed for private Party consultation (R.W. Davies).

67 Letter, the author to Sir Ben Bowen Thomas, 14 November 1972.

68 Letter, Sir Ben Bowen Thomas to the author, 15 November 1972.

69 Letter, Sir Goronwy Daniel to the author, 29 November 1972.

3
'An Active Danger': E.H. Carr at The Times, 1940–46

Charles Jones

During one evening in 1943 with Robert Barrington-Ward, editor of *The Times*, the Duke of Devonshire confided that he had 'still to call your paper publicly the journal of the London School of Economics'. David Bowes-Lyon, a director of the paper, chipped in remarking that *The New York Times* called it the final edition of *The Daily Worker*.[1] This was not an idiosyncratic view of the leftward drift of *The Times* during the war – a drift that more often than not was held to be the responsibility of its leader writer and assistant editor, Edward Hallett Carr, 'The Red Professor of Printing House Square', as he was later referred to. Nor were such views only held by Americans. Carr's opponents went to the very top of the British establishment and came to include Winston Churchill, his son Randolph and later the Labour Foreign Secretary, Ernest Bevin.

This red shift cannot be attributed exclusively to Carr, of course. His chief, Barrington-Ward, was no less convinced than Carr of the need for radical change and consistently emphasised the collective responsibility of the editorial team; and though he frequently toned down Carr's editorials, it was generally with the intention of enhancing more than diminishing their intended political effect. However, it was Carr and no other member of the editorial team who was identified by Lord Elibanks in June 1942 as 'an active danger to the country'.[2] How he became a 'danger', why he expressed the views he did and why in the end his views became unacceptable are at least three of the questions we shall seek to answer in this chapter.

Lure of *The Times*

E.H. Carr left the Foreign Office in 1936 to be free to speak out on the great issues of the day. His views, expressed in a spate of publications over the next three years, amounted to a distinctive and fully developed approach to the study and practice of international relations.[3] Support for Neville Chamberlain's foreign policy was grounded in a characteristic combination of moral and pragmatic considerations. Not only defeated Germany, but a number of the lesser victors had been shabbily treated following the Great War. Many of their initial claims of the 1920s had been justified, and failure to concede them promptly had constituted a needless and damaging provocation leading directly to the breakdown of collective security in the 1930s. More than simply intransigent, the policies of Britain and France had been ineffectual, because neither country had either the will or the means to compel assent. Worse still, Carr believed the strategic position of the victors of 1918 to have been critically weakened by the development of more effective techniques of submarine warfare and aerial bombardment. At the very least, the Democracies needed more time to overcome the obsolescence of their strategic planning and armed forces. To win this, they needed to split the emerging Axis by substantial and selective concessions to one or other of the three principal revisionist powers.[4]

Such arguments, which had led Carr to applaud the Munich Agreement in the first edition of *The Twenty Years' Crisis*, were fully consistent with wholehearted devotion to prosecuting the war once it had begun.[5] Carr went immediately, as Director of Foreign Propaganda, to the newly formed Ministry of Information (MoI), but by April 1940 he had tendered his resignation. The reasons had to do with personal ambition, with the insecure position of the Foreign Publicity Division (FPD) of the MoI, originally set up within the Foreign Office but billeted on the MoI at the outbreak of hostilities, and lastly with the more general weakness of the MoI itself. At the MoI in 1940, as in the Foreign Office in 1936, Carr proved unwilling to submit to the disciplines of public service if this might impede the clarity and effectiveness with which he was able to express his views. After only three weeks he was already starting to chafe at the bit. 'I should very much like, when the thing comes to an end, to be in a position to have a say about terms of settlement, and this job gives me little prospect of that,' he complained to Barrington-Ward.[6] His overriding objective was to have a distinctive and effective voice in the formulation of British policy, and to achieve this he needed an institutional base that would provide him with the necessary authority while allowing him maximal autonomy. Robert Cole perceptively observes that, during his brief tenure, Carr regarded the FPD as a 'miniature Foreign Office'.[7] However it soon became evident that the real Foreign Office would not tolerate any such development and, if unable to strangle the infant at birth, would exercise the role of godfather with Sicilian intensity.[8] It was otherwise with *The Times*, which was to provide the ideal institutional vehicle for Carr's personal project by virtue of its intelligence network, its circulation, and its close relationship with government. Following the success of his debut as a leader writer in 1940, Carr joined the staff as assistant editor in January 1941.[9]

In those days *The Times* was, above all else, a news paper. It had a comprehensive network of correspondents at home and abroad, and its editorial team consequently worked on the basis of copious and generally reliable information which both fuelled and disciplined the broad views of British policy, which it was their business to formulate. In this respect a great newspaper came rather closer than did the Ministry of Information to the ideal propaganda instrument envisaged by Duff Cooper. 'It is an awfully difficult matter, this formulating of war aims,' the Minister mused.

> There are two extremes between which we want to steer a middle course. We do not want to have a lot of professors, out of touch with realities, thinking brilliantly in an academic void, nor do we want purely opportunist propagandists, changing their views from day to day with the course of events. We want something between the two – people who do know what is going on and can keep closely in touch with the course of events, but who are also capable of taking long views and planning for the future.[10]

Here, three months too late, was the brief Carr had wanted at the MoI, and which he now set out to work to at *The Times*.

Propaganda by the mid-twentieth century was fast becoming a matter of numbers. With a circulation of 192,000 on the eve of war, *The Times* fell far short of *The Daily Express* or *The Daily Herald*, each with over 2 million.[11] It did not even come near to the 637,000 claimed by *The Daily Telegraph*. But it had an unchallenged position on the breakfast tables of the British policy-making elites.[12] Viewed from a different perspective, a daily readership of 192,000 dwarfed the 8,965 print-run of the first edition of *The Twenty Years' Crisis*, the 15,000 copies of *Conditions of Peace* printed during 1942 and 1943, or even the 20,000 copies of *Nationalism and After* to be printed in January 1945.[13]

The political alignment of *The Times* was just as important as the class or number of its readership. Under Geoffrey Dawson, the paper had been closely associated with Chamberlain and the policy of appeasement, as Lord Halifax had been through his 1937 talks with Hitler, and

as Carr himself now was following publication of *The Twenty Years'
Crisis*.[14] This reinforced a long-standing assumption that *The Times*
favoured the government of the day. Richard Cockett has suggested
that it was regarded as a semi-official organ overseas throughout the
1930s because of Dawson's very close Cabinet contacts, above all with
Halifax.[15] It was to be the general presumption, especially overseas, that
Carr's policy was identical with official policy which was to exasperate
officials and Ministers most as the divide between the two grew steadily
wider up to the day in 1945 when Churchill finally attacked *The Times*
openly in the House of Commons.[16]

Consistent with this close relationship was the willingness of *The
Times* to publish editorials to order, in support of government policy.
When Sir Samuel Hoare cabled from Madrid in 1941 requesting ener-
getic efforts to prevent Spain from joining the Axis, a Foreign Office
official minuted that 'an inspired *Times* leader would be helpful and
no doubt the News Dept. could arrange for one'. Carr and Iverach
McDonald were spoken to and provided with notes for a leader, which
they promised for the next day. 'Independent Spain', written by Carr,
duly appeared on 24 April 1941.[17] Wartime leaders on Latin American
affairs were generally submitted for comment to R.A. Humphreys of the
Foreign Office Research Department. Indeed some were drafted by
him.[18] In Buenos Aires, the local *Times* correspondent made a rule of
submitting all his copy to the British Embassy for comment.[19] In a
similar spirit, Carr submitted material to the Foreign Office prior to
publication for approval and comment, as did some of the foreign
correspondents working for the paper.[20]

Given this generally close relationship, it was hard for government to
dissociate itself from the line taken by Carr in *The Times*. One of Carr's
1941 leaders, 'Peace and Power', had suggested that a stable post-war
Europe could hardly be assured without recognition of both Soviet and
German power. This simultaneously offended Turks, Yugoslavs, Roma-
nians, Greeks, Poles and Czechs. The Turkish Minister in Madrid was not
alone in regarding *The Times* as 'a spokesman of the British Government'. Knatchbull-Hugessen, in Angora, found it 'virtually impossible to
convince any foreigners ... that the "Times" [sic] is not officially
inspired.' A weary official in London minuted: 'We are at the mercy of
The Times and can only hope for a longish interval before the next
lapse.'[21] On another occasion, State Department officials in Washington
were in doubt about whether a *Times* leader opposing the post-war
dismemberment of Germany was or was not inspired by Her Majesty's
Government.[22] The problem posed by Carr's editorials was that they

were seldom so extreme that they did not reflect the opinion of some faction of government or the Foreign Office. Worse, they sometimes advanced the official consensus, but at a moment that seemed to the official mind to be tactically unsound and therefore damaging to British interests.

Carr and Editorial Policy

Some years ago Alan Foster wrote an article on the attitude of *The Times* towards the USSR in which he argued persuasively for the existence of a coherent underlying philosophy of international relations behind the apparent vacillations of the great newspaper.[23] He reserved treatment of the personal role of Carr to the conclusion, attributed no specific leading articles to Carr, and attempted no comparison of the 'underlying philosophy' of *The Times* with the published and attributable views of its Assistant Editor. Was Foster right to accept the anonymity of the leader writer and the collective responsibility of the team? In doing so he faithfully expressed the view expressed by Barrington-Ward, as Editor, in response to criticism from the Foreign Office. 'It is never safe to attribute the views of *The Times* to this or that individual,' he wrote. 'Whoever may write a given article the opinions expressed are the opinions of the paper. There is really no distinction to be drawn between the Editor and any of his team of leader-writers.'[24]

It is true that there was shared responsibility for the line followed by *The Times*. It is also true that Barrington-Ward adhered to the 'Carr line' in substance even after Carr's resignation and that other members of the team on occasion produced leaders that were assumed to be by Carr. But Barrington-Ward generously and accurately conceded that the vigour and originality of the 'Carr line' were indeed Carr's own and, if only because of the detailed account of the paper's history provided by McDonald since Foster wrote, it would be ingenuous any longer to maintain the stronger version of collective responsibility.[25]

There is a further reason to abandon the official line on collective responsibility. A set of notebooks or logs survives in the archives of *The Times* which provide lists allocating responsibility for the chosen topics of each day to one or, very occasionally, two of the small team of leader writers.[26] The notebooks help establish authorship but do not entirely settle the matter, since a draft might easily be passed from one member of the team to another, and the whole argument of an editorial changed by a few strokes of the editor's pen. However, Carr himself kept a record of his own reviews and newspaper articles at least to August 1940, which tallies precisely with the allocation of topics in the notebooks and constitutes something close to a claim of authorship.[27] It is evident from Foreign Office correspondence and the archives of *The Times* that Carr's personal responsibility for the great majority of the leaders that stand against his name in the notebooks was assumed. Finally, taken as a whole, the Carr leaders are consistent with (and on occasion even identical with!) his published work.

If it is accepted that Carr's stated determination to 'have a say' in the post-war settlement found expression at *The Times*, the questions remain of the precise spin he gave to editorial policy and with what consequences. Which were the significant moments of divergence between Carr's line and the government of the day? The argument is that Carr's radical line on home affairs was much more closely in touch with current opinion – whether of his Editor, Barrington-Ward, of moderate opinion within the Conservative Party, or of the incoming Labour administration – than was the strongly pro-Soviet orientation which arose from his firmly held belief that the future lay with large groupings of states, and that the only way in which Britain could remain a world power was as one of three, alongside the USA and the USSR, in an amicable concert of powers. And even this strongly realist position, premised as it was on maximising rather than satisfying future British power, enjoyed substantial support within the Foreign Office and from Bevin right up to the European spring of 1946.

All of this lay far ahead in 1940, at which point the military and financial position of Britain appeared desperate and a negotiated peace still a lingering possibility.[28] It was at this stage in the war that Carr placed *The Times* firmly behind a radical agenda for post-war economic planning and welfare through a dazzling sequence of leading articles that presented a vision of future British and international social and economic relations at marked variance with both the status quo and Hitler's New Order.[29] In Carr's post-war Utopia the state was to use planning law, selective provision of public housing and an integrated public transport policy to ensure that industrial production and employment were widely dispersed across the country in a manner that would allow the great mass of workers to live close to their jobs while enjoying easy access to the countryside. The inflated size of the metropolis would be dealt with by moving the seat of government to the Midlands. These initiatives would be reinforced by enhanced provision of free education and health services, by the further extension of the social wage through the subsidising of basic foodstuffs in line with a national nutrition policy, and by progressive extension of the principle of state subsidy to embrace essential consumer goods and overseas aid.[30]

The blend of state welfare provision and mixed economy proposed by Carr found favour even within the Conservative Party, where Ministers of a religious (Halifax) or modernising (Beaverbrook) cast of mind rightly feared that Churchill's neglect of social policy would cost them the next general election. They also recognized, in the shorter term, that Britain needed to project an image of social justice and modernity to have any prospect of countering Hitler's New Order or figuring as an ally acceptable to mainstream opinion in the democratic United States of America or the Communist Soviet Union.

It was otherwise with Carr's foreign policy prescriptions, which encountered less firm and consistent approval in official and political circles, frequently alarmed smaller allies and neutrals, and would finally bring him, and *The Times*, into disrepute. The ultimate stumbling block was to be Carr's attitude toward the Soviet Union, but this was in large measure the corollary of two more basic theorems. The first was that, since small nations were no longer able to provide effective security, future international organization must rest on large groupings of states. The second was that Britain could only hope to remain a leading world power at the head of such a grouping of states in a post-war system where the overall management of world affairs was conducted by Britain, the United States, and the Soviet Union acting in friendly conformity. These two routes to a pro-Soviet policy need to be examined in turn before the final step in Carr's argument, and its catastrophic consequences for his intervention in policy-making, are considered.

One tragedy of the Versailles settlement according to Carr had been 'the creation of a multiplicity of smaller units at a moment when strategic and economic factors were demanding increased integration and the grouping of the world into fewer and larger political units'.[31] Carr was determined that the claims of linguistically or culturally identified national minorities should not stand in the way of a workable settlement following the Second World War. The trouble in his view was that small states were no longer viable. Recent tendencies in technology meant that the small size of the typical linguistic unit was no longer adequate to the provision of security and welfare. In the nineteenth century, a small power might still hope to mount a prolonged defence against a large power, imposing very substantial costs, as the Boers had done against the British. Tanks and air power had made this impossible.[32] 'The next war,' he suggested, 'will probably be fought in the main with airborne armies and with projectiles having a range of several hundred miles', adding that 'the whole conception of strategic frontiers may . . . be obsolescent.'[33] Neutrality was no longer a practical policy for small states, which were effectively bound to seek alliances with larger neighbouring states, but such was the pace of modern warfare that neither the old style of alliance nor the inter-war approach to collective security could effectively replace it. 'Paper commitments of mutual assistance are valueless under the conditions of modern warfare unless they involve a pooling in advance of military resources and military equipment, and, above all, a common strategy, common loyalties, and a common outlook on the world.'[34]

The economic history of the inter-war period had delivered a very similar message, Carr maintained. Fragmentation of markets in the inter-war period had imposed costs on all, and these economic costs had too often found expression in political extremism, fuelling further and equally self-defeating nationalist excesses.[35] The answer to Hitler's New Order therefore could not be a return to old European patchwork, but rather to a 'new map . . . not . . . painted in quite so many contrasting and clashing colours' within which 'economic solidarity and a common economic policy will lay the foundations of political harmony'.[36] Smaller European states might wish to 'paddle their own canoes', but would have to do so 'in convoy'.[37]

Offence Taken

The canoeing metaphor poses the question, 'Who can be trusted to provide the escort?' A first hint of the problems of leadership and rivalry in a world of multinational blocs was evident in the welcome accorded late in 1940 to an agreement on post-war political and economic co-operation between the Polish and Czech governments in exile. 'A first step towards a new order in Central Europe', to be achieved with British economic assistance, the new development was nevertheless to be seen in the context of 'the predominant interest which Soviet Russia can naturally claim in the settlement of the affairs of Eastern Europe'.[38] So while many of Carr's leaders on foreign policy questions were a routine and uncontroversial extension of his earlier work at the MoI, the minority, by accepting the need for a Soviet sphere of influence in Eastern Europe as a corollary of the case for large regional groupings, caused offence to small states and embarrassment to the government.

In mid-December 1944 the position adopted by *The Times* on Greece brought things to a head. In whose sphere of influence did the southernmost Balkan state belong? Following a Communist insurrection in Greece on 3 December 1944, Carr and Barrington-Ward opposed the despatch of British troops to support the incumbent right-wing government. Jock Colville, one of Churchill's private secretaries, wrote to the MoI to complain of a leading article by Carr, asking Brendan Bracken to speak about it to Barrington-Ward.[39] A further leading article of 1 January 1945 by Carr finally goaded Churchill into a public denunciation of *The Times* in the House of Commons, which was met with 'the loudest, largest, and most vicious – even savage! – cheer that I have heard in the House,' Barrington-Ward noted ruefully, 'a vent for the pent-up passions of three years, a protest against all that has, rightly or wrongly, enraged the Tories in the paper during that time.'[40]

Yet following Churchill's outburst of January 1945 relations between *The Times* and the British Government, and with them Carr's position, might have been expected to improve. Barrington-Ward was comforted and his resolve stiffened by the support of a number of well-placed acquaintances and friends who thought Churchill's behaviour excessively authoritarian. Encouraging hints of support were received from Max Beaverbrook and Brendan Bracken, who claimed to have restrained Churchill from further excess by reminding him of 'the whole record of *The Times* and its fine work in this war'. John Astor, as proprietor, had been re-reading the leaders that had given offence and found them 'quite soberly expressed, offering advice rather than censure'. Barrington-Ward himself re-read the Greek leaders and was 'once more impressed by their balance and moderation'. Though the balance of correspondence arising from the incident was hostile, the margin was tolerably narrow.[41] It still seemed to Barrington-Ward that by standing firm *The Times* could continue in peacetime to advance British interests through the dual policy of economic growth and Soviet alliance which it had set out so trenchantly during the war. Indeed this was a position to which Barrington-Ward would remain committed as late as January 1947, some months after Carr's departure. '*The Times* ought to have great chances in 1947,' he confided to his diary. 'In particular we can help by swelling the demand ... for production at home (all else hangs upon that) and by promoting a firm but realistically based understanding with Russia, without which there cannot be peace.'[42]

To the consistent support of his Editor on the issue of Anglo-Soviet relations, Carr might have expected, following the general election of July 1945, to have been able to add that of a Labour government more closely in tune with *The Times* than its predecessor. Yet in this Carr was to be disappointed. As time went by the Foreign Office became less and less patient, and by March 1946 the new Labour Foreign Secretary, Ernest Bevin, was every bit as hostile as Churchill had been two years before. In the end, the onset of the Cold War could not be resisted by *Times* leaders, however finely honed.

During this last phase, the rationale for advocating appeasement of the Soviet Union changed from acceptance of the implications of belief in multinational groupings of states to a more general view about the conditions for continued British influence. Movement from the narrower to the broader thesis may be seen in Carr's treatment of Anglo-Soviet relations in the columns of *The Times*. The clearest early statement came at the start of August 1941 in 'Peace and Power'. Post-war leadership in Eastern Europe, Carr proposed, 'can fall only to Germany or to Russia. Neither Great Britain nor the United States can exercise, or will agree to exercise, any predominant role in these regions.... There can be no doubt that British and Russian – and, it may be added, American – interests alike demand that Russian influence in Eastern Europe should not be eclipsed by that of Germany.'[43] By the year's end hypothesis had become orthodoxy. Commenting on Anthony Eden's visit to Moscow, Carr took it for granted that 'in Europe, Great Britain and Soviet Russia must become the main bulwarks of a peace which can be preserved, and can be made real, only through their joint endeavour.'[44]

As the war progressed *The Times* began to be distinguished above all else by this attitude towards the Soviet Union. Carr and Barrington-Ward had explicitly agreed as early as 1942 that at the end of the war Britain would be too weak to prevent the Russians from dominating, if not occupying, the whole of Eastern Europe, at least as far West as Berlin. Still anticipating an early United States withdrawal from Europe and fearful of reviving the Russo-German alliance by ill-judged and ineffectual opposition to Soviet plans, Carr urged that Britain should accept this extension of Soviet influence while striving to maintain a united and prosperous Germany within an integrated post-war Europe.[45]

A number of practical corollaries followed. Most immediately, the need for good relations with the USSR in the post-war world required that Stalin's demands for a second front to relieve pressure on his forces be promptly met. Later, Britain would have to acquiesce in rough Soviet treatment of Eastern Europe. In the longer run, Carr argued, the British government would have to set limits to its relationship with the United States and take the lead in Western European political and economic co-operation. 'It would be the height of unwisdom to assume – he thundered in May 1945 – that an alliance of the English-speaking world, even if it were to find favour with American opinion, could form by itself the all-sufficient pillar of world security and render superfluous any other foundation for British policy in Europe.'[46]

Together these policies were perhaps the only means to any preservation of British power in the longer run, if indeed the task was possible at all. For Carr's consistent objective was for there to be *three* superpowers in the post-war world: the USA, the USSR and the British Commonwealth.[47] But such long-term and general considerations cut no ice with working officials, one of whom minuted in 1943 that 'the leaders [on Soviet and East European affairs] which appear in *The Times* cause more harm than do Mr. Parker's articles', adding that 'those leaders are nearly always the work of Mr. Carr, and it is much more important to get Mr. Carr out of Printing House Square than it is to get Mr. Parker [a fellow traveller with a Communist secretary] out of Moscow'.[48]

The Policy Implications of Carr's Thesis

Just as there was an ideological element in the opposition he encountered over his support of the Soviet Union, so too there may have been in Carr's own position.[49] But the debate about the place of Britain in the post-war international system could also be argued in wholly realist terms, and this was the course Carr generally preferred. The starting point was the relative power of the British state, and the central tenet of Carr's position was that Britain could only maintain parity with the United States and the Soviet Union if the solidarity of the 'Big Three' were maintained. This was because future British power depended crucially on economic success and growth.[50] 'If Britain is to continue to play her old part in the world, domestic reconstruction must be pressed forward,' he insisted. 'For power abroad depends on a healthy economy at home.'[51] A strong economy, in turn, depended on maintaining close trading links and good relations both with Europe and with the English-speaking world. Completing the circle, these links required a balance of maritime and Continental commitments that could hardly be maintained in the face of sustained hostility from either the United States or the Soviet Union.[52] 'Neither the security nor the economic well-being of Great Britain is compatible with a one-sided policy,' he insisted.[53]

Any split would force Britain to choose sides and adopt a role subordinate to one or other of her wartime allies. Though he did not concede it publicly until March 1946, Carr understood very well the extent of British financial and military weakness relative to the USA and the USSR.[54] Fortunately – so it seemed to Carr – the general interest required unity, because no two powers, acting together, had sufficient strength to impose an enduring general settlement and guarantee world security.[55] Moreover, a three-power concert could be justified on moral grounds, he claimed, since no other country besides Britain, the USA and the USSR had made a comparable contribution to victory.[56]

Carr drew a number of consequences from this basic position. First of all, relations with the United States, while amicable, must on no account give any ground for fear of an emerging alliance from which the Soviet Union might be excluded. Secondly, German unity must rapidly be restored before the division of the country into zones created new bones of contention between the Allies.[57] The continued division of Germany, he observed in July 1946, would mean in effect the division of Europe.[58] On this subject Carr consistently maintained the line he had adopted during the war, arguing that 'whatever the safeguards which may still be needed, it is difficult to believe that either economic or political reconstruction can be achieved without the establishment of central agencies of administration run by Germans and comprehending the whole of Germany'.[59] Political unity was in turn the prerequisite for effective German participation in forms of European economic integration, which Carr believed essential to broader British and European interests.[60]

A third consequence of Carr's endorsement of a three-power settlement concerned the atom bomb. To avoid an ephemeral and fortuitous technological advantage to the USA becoming the source of insecurity and suspicion between the Big Three, control of atomic weapons should be forthwith handed over to the United Nations Security Council. While it is easy to endorse Carr's prophecy that 'the withholding of these ... secrets ... may prove to be an advantage dearly bought in terms of future insecurity and suspicion' and possible that he may have been justified in his belief that the effective pooling of atomic weapons would have paved the way to the settlement of other issues, there is not the least inkling in any of Carr's leaders on the subject of any plausible reason why the United States might wish to exchange the certainty of its current monopoly for the chance of better relations in the long run.[61]

Carr's persistent emphasis on the continued co-operation of the Big Three had further implications for British foreign policy. France – and British relations with France – must be marginalized.[62] One reason for this was that France would not willingly concede the political unification and rapid economic recovery of Germany, which he regarded as essential in order to relieve Britain of the costs of feeding its military zone and reassure the Soviet Union about the intentions of the Western Powers.[63] Another reason was that no fourth country must be permitted to claim superpower status.

A fifth corollary of Carr's insistence on three-power hegemony was that the United Nations Organization, useful though this might be, must be subordinated to the Big Three, whose political differences ought not to be paraded in public in New York, but settled quietly at summit or ministerial level. Carr accepted that the UNO possessed certain political and technical advantages over its predecessor, the League of Nations, but characteristically argued that its success must depend on 'the concentration of effective power which it is likely to represent', which, in turn, depended on unanimity of the Big Three.[64] When the Persian government appealed to the Security Council over continued interference in Azerbaijan and the failure to withdraw Soviet troops, the USSR responded by making allegedly analogous appeals concerning British troops in Greece and Indonesia. Carr voiced strong opposition to the Soviet decision to bring before the UN differences which he felt would be better and sooner settled behind closed doors.[65]

Finally, if there must – as Carr reluctantly conceded – be more or less exclusive spheres of influence in the post-war world rather than a multi-lateral settlement jointly concluded and guaranteed by the Big Three, then regional integration and other forms of international co-operation must be conducted in the least provocative way possible.[66] Though the advantages of wartime military co-operation should not be squandered, Carr gradually distanced himself from an early advocacy of joint military planning, standardisation of weapons and shared bases, now preferring to stress economic co-operation.[67] It was important to assuage Soviet fears about the nature of western co-operation by showing it to be non-aggressive. This, he claimed, could best be done by closer economic and financial association with western European states, even if this entailed some loss of sovereignty.[68] A similar line was taken in January 1946 when Carr welcomed an Anglo-Greek financial and economic accord in an editorial that emphasized economic recovery as the path to political stability and urged bulk purchase by Britain of Greek tobacco and currants.[69] Also consistent with this non-aggressive style of international co-operation was the enthusiastic welcome accorded by Carr to Bevin's revival in February 1946 of proposals for economic reorganization of the countries of the Middle East and 'the strengthening of direct economic links between them'.[70]

Dénouement

Abandoning hindsight, it is not difficult to appreciate the general appeal of a post-war concert of powers. Nor were Carr's views initially without support in official and political circles. Graham Ross has shown the extent to which senior figures within the Foreign Office shared Carr's position. As late as 1944, in marked contradistinction to the Chiefs of Staff, the Foreign Office was optimistic about post-war Anglo-Soviet relations. Ross notes 'how much store the Foreign Office was still setting on maintaining co-operation with Russia and how little faith it still had in the United States as a post-war collaborator in Europe.'[71] During 1944, the predominant view in the Foreign Office also favoured a Western European grouping to control German recovery if, as expected, the United States withdrew into relative isolation.[72] This was also Carr's position. Turning to the post-war Labour administration, Sean Greenwood has argued persuasively that Foreign Secretary Ernest Bevin was initially content with the idea of a European union as a 'Third Force' on a par with the USA and the USSR, even arguing, as did Carr, that it should initially be based upon functional co-operation on economic and social issues in order to avoid the provocation that a more formal security arrangement might offer to the Soviet Union.[73]

This concurrence of view would not last. Initially inclined to use British military control of the Ruhr as a springboard to European economic co-operation, Bevin had moved by the end of 1946 to acceptance of a divided Germany.[74] The reason for this was that the practicability of a 'Third Force' policy depended on close co-operation between Britain and France, and this proved to be unobtainable. As early as September 1945 the French blocked an agreement at the first post-war Council of Foreign Ministers to provide for a central German post-war administration. Carr felt that French concerns about a united Germany could be dealt with by imposing international control over the Ruhr.[75] But the decisive moment for Bevin came in the New Year when de Gaulle, barely two months in office, announced his resignation from the Presidency. French intransigence might possibly be overcome, but political chaos and economic collapse were a different matter. Much influenced by gloomy prognostications reaching him from the Paris embassy, Bevin foresaw the Channel ports 'virtually in Russian hands'. He concluded that the project for European economic and social co-operation, and with it the concept of a British-led 'Third Force', was no longer viable. As mistrust between the wartime Big Three deepened, he felt bound to align Britain with the United States.

Not so Carr: late in February, admitting clearly for the first time the incipient breakdown of the wartime alliance but presumably taking a more sanguine view of the French crisis, he was still arguing that for Britain to deviate from strict even-handedness between them would inevitably result in subordination to the United States or the Soviet

Union. The only option for Britain remained the simultaneous strengthening of ties with the Commonwealth and Europe.[76] Early the next month he responded to the Fulton speech, in which Churchill advocated Anglo-United States military alliance and spoke of an 'iron curtain' descending across Europe, by deploring its excessively ideological tone and seizing upon every available straw of conciliation towards the USSR in Churchill's text.[77] A few days later a frank and well-balanced summary of the events that had led to the breakdown of the wartime alliance concluded with a plea to Russia to honour its agreement to withdraw from Persia.[78] Vapid assertions of an underlying common interest in peace of precisely the kind he had once condemned in the early chapters of *The Twenty Years' Crisis* weakened Carr's peroration and can have been no more convincing when repeated a few days later.[79]

Once Bevin had made up his mind, during the early weeks of 1946, that Soviet designs constituted a serious and imminent threat to British security, the unfolding of the Cold War was a matter of time, and the foreign policy that Carr had nurtured with such care throughout the war was doomed. Carr cannot be accused of failing to realise the dangers of confrontation or to foresee the implications of Cold War for British power. It was his all-too-accurate foresight on the central geopolitical issue far more than any ideological preference for centralism and planning that inclined Carr to his passionate attachment to three-power hegemony. In June 1943 he had warned that

> were a rift to occur after the war between Russia, Britain, and America, were mutual suspicion and mistrust to prevail over mutual sympathy and understanding, then any policy for Europe as a whole would be bankrupt from the start. Other countries, enrolling themselves as clients of one or other group, would provide fresh causes of friction by the introduction of their own lesser jealousies and animosities. Germany, from her central vantage point, would quickly regain her freedom of manoeuvre...[80]

Three months later, dismissing as illusory the belief that an Anglo-American alliance could provide 'a self-sufficient guarantee of world peace', he warned that its fallacy consisted in ignoring...the reaction which it would provoke among other nations, and especially in Europe .... It would make the British isles a remote, exposed and not easily defensible outpost of the English-speaking world.'[81]

However accurate in foreseeing the looming Cold War and however ingenious in devising and advocating preventative stratagems, Carr was slow to appreciate the practical implications for policy once the game was lost. Things might have worked out differently. Bevin might have stood his ground and resisted what looks very much like panic in the early months of 1946. But he did not; and one symptom of the panic was the way in which he rounded on *The Times*. Barrington-Ward was summoned to the Foreign Office in March 1946 and subjected to a tirade from Bevin. '*The Times* did great harm. It was taken abroad for a national newspaper. He was going to tell the House of Commons that it was not, and that it was pro-Russian and not pro-British. I had a lot of pink intelligentsia down there and he didn't believe I was in control.'[82] Thenceforward, Carr's chances of exerting any appreciable influence on public affairs were negligible. Realising this, he soon gave up his position at *The Times* and devoted much of the remainder of his long life to a massive history of the Soviet Revolution.

Notes

1 The anecdote is related in Donald McLachan, *In The Chair: Barrington-Ward of The Times, 1927–1948* (London, Weidenfeld and Nicolson, 1971), p. 206n.
2 See *House of Lords Parliamentary Debates*, Hansard, June 2, 1942.
3 These include 'Public Opinion as a Safeguard of Peace' *International Affairs*, Vol. 15, No. 6, November–December 1936, pp. 846–62; 'The Future of the League – Idealism or Reality?' *The Fortnightly*, 140 new series, October 1936, pp. 385–402; 'Great Britain as a Mediterranean Power'. Cust Foundation Lecture. University College, Nottingham, 19 November 1937; 'Europe and the Spanish War', *The Fortnightly*, 141 new series, January–June 1937, pp. 25–34; 'The Twilight of the Comintern', *The Fortnightly*, 143 new series, January–June 1938, pp. 137–47; 'Honour among Nations', *The Fortnightly*, 145 new series, May 1939, pp. 489–500; *International Relations since the Peace Treaties* (London: Macmillan, 1937); *Britain: A Study of Foreign Policy from the Versailles Treaty to the Outbreak of War* (London: Longman Green, 1939); and *The Twenty Years' Crisis, 1919–1939: an Introduction to the Study of International Relations* (London: Macmillan, 1939).
4 This argument is most clearly expressed in E.H. Carr, 'Great Britain as a Mediterranean Power', Cust Foundation Lecture, University College, Nottingham., delivered on Friday, 19 November 1937.
5 Carr, *The Twenty Years' Crisis*, p. 282: 'The negotiations which led up to the Munich Agreement of September 29, 1938, were the nearest approach in recent years to the settlement of a major international issue by a procedure of peaceful change.' This section of chapter 13 was revised in the second edition, and the quoted sentence dropped (1946 edition, pp. 221–2). Further references are to the 1939 edition unless indicated.
6 Archives of *The Times*, Carr to Barrington-Ward, 29 September 1939.
7 Robert Cole, *Britain and the War of Words in Neutral Europe, 1939–45* (Basingstoke: Macmillan, 1990), p. 22.

8   *Ibid.*, pp. 16 and 24; PRO INF1/859, Macmillan to Halifax, 26 October 1939; Halifax to Macmillan, 26 October 1939.

9   McDonald, *The Times*, p. 37.

10 PRO INF1/862, Cooper to Halifax, 27 July 1940. From the context it is clear that the professors with whom Cooper was losing patience were Toynbee's team at Balliol as well as Lionel Curtis and others at Chatham House.

11 I. McDonald, *The History of The Times, V. Struggles in War and Peace, 1939–1966* (London: The Times), p. 63. Wartime paper shortages produced an artificial restriction in circulation, which, however, never fell below 150,000 during the war.

12 Political and Economic Planning, Report on the British Press (London: PEP 1938), quoted in R. Cockett, *Twilight of Truth: Chamberlain, Appeasement and the Manipulation of the Press* (London: Weidenfeld and Nicolson, 1989), p. 25.

13 These and other figures for the print-runs of works published by Macmillan are derived from the Macmillan Edition Books in the British Library. Add. MSS 55909–55930.

14 Cockett, *Twilight*, p. 25 ff, quoting *History of The Times*, IV, p. 915.

15 *Ibid.*, p. 13.

16 McLachlan, *In the Chair*, pp. 239 and 252–3.

17 PRO FO371/26950 C3968/484/41.

18 An example is *The Times*, 21 July 1943, 'Nutrition and Trade' which deals with Latin America and is identified in *The Times'* editorial log as being drafted by Humphreys.

19 PRO FO371/33517 A11406/11/2. David Kelly, Buenos Aires, to Victor Perowne, 2 December 1943, makes clear that the Buenos Aires correspondent of *The Times*, anxious not to damage relations with the new Argentine regime, had been submitting material to the embassy for comment, only to find that the staff of *The Times* in London consistently rendered his copy more hostile to the Argentine government before publication.

20 PRO FO371/26819 C13599/214/36.

21 PRO FO371/30096 R7715/R7720/240/44 1941. The debate as fought out in the correspondence columns of *The Times* and in *The Economist* is summarised in P.M.H. Bell, *John Bull and the Bear: British Public Opinion, Foreign Policy, and the Soviet Union, 1941–1945* (London: Arnold, 1990), p. 60.

22 PRO FO371/39079 C2867/C2868/146/18 1944.

23 A. Foster, 'The Times and Appeasement: the Second Phase', in Walter Laqueur, ed., *The Second World War: Essays in Military and Political History* (London: Sage, 1982), pp. 275–99.

24 PRO FO 371/24761 N6045/1224/59. Barrington-Ward to Laurence Collier, 28 July 1940. On the complexities underlying this bland statement especially those concerning the relationship between Barrington-Ward and Carr, there is no better account than that provided by McLachlan, *In the Chair*, chapter 21.

25 McDonald, *The Times*, p. 134/5.

26 Archives of *The Times*. News International, London.

27 Carr Papers, Box 5. Birmingham University Library.

28 C. Ponting, *1940: Myth and Reality* (London: Hamish Hamilton, 1990), p. 96, identifies the leading advocates as Halifax and R.A. Butler, both close to *The Times*. Ponting argues that the approach was not abandoned until July 1940.

29 Gathered together at the end of the year in pamphlet form, as *Planning for War and Peace: Ten Leading Articles Reprinted from The Times* (London: The Times Publishing Co. Ltd, 1940), these were originally published under the following titles: 'Hazards of Neutrality' (13 July), 'Hitler's Europe' (18 July), 'Britain and Hitler' (22 July), 'Planning for War and Peace' (5 August), 'Bread and Freedom' (13 August), 'Looking Forward' (30 August), 'The Mood of Britain' (5 October), 'The Commonwealth and the Future' (5 November), and 'The Two Scourges' (5 December).

30 E.H. Carr, *Conditions of Peace* (London: Macmillan, 1942), pp. 135–9.

31 E.H. Carr, *The Future of Nations: Independence or Interdependence?* (London: Kegan Paul, 1941). The Democratic Order, No. 1, p. 26. Cf. *The Times*, 1 July 1940. 'The New Europe'. 'Probably the gravest error of the last peace settlement was that it encouraged disintegration at a time when integration was already the crying need.'

32 Carr, *The Future of Nations*, p. 32. This obsolescence of neutrality was hammered home repeatedly in *The Times*. Cf. 1 July, 13 July, 30th August, 16 December 1940, 5 and 9 July, 26 August, 15 September, and 4 October 1941.

33 Carr, *Nationalism and After*, p. 57/8. The paragraph beginning 'Two powerful arguments' was lifted more or less verbatim from *The Times*, 20 September 1944, 'Frontiers of Peace'.

34 *The Times*, 16 December 1940. Cf. 9 January 1941, 'Interdependence', which dwells on Anglo-French military co-operation prior to the fall of France and contrasts it with British military co-operation with the Dominions. The same point about permanent military co-operation is made repeatedly in *The Times*. See 'The Key to the Balkans' (11 March 1941), 'A World Pattern' (15 September 1941), 'Norway Plays Her Part' (14 November 1941), 'Council of War' (24 December 1941), and 'Russia and Poland' (5 December 1941), the last of which jauntily hails military co-operation between the two Allies as 'a happy precedent for future Russo-Polish relations'.

35 Carr, *The Future of Nations*, p. 43.

36 *The Times*, 2 September 1940, 'The Map of Europe'.

37 *The Times*, 30 August 1940, 'Looking Forward'.

38 *The Times*, 12 December 1940, 'Active Diplomacy'.

39 PRO FO371/43709 R21228/73/19.

40 McDonald, *The Times*, p. 122.

41 McDonald, *The Times*, pp. 123–5, quoting Barrington-Ward's diary.

42 McDonald, *The Times*, p. 127, quoting Barrington-Ward's diary entry for 1 January 1947.

43 *The Times*, 1 August 1941, 'Peace and Power'.

44 *The Times*, 29 December 1942, 'Mr. Eden's Mission'.

45 McDonald, *The Times*, pp. 104–7.

46 *The Times*, 23 May 1945, 'Conditions of Confidence', quoted by McDonald, *The Times*, p. 135.

47 See No. 4 of Fox's Carr memorial lecture, 1984, and W.T.R. Fox, *The Superpowers: The United States, Britain, and the Soviet Union – Their Responsibility for Peace* (New Haven, Conn.: Yale University Institute of International Studies, 1944), therein referred to. Maintenance of Britain as one of three preeminent world powers was the central plank of Carr's programme, returned to again and again in the leader columns of *The Times*. Examples include 23

March 1943, 'Great and Small Nations'; 29 July 1943, 'Concerted Policy'; 25 September 1944, 'Security and Power'; and 23 May 1945, 'Conditions of Confidence'. There are many others.

48   PRO FO371/56866 N3041/3041/38.

49   Timothy Dunne, 'International Relations Theory in Britain: the Invention of an International Society Tradition' (Unpublished D.Phil. thesis, Oxford 1993), p. 33.

50   *The Times*, 26 October 1946, 'Peace, Trade and Output'.

51   *The Times*, 8 February 1946, 'After the Debate'.

52   *The Times*, 4 December 1945, 'The Three-Power Pattern'. See also 11 December 1945, 'Agenda for Moscow'; 8 January 1946, 'UNO'; 8 February 1946, 'After the Debate'; 22 February 1946, 'Britain and the World'.

53   *The Times*, 25 September 1946, 'The British Role'.

54   *The Times*, 7 March 1946, 'British Foreign Policy'.

55   *The Times*, 8 November 1945, 'Policy and the Atom'; see also 21 September, 'Italian Colonies,' and 3 October 1945, 'A Failure to Retrieve'.

56   *The Times*, 4 October 1945, 'After the Setback'.

57   *The Times*, 25 October 1945, 'A Call for Unity'. See also 11 March 1946, 'The German Deadlock': continued division of Germany threatened to provoke 'dissensions and rivalries between the allies by inviting constant and competitive intervention'. Deploring the divergence already evident between the zones of occupation he hoped in vain for a belated solution from the imminent Four-Power Conference.

58   *The Times*, 29 July 1946, 'The Peace Conference'.

59   *The Times*, 25 October 1945, 'A Call for Unity'.

60   *The Times*, 13 November 1945, 'German Unity'. See also 5 November 1945, 'Harnessing German Industry'.

61   *The Times*, 23 November 1945, 'The Atom and After'. See also 31 October, 'The Explosive Atom'; 8 November 1945, 'Policy and the Atom'; 16 November 1945, 'Peace and the Atom'; 11 December 1945, 'Agenda for Moscow'.

62   *The Times*, 11 December 1945, 'Agenda for Moscow' has strong anti-French implications. For a comprehensive indictment see *The Times*, 22 January 1946, 'General de Gaulle's Challenge'.

63   On French intransigence and Carr's remedy see *The Times*, 11 December 1945, 'Agenda for Moscow', and 12 December 1945, 'Control over Germany'.

64   *The Times*, 8 January 1946, 'UNO'; 18 January 1946, 'Mr. Bevin's Speech'. See also 4 November 1946, 'The United Nations'.

65   *The Times*, 6 February 1946, 'UNO and the Powers'. Carr described the Soviet move as 'a reprisal'. Two days later he returned to the same theme, advising that differences between the Big Three 'will be settled not by resounding declarations of principle but by the quiet conciliation of particular interests, not by public recrimination, but by amicable private discussion'. *The Times*, 8 February 1946, 'After the Debate'. See also 21 January 1946, 'Procedures for Persia', and 23 January 1946, 'The Soviet Appeals'.

66   *The Times*, 3 October 1945, 'A Failure to Retrieve'; 5 June 1946, 'Mr. Bevin's Review'. See also *The Times*, 22 February 1946, 'Britain and the World'. The same argument against public diplomacy is extended to peace negotiations in *The Times*, 17 October 1946, 'Publicity and Peace'.

67   *The Times*, 7 March 1946, 'British Foreign Policy'.

68   *The Times*, 24 November 1945, 'Mr. Bevin's Review'.

69   *The Times*, 26 January 1946, 'Recovery in Greece'.

70   *The Times*, 8 February 1946, 'After the Debate'.

71   G. Ross, 'Foreign Office Attitudes to the Soviet Union, 1941–45', in W. Laqueur, ed., *The Second World War: Essays in Military and Political History* (London: Sage, 1982), p. 266.

72   S. Greenwood, 'Ernest Bevin, France, and "Western Union": August 1945– February 1946', *European History Quarterly*, No. 14, 1984, p. 320.

73   Greenwood, 'Bevin, France', pp. 323–5. See also *The Times*, 24 November 1945, 'Mr. Bevin's Review'.

74   S. Greenwood, 'Bevin, the Ruhr and the Division of Germany: August 1945– December 1946', *The Historical Journal*, Vol. 29, No. 1, 1986, p. 203.

75   *The Times*, 11 December 1945, 'Agenda for Moscow'; 15 December 1945, 'Control over Germany'.

76   *The Times*, 21 February 1946, 'Policy in the Making'.

77   *The Times*, 6 March 1946, 'Mr. Churchill's Speech'.

78   *The Times*, 14 March 1946, 'The Three Powers'.

79   *The Times*, 19 March 1946, 'The Common Interest'.

80   *The Times*, 3 June 1943, 'Germany's Last Hope'.

81   *The Times*, 30 September 1943, 'Foundations of Peace'.

82   McDonald, *The Times*, pp. 139–40.

II
The Russian Question

4
Carr's Changing Views of the Soviet Union

R.W. Davies

Carr embarked on his 14-volume *History of Soviet Russia* in 1944 at the age of 52, and completed it 33 years later at the age of 85. For Carr the writing of the *History* was the culmination of his life's work and his most important contribution to human knowledge.

Carr's view of the world scene, reflected in the 14 volumes of his *History of Soviet Russia*, is often depicted as both detached and pragmatic. A.J.P. Taylor, one of his most sympathetic critics, described Carr as 'an Olympian among historians'. Others have often stressed that his uncompromising belief in the inexorable determinism of human progress led him always to side with the victors, and write from their point of view. Accordingly, they argue, it was quite natural that in the later 1930s he advocated the appeasement of the triumphant Nazi regime, while in the 1940s he called for cooperation with and concessions to Stalin's Soviet Union.

There is an element of truth in this assessment. Both as historian and as public figure, Carr tended not to take seriously groups, individuals and causes whose policies were impracticable and doomed to failure. In his account of the Russian Revolution, Constitutional Democrats, Mensheviks and anarchists all appeared in his pages but were not granted much space. When I was working with him on *Foundations of a Planned Economy, 1926–1929*, Vol. 1 (1969) he argued that in a history of the Soviet 1920s it would be ridiculous for the economist Bazarov to receive as much attention as the leading Gosplan officials who were making policy. And I was able to persuade him to devote more attention to speeches by Stalin, whose utterances he held in low esteem, on the grounds that Stalin deserved at least as much space as Bukharin. Carr was also contemptuous of the universal tendency of statesmen to wrap policies based on national interest in an envelope of moral righteousness, a cover-up to

91

which he believed Americans were particularly prone. He insisted that it was a historian's job to cut through the moralising flim-flam and reveal the national, economic and social mainsprings of political action. The literary critic D.S. Mirsky, in his preface to Carr's first major work, *Dostoevsky, 1821–1881: a New Biography* (1931), commented that 'there is no nonsense in Mr. Carr's book'. The absence of speculative and moralising 'nonsense' in almost all his writings was one of Carr's great strengths (though occasionally a weakness).

Yet this assessment of Carr's world outlook misses its most important characteristics. In 1937 he published *Michael Bakunin*. In an interview on the occasion of the completion of his *History*, over 40 years later, he remarked about his biography of this notorious anarchist: 'I'd almost say it was the best book I ever wrote.'[1] Yet Bakunin was certainly someone whose policies were impracticable and doomed to failure. In the biography Carr describes his career as 'barren of concrete result'. So why this fascination with Bakunin? Carr explained:

> Bakunin is one of the completest embodiments in history of the spirit of liberty – the liberty which excludes neither licence nor caprice, which tolerates no human institution, which remains an unrealised and unrealisable ideal, but which is almost universally felt to be an indispensable part of the highest manifestations and aspirations of humanity.

Carr contrasted Marx and Bakunin: both wanted to tear down the existing order, but one was a statesman and constructive revolutionary who sought the rule of a new class, the other a visionary and prophet, who predicted and favoured a spontaneous revolt of the least civilized which would achieve the domination of the individual and destruction of the state, but was curiously permissive to dictatorship. For Carr, Marx and Bakunin represented the conflicting realistic and utopian elements in the movement against capitalism.

Carr returned to the tension between realism and utopianism in the short autobiographical memoir which he wrote in the late 1970s:

> Perhaps the world is divided between cynics, who find no sense in anything, and Utopians who make sense of things on the basis of some magnificent unverifiable assumption about the future. I prefer the latter.[2]

As I see it, an understanding of Carr's assessment of the Soviet experience has to be grounded in his view that in human affairs it was through the interplay between utopianism and realism that society progressed; he assessed the October Revolution and its aftermath as a bold and major attempt to combine utopianism and realism, and create a new society by the use of political power.

In his assessment of the Soviet experiment, Carr went through several major personal revolutions in the course of his long life, closely associated with his changing view of society and politics generally. Carr's personal intellectual history helps us to understand how he came to the view of the Soviet system which he reached during the Second World War, and which led him to write his *History*. In this chapter, I deal primarily with his changing views before the Second World War; these have received little attention in writings about him. His publications and unpublished writings of the time are my main source of information, and in particular his many book reviews. Until he took up the Woodrow Wilson Professorship of International Politics at Aberystwyth in 1936 Carr was working in the Foreign Office, and many of his reviews were published anonymously, or with the initials 'E.C.' or 'E.H.C.', or over the pseudonym 'John Hallett' (John being the first name of his only son, and Hallett his mother's surname). In the course of the 1930s Carr reviewed most important and some trivial books about Russia. (The vast and broad background knowledge of Soviet affairs and Russian history which he acquired helped to enrich his *History*.) These reviews, together with articles and reviews on a wide range of historical and contemporary topics, appeared in the *Spectator*, the *Fortnightly Review*, the *Christian Science Monitor*, the *Sunday Times*, and the *Times Literary Supplement*.[3]

Before the Storm: 1917–30

As a schoolboy and a young man Carr, under the influence of his father, was a Lloyd George Liberal, believing strongly both in free trade and in Lloyd George's social and budgetary reforms. His school-fellows were nearly all orthodox Conservatives, and Liberals like Carr were a despised minority. But his radicalism did not go beyond Lloyd George. There was no sign that Carr, either as a schoolboy or as a university student, took any interest in socialism or the labour movement, or in Tsarist Russia and its revolutionaries.

But at Cambridge, where he took a double first in Classics in 1916, he acquired a significant insight into what history was about. According to his memoir, he was taught history by a 'rather undistinguished' specialist in the Persian wars, who argued that Herodotus' account of them was 'shaped and moulded by his attitude to the Peloponnesian War, which was going on at the time he wrote'. This 'fascinating revelation' strongly and permanently influenced Carr's view of history and historians.

His interest in Soviet Russia began partly by chance. After graduation Carr, who was unfit for military service, took a temporary post as a Foreign Office clerk. A year later, following the Bolshevik Revolution, he was appointed as junior member of a three-man team concerned with the Russian problem. After other posts, including membership of the British delegation to the Paris peace conference in 1919, he served between January 1925 and the summer of 1929 as second secretary in the British legation at Riga. In Riga Russia was the constant topic of interest. Carr learned Russian in 1925; and visited Moscow for the first time in 1927.

He was thus concerned with the Russian Revolution and its aftermath from the very beginning. He found much smugness among his fellow officials. The commercial attaché in Petrograd told him that the Bolsheviks would not last more than a week or so. In Riga, where the headquarters of British intelligence in Eastern Europe were located, he met with the 'narrowness and bigotry' of the two top people in intelligence, ex-residents of Russia who had lost their fortunes in the revolution. In his memoir Carr comments that 'from the first, owing to some *esprit de contradiction*, I refused to believe' that Bolshevism would not last; 'I studied eagerly every bit of news, and the longer the Bolsheviks held out, the more convinced I became that they had come to stay.'

But in the mid-1920s his dissent from conventional views was very limited. Like others who took part in the peace conference, he was outraged at the French and British unfairness to the Germans – to this extent he was critical of those who made the post-war world order. But he remained a firm Liberal, and in his memoir he recalled that at this time he 'knew nothing of Marxism; I'd probably never heard of Marx.' There is no indication that he took seriously the communist challenge to capitalism.

His world view was, however, modified in one important respect while he was at Riga. This development deserves description in his own words:

I began to read a lot of Russian nineteenth-century literature. The authors who influenced me most deeply were (in that order) Dosto-evsky and Herzen. I now perceived for the first time that the liberal moralistic ideology in which I had been brought up was not, as I had always assumed, an Absolute taken for granted by the modern world, but was sharply and convincingly attacked by very intelligent people living outside the charmed circle, who looked at the world through very different eyes. In other words, the first challenge to the bourgeois capitalist society came, so far as I was concerned, not from Marx or from the Bolsheviks, but from Russian nineteenth-century intellectuals, who were not in any strict sense revolutionaries at all.

Gradually Carr also came to take an active interest in Bolshevik social aims and achievements. His first recorded article on a Soviet theme appeared in the *Christian Science Monitor* in April 1929,[4] and dealt with the illiteracy campaign. The article noted that the 1926 census showed that while literacy had improved since 1920 it was lower in the 11–16 than in the 16–24 age group. Hence the importance of the extension of elementary education provided for in the five-year plan. While the spread of 'half education' had unfortunately lowered the standard of Russian literature, 'it would, however, be unfair to minimize the achievements of the Soviet régime' in the educational field:

> elementary education has become one of the handmaids and instruments of the Soviet system. To become literate in Soviet Russia today is to become a good Communist; and this is sufficient to explain the strenuous efforts of the authorities to spread education among the masses.

Carr by this time had firmly formed the view that there was nothing to be said for the role of the 'White' Russians during the civil war (perhaps he had held this view since 1919?). In a review of an English translation of Wrangel's memoirs, he bluntly declared:

> it is no longer possible for any sane man to regard the campaigns of Kolchak, Yudenich, Denikin and Wrangel otherwise than as tragic blunders of colossal dimensions. They were monuments of folly in conception and of incompetence in execution; they cost, directly and indirectly, hundreds of thousands of lives; and, except in so far as they may have increased the bitterness of the Soviet rulers against the 'white' Russians and the Allies who half-heartedly supported them, they did not deflect the course of history by a single hair's breadth.[5]

In spite of his approval of Soviet educational policy, in 1929 and 1930 Carr, to judge by his writings, was not yet impressed by Soviet achievements in other respects. He wrote informatively and sympathetically about the poetry of the early Soviet period, singling out Mayakovsky's 'brilliant talent' and 'moments of real beauty' for special praise. Among Soviet prose writers he particularly admired Babel, who combined his allegiance to the regime with 'a capacity for looking at his subjects simultaneously from within and without'. But he dismissed propaganda novels such as Gladkov's *Cement*: 'it is a solid, ponderous straightforward tale innocent of any approach to grace or subtlety.'[6] Carr displayed a somewhat patronising agnosticism about the Soviet regime. In the summer of 1930 he compared Loyola, the founder of the Jesuits, and Lenin as 'fanatics of narrow, but piercing vision and iron will'.[7] In a review of Trotsky's autobiography he commented:

> it is odd, and rather pathetic, that Trotzky still retains unimpaired his faith in the Soviet system, and interlards his narrative with denunciations of the western parliamentary democracies. One would have thought that some things, at least, are better ordered under a democratic regime.[8]

Reviewing Aylmer Maude's *Life of Tolstoy* at this time he criticised Tolstoy for 'the characteristic Russian contempt for the practical consequences of applying ideas which he believed to be just' and praised Maude's 'apposite' dictum that 'Even today the U.S.S.R. is more concerned about maintaining Marxian principles than about seeing that the people secure decent food, clothing and housing.'[9]

'Thoroughly pro-Soviet', 1931–35

Carr's view of the Soviet regime changed fundamentally (though temporarily) as a result of the economic crisis which struck the capitalist world in 1929 and reached its nadir in 1931. Simultaneously the first five-year plan seemed to demonstrate that there was an alternative to the chaos of capitalism. In his memoir Carr describes himself as having been 'thoroughly pro-Soviet (a dissident view at this time)'. He recalls that he admired Litvinov's exposure of western hypocrisy about disarmament, deplored the campaign against Soviet 'dumping' and assessed the five-year plan as 'the answer to the anarchy of capitalism'.

His new approach was reflected in two reviews which appeared in the summer of 1931, and, in startling contrast to his previous publications, were enthusiastic about Soviet economic developments. In August, he reviewed *Red Bread*, by Maurice Hindus,[10] an American of Russian origin who returned to the Soviet Union and his native village during the summer of 1930. In his review Carr sets out the positive assessment of the collectivization of agriculture from which he never later departed:

It is easy now to see that the ambitious enterprise of 'collectivising' the farm was both a political and an economic necessity for the Soviet Government. A political necessity, because it was impossible, in a country more than ninety per cent agricultural, to maintain indefinitely a communist system while agriculture was still organised on an individualistic basis. An economic necessity, because the mechanisation of modern agriculture is making the cultivation of cereals by small holders more and more unprofitable, and cereals must perforce remain the staple product of Russian agriculture. The 'Stolypin' reforms of the decade before the war, which were inspired by bureaucratic study of western methods and aimed at the development of 'peasant proprietorship' could never have got to the root of the problem. In Russian conditions, the collective farm seems to be the only permanent alternative to the large estate of the capitalist landowner; and the Soviet government was therefore bound sooner or later to stake everything on the experiment.[11]

In the following month Carr reviewed M. Ilin's *Moscow Has a Plan: a Soviet Primer*,[12] a lively Soviet propaganda booklet, originally published for a Soviet audience. This review was even more remarkable:

Try as he may the reader will find it hard not to be impressed by the hammer-like intensity with which the main points of the Five Year Plan are driven home – the electrification, the doubling of coal production, the creation of large scale mechanised agriculture through the medium of the collective farm. And to follow all this, town planning, health services, universal instruction, and the organisation of sport and recreation. 'Our whole life, down to the kitchen pot, must be changed'! You feel that these people have faith, and that it is this faith which implanted in the masses, forces them to undergo the many privations which the Five Year Plan entails (and of which, naturally, nothing is said in this book). They have discovered a new religion of the Kilowatt and the Machine, which may well prove to be the creed for which modern civilisation is waiting....

...The important question for Europe at the present time is not whether the Five Year Plan will be completed in four years...or whether the output of Soviet factories is up to western standards; but whether Europe can discover in herself a driving force, an intensity of faith, comparable to that now being generated in Russia.[13]

A year later he reviewed Lancelot Lawton's two-volume *Economic History of Soviet Russia* (1932),[14] which became a standard work in the 1930s. He brusquely dismissed Lawton's attempt to show that the Soviet economic system did not work; and praised Maurice Dobb's positive assessment of the Soviet economy: 'as regards economic development,' Carr wrote, 'Professor Dobb is conclusive.'[15]

In these years Carr also wrote about Lenin and Trotsky, and the Bolshevik Revolution, in far more sympathetic terms than he had in 1929 or 1930. He commended Trotsky's *History of the Russian Revolution*[16] and W.H. Chamberlin's two-volume *The Russian Revolution, 1917–1921* (1935), for their insistence that the revolution – and the civil war which followed it – were not made from above but by the mass of the people:

There are only two histories of the Russian Revolution which matter: Trotsky's, which appeared in English three years ago, and Mr. Chamberlin's, published last week...

Both Trotsky and Mr. Chamberlin rightly insist on the spontaneity of the revolution. It was not, as nearly every foreigner believed at the time, the work of a band of fanatics or agitators inciting the masses to violence. Again and again it was the masses who drove their hesitating and temporising leaders further and further down the path of revolution. The makers and heroes of the revolution were in fact, as the Bolshevik legend proclaims, the proletarian and the peasant...

[Like the March 1917 revolution], the November revolution was also forced on its leaders from below. But it had the fortune to find in Lenin a leader who, unlike the Milyukovs and Kerenskys, understood what it was all about. The genius of Lenin was as the interpreter rather than as the creator of the revolution.[17]

Carr's sympathy for the revolution and for the achievements of the Soviet regime did not blind him to its dark sides. In his review of Maurice Hindus, while sympathizing with his positive view of the collectivisation of agriculture, he gently derided Hindus because he 'looks at the kolkhoz through rose-tinted glasses of a familiar American pattern'. Hindus, Carr pointed out, was not in the Soviet Union in the first months of 1930, 'when "shock brigades" travelled about the country forcing the peasant into the collective farms, when thousands of the *kulaki*, or prosperous farmers, were deprived of everything they had and deported to northern Russia, and when peasants all over the country were killing off their stock rather than hand it over to the *kolkhozi*.' Elsewhere he reviewed a favourable book about the Soviet economy by Louis Segal jointly with a collection of letters from prisoners in the timber camps, and chided Segal for his bias:

> The letters contain little evidence of deliberate cruelty, but much of the almost intolerable hardships which fall on an outlawed and persecuted class in a land where even the favoured are not living much above subsistence level. Here is an achievement of the Five-Year Plan not mentioned by Mr. Segal.[18]

Through his access to Foreign Office papers, Carr was well acquainted with reports about the disastrous famine of 1933.[19] When the first detailed book about the famine was published three years later, Carr in his review castigated foreign visitors who had denied the existence of famine. He condemned Edouard Herriot, ex-Prime Minister of France, who spent a fortnight in the Soviet Union 'in a heavily conducted and heavily banqueted tour' and 'took it on himself to announce to the world on his return that there was no famine'; Carr castigated Herriot as 'hasty and irresponsible'. He added that 'Mr. Bernard Shaw makes an equally vulnerable target.'[20]

Carr was always extremely critical of western writers who, in their enthusiasm for the Soviet system, ignored or played down its defects. While praising Dobb's economics, he roundly condemned Dobb for being 'hopelessly biassed'; he either ignored 'the darker sides of the Soviet régime' or 'tries to defend them by transparent sophistries'.[21] Maurice Hindus, Carr noted, 'like other writers who go in and out of Soviet Russia . . . is obliged to put a seal on his tongue in criticizing certain aspects of the Soviet régime'.[22] And as for Beatrice and Sidney Webb's two-volume *Soviet Communism: a New Civilisation?* (1935), while he conceded that 'as an exposition of facts this book is both stimulating and illuminating', he diagnosed 'the fundamental weakness . . . that it attempts to fit the Soviet Union into a mould for which it was never intended and to judge it by standards which it has never accepted.'[23]

In discussing the Soviet political system in the early 1930s, Carr frankly described the role of the OGPU. He took it for granted that the public trials during the first five-year plan were entirely based on 'confessions extorted from the defendants by methods known to the OGPU'; and he compared the OGPU as a 'state within a state' with Ivan the

Terrible's *oprichnina*.[24] He noted the baleful effects of Soviet dogmatism and orthodoxy: as a result, Russian literature 'has been virtually dead since 1926'.[25]

Nevertheless, Carr was convinced that the Soviet system, and Marxism, were a serious challenge to capitalism. 'Bolshevism,' he wrote in 1932, reviewing a book which rejected Soviet ideals as unachievable, 'will be measured not against the absolute ideal posited by Dr Gurian, but against the practical achievements of the rival capitalist system; and the failure of the latter, and in particular its failure to adjust its international differences, will continue to constitute the most effective argument in the Bolshevik armory.'[26] In the following year, on the occasion of the 50th anniversary of the death of Karl Marx, he concluded that developments since Marx's death, including the Russian Revolution, 'give Marx a claim to be regarded as the most far-sighted genius of the nineteenth century and one of the most successful prophets in history':

> There are now few thinking men who will dismiss with confidence the Marxian assumption that capitalism, developed to its highest point, inevitably encompasses its own destruction. The idea is once more abroad that the capitalist system has received notice to reform or quit.[27]

'Disillusionment and Revulsion', 1936–39

In his memoir Carr described the sea-change in his views in the mid-1930s:

> From about the beginning of 1935 ... ignorance or concealment were no longer possible. The whole period of the purges was one of disillusionment and revulsion, the intensity of which was, I suppose, accounted for by my previous enthusiasm. I became very hostile to the USSR.

Carr's memoir was written 40 years after this period. Whatever his private change of heart, in his writings the major shift did not take place as early as 1935 or even in the first half of 1936. In 1935, as we have seen, he was still writing about Soviet developments in a generally positive spirit. In 1936 he still attempted to explain the dark sides of Soviet development in terms not so much of the system but of the historical circumstances. In his review about the famine, he explained, more in sorrow than in anger:

In Russia human life has always been, to put it brutally, the cheapest and most abundant of commodities. It will require centuries of evolution to alter this tradition. Meanwhile, policies can be carried out in Russia with far less regard to the cost in human material than would be possible elsewhere. The building of the Socialist State, and the collectivisation of agriculture which is an essential part of it, is one of these policies.[28]

The turning point for Carr was certainly the Great Purges of 1936–8. He wrote about the purges with the bleak certainty that the accused were innocent of the crimes of which they were accused. His article on the first major public trial of August 1936, which was entitled 'The Twilight of the Bolsheviks', derided 'the liberal friends of the Soviet Union, who took at its face value the new "democratic" constitution', and described the trial as a 'public reversion to terrorist methods' an 'atrocity'. Stalin alone remained of the seven original members of the Politburo, 'bloodstained, but victorious', but this would not be the end of the 'holocaust'.[29]

Nine months later, in May 1937, Carr visited the Soviet Union for the first time since 1927. He published a series of articles entitled 'Lenin: Stalin' anonymously in *The Times* after his return. Stalin was assessed as having constructed 'the most powerful and arbitrary State machine yet known in history'; 'the suppression of free thought is carried to the pitch of perfection'. Carr continued to acknowledge Soviet industrial achievements. 'The central and fundamental fact about contemporary Russia is that the country is in the throes of an industrial revolution comparable with that which transformed Western Europe 100 years ago', a revolution which had done much for the industrial workers, now far greater in numbers. This revolution had 'brought into power in Russia, as it did in the West... a new social stratum, appropriately defined as a "middle class"', which was slowly but surely acquiring benefits and privileges. This was a 'new bourgeoisie'. But it was not quite the same as the bourgeoisie in Western Europe, because 'classes in the Soviet Union have not yet crystallized, and may never crystallize'.

Carr now described the fate of the peasantry more starkly than in his previous writings. Ever since the 'scissors' crisis' of 1923, he wrote, 'the agriculturalist in the Soviet Union has had a raw deal'; 'the Russian peasant still, as of old, gets all the kicks and few of the halfpence'. He concluded that 'Soviet Socialism is, after all, only capitalism writ large'.[30]

These articles of July 1937, though published anonymously, did not display the extent of the revulsion which Carr recalled having felt at that time. But from 1936 onwards Carr ceased to present the Soviet Union as offering a fundamental challenge to the West. Instead, he now saw it as an authoritarian or totalitarian regime similar to that of Nazi Germany. 'The Stalin régime was built up on a system of brutality, espionage and hypocrisy beyond anything of which bourgeois democracy was capable,' he wrote in a review of *Assignment in Utopia* (1937), written by the American journalist Eugene Lyons in disillusionment with Soviet Communism.[31] And reviewing *A False Utopia: Collectivism in Theory and Practice* (1937), a book written by W.H. Chamberlin in the same disenchanted spirit, Carr noted that Chamberlin 'has no difficulty in showing that the machinery of both dictatorships is the same in its essential features'.[32] In a talk to the Royal Institute of International Affairs at this time he claimed that, because of the long German tradition of individual freedom, Germany under the Nazis, which he also visited in 1937, was 'almost a free country as compared with Russia'.[33]

Carr's disillusionment with the Soviet Union, together with his long-established sense of indignation at the treatment of Germany in the Versailles Treaty, played a significant part in his failure to recognise the menace of Nazi Germany and world fascism. In his memoir he explains:

> One result of my preoccupation with the Russian horrors was a neglect of what was going on in Germany. I don't think it was till 1938, after the occupation of Austria, that I began to think of Hitler as a serious danger. No doubt I was very blind.

'A Great Achievement and a Historical Turning-Point', 1941–80

During the Second World War Carr's view of Soviet development underwent a further major change. He summed up his final personal mental revolution in his memoir:

> of course the event which influenced me – and most other people at the time – enormously, was the entry of Russia into the war. In *The Times* [of which he was Assistant Editor] I very quickly began to plug the Russian alliance; and, when this was vindicated by Russian endurance and the Russian victory, it revived my initial faith in the Russian revolution as a great achievement and a historical turning-point. It was obvious that the Russia of the second world war was a very different place from the Russia of the first – in terms of people as well as material resources. Looking back on the thirties, I came to feel that my preoccupation with the purges and brutalities of Stalinism

had distorted my perspective. The black spots were real enough, but looking exclusively at them destroyed one's vision of what was really happening. . . . I became intensely interested in what the Russians had done, and how far this had any lessons for western society; and this tied up with my interest in the Marxist critique of capitalism and the bourgeoisie.

It was with this outlook that Carr embarked in 1944 on his *History of Soviet Russia*. The post-war writings in which he expressed his general view of the Soviet Union are easily available and have been frequently discussed by others; and I shall not deal with them in detail here.[34]

But in assessing his approach to the Soviet experience in his *History* several aspects of it should be borne in mind. First, when he wrote his *History* he was thoroughly imbued with enthusiasm for economic planning as an important part of the solution to the problems which beset the whole world. The titles of the six lectures broadcast in 1950, and published the next year as *The New Society*, make clear both his view about the general direction in which the world was going, and his approval of what was happening:

> The Historical Approach
> From Competition to Planned Economy
> From Economic Whip to Welfare State
> From Individualism to Mass Democracy
> The World Transformed
> The Road to Freedom.

In his book *The Road to Serfdom* published in 1944 Hayek strongly attacked Carr as one of those whose works were 'preparing the way for a totalitarian course in this country'.[35] The final chapter of Carr's *New Society* argued that a world revolution was taking place 'in Europe, in Asia (perhaps at this moment most of all in Asia), in Africa, in the Americas'. The Road to Freedom was to adapt oneself and one's country to this revolution. 'Freedom means freedom for all and therefore equality, and . . . freedom, if it means anything at all, must include freedom from want.' This could be achieved only by 'the creation of abundance through the right allocation of our human and material resources to the requirements of production'. Democracy could survive only if it was reconciled with 'planning for socialism'.

Now that the Soviet system is no more, it is worth recalling that Carr's view of the prospects for planning, based on Soviet experience, were not unusual or eccentric in the first quarter of a century after the Second World War. It is true that enthusiasm for Soviet planning was rarely heard in 1951 when Carr gave these lectures – Stalin was still firmly in power and the Cold War was at its most intense. But five years later in the days of Khrushchev, the dark sides of the Soviet system were dropping away and Soviet economic progress seemed undoubted. Well-informed liberal economists like the late Professor Peter Wiles believed that Soviet economic growth presented a major challenge to capitalism. The American engineer Seymour Melman proclaimed that this challenge was embodied in the rapid progress of the Soviet machine-tool industry. A senior Professor of Chemistry at the University of Birmingham even persuaded the authorities to provide him with a smart new building when he reported the results of his investigation of chemical research in Moscow!

A second aspect of Carr's approach to the history of the Soviet Union is equally important. It is commonly assumed that he regarded the Soviet road to the future, or some minor modification of it, as a model for Western society. But he saw the Soviet system as a challenge rather than as a model. This was made clear even in the most one-sided of his books, *The Soviet Impact on the Western World*, published under the influence of the great victory over fascism in 1946. In this book he exaggerated the power of the Soviet challenge, and greatly underestimated Soviet deficiencies. But he looked forward to 'not an out-and-out victory either for the western or the Soviet ideology', but 'a compromise, a half-way house, a synthesis between conflicting ways of life'. 'The fate of the western world will turn on its ability to meet the Soviet challenge by a successful search for new forms of social and economic action in which what is valid in individualistic and democratic tradition can be applied to the problems of mass civilization.'

In terms of international politics, he envisaged that Britain's future lay in an alliance with Western Europe. In Carr's view, an appropriate corollary of Russian domination over Eastern Europe, which he regarded as inevitable and even appropriate, would be more intimate links between Britain and Western Europe. These would include economic planning in common and a joint military organisation. In this framework Europe must 'find an answer based on principles which diverge both from the Soviet ideology of state monopoly and from the American ideology of unrestricted competition'.[36]

A third common misunderstanding of Carr's post-war viewpoint is the assumption that it remained more or less static after 1945. During the Cold War, Carr's unorthodox views, and the intolerance displayed towards him by his former associates in the British Establishment, isolated him from the circles in which he had moved before and during the war. At the same time the intolerance and one-sidedness in British and American policy towards Russia (as compared, say, with the attitude to the Shah's Iran or Communist China) continued to arouse his indignation throughout the rest of his life. These circumstances no doubt acted as a brake on his rethinking about the Soviet system. But during his decades of work on the *History*, his view of Soviet history changed substantially. He continued to believe that any Soviet leader, including Lenin if he had lived, would have had to carry out some kind of 'revolution from above' in order to solve the basic Soviet problems of the 1920s. But he came to the conclusion that Lenin, in contrast to Stalin, would have been able to 'minimize and mitigate the element of coercion'.[37]

His mature assessment of the Stalin regime is summarised in two chapters of the political volume of *Foundations of a Planned Economy*, 'Class and Party', and 'The New Soviet Society'. While in Carr's view this was a new society and a monumental achievement, it was also a society which had seen 'the substitution of the Party by the proletariat, resulting by slow stages in the rise of a privileged bureaucracy, the divorce of the leadership from the masses, the dragooning of the workers and peasants, and the concentration camps.' Moreover, 'Stalin's personality, combined with the primitive and cruel traditions of Russian bureaucracy, imparted to the revolution from above a particularly brutal quality.'[38]

How did this darker if still positive assessment of the results of the Bolshevik Revolution affect his view of the world and of the place of the Soviet Union in the history of the twentieth century? By the 1970s, if not earlier, Carr had come to consider himself, with qualifications, a socialist. He referred in his memoir to what he described as 'my unverifiable Utopia':

> I suppose I should call it 'socialist' and am to this extent Marxist. But Marx did not define the content of socialism except in a few Utopian phrases; and nor can I.

Carr however was convinced that what had been established in the Soviet Union was not socialism. But he was already 72 when Khrushchev fell, and did not find the energy in the Brezhnev years to assess the changes which were taking place beneath the surface in the Soviet Union. Asked about the prospects of a breakthrough to a socialist society in the USSR, he drew attention to the huge increase in numbers and in standard of life of the Soviet proletariat, and commented somewhat enigmatically:

> If one wanted to indulge in flights of fancy, one might imagine that this new proletariat will one day take up the burden which its weak forebears could not carry sixty years ago, and move forward to socialism. Personally I am not addicted to such speculations. History rarely produces theoretically tidy solutions. Soviet society is still advancing. But to what end, and whether the rest of the world will allow it to pursue its advance undisturbed – these are questions which I shall not attempt to answer.[39]

In the preface to the second edition of *What is History?*, completed shortly before his death, he claimed that 'the erection of insurmountable barriers to communication on one side and the incessant flow of Cold War propaganda on the other, render difficult any sensible assessment of the situation in the USSR.'[40] Like almost everyone else, old and young, he did not anticipate that Communism would collapse.

While agnostic (though on the whole positive) about the future of the Soviet Union, he had come to the pretty firm conclusion that no fundamental change in the social order was likely in the West. Even before the election of Thatcher and Reagan he decided that 'this is a profoundly counter-revolutionary period in the West'.[41] Instead his hopes turned not to the USSR but to the Third World:

> I think we have to consider seriously the hypothesis that the world revolution of which [the Russian Revolution] was the first stage, and which will complete the downfall of capitalism, will prove to be the revolt of the colonial peoples against capitalism in the guise of imperialism rather than a revolt of the proletariat of the advanced capitalist countries.[42]

How, then, would Carr have reacted to the fall of Soviet Communism in 1991 – if he had lived and retained his faculties to the age of 99? I don't think the demise of the one-party dictatorship would have troubled him. But he firmly believed that the Bolshevik Revolution and the Soviet Union had great accomplishments to their credit. In 1978, while describing the Bolshevik notion of establishing a dictatorship of the proletariat in Russian conditions as a 'pipe-dream', he claimed that the Russian Revolution had created something of permanent value:

something was done which has not been done in the West. Capitalism has been dismantled and replaced by planned production and distribution; and, if socialism has not been realized, some of the conditions for its realization have, however imperfectly, been established.[43]

The collapse of the Soviet planned economy would have appalled him.

Notes

1 Interview with Richard Gott, *Guardian*, 25 November 1978.
2 The ten-page typescript of this memoir is in the E.H. Carr Collection in the University of Birmingham, and is reproduced in this volume at pp. xiii–xxii.
3 Carr's collection of these reviews, in chronological order, is in the Birmingham Carr Collection.
4 *Christian Science Monitor*, 25 April 1929.
5 *Fortnightly Review*, January 1930, pp. 139–40; review of *The Memoirs of General Wrangel* (London: Williams & Norgate, 1929).
6 *Fortnightly Review*, February 1930, pp. 241–50; March 1930, pp. 362–72.
7 *Fortnightly Review*, September 1930.
8 *Christian Science Monitor*, 19 July 1930; L. Trotsky, *My Life* (London: Thornton Butterworth, 1930).
9 *Christian Science Monitor*, 9 August 1930; A. Maude, *The Life of Tolstoy*, Vol. 2, *Later Years* (London, Humphrey Milford for Oxford University Press, 1930).
10 London: Jonathan Cape, 1931.
11 *Fortnightly Review*, August 1931.
12 London: Jonathan Cape, 1931.
13 *Fortnightly Review*, September 1931.
14 *Spectator*, 1 October 1932.
15 *Spectator*, 6 August 1932, reviewing M. Dobb, *Soviet Russia and the World* (London, Sidgwick & Jackson, 1932).
16 Published in three volumes (London: Gollancz, 1932–3); current one-volume edition is London: Pluto Press, 1977.
17 *Sunday Times*, 6 October 1935; see also his second review of Chamberlin in *Fortnightly Review*, November 1935.
18 *Spectator*, 18 July 1933, reviewing *inter alia* L. Segal, *Modern Russia* (London: Industrial Credit and Services, 1933) and *Out of the Deep: Letters from Soviet Timber Camps* (London: Geoffrey Bles, 1933).
19 See his despatch of 30 September 1933, from Geneva, where he was a member of the UK delegation to the League of Nations. The despatch is reprinted from the PRO archives in *The Foreign Office and the Famine: British Documents on Ukraine and the Great Famine of 1932–1933* (Kingston, Ontario: Limestone Press, 1988), pp. 322–8; Carr reported that 'it was obvious from the first that it was politically impracticable' for the League to take any action.
20 *Spectator*, 7 August 1936; this is a review of E. Ammende, *Human Life in Russia* (London: Allen & Unwin, 1936).

21 *Spectator*, 6 August 1932.
22 *Spectator*, 23 June 1933.
23 *Fortnightly Review*, February 1936.
24 *Spectator*, 6 August 1932; *Christian Science Monitor*, 6 May 1933.
25 *Spectator*, 23 June 1933; review of Hindus' *The Great Offensive* (London: Gollancz, 1933).
26 *Fortnightly Review*, 1932, pp. 391–2; W.Gurian, *Bolshevism: Theory and Practice* (London: Sheed & Ward, 1932).
27 *Fortnightly Review*, March 1933, pp. 319, 321.
28 *Spectator*, 7 August 1936.
29 *Spectator*, 28 August 1936.
30 *The Times*, 5, 6 and 7 July 1937.
31 *Times Literary Supplement*, 14 January 1938.
32 *Fortnightly Review*, November 1937. See also 'Hitler's Gospel and Stalin's', *Spectator*, 16 September 1938.
33 Typescript of talk of 12 October 1937, in the Carr Collection, University of Birmingham.
34 The main books by Carr are *The Soviet Impact on the Western World* (London: Macmillan, 1946), *The New Society* (London: Macmillan, 1951), *1917: Before and After* (London: Macmillan, 1969) and *From Napoleon to Stalin, and other Essays* (London: Macmillan, 1980); the last two books include many of the book reviews which appeared anonymously in *The Times Literary Supplement*. My own account of Carr's wartime and post-war view of the Soviet Union will be found in *The Proceedings of the British Academy*, lxix (1983), pp. 488–93, 508–10.
35 F.A. Hayek, *The Road to Serfdom* (London: Routledge & Kegan Paul, 1976, first published 1944), pp. 137–41.
36 E.H. Carr, *Nationalism and After* (London: Macmillan, 1945), pp. 87 ff.
37 *From Napoleon to Stalin* (London: Macmillan, 1980), p. 339.
38 *A History of Soviet Russia*, Vol. 2 (London: Macmillan, 1971), p. 448.
39 Interview with Perry Anderson, *New Left Review*, No. 111, September–October 1978, pp. 32–3.
40 *What is History?*, 2nd edition, ed. R.W. Davies (Harmondsworth: Penguin, 1987), p. 5.
41 *New Left Review*, No. 111, September–October 1978, pp. 35–6.
42 *Ibid.*, p. 35.
43 *Ibid.*, pp. 32–3.

5
The Soviet Carr

Stephen White

Carr's death in 1982 went unnoticed in the Soviet historical journals and his work itself was not available to Russian readers until 1990, when the first of an intended four-volume set of his *History of Soviet Russia* was published in a large edition. His name, as a leading journal put it in 1991, had up to this point been 'almost unknown to a broad Soviet readership', although specialists were aware of his work and regarded it with great respect even though they could not yet say so in their publications ('Carr,' as one of them remarked, was a 'whole research institute').[1] Carr had in fact become an object of study at a much earlier stage through the substantial numbers of Soviet authors whose business was the refutation of 'bourgeois falsifiers', and through the smaller but more interesting group of Soviet historians who were allowed to read his work in the original and who engaged seriously and in public with his philosophy of history and with his examination of 'continuity and change' in the Soviet historical experience.

The 'growing influence of the Soviet Union', it was claimed in many of these early works, had been 'reviving reactionary bourgeois historiography'. Acting at the behest of their Cold War paymasters, western scholars had been doing their best to distort the history of the Soviet state and its 'consistent struggle for peace and peaceful coexistence with the capitalist countries', and minimizing its social and economic achievements. Carr, in this connection, had argued that there was 'chaos' in the countryside after the October Revolution and that 'all the efforts of the Soviet government to do anything about it had ended in failure'.[2] But Carr was generally exempted from the most serious attacks in such work: he and his colleague R.W. Davies were, for instance, among the 'few bourgeois authors' to admit that Soviet rates of growth had been higher than those of the tsarist period, and his *History* was acknowledged as 'one of the most fundamental works in bourgeois sovietology'.[3]

As Carr would himself have concluded, Soviet students of his work were a reflection of the nature of the period in which they wrote. At first a 'bourgeois falsifier', Carr gradually became a scholar who had taken 'certain steps' towards a Marxist methodology, and then one whose 'fairly objective' analysis was one with which Soviet historians could themselves engage; a scholar who continued to base himself on a 'bourgeois world outlook' and (writing with R.W. Davies) gave a 'distorted representation of the key issues in Soviet society in the late 1920s', but who at the same time had 'departed in important ways from the traditional approaches that had for decades been dominant in bourgeois historiography'.[4] By the Gorbachev and early post-communist years his work began to receive a more considered evaluation, combining admiration for its command of sources and literary style with reservations about his neglect of archives and (as the Soviet system collapsed) his now too optimistic belief in progress and planning. In what follows I shall concentrate upon the development of this more considered critique, concluding with some more general reflections on Carr's influence on the study of history in the USSR and in the post-communist Russia that succeeded it.

Early Assessments

It was, it seems, the philosophy of history that first attracted the attention of Soviet journals to the work of E.H. Carr. It was already clear that he occupied a 'prominent place' in bourgeois historiography; but he had a particular value, Soviet reviewers suggested, for 'reactionary historians' who represented force as the 'main and decisive factor in international relations'. Carr had been one of the 'pioneers of the canonisation of force' during the pre-war years, and had made clear in his preface to the *Twenty Years' Crisis* that it was directed against those who neglected its importance. This clearly left little room for a philosophy of history. But his Trevelyan lectures of 1961, for Soviet writers, marked a new stage in his thinking, and one that had been welcomed by British Communists.[5] There had been no fundamental change in Carr's attachment to the role of force: the difference was that the balance between socialism and capitalism had changed, and that 'not only law, but also overwhelming might' were now on the side of socialism. Soviet reviewers also noted Carr's dictum that history was meaningful for British historians when it was developing in the right direction, as they saw it; but with international developments were now moving towards a very different destination, belief in a meaningful destiny had 'become a heresy'. A 'social structure in decline', Soviet reviewers explained, could not develop an 'ideology underpinned by a belief in progress'.[6]

Carr's *History* was still in progress, but his methodology received a very careful interim examination in these early years from Irina Olegina, of the History Faculty of Leningrad University, first in an article and, rather later, in two books.[7] There was no doubt, for Olegina, of Carr's standing as an historian of Russia, at least within the 'bourgeois literature'. Several features helped to distinguish his work from that of others, including the rich range of sources on which he drew and his respect for Marxist approaches. Like many of his other reviewers, not just in the West, Olegina was particularly attracted by the chapter on the 'legacy of history' in the first volume of *Socialism in One Country*, and by Carr's use of an explanatory framework conceived in terms of 'continuity and change'. Surprisingly, in the Soviet view, Carr had not seen the revolution itself as a sudden shift, on the grounds that no revolution of a Marxist kind could take place in an overwhelmingly agrarian country. There was a second assumption as well: that Russian and Western patterns of development could be sharply distinguished. This led to a characteristically jerky pattern of development: forward movements, under the coercive auspices of the state, were succeeded by no less violent reversions to a more traditionally Russian pattern. The October Revolution, from this perspective, was simply the latest in a sequence of revolutions from above that addressed the same dilemma: would Russia follow a western model, or one that reflected the country's own traditions?[8]

For Olegina, this was an interpretation that rested on arbitrary and bourgeois foundations. It assumed, for a start, that the development of industry meant the exploitation of the countryside: but there could be no relationship of this kind under socialist conditions. And there were serious problems with the thesis of 'continuity'. For instance, Carr had attempted to draw parallels between Soviet economic development and the tsarist economy under Prime Minister Witte. But an economic policy was not the same as planning in a Soviet sense, which involved the political direction of the economy as a whole in the interests of ordinary people rather than a financial oligarchy. Equally, the defence industry had a different function under socialist conditions: there was no compelling economic need for military spending and it was simply a burden that had been imposed by the need to defend the revolution against the western powers. Military spending, indeed, was at its lowest in the 1920s at precisely the time that the first steps were being taken to industrialise: it had fallen from 17.7 per cent of the state budget in 1923/4 to 12.3 per cent by 1927/8, and there had been no increase in the number of men under arms.[9]

Overall, for Olegina, Carr's were the typical assumptions of bourgeois historical science: a 'denial of the objective basis for a proletarian revolution in Russia, a search in the Russian past for analogies with the present, [and] an identification of capitalist and socialist industrialisation in their aims and in the methods by which they were realised'.[10] His work was full of contradictions; indeed it was bound to be, as Carr had 'eclectically combined very different conclusions'. His theory of continuity and change quickly collapsed when he embarked on the analysis of concrete events, and it played no part in his more general philosophy of history; in the end, Carr had to resort to voluntaristic explanations in terms of the 'dominance of politics'. It was this combination of opposites, his attempt to steer a 'middle way' between the prejudiced theories of his bourgeois colleagues and the methodology of Marxism, that gave Carr his 'rather distinctive position in Western historical science'. There remained every reason for Soviet historians to welcome the 'progressive tendencies' in his work, and to support his call for 'realism and common sense' in the face of much wider differences between East and West.[11]

Evolving Perspectives

These were serious, but somewhat formulaic criticisms. A more nuanced view began to emerge in the late 1960s, as theses were prepared on Carr's historiography and as it began to receive a more respectful hearing; but the discussion was still confined to less prominent outlets, among them a collection edited by the later dissident, Mikhail Gefter, in 1969.[12] Gefter's book was sent to the press in October 1968, two months after the liberal reforms of the Prague Spring had been crushed by Warsaw Pact armies; but it took its origins from the shift in historical thought that had taken place under the influence of the 20th Congress of the CPSU, and continued the reconsideration of methodology that had been initiated at a conference on history and sociology in 1964. There were two related concerns, in this discussion: that history was becoming too isolated from empirical investigation, and, on the other hand, that it was becoming too detached from long-standing and much wider issues of social development.[13]

Gefter's volume included the first extended publication on Carr by the historian Abram Neiman, of Gor'ky State University.[14] Carr, in this context, was a representative of 'non-Marxist' rather than of bourgeois thought, and a scholar whose philosophy of history reflected the influence of Marxism. Neiman's starting point was the 'complex and divergent processes' that were taking place in British historiography, and the more general 'crisis' in traditional approaches.[15] Carr's work was of special importance in this connection, as he was 'one of the major English academic historians' and one whose work had been warmly applauded by *Marxism Today*.[16] Neiman drew particular attention to Carr's 'lively, publicistic style', which had earned him a reputation as an outstanding essayist in the 'spirit of the great English tradition.'[17] Neiman's own contribution was to the study of Carr's philosophy of history, as set out in his Trevelyan lectures: an attempt, Neiman suggested, to overcome the theoretical shortcomings that had emerged in the dominant tradition in historical thought, and at the same time to adapt the values of the liberal Victorian era to the very different circumstances of the mid-twentieth century.[18]

Carr's philosophy of history, as Neiman explained, was an 'eclectic' one, combining Fabian socialism, Keynesianism and labourism. It was also one that had evolved gradually over the years. Writing in 1934 Carr had seen Marxism as a set of 'dogmas', but by the time of his 1961 lectures he was speaking of Marxism as a developing body of thought and defending it against Karl Popper.[19] The development of Marxism in accordance with changing conditions, Carr had written, was itself a demonstration of one of the fundamentals of the theory.[20] Carr's work, as Neiman noted, had attracted heavy criticism for its tendency to conceive of history as a '"progressive and dynamic" process', and in a way that could be considered 'eccentric'.[21] But representatives of a more democratic approach to historical thought appreciated his attempt to develop an unprejudiced understanding of the world's first socialist state. For British Marxists, and evidently for Neiman himself, together with the 'real contradictions' of Carr's philosophy of history, there was a need for 'cooperation and dialogue' in a 'popular front of historians' that could counter a 'front of reaction'.[22]

Writing some years later, Neiman widened his analysis to Carr's writings on the Russian revolutionary movement, and more particularly his writings of the late 1930s on international relations.[23] Carr's work of this period drew directly on his own experience, and for Neiman it had the character of 'eyewitness history' and the literary form of *publitsistika* or current affairs writings. But it was these works that had identified Carr as 'one of the most important bourgeois students of the history and theory of contemporary international relations', indeed as 'one of the main theorists of so-called political realism'.[24] It was a theory on which Carr drew in his later works, for instance in *Nationalism and After* (1945) and *German–Soviet Relations between the Two World Wars* (1952) – a study that belonged to the third and best-known cycle in Carr's work, the one in which he had begun to explore the October Revolution and its consequences. But it had its origins, for Neiman, in Carr's studies of the Russian revolutionary movement, and of Marxism. Neiman's particular concern was the evolution of Carr's methodology as formulated, above all, in his work on international relations and the philosophy of history.

Theories of international relations, Neiman suggested, had evolved in two main stages since the war: first of all, an 'idealist' model had gradually given way to a rather vaguely defined 'political realism'. The second period, from the 1960s, had seen the emergence of a newer 'scientific' methodology, in self-conscious opposition to more 'traditional' approaches. Carr was involved in both controversies: Hans Morgenthau, the patriarch of 'political realism', had welcomed Carr's contribution as one of the 'first importance', and it had been central to the re-evaluations of the 1960s.[25] An analysis based on the 'real relationship of political forces' was certainly closer to Marxism than one based on abstract moralising, Neiman noted, although the notion of 'force' remained ambiguous. But for all its merits, Carr's concept of 'force' was no substitute for the 'only scientific – Marxist, class – analysis of history and politics', and his work was characterised by reformist illusions of 'social compromise', not only in domestic affairs but also in relations between states – an approach that had led to his support for appeasement and for those, like Neville Chamberlain, who had promoted it.[26]

The Limits of 'Bourgeois Objectivism'

If Olegina's concern was methodology and Neiman's the philosophy of history, Violetta Chernik embraced both in a series of writings from the 1970s up to the 1990s. In an early postgraduate essay Chernik focused initially on Carr's writings on post-revolutionary economic policy and on the New Economic Policy in the Soviet countryside.[27] As an 'outstanding representative of contemporary bourgeois scholarship', Carr was a particularly appropriate means of identifying the 'limited nature, inconsistency and contradictory nature of bourgeois objectivism'. For Chernik, writing in 1973, Carr had been wrong to distinguish war communism and NEP as sharply as he did: they were part of a single historical process, whose purpose was the transition from capitalism to socialism. This was apparent in the early start that had been made to the socialisation of production, including the nationalisation of banking – 'one of the commanding heights of socialism in the Russian economy' – and of some of the leading industrial enterprises.[28]

Carr, in Chernik's view, had been too heavily influenced by Leon Kritsman, and by his sharp distinction between the 'heroic' early months of the revolution and the war communism that had followed them, and he had also been unduly influenced by other Soviet economists of the 1920s. He was accordingly inclined to overemphasize the negative consequences of war communism, which had their origin not so much in war communism itself as in the economic difficulties that had themselves given rise to the policy. Carr was much closer to Soviet historians in his explanation of the transition to NEP, and 'fairly objective' in his analysis of the factors that were involved. But here as elsewhere he was attempting to take a position 'somewhere between the contending forces – between Soviet and reactionary bourgeois historiography', leading to 'inconsistency and contradiction'.[29] Equally unacceptable were Carr's periodization of NEP and his reproduction of 'outmoded ideas about the contradictions between the objective conditions of Russia in the 1920s and the tasks of the construction of socialism'.[30]

Chernik's doctoral dissertation, four years later, dealt more generally with the historiography of Soviet agrarian history in the 1920s, but it drew particular attention to Carr as 'one of the most important and notable representatives of bourgeois objectivism' in this connection.[31] His *History of Soviet Russia* was acknowledged as the 'most fundamental work on the history of the USSR not only in English but in the whole of bourgeois historiography'. But again Carr's 'eclecticism' was faulted – a combination (this time) of Fabian socialism, Keynesianism, the 'welfare state' and convergence. And although Carr had certainly been influenced by Marxism, its contribution to his own work 'should not be exaggerated'; like some others, it involved 'at best' the absorption of some aspects of a Marxist methodology and a recognition of 'some categories of Marxist economic theory', and it might even be seen as an attempt to 'breathe new life into decrepit bourgeois dogmas'.[32] Chernik took particular exception to Carr's emphasis on continuity, which was at odds with the very nature of socialist revolutions and another attempt to discount Leninism as a purely Russian phenomenon. Equally, the attempt to present socialism as a response to purely Russian conditions was at odds with a wider conception of the twentieth century as an 'epoch of the transition from capitalism to socialism'. Carr's whole work, accordingly, was 'irreconcilable with the objective study of the history of the USSR in the Soviet period'.[33]

If this was a 'Brezhnevite' characterization, redeemed only by its direct quotations and recourse to some of the less favoured contemporary sources on the 1920s, Chernik's later writings reflected a *perestroika* and even a post-communist perspective. By 1988, Carr was a scholar whose 'unquestioned theoretical gifts, personal integrity and efforts to remain unprejudiced' could be more warmly welcomed, although it was still necessary to insist that only Marxism-Leninism provided an entirely satisfactory understanding of the 'law-governed nature of the historical process'.[34] Chernik's concern was once again Carr's writings on Soviet rural development, as part of a body of work which was 'one of the most fundamental in bourgeois historiography' and one that attached decisive significance to the peasantry in the explanation of social change. But there was a political purpose in such an emphasis: it limited the historical significance of the October Revolution by suggesting that it was inappropriate for developed nations, and suggested at the same time that it was not a sensible option for the postcolonial world – another example of the 'close link between history and politics' to which critics of Carr in the West, like the 'English historian A. Nove' (*sic*), had themselves drawn attention.[35]

Carr, in this connection, could best be seen as the leading representative among western historians of an 'objective orientation'. A study of his work, Chernik suggested, was important for two reasons: it showed the 'growing authority of Soviet historical science abroad and its influence on bourgeois historiography', and at the same time it demonstrated the limitations of bourgeois objectivism. Carr's work, admittedly, was distinguished from that of others by its factual nature, and by its effort to recreate the nature of the period itself. His sources were part of the reason for his achievement, with their heavy emphasis upon land legislation, statistical collections and the contemporary press as well as the writings of the political leadership. This helped Carr, for instance, to come to the 'very important and correct conclusion' that it was the Bolsheviks whose programme best corresponded with the interests of the peasants, and especially their poorest members.[36]

It was Carr's willingness to understand the class forces that operated in the early post-revolutionary period that, for Chernik, most clearly distinguished Carr from the work of 'other bourgeois historians'. Indeed no Western historian before Carr had given so much attention to the socioeconomic development of the Soviet countryside, and to the changes that were taking place in its social and property structure. For

Taniuchi and Shanin, at least in Chernik's interpretation, the peasantry was a unitary force and there had been little response to the attempts the Bolsheviks had made to appeal to their poorest elements. And yet an understanding of the class nature of the agrarian revolution was 'fundamental' to an understanding of the course of developments at this time. Carr, by contrast, followed Soviet historians in identifying a narrowing of social differences in the countryside, and was mistaken only in suggesting that the Bolsheviks had taken no account of it – it was, rather, the reason for their orientation in these years towards the middle peasantry, whose position had become dominant.[37]

By the later volumes of his *History*, working now with R.W. Davies, Carr (for Chernik) was beginning to show the positive influence of Soviet historians, although he still entertained a number of 'bourgeois prejudices' about socialist agriculture, and too often used his sources 'uncritically' in such a way that he identified with 'opponents of the party line'. Satisfied at the start of his work with a 'quick review' of the situation in the countryside during the revolution and civil war, Carr had moved on to a full-length study of changes in the rural economy in the 1920s – a study which in its sources and argumentation showed the 'direct influence of Soviet historiography', and in which Carr 'most clearly departed from the positions of the reactionary wing of bourgeois historiography'. Indeed, it was surely (in the celebrated phrase) 'not accidental' that his work was organized around the kinds of questions that were usually considered by Soviet, but never by bourgeois historians – such as 'the mechanisation of agriculture' or 'land husbandry'.[38]

All of this, for Chernik, did not make Carr a Marxist, but the influence of Soviet writings was clearly apparent in these later works in which he displayed an interest in various aspects of the Soviet countryside before collectivisation which were not just neglected in bourgeois historiography but which contradicted it. There was still evidence of 'bourgeois objectivism' in Carr's emphasis upon the 'psychological unity' of the peasantry; what 'unity' could there be in a countryside riven by class struggle? Carr, Chernik concluded, had taken 'certain steps' towards a genuinely scientific account of his subject, and had done so with more impartiality than other foreign historians and with a greater degree of attention to the writings of Soviet leaders and the documents of the ruling party. But it was only Marxism-Leninism that made possible a genuine understanding of the historical process, of the interaction of objective and subjective factors, and of the inevitable triumph of the socialist cause.[39]

This was still a 'Soviet Carr', especially in its insistence that Carr's development reflected the influence of Soviet historians[40] and in its

reluctance to concede more than a partial validity to Carr's interpretation of developments in the Soviet countryside. Readers of Chernik's
work up to this point would accordingly have been surprised by the
rather different views that were put forward in her contribution to a
collection that was published in 1992, in a post-communist Russia. The
title of the collection was 'The People: Creator or Hostage of the October
Revolution'; it stemmed from a conference on theoretical and methodological aspects of the study of the revolution that had taken place in
1989, but the book itself was signed for the press in January 1992 after
what were presumably extensive editorial changes.[41] Chernik's chapter
on 'E.H. Carr on the October Revolution' was part of a more general
attempt to escape from a 'narrow class approach' to historical developments, allowing more scope for 'general human values' and for what
was valuable in Menshevik and Socialist Revolutionary interpretations;
the Mensheviks, in particular, had 'properly grasped the tragedy of the
Bolsheviks who headed the revolution in a country that was poorly
prepared historically for a breakthrough to socialism'.[42]

Carr's *History* was by now the 'most significant study of the revolution
and the succeeding decade, not only in England'; the clear implication
was that it had superseded Soviet and Russian interpretations of the
same subject. Carr's earlier work on Dostoevsky, Herzen and Bakunin
was enthusiastically cited, as well as his other writings on international
politics and the philosophy of history and his more recent book on the
Russian Revolution from Lenin to Stalin.[43] As Chernik noted, Russian historians generally took a 'moderately approving' view of Carr's work,
together with a 'mass of reservations'. As an objective historian, he saw
the October Revolution as the beginning of a world revolution, but he
also acknowledged the retreat from a revolutionary perspective as the
international context changed in a way that undermined the Bolsheviks'
initial assumptions.[44] Carr was particularly noteworthy for his careful
use of sources, to such an extent that others could use his evidence to
attack his own conclusions. Soviet historians, Chernik concluded, sometimes suggested that there were 'some elements of truth' in the work of
non-Marxist historians. But why only 'some elements'? Why could foreign scholars, who had made an honest and rigorous assessment of the
October Revolution from their own positions, not simply be right?[45]

Carr after the Soviet Union

This was obviously an abstract discussion so long as Carr's own writings
were held in the closed stacks of Soviet libraries and were not more

widely available in Russian translation. For Chernik, in 1992, there were few more urgent tasks than to translate and publish the work of Carr and other 'bourgeois scholars' so that Russian historians could have a fuller, more adequate range of commentaries on the events with which they dealt.[46] By this time a first instalment of the *History of Soviet Russia* had in fact appeared, and in a substantial edition of 100,000 copies. In the past, Al'bert Nenarokov explained in his Preface, Carr had 'automatically been ranked with the falsifiers'; but by the standards that prevailed in 1990 his *History* was a 'scrupulous, professionally conscientious work' and Carr himself was an 'honest, objective scholar, espousing liberal principles and attempting on the basis of an enormous documentary base to create a satisfactory picture of the epoch he was considering and of those who were involved in it, to assist a sober and realistic perception of the USSR and a better understanding of the great social processes of the twentieth century'.[47] It was one of Carr's especial virtues that he was able to show events 'in all their contradictoriness and dialectical interrelation'. He was writing, as Nenarokov pointed out, 'under the powerful influence of the successes of the Soviet Union in the socioeconomic field, the growth in the authority and power of the USSR [and] its influence on the world arena both in the period he studied and after the war'. What was published in 1990 was 'Book 1', consisting of a translation of the first two volumes of *The Bolshevik Revolution*. There were to be four books eventually, incorporating seven of Carr's English-language volumes. All of this was simply a 'first step' in acquainting the Soviet reader with this 'voluminous work':[48] in the event, only Book 1 was ever published.

Nenarokov, in his introduction, had some historian's criticisms of Carr and his approach. He was, for instance, too inclined to see Soviet history as a choice between Stalin and Trotsky, neglecting the Bukharinist alternative (there was additional evidence of his views in his dismissive review of Stephen Cohen's biography of Bukharin, which had by this time appeared in a Russian translation).[49] Some of Carr's virtues, for earlier Soviet reviewers, were now his shortcomings: for instance, the titles of some of his chapters were (for Nenarokov) in the tradition of the Stalinist *Short Course*, and he could use a term like 'right deviation' without quotation marks in his chapter on the Bukharinist opposition. The discussion of Trotsky's position was no more satisfactory. And he was writing without access to the Soviet archives, which by this time were beginning to reveal their riches. None the less, for Nenarokov, Carr had 'shown brilliantly what could be done through a close study of the press, central and local: newspapers, journals, all kinds of weeklies and bulletins, including specialised and departmental ones'. He was equally at home in the proceedings of party and state bodies, official statistics, collections of laws, and the writings of the Bolshevik leaders and their opponents. All of this was the clearest possible demonstration of the value of a 'respectful attitude to the written sources of earlier years'. And not least, the *History* was written vividly and with character, in what was an 'acknowledged classic of English historiography'.[50]

Yet for all the respect that has been accorded to his work after 1991, Carr remains fairly remote from the contemporary concerns of Russian historians. Only a small proportion of his work has been translated, and it is cited in whatever language much less often than the work of other foreign scholars, such as Richard Pipes, Mikhail Geller or Guiseppe Boffa. Part of the explanation, in the post-communist 1990s, is precisely the sympathy towards Marxism that made Carr the least objectionable of the bourgeois historians in the Soviet period. But there are other reasons. They include Carr's factual emphasis, which left little room for the kinds of overt theorizing that have always attracted Russian historians, and the absence of a 'school of Carr' among British or Western historians, devoted to extending Carr's work in the same way that the leading Soviet and pre-revolutionary Russian historians established their own traditions through the departments they headed over many years.

The criticisms of Carr that Soviet historians put forward, in fact, could have been taken further. Carr's Soviet readers generally welcomed the increasing attention that he gave to social and economic history as his work developed, and particularly in the volumes that he coauthored with R.W. Davies. But they could well have questioned the proportion of his work that came to be devoted to international affairs – not simply Soviet foreign policy, but the Communist International and the domestic politics of communism in other countries. They could equally have pointed to the neglect of cultural and intellectual history – a surprising omission, given Carr's earlier work on Russian social thought.[51] It could even be argued that top-level politics came to be neglected in favour, if not of the glass industry, then of transport, the harvest and armaments; even the organization of *Foundations of a Planned Economy* echoed the old metaphor of base and superstructure, with two volumes on the economy preceding a single one on domestic politics.[52]

The criticisms of Carr that were put forward by Soviet and Russian historians were clearly a product of the time and of the academic environment within which they were formulated. Much of what they wrote was obliged, rather pointlessly, to demonstrate that Carr was not a Marxist-Leninist; and the manner in which the criticism shifted ground in accordance with changing requirements, from Carr the 'falsifier' to Carr the 'objectivist' and then to Carr the model for Russian as well as other historians, did little credit to the authors involved. There was a heavy emphasis upon Carr's writings on the Soviet countryside, very little – for understandable reasons – about his account of the promotion of world revolution through the Communist International and its affiliates.[53] But there were criticisms that, much later, are still worth pondering. Perhaps the most central is the question of 'continuity and change', addressed most directly by Olegina. The theory itself occupies a very small place in Carr's *History*, the celebrated first chapter of *Socialism in One Country*, and yet it raises larger questions, which are still current, about the relationship between the Soviet period and the longer perspective of Russian history.

Was the Soviet experience, for instance, a radical departure, or an organic development? Was the October Revolution no more than a coup by political authoritarians, or did it reflect popular consensus (as even post-communist histories have accepted) and embody a wider range of human values, including peace itself, as Pavel Volobuev has reminded us?[54] And is post-communist Russia, from the same perspective, a break with the past and a state that has made a 'transition to democracy', or a reversion to a late tsarist and earlier Soviet pattern of consultative but not directly accountable government? Carr was scarcely damaged by his Soviet critics; it may be more accurate to conclude that they have helped us to identify some of the larger issues that were often concealed behind the detailed exposition through which his *History of Soviet Russia* has addressed its successive generations of readers.

Notes

1 *Svobodnaya mysl'*, No. 16, 1991, p. 20; and for the Soviet historian's comment, R.W. Davies, personal communication, 12 November 1997. (Davies lectured on Carr in the Institute of the History of the USSR in the early 1980s; 'there were a lot of questions, but no hostility to Carr'.) The closed stacks of the Lenin Library contained a 'handsome secret edition [of his *History of Soviet Russia*] of which every copy was numbered': R.W. Davies, *Soviet History in the Yeltsin Era* (London: Macmillan, 1997), p. 87.

2 A.M. Nekrich et al., eds, *Protiv burzhuaznoi fal'sifikatsii istorii sovetskogo obshchestva* (Moscow: Izdanie VPSh i AON pri TsK KPSS, 1960), pp. 5, 121, citing the 'two-volume [sic] work *The Bolshevik Revolution 1917–1923*' at Vol. 2,

pp. 37–8 (Carr, in fact, noted that the evidence was 'fragmentary and misleading' and relied heavily on the testimony of the first People's Commissar of Agriculture).

3 See respectively V.E. Lyzlov in T.V. Bataeva, ed., *Kritika burzhuaznoi istoriografii istorii SSSR* (Moscow: Izdatel'stvo universiteta druzhby narodov, 1985), p. 13, and the review of *Foundations of a Planned Economy* in *Istoriya SSSR*, No. 5, 1974, p. 190.

4 *Istoriya SSSR*, No. 5, 1974, p. 198. Bob Davies was invited to consider a draft of this review, and objected to the statement that he and Carr had 'absolutised' finance: the version that was published maintained that they had 'absolutise[d] specific forms of economic management', in practice fiscal measures (*ibid.*, p. 193).

5 E.J. Hobsbawm, 'Progress in History', *Marxism Today*, February 1962, p. 47.

6 N.N. Yakovlev, 'Razdum'ya angliiskogo istorika', *Novaya i noveishaya istoriya*, No. 1, 1963, pp. 173–4.

7 I.N. Olegina, 'O trude E.Kh. Karra "Sotsializm v odnoi strane"', *Istoriya SSSR*, No. 4, 1963, pp. 188–205. (It is a pleasure at this point to acknowledge the assistance that was rendered to me by Dr Olegina in 1975 during my first exchange visit to what was then still the USSR.)

8 *Ibid.*, pp. 188–90.

9 *Ibid.*, pp. 195–6.

10 *Ibid.*, p. 204.

11 *Ibid.*, pp. 204–5. Olegina's book, *Industrializatsiya SSSR v angliiskoi i amerikanskoi istoriografii* (Leningrad: Izdatel'stvo Leningradskogo universiteta, 1971) extended her critique to foreign policy (chapter 4). In her article with O.I. Velichko, 'Industrializatsiya SSSR i ee traktovka v sovremennoi burzhuaznoi sovietologii', in V.S. Vasyukov, ed., *Kritika burzhuaznoi istoriografii sovetskogo obshchestva* (Moscow: Politizdat, 1972), Olegina insisted that the example of Carr showed that 'even the most objective bourgeois historians' were unable to understand the 'essence of socialist industrialisation in the USSR' and that it was a 'component part of the Leninist theory of the construction of socialism in a single country' (pp. 136–99, at p. 153). Her book *Kritika kontseptsii sovremennoi amerikanskoi i angliiskoi burzhuaznoi istoriografii po problemam industrializatsii SSSR* (Leningrad: Izdatel'stvo Leningradskogo universiteta, 1989) repeated these criticisms (see pp. 36–45, 81–4, 126–8). The two reviewers of *Foundations of a Planned Economy* in *Istoriya SSSR* had noted 'clear conceptual differences' between the two authors, but did not elaborate (No. 5, 1974, p. 192); Olegina was unusual (as R.W. Davies has commented) in noticing a genuine difference between the two authors, rather than the imaginary differences that other Soviet reviewers had claimed to identify (personal communication, 12 November 1997). See Olegina's 'Angliiskaya I amerikanskaya burzhuaznaya istoriografiya o sootnoshenii NEPs I politiki sotsialisticheskoi industrializatsii SSSR', in *Ekonomicheskaya politika perekhodnogo perioda v SSSR: problemy metodologii i istorii: vsesoyuznaya sessiya*, Vol. 2, 1981, pp. 232–5 (I am grateful to Bob Davies for calling my attention to this item).

12 It was, indeed, for this collection that Gefter (who died in 1995) was criticized in the press and then, for his 'incorrect reaction', disciplined by his party branch; his section within the Institute of General History of Academy

of Sciences was dissolved and he was no longer allowed to publish his work (*Izvestiya*, 18 April 1997, p. 6).

13 M. Gefter, ed., *Istoricheskaya nauka i nekotorye problemy sovremennosti* (Moscow: Nauka, 1969), p. 5. For the conference see *Istoriya i sotsiologiya* (Moscow: Nauka, 1964).

14 A.M. Neiman, 'Nekotorye tendentsii razvitiya sovremennoi nemarksistskoi istoricheskoi nauki v Anglii i teoretiko-poznavatel'nye vozzreniya E. Kh. Karra', in Gefter, ed., *Istoricheskaya nauka*, pp. 177–91.

15 Quoting Geoffrey Barraclough, *History and the Common Man: A Presidential Address* (London: Historical Association, 1967), p. 14.

16 Carr was 'not a Marxist', according to E.J. Hobsbawm in this review, but an historian who admired and defended Marx and who cited him more than any other writer ('Progress in History', p. 47).

17 Neiman, 'Nekotorye tendentsii', p. 181; for the quotation on Carr as an essayist see the review of his *New Society* in the *International Journal*, Vol. 7, No. 4, 1952, p. 303.

18 Neiman, 'Nekotorye tendentsii', p. 181.

19 *Ibid.*, p. 189. Carr's defence of Marx against Popper appears in *What is History?*, Second edition (London: Macmillan, 1986), pp. 59–60, 85–7.

20 Neiman cited Carr's *Studies in Revolution* (London: Macmillan, 1964), p. 36.

21 See respectively the *Catholic Historical Review*, Vol. 35, No. 2, 1963, p. 158, and *History and Theory*, Vol. 3, No. 1, 1963, p. 136.

22 Neiman, 'Nekotorye tendentsii', pp. 190–1.

23 A.M. Neiman, 'E. Kh. Karr: ot "politicheskogo realizma" k "novomu obshchestvu"', in *Istoriya i istoriki. Istoriograficheskii ezhegodnik 1978* (Moscow: Nauka, 1981), pp. 96–112.

24 *Ibid.*, p. 97.

25 *Ibid.*, p. 98.

26 *Ibid.*, pp. 101–4. Neiman contributed a shorter version of these remarks to M.V. Nechkina et al., eds, *XXV s'ezd KPSS i zadachi izucheniya istorii istoricheskoi nauki*, part 2 (Kalinin: Kaliningradskii gosudarstvennyi universitet, 1978); see his 'E. Kh. Karr: metodologiya issledovaniya mezhdunarodnykh otnoshenii', pp. 185–9.

27 V.V. Chernik, 'Voennyi kommunizm i novaya ekonomicheskaya politika v sovetskoi istoriografii i v kontseptsii E. Kh. Karra', in A.M. Anfimov et al., eds, *Problemy otechestvennoi istorii. Sbornik statei aspirantov I soiskatelei Instituta istorii SSSR* (Moscow: Institut istorii, 1973), pp. 159–81. Carr, recalled R.W. Davies, was 'quite contemptuous' of this paper, 'not because it was critical of him but because (according to him) it had grossly misunderstood what he had to say' (personal communication, 12 November 1997).

28 *Ibid.*, pp. 160, 168.

29 *Ibid.*, pp. 172, 174–5.

30 *Ibid.*, pp. 175, 178. For another early study see Chernik, 'Problemy sotsial'no-ekonomicheskogo razvitiya sovetskoi dokolkhoznoi derevni v anglo-amerikanskoi istoriografii', in *Problemy sotsial'no-ekonomicheskogo razvitiya sovetskoi derevni* (Vologda, 1975).

31 V.V. Chernik, *Problemy agrarnoi istorii sovetskogo obshchestva (1917–1929) v sovremennoi angliiskoi burzhuaznoi istoriografii* (avtoreferat kandidatskoi dissertatsii, Moscow: Institut istorii Akademii nauk SSSR, 1977), p. 5.

32 *Ibid.*, pp. 6, 9.
33 *Ibid.*, pp. 10–12.
34 V.V. Chernik, 'Problemy razvitii sovetskoi derevni v istoricheskoi kontseptsii E. Kh. Karra', in A.N. Sakharov, ed., *Sovremennaya burzhuaznaya istoriografiya sovetskogo obshchestva. Kriticheskii analiz* (Moscow: Nauka, 1988), pp. 116–42, at p. 139.
35 *Ibid.*, pp. 116–17.
36 *Ibid.*, pp. 118–19, 127.
37 *Ibid.*, pp. 129, 130, 134.
38 *Ibid.*, pp. 135–6.
39 *Ibid.*, pp. 136–9.
40 There are in fact few references to subsequent Soviet scholarship in the first volume of Foundations of a Planned Economy, but many to the Trotsky archive and to the contemporary work of other oppositionists.
41 P.V. Volobuev et al., eds., *Oktyabr'skaya revolyutsiya. Narod: ee tvorets ili zalozhnik?* (Moscow: Nauka, 1992).
42 *Ibid.*, pp. 7–8.
43 V.V. Chernik, 'E. Kh. Karr ob Oktyabr'skoi revolyutsii', in *ibid.*, pp. 365–73, at pp. 365, 364–5, 366.
44 *Ibid.*, pp. 367, 370–1.
45 *Ibid.*, pp. 372–3.
46 *Ibid.*, p. 373.
47 E. Kh. Karr, *Istoriya Sovetskoi Rossii*, Book 1 (Moscow: Progress, 1990), pp. 9–10.
48 *Ibid.*, pp. 10–11.
49 Carr, Nenarokov recalled, was 'one of the most forthright critics' of Cohen's biography (*ibid.*, p. 12).
50 *Ibid.*, pp. 12, 13, 14 (Nenarokov also noted 'a few inaccuracies and mistakes': p. 14). An interview with Carr ('Revolyutsiya v Rossii i Zapad' appeared in *Svobodnaya mysl'*, No. 16, 1991, pp. 20–5); his *Russian Revolution from Lenin to Stalin* also appeared in translation (Moscow: Inter-Verso, 1990).
51 Alec Nove in the *Times Literary Supplement*, 11 January 1980, p. 37.
52 On the glass industry, see R.W. Davies' memoir, '"Drop the glass industry": collaborating with E.H. Carr', *New Left Review*, No. 145 (May–June 1984), pp. 56–70.
53 Where Carr's writings on Soviet foreign policy was discussed it was routinely to reject his view that the early Soviet state had 'in principle' conducted policies that were hostile towards the capitalist powers: see for instance V.A. Ovsyankin, ed., *Protiv burzhuaznoi fal'sifikatsii istorii sovetskogo obshchestva* (Leningrad: Izdatel'stvo Leningradskogo universiteta, 1967), p. 18.
54 As a recent text affirms, the elections to the Constituent Assembly in November 1917, in which the 'bourgeois parties' won just 13 per cent of the vote, showed the 'rapid radicalisation of the masses' (V.P. Dmitrenko, ed., *Istoriya Rossii. XX vek* (Moscow: AST, 1996), p. 174). Volobuev is quoted from his preface to *Oktyabr'skaya revolutsiya*, p. 5.

6
E.H. Carr and Isaac Deutscher: a Very 'Special Relationship'

Michael Cox

> *It is very difficult or perhaps impossible for him to get out of his skin, theoretically and ideologically. He is steeped in English empiricism and rationalism, his mind is very far from what to him are abstract dialectical speculations, and so he cannot really break down the barrier between his own way of thinking and Marxism.*
>
> Isaac Deutscher on E.H. Carr (1955)[1]

> *He calls me 'a great respecter of policies and a despiser – sometimes – of revolutionary ideas and principles', and speaks of 'my impatience with Utopias, dreams and revolutionary agitation'... But does not Deutscher lean to the other side? Are not his eyes sometimes so firmly fixed on revolutionary Utopias and revolutionary ideas as to overlook the expediencies which often governed policy – even in the Lenin period?*
>
> E.H. Carr on Isaac Deutscher (1969)[2]

> *At first sight their personal amity might seem puzzling: on one side, a self-educated former member of the Polish Communist Party, an exile from Hitler and Stalin stranded in London and on the other an English historian who was an unmistakable product of Cambridge, a former member of the Foreign Office, schooled in a diplomatic service famous as a bastion of British traditionalism.*
>
> Tamara Deutscher on E.H. Carr and Isaac Deutscher (1983)[3]

Along the long road that led from the Truman Doctrine in 1947 to the final collapse of Soviet power over 40 years later there were an almost infinite number of intellectual battles and skirmishes surrounding the Cold War. Some of these took place in public, but many tended to be

125

fought out in the pages of academic journals, magazines and books that were read by few but thought at the time to be deeply significant. Given the turbulent times, most of these encounters tended to be highly polemical, several became the subject of litigation, though some – like the great 1960s debate about the origins of the Cold War – helped redefine the way historians thought about the world around them. In the end, however, nearly all of these discussions returned to the same set of questions: about who started the conflict, which of the two sides (if any) held the moral high ground, on whose side should one stand and what attitude should one adopt towards the two principal antagonists? On these particularly dangerous rocks any number of reputations were made and unmade, friendships broken and forged, careers wrecked.

But it was the 'Russian Question', ultimately, that was to become the litmus test for most western intellectuals; and where one stood on this single issue determined one's political loyalties, pitting democratic socialist against communist, Marxist against Marxist, conservative against liberal, and the Left as a whole against their various political opponents. The 'line' one took on Soviet Russia – whether you were for it or against it, characterized it as a workers' state or a new form of totalitarianism, progressive or reactionary, an aggressive threat or an insecure power more sinned against than sinning – defined you in ways that must now seem faintly bizarre. But that is the way things were in a bipolar world that not only divided the superpowers and gave rise to that most geographically specific of all Cold War terms – 'East' and 'West' – but divided people within the 'West' as well. Nor should we be so surprised by this. The Cold War after all was something from which none of us could escape: it shaped our political choices, inserted itself into our economic lives, led to wars that killed millions, justified the most brutal forms of repression, spawned a vast ideological apparatus, legitimized surveillance, made ideas an issue of national security and for the better part of 40 years threatened to destroy us all. Little wonder the Cold War was discussed and theorized in such minute and bitter detail. In many ways 'it was the most important relationship in our lives'.[4]

If the Cold War in general and the Russian Question in particular helped define an era, it also helped create and sustain one of the more interesting intellectual partnerships of the period between the former diplomat and one-time assistant editor of *The Times*, E.H. Carr, and the Polish Jewish émigré and writer, Isaac Deutscher. They arrived at the Finland station called the Soviet Union by very different routes however; and it might be worth pausing just to see how.

Carr's interest in Russia was at first entirely professional, but after having entered the Foreign Office in 1916 he developed a genuine affection for Russian culture and later a positive, though by no means uncritical attitude towards the Soviet experiment – the greatest challenge to a failing western civilization as he saw it. This sympathy, of course, had nothing to do with Marxism but a recognition that the liberal certainties he had shared before 1914 no longer made much sense, and that if the world was to be reborn, some form of planning was necessary. He did not, however, equate planning with the expansion of workers' control; nor did he ever seem to advocate democratic planning. His perspective on the question was essentially that of the policy expert who looked at the world through the eyes of a policy-maker – in other words, through the eyes of the state rather than someone seeking to change or even overthrow the state. As Tamara Deutscher observed, fairly I think, Carr was an extraordinary man of great principle but he was hardly a revolutionary. And this is perhaps why he came to have a genuine interest in the USSR – not because it was a Utopia on earth but precisely because it had abandoned what he thought was its earlier 'unrealistic' rhetoric and settled down.[5]

Isaac Deutscher's interest in the Soviet Union arose from a quite different set of concerns. Born into a Jewish family in 1907, he joined the illegal Polish Communist Party 20 years later, and then four years on, in 1931, headed the first anti-Stalinist opposition in the party – that is until he was expelled from the organization the next year on the charge of Trotskyism. An admirer of Trotsky's but never an acolyte, Deutscher always approached the issue of the USSR therefore as a critical Marxist rather than a disenchanted liberal; someone moreover who had known what it was like to be hunted and hounded by the political apologists of Stalinism. Thus he looked at the Soviet Union not through the eyes of someone who was fascinated by Russia *per se* (like Carr) but as a revolutionary who was only really interested in the system there to the extent that its actions impacted on the cause of socialism elsewhere.[6] Deutscher did not belong to any party or faction and made clear his differences with the organized followers of Trotsky. As he put it rather forcefully in a private letter to the French Trotskyist Pierre Frank, he was not and 'never' had 'been a believer in the Fourth International'.[7] He remained as he once put it *au-dessus de la mêlée*.[8] Yet Deutscher was always an activist in search of action and when given half a chance, as he was increasingly in the 1960s, he threw himself into the struggle, and nowhere more vigorously than in the United States where he played a crucial role in the early development of the anti-Vietnam War movement.[9]

But in spite of these important differences, the paths of the two men not only crossed, but did so (not coincidentally) when the Cold War was just beginning to take shape in 1947.[10] Thereafter, they became and remained very close friends for the better part of 20 years. Indeed, in the life of Carr there was nobody with whom he ever achieved the same degree of intimacy. A close reading of their rather extensive correspondence over two decades also indicates that Carr was not only close to Deutscher, but also tended to draw upon his wealth of knowledge and, I would suggest, his more general theory of Stalinism as well. The relationship therefore was not just personal, or even just intellectual, but deeply political. Carr in turn helped and supported Deutscher. He reviewed at least eleven of his books,[11] discussed his work with him in often minute detail, and later ensured that he would give the influential Trevelyan lectures that were later published in 1967 under the title *The Unfinished Revolution*. Ostensibly the relationship was one between equals: one might even say that it was the most equal relationship Carr ever had. But there was always a somewhat asymmetrical quality to it. Carr may have had the official academic position and the status always denied Deutscher; yet Deutscher always tended to be far more critical of Carr than Carr ever was of Deutscher.[12] Indeed, Carr sometimes gave the impression of standing in awe of Deutscher. Carr, as others have noted, did not suffers fools easily. Nor was he always the most charitable of reviewers. With Deutscher, however, it was always different. From his several reviews of Deutscher's first major book published in 1949 (he did four altogether of the *Stalin* volume!),[13] through to the short obituary he wrote following Deutscher's sudden death in 1967, there was a tone of respect that one rarely encounters in his dealings with other writers. The former mandarin from the Foreign Office who held one of the more prestigious Fellowships, in one of the more prestigious Colleges in Cambridge, clearly revered this 'admirer of Lenin'[14] to an extent that was virtually inconceivable with anybody else.

This relationship, born out of a shared interest in the early history of the Soviet Union, and forged in a period of Cold War when these two dissident figures played an enormous role in the intellectual life of Britain, is the subject of this chapter. Based in large part on original sources, it begins with a brief biographical sketch of their relationship. What this reveals, or confirms, is the extent to which the two men collaborated over a period of 20 years. The chapter then goes on to explain why they collaborated so closely and what it was that bound them together. It continues with an equally important analysis of their differences – which were real and profound. And it concludes with an assessment of their work on the USSR. Here we try to move beyond the relationship itself and try to answer two critical questions: Did they get the Soviet Union wrong, and if so why? And should we in the post-Soviet era be at all concerned with what Carr and Deutscher said about a system that no longer exists?

Carr and Deutscher: Partners in History

our relations have a rather special character...

Carr to Deutscher (1954)[15]

The coming of war in 1939 irrevocably transformed the lives of E.H. Carr and Isaac Deutscher – though in rather different ways. In the case of Carr it simply meant abandoning his post in the Department of International Politics in Aberystwyth, at least while hostilities continued. For Deutscher it involved an entire change in life circumstances, and having arrived in London just before the German invasion of Poland, he now found himself in the unenviable position of being a total stranger in a strange country whose language he could hardly understand. His early days in England and then Scotland were, it seems, deeply traumatic ones. But the young Jewish émigré (whose close family later perished in Auschwitz) was very determined, and like Carr had an enormous capacity for hard work, a strong sense of his own very great ability and a penchant for writing. Almost inevitably this led both – quite independently – into journalism: Carr to *The Times* where he vigorously promoted the idea of a permanent post-war alliance that would include the United Kingdom, the United States and the Soviet Union; and Deutscher to the *The Observer* and *The Economist*, where he became a regular writer on international affairs in general and Russian affairs in particular. The two men made excellent journalists and the two (quite separately, of course) quickly acquired a wide and appreciative readership. And while neither knew the other, both were interested in the same fundamental questions: how was the war going to change the landscape in Europe and what position would the new USSR hold in the new world order about to emerge out of the ashes left behind by the destruction of German fascism?

Carr and Deutscher also had something else in common: a desire to write serious work on Soviet history. Journalism may have paid the bills and given the two an audience they could not otherwise have reached, but it did not satisfy their intellectual longing. In 1944, therefore, Carr made the decision in principle to embark on his *History of Soviet Russia*, though he had absolutely no idea it would take him 30 years to complete. Two years later Deutscher 'withdrew from full-time journalism at a stage' when, according to his friend Daniel Singer, 'he was in a position to command the most rewarding jobs', and began working on a biography of Stalin.[16] But of the two it was Deutscher who had to make the greater intellectual sacrifice. As an historical materialist he was no great fan of the biographical form, but assumed (correctly as it turned out) that the English loved biography and would thus purchase a volume on Stalin more readily than they would a massive tome on the Five Year Plans. This in turn would help subsidize his most cherished project: a full-length study of the life and times of Lenin.

Carr and Deutscher thus encountered each other when they had already made the key decisions that would, in effect, determine the course of the rest of their lives. Meeting for the first time in early 1947 – only a couple of weeks after the United States had embarked on the policy of containment – the two obviously had much in common. Carr, we are told by his biographer, was much taken with Deutscher, though what Deutscher felt about Carr is less clear. By all accounts, he and his wife Tamara admired his earlier work on Russian revolutionaries in the nineteenth century but were less than enthused by his harsh views on the post-war fate of small nations in Eastern Europe. Significantly, Deutscher and Carr could never agree on Poland. Carr had little time for their claims; Deutscher did. But even this did not prevent the relationship from blossoming. Nor did it prevent Carr from trying immediately to support Deutscher. It was in fact Carr, using his connections at the Royal Institute of International Affairs, who helped Deutscher get involved in a project that finally culminated with Deutscher's book on *Soviet Trade Unions* in 1950.[17] He then reviewed the book – very favourably – in the *Times Literary Supplement*.

It was Deutscher's proposed study on *Stalin* however that fired Carr's imagination. To say that he was enthused would be something of an understatement. Indeed, having looked at a few draft chapters he wrote back to 'my dear Deutscher' in July 1948 saying that the 'chapters' he had read were 'brilliant' and 'that if the rest' of the book was 'up to the sample' he had seen, then 'we shall have a really good biography of S [Stalin]'. Communication about the book did not end there, however. In December of the same year Carr actually read the whole *Stalin* manuscript in proof stage and sent it back to Deutscher with 'really only one or two trivial' suggestions.[18] The following May Carr then received a most remarkable letter from Deutscher. In this, Deutscher not only explained to Carr what the book was trying to do (in case he had not got the point), but almost appeared to be advising Carr on how best to review the book as well. Deutscher trusted Carr, of course; but he did have a concern which he then decided to share with Carr. As he put it, the *Stalin* book was dialectical in character and he was worried, therefore, that the 'English aversion to dialectics' (and possibly Carr's as well) might mean that readers would not fully appreciate its subtlety. Naturally, he left it to Carr, 'my dear prospective critic' as Deutscher referred to him, 'to say whether or not' his 'performance' in print corresponded to his original 'design' or in 'what particular point the design itself was wrong'. But he clearly hoped Carr's review would be a good one. 'I shall be anxiously awaiting your verdict,' he concluded.[19]

He had little reason to worry. Carr's review in the *Times Literary Supplement* was glowing[20] and his two broadcasts dealing with the book, equally positive.[21] To add to Deutscher's sense of intellectual well-being, Carr followed up with an exceptionally strong review in the American magazine, *The New Republic*. In this he recommended the book to his US readers and praised it, amongst other things, for presenting a 'complex' picture of Stalin which correctly focused on the 'dual significance of Stalin's career'. Indeed, 'the real merit of Deutscher's book', he suggested, was that it 'depreciated neither the magnitude of Stalin's work and place in history nor the heavy cost at which they have been achieved'. For this reason, amongst many others, Deutscher's 'outstanding biography' (Carr referred to it elsewhere as an 'objective and absorbing account of the most complex political personality of the contemporary world') had a great deal to recommend it to the 'student of politics'.[22]

Deutscher could not have been more delighted, and in a short letter to Carr written the day after Carr's review appeared in *The Times Literary Supplement*, he manifested both gratitude and insecurity in equal measure. He could barely contain himself. 'I have been truly moved,' he wrote; 'and (let me admit this) somewhat surprised by your review. I did not expect that you would express so high an opinion about the book.' Carr's review, he continued, was not just 'masterly' but 'brilliantly managed to analyse and compress' in 'one article' what it had taken Deutscher himself one and half years to write. In fact, there were passages in the review which Deutscher thought were so good that he 'wished' he could have incorporated them into the book itself. It was a most pleasurable experience; so good that 'even now' he wondered whether or not Carr had treated the book with too 'much indulgence'. But he could hardly complain, and for the time being he would simply allow himself 'the enjoyment of the occasion'.[23]

If Carr's extraordinarily favourable review of the *Stalin* volume helped cement the relationship, so too did Deutscher's subsequent reviews of Carr's *History*: three on *The Bolshevik Revolution*, one on *The Interregnum* and three more on *Socialism In One Country* – all published in the 1950s. Though far less effusive than Carr's reviews of his own work, Deutscher was none the less clear in his own mind that Carr stood head and shoulders above his peers when it came to the early history of the USSR. In Deutscher's opinion there was no academic rival to Carr: he was, in his view, 'the first genuine historian of the Soviet regime' and whatever his limits – and Deutscher made these clear – his '*History* must be judged a truly outstanding achievement'. He might have also added that he had done a great deal of work on some of the volumes as well, something that Carr readily accepted in his various acknowledgements.

But if Deutscher was impressed with Carr's attempt to write the early history of Soviet Russia, Carr was almost ecstatic when it came to Deutscher's three volumes on Trotsky. He reviewed each in turn and paid all the highest compliment. But he was particularly taken it seems with the first volume, *The Prophet Armed*, which covered the years 1879 to 1921. This was especially brilliant he felt: much better in fact than Deutscher's earlier biography on *Stalin*, which though 'dramatic and unsuperseded' could not compare with this new book which was not only 'more penetrating' but 'more mature' as well.[24] But all three books were outstanding in his opinion. As Carr later put it, the trilogy was almost that perfect coming together of great subject matter on the one hand, and outstanding writer on the other. Indeed, Deutscher according to Carr had done what few before had managed to do, and what Carr himself always doubted was possible: to make good biography into good history.

The plaudits did not end there however, and continued into the 1960s following the publication of Carr's *What is History?* in 1961. Having already been informed by 'the Prof' (as Deutscher referred to Carr) that Carr was going 'to answer, among other things, the foolish remarks of Popper, Isaiah Berlin etc. about history in general and revolutions in particular', he was more than pleased with the outcome. First he wrote to Carr following the broadcast of the lectures. Both he and Tamara he noted had very much 'enjoyed listening to these lectures on the radio – it was really a delight to hear you in such excellent form'.[25] Then he wrote the anonymous review of the book itself in the *TLS*. True to form, he took Carr to task for some of the volume's theoretical and methodological shortcomings. None the less, *What is History?*, he concluded, was a fine book written by a fine man 'one of the most unorthodox, radical and open-minded British liberals of his generation'. Whether Carr liked being referred to as a liberal is not at all clear. But it did not seem to alter his attitude towards Deutscher whose work he continued to praise – both in private and in public: and there was no event more public than the Trevelyan lectures which Deutscher gave six years later. Having urged Deutscher in the first instance to focus as much as possible on the Russian revolution rather than making his six presentations too general ('these lectures,' he argued, 'will give an impetus' to the 'hitherto neglected treatment of Russian history' here in Cambridge)[26] he was more than pleased with the final product. Once again, Carr could hardly contain his enthusiasm, and while not completely uncritical of *The Unfinished Revolution* (did Deutscher perhaps fail 'to do justice to' the 'dilemma which the makers of Soviet foreign policy faced from the beginning and still face today' he asked?) he concluded with a ringing endorsement of this 'remarkable and masterful book'.[27]

The reviews only illuminate one side of the relationship. There were other dimensions to it – mainly professional (the two men were constantly exchanging letters on matters of detailed research) but also personal. And if we accept that 'the personal is political', then this very political relationship was very personal indeed. This comes out in all manner of ways: in the warm tone of their numerous private exchanges, the frequent meetings at each other's house, the length to which they went to support the other in times of adversity, and, of course, in the enemies they had in common – most obviously Isaiah Berlin, who had scuppered Deutscher's chances of getting a Chair in Sussex in 1965, and whose outward display of charm and civility could not disguise his very deep hostility to Carr as an intellectual and, one suspects, as a human being as well.

The bond between the two men therefore was a powerful one; how powerful was most clearly revealed when Deutscher suddenly died in August 1967 – quite literally a few days after Carr's review of *The Unfinished Revolution* appeared in the *TLS*. The shock within the Carr family was palpable; Carr himself was very badly shaken, so much so that he found it almost impossible to write something about his old intellectual comrade-in-arms. Tamara, however, was especially keen for him to do so, and in the end (after some persuasion) he responded with a short and somewhat restrained appreciation which appeared in the *Cambridge Review* in 1967. This was followed two years later by a new 'Introduction' to a reissue of Deutscher's *Heretics and Renegades*. Finally, in 1970, he penned a small, but incisive review on Deutscher's posthumously published short study on *Lenin's Childhood*. In this, the last thing he ever wrote about Deutscher, Carr was typically generous. 'Isaac Deutscher,' he noted, 'possessed the capacity unequalled among historians of his generation to combine the imaginative and intellectual approaches to history.' This was a rare if not almost unique talent, and for this reason – there were many more – this last fragment about Lenin deserved to be read: not just because it afforded us insight into what might have been one of the great books that was never written about 'the making of the greatest revolutionary of our age', but as a tribute to Isaac Deutscher who in Carr's words was 'a great biographer and historian'.[28]

Carr and Deutscher: The Shared Outlook

> *Since Castor and Pollux, and Don Quixote and Sancho Panza, there have been few such unusual pairings.*
>
> Leopold Labedz on Carr and Deutscher (1988)[29]

> *In the middle of writing his work, Carr came under the influence of Isaac Deutscher.*
>
> Norman Stone on E.H. Carr (1983)[30]

Not surprisingly, the very close relationship between these two very different men has been the subject of some speculation. After all, it did not look like a 'natural' partnership. They came from remarkably different backgrounds and, as we shall see in the next section, disagreed quite fundamentally on certain key questions. Yet the combination worked and worked at many levels, to their mutual advantage and to the great dismay of their many ideological opponents who viewed these intellectual partners in crime – for that is how Carr and Deutscher came to be seen by some of their enemies during the Cold War – as waging a systematic and highly effective campaign to sell Stalin and Stalinism, not to mention Trotsky and Trotskyism, to an unsuspecting British public.[31]

Clearly, one reason why Carr and Deutscher were drawn together was their mutual interest in the early history of Soviet Russia. With one or two exceptions, nobody else of comparable stature shared their enthusiasm. Nor did others working in the field have their detailed and intimate knowledge of the period. Not surprisingly therefore they tended to be pulled into each other's orbit. Indeed, one suspects that even if they had not agreed on so many issues, the sheer logic of what they were doing, and the quite terrifying scale of the scholarly mountains they were trying to climb separately, would have impelled them together – almost like two climbers on a steep rock face, who having embarked on a course of action, find they have no alternative but to rely on one another, less they fall to their deaths!

But even this would not have been enough to make the relationship so close. Carr we know from his own papers worked with several academic colleagues; yet he never became as involved with them as he did with Deutscher. Nor did he review their work with such enthusiasm or admire them in the way he admired Deutscher. But as Haslam makes clear in his study of Carr, Carr did not just admire Deutscher but was drawn towards the man and formed 'a curious emotional bond' with him. This he suggests was partly for political, partly for academic and partly for psychological reasons. 'It was easy to see what drew Carr towards him,' says Haslam. 'He was a revolutionary by outlook, an outstanding intellect and a pugnacious publicist who could easily wound less armoured minds.' According to Haslam, Carr was also drawn to Deutscher because he appeared to remind him of those romantic exiles he had studied and written about so affectionately during the 1930s. For this reason he found Deutscher 'not only fascinating but also endearing'. It is even possible that the 'realist' Carr was attracted towards the Polish émigré because he seemed to embody those 'utopian' ideals which he found easy to criticize in others yet still found so compelling. Thus Deutscher, the radical Marxist who still believed fervently in the political mission of the working class and the ideal of a classless society, attracted Carr for the same reason as he had originally been drawn towards the nineteenth century Russian anarchist, Michael Bakunin – the subject of Carr's fifth book and fourth biography published in 1937. Because he dared to dream big dreams and construct in thought that which he hoped one day would be created on earth.[32]

These insights into Carr's psychology make a good deal of speculative sense. But they remain just that – speculation: they also leave the question unanswered as to why the two formed the relationship they did and why that relationship lasted so long. Certainly, it was linked to the Cold War and the politically hostile environment they inhabited: it was not unconnected either to their joint refusal to condemn the Russian revolution and the revolution's principal leader, Lenin, a man they admired enormously.[33] Yet even this only takes us part of the way towards an explanation. The clue has to be sought elsewhere, and the best place to look for the clue is in Soviet history itself.

Basically, when Carr and Deutscher set out on their voyage of intellectual discovery they carried little in the way of provisions, but they did take one major navigational aid with them: a belief that whatever Stalin had done in the 1920s and 1930s he had at least preserved something of the essential core of the original revolutionary aim of creating a more equal, more dynamic and more literate society. He had, quite obviously, abandoned the pristine goals of the Bolsheviks and, in the process, destroyed the Bolshevik Party as well. He had also fatally severed the connection between the cause of world revolution – something that Carr never believed in – and the cause of socialism. To this extent he had betrayed the revolution. But he had not abandoned the cause of socialism completely. Some umbilical cord, however tattered and frayed, continued to connect the Stalinist system in all its mire with the aspirations of 1917.[34]

This attempt to retrieve something progressive from the Soviet experience was in turn linked to the way in which both Carr and Deutscher understood the dynamics of industrialization. In his own work, Carr had deliberately stayed away from the 1930s on the grounds that there was not enough sources to make a thorough investigation of the Five Year Plans possible. Nevertheless, he had a view, and the view, like Deutscher's, was fairly clear: industrialization was inevitable because the USSR was isolated and surrounded on all sides by hostile capitalist states: it was also necessary because there was no other way to build the foundations of a more mature, advanced society in which the working class would one day become the majority. Admittedly, the means employed to achieve fast economic growth were crude. Deutscher at one point referred to them as being 'barbarous'.[35] Moreover, there were huge costs involved. As Carr conceded in one of the last volumes of his *History*, 'seldom perhaps in history had so monstrous a price been paid' for achieving a desired objective. Yet at the end of the day, the objective – namely industrialization – had been undertaken and, in his own words, had turned out to be a 'monumental achievement'.[36] Deutscher agreed, without reservation. As he noted in his *Russia After Stalin*, a critically important study published in 1953, 'The core of Stalin's genuine achievement' he opined 'lies in the fact that he found Russia working with the wooden plough and left her equipped with atomic piles'.[37]

Finally, Carr and Deutscher took a more or less identical view of the contradictory nature of Stalinism. Deutscher in particular felt that the economic logic of the Soviet system would inevitably bring about political change – a view he expounded at great length after 1953. Carr was more sceptical, as he made clear in one of his more critical reviews of Deutscher.[38] Yet even he seemed to agree with Deutscher that Stalinism by fostering rapid growth and generating widespread sociological change had, in effect, created its own gravedigger. To this extent the revolution remained 'unfinished'. And even if this did not lead directly to democracy or greater working class control over Soviet society, the future for the planned economy remained relatively bright. This remained Deutscher's position until his death in 1967; and it was Carr's too while Deutscher remained alive. Indeed, as he emphasized in 1969, while the 'phenomenal achievements' of the USSR over the past forty years were unlikely to be matched in the future, the socio-economic foundations of the system were secure. More than that, the utopian aspirations of the past had not yet withered away entirely. For this reason the society had not and was not likely to stagnate in the future.[39]

Carr and Deutscher: The Differences

In general I would hazard the guess that Carr is not 'your kind' of historian.
Ernest Simmons to Isaac Deutscher (1955)[40]

Carr and Deutscher thus agreed that there was something worth defending in the Soviet Union, especially at a time of Cold War when the massed ranks of reaction in their view were mobilizing their not inconsiderable resources to attack the cause of progress around the world. Under such circumstances it would have been the height of political folly, they believed, to have attacked the USSR too openly. They would not be apologists. On the other hand, they were not going to be drawn into any anti-Soviet campaign and denounced others on the left who, in their opinion, had been. Orwell was especially singled out for having helped the enemy. In their view, his various works, though brilliant as polemic, were used (and used most effectively) by the establishment in their larger ideological campaign against the left. Hence, what Orwell might have regarded as a powerful statement against Stalinism ended up being deployed against his own side. Such was the fate, they felt, of all heretics turned renegade in the Cold War after 1947.[41]

The solidarity between the two men was thus real. But the differences should not be underestimated either; and the more one explores these, the more remarkable seems their united front against the world at large. Remarkable too is the fact that both men were fully aware of these differences, discussed them openly and yet continued to work closely together.

At the heart of the great divide, of course, was a fundamental difference in outlook and philosophy. Deutscher had been formed in a revolutionary environment in Poland, and quite consciously still regarded himself as part of a larger political movement whose goal was to change the world in the direction of socialism. Carr was cut from a different cloth, and while he opposed the West and made some really quite dramatic statements (even late in life) about the long-term decline of capitalism, at the end of the day he remained uncertain about the future. He was very sceptical indeed about the possibility of revolution, at least in the advanced countries. And he was especially doubtful about the working class. In his view they were either counter-revolutionary or politically incapable of taking power. Deutscher, on the other hand, was as orthodox on this question as it was possible to be. Indeed, in his various discussions with the New Left in the United States in the 1960s, he berated them in no uncertain terms for abandoning the working class and looking for vanguards elsewhere. Go out, he virtually shouted at them, find the working class, educate them and lead them towards socialism. One could hardly imagine 'the Prof' urging this on the editorial board of the *New Left Review* – and he didn't.[42]

This divide in perspective complicated the relationship between Carr and Deutscher in a number of important ways. However, it manifested itself directly in at least two large disagreements, one concerning the nature of the Russian Revolution and the other revolving around the issue of method. Let us deal with each in turn.

The first open dispute occurred in the mid-1950s. Deutscher had been asked by the influential Glasgow-based journal, *Soviet Studies*, to provide a lengthy review of Carr's more general contribution to the study of Soviet history. Typically, he took the job seriously; typically, he did not mince his words. But he was not insensitive to the problems that were likely to be caused and thus decided to consult Carr: and it was only after some lengthy negotiations between the two men that he finally sent in the offending article.[43] This appeared in the May 1955 issue under the rather gentle title 'Mr E.H. Carr as Historian of Soviet Russia'.[44]

At one level the Deutscher review was not at all unfavourable. But there was a problem, one to which Deutscher had already alluded in some of his earlier reviews of Carr: and the problem, basically, was that Carr was always inclined to look at the revolution from the top down rather than the bottom up. Inevitably, this skewed his perspective and lent his account a rather formal character. He also appeared to have little interest in revolutionary ideas. As a result, he was constantly trying to normalize the revolution – almost treating it as if it was some madcap event led by wild-eyed ideologues with no real grasp of the world around them, which would, hopefully, settle down (sooner rather than later) and allow more stable people with a sensible outlook to run the show: people presumably like Stalin, and though Deutscher did not draw that conclusion, that was certainly implicit in what he was saying.

Deutscher, however, was especially caustic about Carr's handling of Lenin. Carr, he felt, tended to treat Lenin too uncritically and his various opponents like the Left Communists much too harshly. He also had a tendency to overstate Lenin's role, and in some of his early letters to Carr he chastised him too for not saying enough about Trotsky. Much more seriously though was his attitude towards Lenin. Lenin the revolutionary who challenged power and talked about the withering away of the state he seemed to find faintly naïve. Lenin the builder of state power he admired. The implication was clear: Carr did not really understand what motivated Lenin and thus probably did not understand the revolution as a dynamic event either.

If Carr was wounded by Deutscher's remarks (and there is every indication that he was)[45] he was even more non-plussed by what happened a few years later. The roots of this altercation went back to the very beginning of the relationship, but assumed a more precise form in the early 1960s. There were hints of it in Deutscher's otherwise positive review of *What is History?* in late 1961, followed in 1963 by Carr's own review of Deutscher's third volume on Trotsky. But the issue came to a head when a lengthy item written by a critic landed on Carr's desk in December of the same year. Carr was somewhat taken aback by the large package and its contents. As he noted in a letter to Deutscher, 'you might be amused to see the enclosed essay from a Marxist in America who has written to me once or twice before, and who attacks us both from opposite angles on this problem of accident in History'.[46] Deutscher was probably not amused because he knew the person in question very well – Roman Rosdolsky. Moreover, while he had no reason to be overly keen on Rosdolsky, who had in the past attacked Deutscher for being too soft on the Soviet Union, he regarded him as a 'very old friend' who, 'academically' at least, was 'the best Marx scholar alive'. He also reminded Carr that it was none other than Deutscher himself who had drawn Rosdolsky to Carr's attention some 'years ago' – something that Carr had obviously forgotten in the intervening period.[47]

The arrival of the Rosdolsky paper[48] seemed to set off something in Deutscher. But instead of responding to the criticisms made of himself used the occasion to try to educate Carr into the meaning of Marxism and dialectics. All he managed to do, though, was simply confirm that the theoretical gap between the two was too wide ever to be bridged – as Deutscher had always known. Carr had undoubtedly absorbed a lot of

Marxism, but at heart remained, in Deutscher's view, a British empiricist 'in spite of his explicit criticisms' of that particular 'tradition'.[49] As he had observed in 1955, Carr just could not 'get out of his skin theoretically and ideologically . . . and so he cannot really break down the barrier between his own way of thinking and Marxism'.[50] Deutscher, on the other hand, remained a committed historical materialist who in his own words really did believe that Marx could not be improved upon. Moreover, in his view, the only Marxist in the twentieth century who had even begun to get close to developing some of Marx's original insights was Trotsky himself. And this is why he was interested in the man: not just because of his historical role but also because of his contribution to Marxism. Indeed, Trotsky's real tragedy, according to Deutscher, was not that he was defeated politically (as he pointed out in his last volume on Trotsky, even in defeat there was victory),[51] but that he was ahead of his time. However, his time would come – one day – and at that point Marxism would be reborn.

Deutscher's reflections on the age did not provoke a response in Carr. Nor were they likely to. For as was clear, what motivated Deutscher and what interested Carr were very different things. Deutscher obviously looked forward to a new upsurge of revolution and a rebirth of Marxism in the process: Carr continued to look back towards Russia and the revolution whose tortured course he had plotted in such careful detail. And while Carr accepted that Marxism had a good deal to teach us, and was prepared to defend and encourage those many Marxists he knew, he could never share in their enthusiasms. As he remarked in one of the very last things he wrote just before he died in 1982, 'am I a Marxist?' Perhaps, he replied. Marx after all was a very great thinker whose analysis of capitalism represented 'an enormous advance in knowledge'. On the other hand, the idea that there will ever be world revolution was merely utopian and to that extent, therefore, 'I suppose I am not a Marxist'.[52]

Carr and Deutscher – After the Soviet Union

Feudal and even bourgeois property relations may be compatible with economic stagnation or a sluggish tempo of growth. National ownership is not, especially when it has been established in an underdeveloped country by way of a proletarian revolution. The system carries within it the compulsion to rapid advance, the necessity to strive for abundance and the urge to develop.

(Deutscher, 1967)[53]

No society entirely devoid of utopian aspirations will escape stagnation.
Soviet society has not stagnated.

(Carr, 1969)[54]

This brings us finally to the issue of the collapse of the Soviet experiment – an event that Carr and Deutscher neither anticipated nor could anticipate given their views about the superior character of Soviet planning. Indeed, not only did they fail to anticipate the possibility of economic implosion, but actually ruled it out as being theoretically inconceivable. Both were quite explicit: capitalist restoration was simply impossible. To this extent therefore they got the Soviet Union utterly wrong and there is little point denying it. But let us be clear. They were not the only people who got the USSR wrong or failed to anticipate the subsequent demise of the Soviet system. With one or two notable exceptions, nearly everybody else failed as well – including, by the way, most of the retrospectively wise critics who now hold Carr and Deutscher to account before the bar of History. So if we are to criticize Carr and Deutscher, we should at least be fair and not only take them to task but also the Conservative Right – who felt the USSR could never change because of its totalitarian character – the experts in international relations – who assumed that bipolarity was a permanent condition – students of European security – who believed the Soviet Union would never get out of Eastern Europe – the CIA who until the bitter end argued that the Soviet system could muddle along – and the overwhelming majority of the Left who either thought Soviet planning represented the wave of the future or that the system could be progressively reformed, from above or below. Hence, if Carr and Deutscher had their illusions about the former USSR – and they did – they shared these with nearly everybody else.[55]

But does any of this really matter any longer? And should we be concerned – except as archeologists and archivists – about what Carr and Deutscher once said about the former Soviet system? I would suggest we should be: partly because by re-examining their role during the Cold War we can much better understand what the conflict was all about and why it precipitated such bitter debate in the West itself; partly because by coming to terms with Carr and Deutscher, we can more sensitively appreciate the radical dilemma before 1989 – namely, what were those opposed to the West supposed to say about a system which, on the one hand, was deeply repressive and highly inefficient but, on the other, the only effective block to the further expansion of capitalism; and partly because the putative mistakes made by left-wing critics like Carr and Deutscher before the demise of the Soviet system are still being used by the apologists of liberal capitalism to justify their claim that there is really no serious historical alternative to the market. To those who think there still might be, it is thus essential to come to terms with their own history, warts and all: and perhaps there is no better place to start than with the writings of E.H. Carr and Isaac Deutscher who formed a very special relationship between 1947 and 1967.

Notes

1   Quoted in Jonathan Haslam, *Vices of Integrity: E.H. Carr, 1892–1982* (London: Verso, 1999), p. 140.

2   See E.H. Carr, 'Introduction', in Isaac Deutscher, ed., *Heretics and Renegades and Other Essays* (London: Jonathan Cape, 1955), pp. 3–4.

3   Tamara Deutscher, 'E.H. Carr – A Personal Memoir', *New Left Review*, No. 137 (January–February 1983), pp. 78–9.

4   See my 'The End of the Cold War and Why We Failed to Predict it', in Allen Hunter, *Rethinking The Cold War* (Philadelphia: Temple University Press, 1998), p. 157.

5   While Carr applauded total planning in the USSR, he did not necessarily advocate it for Britain. 'Britain's own domestic outlook', he noted in 1947, was 'equally far removed from the thorough-going state regimentation of the Soviet Union and from the unplanned *laissez-faire* capitalism of the United States.' See his 'Foreign Policy Begins At Home', *The Listener* (31 October 1946), p. 585.

6   On Deutscher's early years, see Ludger Syre, *Isaac Deutscher: Marxist, Publizist, Historiker: Sein Leben und Werk, 1907–1967* (Hamburg: Junius Verlag, 1984), pp. 22–158, Tamara Deutscher, 'Introduction: The Education of Jewish Child', in Isaac Deutscher, ed., *The Non-Jewish Jew and Other Essays* (London: Oxford University Press, 1968), pp. 1–24; and Daniel Singer, 'Armed with a Pen', in David Horowitz, ed., *Isaac Deutscher: The Man and His Work* (London: Macdonald, 1971), pp. 19–56.

7   Letter from Deutscher to Pierre Frank, 10 November 1958, *Deutscher Papers* (International Institute of Social History, Amsterdam).

8   Isaac Deutscher, *Heretics and Renegades*, p. 20.

9   See Steve Unger, 'Deutscher and the New Left in America', in Horowitz, *Isaac Deutscher: The Man and His Work*, pp. 211–25.

10   The first letter between them is dated 31 January 1947 and is written by Carr to 'Dear Deutscher': this rather formal note was maintained until 1949 when Carr began to address Deutscher as 'my dear Isaac' and Deutscher started to refer to Carr as 'my dear Prof', *Deutscher Papers*.

11   In Britain, Carr reviewed all Deutscher's books (with the exception of *Lenin's Childhood* (1970) in *The Times Literary Supplement*. Five of these, *Soviet Trade Unions* (1950), the Trotsky 'trilogy' (1954, 1959 and 1963) and *The Unfinished Revolution* (1967) are collected in E.H. Carr, *1917: Before and After* (London: Macmillan, 1969), pp. 128–76.

12 See however Carr's somewhat mild criticism of Deutscher for tending 'to exaggerate the personal elements inherent in Stalinism' in his *Russia and After*, and for assuming there was a necessary connection between further Soviet economic development after 1953 and democracy. See his 'The Heritage Of Stalinism', *The Times Literary Supplement*, 28 August 1953 and 'Recoil Against Stalinism', *The Times Literary Supplement*, 20 May 1955.

13 For Carr's very positive review of *Stalin*, see his 'The Dialectics of Stalinism', *The Times Literary Supplement*, 10 June 1949. Carr actually reviewed *Stalin* four times! His other reviews were a radio programme 'Stalin' for the Third Programme 30 June 1949, another transmission 'Stalin: A Political Biography' that went out for the BBC on 27 August 1949 (see *Carr Papers*, University of Birmigham) and 'The Riddle of a Public Face', *New Republic*, 28 November 1949, pp. 19–21.

14 The phrase was used by Carr in his 'Isaac Deutscher: In Memoriam', in E.H. Carr, ed., *1917: Before and After*, pp. 177–8.

15 Quote from letter sent by Carr to Deutscher, 16 November 1954, *Deutscher Papers*.

16 Daniel Singer, 'Armed With A Pen', p. 42.

17 See the letters between Carr and Deutscher dated 21 January 1947, 20 March 1947, 21 March 1947, 5 June 1947, 16 June 1947 and 18 September 1947 dealing with Deutscher's research on his book on Soviet Trade Unions. He hoped to have this volume ready by the end of 1947 – along with the volume on Stalin. In the end *Stalin* appeared in 1949 and *Soviet Trade Unions* in 1950, both published by Oxford University Press. See *Deutscher Papers*.

18 Letter from Carr to Deutscher, 3 December 1948.

19 Letter from Deutscher to Carr, 3 May 1949, *Deutscher Papers*.

20 Carr wrote about Deutscher's *Stalin*: 'the present biography will not easily be superseded'. See his 'The Dialectics of Stalinism', *The Times Literary Supplement*, 10 June 1949.

21 The two Carr broadcasts on the Deutscher book were 'Stalin' (30 June 1949) and 'Stalin: A Political Biography' (27 August 1949). Transcripts of these can be found in the *Carr Papers*. The University of Birmingham, Special Collection.

22 See E.H. Carr, 'The Riddle of a Public Face', *The New Republic*, 28 November 1949.

23 Letter from Deutscher to Carr, 11 June 1949, *Deutscher Papers*.

24 See Carr's 'Trotsky and Bolshevism', *The Times Literary Supplement*, 19 February 1954.

25 Letter from Deutscher to Carr, 2 December 1961, *Deutscher Papers*.

26 Letter from Carr to Deutscher, 7 July 1965, *Deutscher Papers*.

27 See Carr's review, 'Fifty Years On', *The Times Literary Supplement*, 3 August 1967.

28 See E.H. Carr, 'Early Influences', *The Sunday Times*, 20 November 1970.

29 Leopold Labedz, 'E.H. Carr: An Historian Overtaken by History', *Survey*, Vol. 30 (March 1988), p. 104.

30 Norman Stone, 'Grim Eminence', *The London Review of Books*, 20 January 1983, p. 7.

31 See Leopold Labedz's double review of Carr and Deutscher together in *Survey*, Vol. 30 (March 1988), pp. 33–111.

32   Haslam, *The Vices of Integrity*, pp. 138–40.
33   See Michael Cox, 'Will the Real E.H. Carr Please Stand up?', *International Affairs*, Vol. 75, No. 3 (July 1999), pp. 643–53.
34   Nor did Deutscher change his mind on this question. In a new 'Preface' to his original *Stalin* (Harmondsworth: Pelican, 1966) he argued: 'I have seen no reason to alter my narrative or my interpretation of Stalin's career' (p. 10).
35   Isaac Deutscher, *Russia after Stalin* (1953; London: Jonathan Cape, 1969) p. 54.
36   E.H. Carr, *Foundations of a Planned Economy, 1926–1929: 2* (1971: Harmondsworth: Penguin Books, 1976), p. 477.
37   *Russia after Stalin*, p. 55.
38   See Carr's 'Recoil against Stalinism', *The Times Literary Supplement*, 20 May 1955.
39   See Carr's 'Editor's Introduction' in N. Bukharin and E. Preobrajensky, *The ABC of Communism* (Harmondsworth: Penguin Books, 1969), p. 51.
40   Letter from Ernest Simmons to Isaac Deutscher, 10 June 1955, *Deutscher Papers* (Amsterdam).
41   For Deutscher's critique of Orwell, see his '1984 – The Mysticism of Cruelty', in his *Heretics and Renegades and Renegades*, pp. 35–50.
42   For Deutscher on the working class, see his *Marxism in Our Time* (Berkeley: The Ramparts Press, 1971), pp. 71–3, 227–54.
43   The correspondence between Carr and Deutscher can be found in the *Deutscher Papers*.
44   See *Soviet Studies*, Vol. 6, No. 4 (April 1955), pp. 237–350.
45   See his defensive remarks in his 'Introduction' to Deutscher's reissued edition of *Heretics and Renegades*, pp. 3–4.
46   The letter from Carr to Deutscher dated 17 December 1963 can be found in both the *Carr Papers* in Birmingham and the *Deutscher Papers* in Amsterdam.
47   Letter from Deutscher to Carr, 23 December 1963, *Deutscher Papers*.
48   The full text of Rosdolsky's remarkable piece can be found in *The Carr Papers*. Its full title is 'Prof. E.H. Carr und Isaac Deutscher über die Rolle der Zufalis der Grossen Manner in der Geschichte' (28pp).
49   Quoted from Isaac Deutscher, 'Between Past and Future', in his *Ironies of History: Essays On Contemporary Communism* (London: Oxford University Press, 1966), pp. 199–206.
50   See the quote in note 1.
51   Isaac Deutscher, *The Prophet Outcast, Trotsky: 1929–1940* (London: Oxford University Press, 1963), pp. 510–23.
52   See his 'autobiography' written in 1980 for Tamara Deutscher and reprinted in full in this volume.
53   Isaac Deutscher, *The Unfinished Revolution: Russia 1917–1967* (London: Oxford University Press, 1967), p. 37.
54   E.H. Carr, 'Editor's Introduction', in N. Bukharin and E. Preobrajensky, *The ABC of Communism* (Harmondsworth: Penguin Books, 1969), p. 51.
55   I explore these issues in Michael Cox, *Rethinking The Soviet Collapse: Sovietology, The Death of Communism and the New Russia* (London: Cassell/Pinter, 1998).

7

E.H. Carr, the Cold War and the Soviet Union

Hillel Ticktin

Introduction

As Michael Cox has argued in the introduction, Carr played a critical intellectual role in the post-war period as sympathetic analyst of the early Soviet regime and credible critic of the West. For both these related misdemeanours he was frequently taken to task and attacked by his many enemies. Nor have the critics gone away and, following the publication of his biography by Jonathan Haslam (a fair but not fawning account of Carr's life), they once more emerged from the woodwork.[1] Indeed, one of the most striking things about the various reviews, with one or two notable exceptions, was that they virtually ignored the book but attacked Carr in person for being, amongst other things, a 'cold-blooded colossus', a 'turgid' writer more likely to turn people off history than onto it, a 'very cold fish' who had no interest in human beings, and a 'horrible history man' whose work on the former USSR was now obsolete but who unfortunately did not live long enough to see the object of his fascination disintegrate in 1991. Even in death Carr appears to have the capacity to rile those with whom he had disagreed when alive.[2]

To the outsider the bitter and unpleasant tone of these attacks must come as something of a surprise; after all Carr died in 1982 and the Cold War came to an unexpected conclusion seven years later. Yet the struggle, it would seem, goes on, making a serious evaluation of Carr's ideas and his place in history very difficult. However, such a discussion has to take place – partly because Carr is too significant a figure to be left to the tender mercies of his enemies, partly because he was a major influence on a generation of people, and partly because, by understanding Carr and the debates in which he got involved, we can better understand the world he inhabited after 1947 and the pressures which the Cold War in particular had upon intellectual debate at the time.

Carr however never really understood the Cold War as a complex phenomenon: for him there were two sides in opposition and the role of the intellectual was not so much to support one side against the other (he was never that crude) but to refuse to engage in what he viewed as propaganda against the USSR. As he made clear in his 1978 interview with the *New Left Review*, those who indulged in such activities were only giving moral heart to Cold War warriors in the West. Not surprisingly, this somewhat defensive stance rather limited his own understanding of the Soviet system. His analysis was further impaired by an inability to transcend his particular background. The product of an elitist system and an effective member of the elite itself until the onset of the Cold War, Carr always tended to view the world from the perspective of the rulers rather than the ruled – including those who ruled the former USSR. In this sense, his critics are entirely wrong when they accuse Carr of being a closet communist or fellow traveller. His problem, if it can be defined as such, was not his overt left-wing ideology – Tamara Deutscher once described him more correctly as a discontented liberal, 'who had become exceedingly impatient with the anarchy of modern capitalism'[3] – but his own training and formation. Indeed, even when Carr became a dissident he never really managed to break from his 'own people', and this left him in the most ambivalent of positions of being outside an establishment to which he was ostensibly opposed but yet remaining part of it. As Isaac Deutscher once observed, Carr was honest and open-minded in ways that most of his peers were not; an expatriate from his own class who, because of his background, had the confidence to attack them. And that is why they hated him so. But ultimately, he could never quite detach himself from his moorings.[4] Brave in his own way and an irritant, Carr was thus a tremendous paradox: admired by the Left but never quite of it (even in 1980 he could not quite make up his mind whether he was a socialist or not), disliked by liberals and conservatives alike, yet maintaining good personal relations with people like Lewis Namier and Isaiah Berlin, and ready to defend Marxism but never willing to make the intellectual journey from his own very special brand of materialist empiricism to historical materialism.

Before exploring these issues in more detail, however, it might be helpful first to look at the Cold War as a system and the impact which this had on intellectuals in the West after 1947.

The Cold War as a System

The Cold War was a complex form of interaction between capitalism and Stalinism which served to support the structures of both systems. Thus the USSR became dependent on world capitalism as a 'threat', while the Soviet Union served to unite and legitimize western capitalism.[5] Indeed, the Cold War can be understood more precisely as a particular system that expressed both an antagonism between two sets of social relations but helped bolster capitalism during a specific period of decline.[6] Moreover, though the existence of the Soviet Union was a manifestation of that decline, precisely because of the Stalinist form it assumed that decline was arrested – in part because of the foreign policy it pursued but, more importantly, because the idea or ideal of socialism became identified with repression and inefficiency. To this extent the USSR became what might best be described as a deterrent state ostensibly opposed to what existed in the West, but in a deeper sense helping strengthen the institutions of the West, especially in the post-war period.

This, however, is not how things looked to most people. The USSR, it seemed to them, was a single-minded opponent that threatened the very foundations of democratic capitalism. As a self-proclaimed 'superpower' it also looked exceedingly powerful even though it was systemically weak. It even had the appearance of being economically dynamic when in reality it was in advanced state of decline from the late 1960s onwards. Thus, although it limited American reach, it never seriously challenged the US in any meaningful way. Indeed, the very idea that America might have found the relationship with the USSR at all useful struck most observers at the time of the Cold War as being faintly absurd. Yet that was the reality. The very existence of the USSR after all helped justify its own high military expenditure; it also proved a useful discipline over its own workforce; and of course it made it possible for the American state to stigmatize and thus marginalize all anticapitalist intellectuals by claiming they were close to, or working for, the Soviet Union. In many respects the USSR was an ideal competitor.

The Cold War thus wore a mask – several in fact. It was never quite what it seemed to be. The political consequences of the Cold War, however, were all too plain to see. Confronted with an antagonism between what some viewed as a conflict between freedom and despotism – and others imperialism and progress – intellectuals in the West were forced to choose between one or other of the antagonists. There could be no neutrality in a bipolar world where one camp stood in stark opposition to the other. The fact that the opposition hid a deeper interdependency was simply ignored. The fact that the Soviet Union also represented a block to socialism rather than the real thing was also swept under the table as idle speculation, especially by those engaged in the conflict and who had an interest in perpetuating this myth: the West better to discredit the ideal of socialism and the East to mobilize left-wing support abroad. In a two-camp world one was thus almost forced to choose sides and not remain aloof from the struggle going on in what Deutscher liked to term 'The Great Contest'.[7] Such was the confusing and complex world which E.H. Carr inhabited.

E.H. Carr and the Cold War

If we define the intellectual as someone who follows ideas honestly to their conclusion whatever the cost, then it is hardly surprising to discover that there are so few genuine intellectuals in the world. During the Cold War, of course, the pressures were immense and few avoided the choices open to them of taking sides. Some did, and attempted to stand outside the usual reward system and engage in original, path-breaking analysis. But this required courage and the psychological strength; it was also extremely isolating. And very few people were equal to the challenge. Isaac Deutscher, to take the obvious contemporary of E.H. Carr, went some of the way along this road but in the end produced a book on Stalin which allowed him to remain a critical supporter of both Stalin and the USSR, a position that Carr heartily endorsed.[8] Carr was less of an outsider but could hardly be characterized as a hardy intellectual standing against the stream. Furthermore, he was no Marxist, even though his work was appreciated by Marxists and by those who stood in neither camp.[9] Which leads to the key questions: what precise role did he play in the Cold War; and to what extent was he able to achieve an understanding of the Soviet sytem? Let us look at each question in turn.

In so far as any intellectual broke with the dominant pro-NATO viewpoint, the ideological control exercised by the Cold War was thereby weakened. The McCarthy era, whose effects lasted a long time, was critical in cowing American and British academics and writers. By controlling criticism, the ruling class in the West was also able to prevent the emergence of a viable critique of capitalism. Any criticism of the consensus which came from intellectuals therefore disrupted the operation of the Cold War itself. Even if the critique was limited, or muddled, it could create problems. This is why the Cold War assumed such an intense ideological form. McCarthyism, from this viewpoint, was important and functional to the Cold War. This in the first instance is why Carr posed a problem, even though he never represented a serious threat.

There are those who argue that a good history or a good account is necessarily objective, does not take sides and can be used and appreciated by everyone regardless of their assumptions. There is, obviously, some truth in this assertion, but the truth is banal. In a battle between good and evil no one can be above the fray as indeed those who waged the Cold War in the West firmly believed. Moreover, every historian has his assumptions as E.H. Carr's little book on historiography[10] seeks to show. His strength lay in the fact that he did not shirk the issue, as it were. And yet he did, while appearing not so to do.

Norman Stone's self-serving attack on Carr[11] was very much part of the Cold War and it served the author's purpose. Its underlying thesis was that Carr was pro-Soviet, a point with which this chapter does not disagree. The style more than the content of the review illustrated as clearly as possible the fact that Carr was seen as part of the other side by a section of the Cold War academics. Perhaps Norman Stone is an extreme case of a Cold War warrior, but he illustrated the dilemmas and the problems of the time. Richard Pipes, who did not descend to such personal lengths, was a completely different example of an academic who appeared to be governed largely by ideology. In fact, the Cold War in ideological history seems to have been fought out between Carr and Deutscher on the one side and the academics like Pipes, together with the journals *Encounter* and *Survey* on the other. On the Carr side, Bob Davies and Alec Nove, among others, came to Carr's defence against both Norman Stone and Leo Labedz.[12]

Pipes' apparently more measured attacks appear far more vituperative when properly examined. I shall take one instance as an illustration of the problem. He attacks E.H. Carr's *Bolshevik Revolution Vol 2*[13] in his *Russia under the Bolshevik Regime, 1919–1924* on the grounds that Carr gives only one paragraph to the famine of 1921, where he dismisses the calculation of the numbers involved as unreliable. This Pipes claims as the reason why there is only one paragraph.[14] Pipes goes on to say that 'similar reasoning has been adduced by neo-Nazi historians for ignoring the Holocaust'.[15] This is a breathtaking misrepresentation, as Carr does not give any reason for the number of words he devotes to the famine and in fact he provides closer to two pages on the subject, with enough footnotes for it to be pursued. None the less, Pipes turns the famine into a major political issue, attributing it to the Bolshevik policy of confiscation of the 'surpluses'. Carr does not give any cause, though the Pipes conclusion, on Carr's evidence, would be rational. Pipes does not really add anything more of substance, although he spends more words on the subject. Nor does he illuminate the issue. After all, the real question is whether the famine could have been avoided. It is absurd to argue that if the Bolsheviks were not Bolsheviks there would have been no famine. They clearly did not want the famine and there is no evidence that it followed from their peacetime policy or programme. One could equally argue that if there had been no Civil War there would have been no famine. Therefore, had the Western Powers not supported the Whites there would have been no famine. Hence, if one is to use the Pipes' argument, one might conclude that the famine was the fault of the Western Powers or the Whites and so of the old order.

The issue, in short, either deserves a few paragraphs or a separate book, but it is absurd to suggest it was an attempt by Carr to gloss over or hide the issue. None the less, this was symptomatic of the Cold War scholars' attitude to Carr. The Pipes book was actually written during the Cold War but appeared after it was over, as he tells us in the preface. The essential point here is that both sides of this debate were operating with a confused analysis. At the risk of oversimplification one may say that Pipes saw the Bolsheviks and Stalinism as a seamless web whose purpose was wholly evil. The famine was, therefore, part of their evil design. The Cold War ideology required extremists like Pipes to maintain a doctrine, which was otherwise highly dubious. Carr, on the other hand, appeared to sympathize with those who, he thought, were trying to improve the lot of the majority but he fell into the trap of supporting, however critically, the Stalinist regime.

The journal *Soviet Studies* played its own role in this ideological Cold War. Founded in 1949 by Jack Miller and Rudolf Schlesinger, with the backing of Glasgow University, it appeared to be above the ideological fray; E.H. Carr was one of its original contributors and supporters, writing in the first issue.[16] In fact, Jack Miller was a member of the Communist Party at the time. Rudolf Schlesinger had been expelled from the Communist Party but remained a loyal if idiosyncratic supporter of the Soviet Union to the end. *Soviet Studies* was anything but impartial at the time. Jack Miller left the Communist Party in 1955 and *Soviet Studies* later changed, falling under the influence of Alec Nove.

Leo Labedz was also one of Carr's main opponents, and one can read his statements in the *Times Literary Supplement* among other places (including *Survey*, the journal he edited).[17] He did not spare his words in criticizing Carr. The antagonism between *Survey* and *Encounter* and *Soviet Studies*, and later, between Carr and Deutscher on one side and the

CIA academics and writers, on the other, was considerable. 'Carr was no crude whitewasher of Stalin; he was, like Deutscher, a very subtle apologist,'[18] Labedz remarks. He quotes Leonard Schapiro to the effect that Carr provided the information 'with consummate skill and clarity' but, Schapiro continues, he failed to see the effects of policies on the ordinary population of the country. He looked at the Soviet Union through the eyes of the officials, particularly that of Lenin.[19]

It is extraordinary for someone like Schapiro to have produced such an argument when he was hardly a socialist, populist nor even a man of the people as it were. In contrast to the above, Schapiro argued that 'It is this mass democratic character of totalitarianism which distinguishes this form of rule from anything that has gone before.' The meaning of 'mass democratic character' is made clear in the preceding sentences:

> the mass appeal of Bolshevism delves much deeper into the dark recesses of the mob mind. It draws response from the fear of freedom, the envy, the anti-intellectualism, the chauvinism – in short all the characteristic ambience of the mass man . . . with his own mass morality, his crude egalitarian and levelling aspirations and his herd paranoia.[20]

If any statement is undemocratic this is. The Cold Warriors were not just attacking Carr for being soft on Stalin and Stalinism but more fundamentally for being soft on socialism, too much on the side of the people. They were not themselves on the side of the proletariat, the oppressed or the exploited. There can be no question that they were right: Carr was too uncritical of Stalin and Stalinism; but their critique was little more than a defence of the West. Whereas Carr spoke of oppression and the need for equality, even though he could not see the way towards it, they stood for an unequal society. Carr admired the 'spirit of liberty' evidenced for him in Bakunin.[21] They, on the other hand, were an entirely unsavoury collection, not unconnected with serving the needs of official British and American foreign policy.

One could conclude that Carr survived the attack on his integrity by these Cold Warriors precisely because his attackers were, themselves, so closely identified with a discredited right-wing politics in the minds of most intellectuals. Few were taken in by their attempted identification with workers. None the less, they were the establishment both in academia and in the service of the state, and their articles established the orthodoxy. This orthodoxy, in turn, informed much of the popularization of the Cold War ideology that was relayed through the media. E.H. Carr's dissidence went beyond that of such as Nove because he appeared to chronicle a genuine attempt to change the world for the better. By so doing, he created a space for others to go beyond him. This logically leads to the question of what lay beyond him and that must lead to the question of Marxism.

Marxism and E.H. Carr

When considering whether E.H. Carr was a Marxist or soft on Marxism there are two questions to be discussed. In the first instance, there is his attitude to Marxism and so to Marxist historians and Marxist activists. In the second instance, there is the question of what is Marxist history. We need to consider both in order the better to understand Carr's viewpoint.

I will first discuss the question of Marxist history. There have been many historians who have belonged to communist parties and also many historians who have seen themselves producing historical work which is Marxist. The fact that they proclaim themselves to be Marxist or communists does not necessarily make their work Marxist. It might make it left-wing, or more objective, or less right-wing, or socialist-oriented, but it does not automatically make it Marxist. The reason for the qualification is not pedantry or sectarianism, but rather reflects the difficulty of being a genuine Marxist historian. Marx himself wrote history as exemplified in *Capital*, most particularly in the last section, where he discussed the origins of capitalism. There he traced history through an understanding of historical laws, forms and categories. To be a Marxist historian one must do the same thing. This involves a profound knowledge of political economy. Few historians have such knowledge and even with such knowledge, it is difficult to apply political economy to history. As a result, there have been very few serious Marxist historians.

Why is this point important? The reason lies in the context in which Carr was writing. Most historical writing of the Left was either openly Stalinist or strongly influenced by Stalinism.[22] In most cases where it was not, it lacked the criteria I have given for a genuine Marxist history. On the other side, the Right produced history which declared itself objective although it was openly biased or at the very least, used prejudicial assumptions.

It is not possible for an historian to have no viewpoint on the ideals of the October Revolution. It is also not possible for a historian to produce a history which has no view on the mass killings which occurred in this period. The historian must decide on his focus and carefully state his assumptions if he is honest. But he cannot pretend to have no viewpoint. The highest tribute which can be paid to a historian is not to declare him objective – when that is usually merely a statement that the speaker likes or agrees with his work – but to declare him to be honest.

And in reality that is what Carr appears to have been. He did not comprehend Marxism, nor the Russian Revolution, nor the nature of the epoch, but at least he struggled to understand all three. He saw the decline of capitalism, the contradictions of the Russian Revolution and the conflicts inherent in Stalinism. Carr made his views quite plain in reviewing Deutscher. He regarded the Marxist concept of Socialism as utopian, ethically defensible, but practically impossible.[23] Carr argued, in the gentlest way possible, that Deutscher was going too far in accepting the possibility of a classless society. He saw the ideal of equality as being nebulous. 'But the Utopia of Equality, of the classless and stateless society, is more intangible, and more difficult to define or describe.'[24] Indeed, his theoretical grasp of Marxism was so poor that he appears entirely muddled when discussing Deutscher's Marxism.[25]

One can easily quote Carr's description of the debates of the 1920s to show that he has at best a superficial understanding of the questions at issue. That is not surprising because few historians have understood them. It could be argued that because he was not a Marxist, his discussion has little reference to the topic. But Carr was dealing with Marxist topics, which required an understanding of Marxism. Furthermore, he saw himself as standing on the side of human liberty. As Marxism, above all, stands for human emancipation, he would have had to come to terms with it. Clearly one can be a non-Marxist and deal with Marxist topics provided one has a full understanding of the issues involved. Carr had some understanding but it is clearly limited and to that degree his work is limited.

R.W. Davies has attempted to answer the question of Carr's Marxism in his afterword in the second edition of *What is History?*.[26] There he shows that Carr was sceptical about the revolutionary role of the proletariat but saw Western society as in decline or decay. He saw the overthrow of Imperialism as a stepping stone to socialism but found socialism undefinable. He remarks that Marx did not define socialism. In the sense in which he seems to mean it, it is untrue. A society without the law of value and therefore money, which is no longer subject to the division of labour, in which there is abundance, in which everyone takes part in governing is already largely defined in relation to the present.

The many other features that are also required to fill in the details cannot be known. But these features alone do give us a goal towards which to work. Furthermore, it is hard to call anyone a Marxist who does not start with the revolutionary role of the proletariat. Marcuse may have rejected the idea, but then he was not fully a Marxist. Carr, however, seems to have accepted even less of the theory of Marxism than did Marcuse.

The importance of this discussion is to understand the role that Carr played in the Cold War. One can only conclude that Carr was sympathetic to Marxism but was not a Marxist. He chronicled Marxism but did not fully understand it. It was this ambiguity which allowed him to play the role he did in the Cold War, standing opposed to the Cold Warriors, while not being part of the socialist movement, while being tolerant of Stalinism though not being a Stalinist himself.

Carr and the Cold War – again

We can now revert in more precise form to the question of Carr's role in the Cold War. Carr was an intellectual in the sense that he took ideas seriously and tried to develop them in a critical way, which necessarily involves criticizing the old order – in this instance capitalism. However, he did not do so directly, neither did he support a coherent alternative viewpoint. Rather he was much like an artist who produces art as he sees it. In so far as art is good art, it necessarily criticizes the deficiencies of society around it. The artist may not understand that he is doing that, the ordinary viewer may not understand it either but the critique remains.

Cold War intellectuals like Labedz and Pipes were never intellectuals but bureaucrats of knowledge, if not worse. They derived many benefits from supporting the status quo. This is not to say that they were not right on many factual issues pertaining to the Cold War, but instead of using their knowledge to support change in the West they preferred to support the establishment, of which they became stars.

Their interpretations of the actions of the Bolsheviks in particular were misanthropic to the point of lunacy. All great revolutions have to be declared non-revolutionary by the establishment. Such was the fate of the French Revolution and such is the current attitude towards the Russian Revolution. The revolution must be shown to be a failure, the revolutionaries must be shown to have been fallible human beings, as corrupt as possible, and if not corrupt then sadistic. This is an easy exercise, much indulged in by such as Volkogonov and following him

Pipes. It is interesting that Carr himself fell into the category of those to be subjected to the same treatment, in his case by Norman Stone.

Academics who follow this trend may do so for the best of motives. They find evidence in archives showing the murderous nature of one or other revolutionary and publish the results in respectable journals. That they are able to publish those results, while others, who have contrary opinions on the same evidence, is not accidental. Everyone has to survive, and the publish or perish culture in which we live produces particular kinds of academics. They may be honest by their own lights, but they are dishonest judged by history. The venal nature of many writers and academics is partly unconscious but the distortion remains.

Those who struggle against the tide and try to establish the truth to the best of their ability are intellectuals, even if they are muddled. In this sense, Carr was an intellectual. But at the same time he had access to journals such as the *TLS* and so was part of an academic establishment. But what are we to make of his attitude towards Bakunin?[27] He shows clearly that Marx was right against Bakunin, that Bakunin was anti-Semitic, and that he endorsed the monstrosities of Nechaev; yet he still sees him as a liberated free spirit. Carr was a contradictory liberal, whose subjective understanding of history was more limited than what flowed from his own writings. Put more positively, Carr had a grasp of history which went beyond his own theoretical comprehension.

Carr's influence on the Cold War was, therefore, all the greater. He could not be accused of being a Communist or a Marxist. He could only be accused of being soft on the Soviet Union.

E.H. Carr, the Cold War, Soviet Studies and the Influence of his Work[28]

We can now categorize E.H. Carr in this context. In my view, we can divide Soviet Studies into seven schools of thought.

1. On the Right we have the Cold War warriors such as Pipes and Solzhenitsyn who saw the USSR as a monolith which could not change except from the outside, yet it threatened to take over the world. Lenin, naturally, was a monster and Trotsky was also a monster who had the additional defect of being a loser.
2. Still on the Right were the CIA 'intellectuals' who were the 'liberal warriors' who stood for civil rights, even though the CIA itself had no trouble ignoring human rights when necessary. *Encounter* belonged to this category. This group saw the Soviet system in

change. The CIA like the KGB knew the facts about the Soviet Union. They knew that it was fundamentally weak and thus no serious competitor for the United States.

3. Some academics, such as those engaged in the Harvard Project, who were funded by the military, fell into this category but in a subset of their own, in so far as they adopted a less hysterical and more analytical approach.

4. In this category were those people who wanted to be fair to both sides. These were usually liberals in Europe, who could see the deleterious effects of the Cold War in their own countries and preferred to see gradual reforms in the USSR. Alec Nove was part of this tendency. By and large they were part of the academic establishment but not of the ruling class. Often social democrats, they tended to look for the positive aspects in the Soviet Union, while not ignoring the crimes committed there. Many British academics fitted into this category partly because it was, by and large, the attitude adopted within Europe by a section of the establishment.

5. Moving to the Left, we had more left-wing academics and writers such as Deutscher who looked at the USSR as a workers' state which had gone wrong. He tended to interpret Trotsky in a more liberal light, so allowing him to see the USSR in a less critical way. None the less, although writers in this category overlapped with the previous group, they were distinct in seeing the USSR as somehow a deformed form of socialism.

6. Still further to the Left we have had writers (including this author) and the *Critique* School who saw nothing positive in the USSR after the 1920s. Stalinism was an historical abortion which has delayed the move to socialism by a century or more. It was a system though not a mode of production. This school had the advantage of arguing that the Soviet Union was unviable.

7. Various other schools took a more charitable view of the USSR, but rejected the view that it was socialist and saw little in it that had advanced humanity. Such were the various state capitalist viewpoints and indeed the bureaucratic mode of production school.[29] The problem with the arguments of these schools was that they were often produced a priori, without knowledge of the Soviet Union, and really only using the subject of the Soviet Union in order to further their own political agenda.

Where did E.H. Carr fit in these categories? Clearly he was not a Marxist or a Cold War warrior and so did not fit into categories 1, 2 or 5. That leaves him between Isaac Deutscher and Alec Nove. He was a liberal who went beyond liberalism and did his best to portray events as he saw them. He was wrong on the nature of the Soviet Union and in so far as he did not have a category of a free capitalism on the one side or of socialism-communism on the other, he did not have the theoretical categories to understand events in their world historic context. There will be those who would want to argue that he did not need such categories. The duty of the scholar is to simply paint the canvas as he sees it. No self-respecting and genuine scholar (as opposed to the bureaucrats of knowledge) can actually believe this. It does not even square with Carr's understanding of history. The theoretical assumptions made in depicting ideas or movements are absolutely crucial for the production of the painting.

Carr tended to take the ideas of the protagonists as the ideas that he needed to work with. Hence his portrait of Trotsky is not unfair. But then his portrait of Stalin may not be unfair to Stalin, but it is unfair to the people of the Soviet Union and mankind. It has been suggested that the problem with Carr was that he was a Hegelian, who, therefore, worshipped authority. This is a misinterpretation of both Hegel and Carr, but it is misinterpretation that has a grain of truth.

Carr then sits between Nove and Deutscher in academia, somewhere between those who took a liberal social democratic attitude to the USSR and those who took an attitude at once more critical and more favourable. In the context of the Cold War, this made Carr an enemy of the Cold War warriors. It also put him together with Deutscher as an icon of the Left.

E.H. Carr's Place in History after the Cold War

E.H. Carr's works are very much part of the Cold War and we have to ask the question of whether his works can survive it or what place his work will have in history. His multi-volume history of the Russian Revolution is his testament to humanity. His work on the Russian Revolution down to 1927 or so, as opposed to his writings on Stalinism and its rise, which form a part of his History, has its own influence.

There have been many attacks on the Russian Revolution, from the day when it was consummated. The viciousness of the attacks, like those in *The Times*, which said that it could not last even a short time, are a tribute to its success. The Russian Revolution overthrew the capitalist order on a world scale and by winning the civil war it showed that it was not just an idea but a material reality. However, the Revolution could be damned in a number of ways.

One way was to declare it evil in both intention and deed. Such is the view of Pipes, Schapiro and the most virulent Cold War warriors. This doctrine never worked. It could not work because Marxism is so much a humanist doctrine that it makes no sense to attribute bad motives to the protagonists. Clearly Carr did not go along with this.

Another tack is to say that Lenin and Trotsky were undemocratic, who believed that the end justifies the means and were only involved in politics for self-aggrandisement. Volkogonov and others have adopted this line and it was a common viewpoint during the Cold War.

A third view is to argue that 1917 was a wrong policy and that the Bolsheviks were caught up in their own mistakes. This is more or less a Menshevik argument.

For millions the world over, however, the spectacle of a revolution in the name of human emancipation was itself liberating. Honest intellectuals, ordinary peasants and workers welcomed the revolution and continue to do so. The constant abuse, distortions of history and general vilification of the Russian Revolution has only served to intensify its importance. Carr's history helped to provide the empirical detail to support this viewpoint.

Hence, looked at from the perspective of those who reject the concept of socialism itself, the Russian Revolution could only be brought to earth with a more prosaic form of attack. This was particularly important with the waning of the influence of the Cold War and in the post-Cold War period. This is where Orlando Figes' book serves its purpose.

He has written a book which stands in competition with E.H. Carr's work on the revolution. He has three differences which highlight the importance of Carr's work. In the first place, his work is almost novel-like in ascribing motives and telling stories, often without footnotes. Thus he attributes Trotsky's failure to take power against Stalin to Trotsky's fear of losing the battle. He then produces a story of Trotsky losing his temper over a chess match, when in New York, years earlier. This behaviour he finds typical of Trotsky, without any evidence. While he footnotes the chess match he cannot footnote the generalization. He is entitled to his psychological assumptions and his psycho-history but the political goals and known political behaviour of Trotsky provide us with a better understanding of his actions.[30]

In the second place, he calls his work a social or popular history but there is no understanding of mass psychology or the needs or wishes of the masses. Instead he emphasizes the use of terror. He gives particular importance to the killing of the Imperial family as marking a declaration of terror. In fact, he argues the terror really began with the taking of power itself, so his argument becomes monarchist. At this point he attacks Carr for not paying more attention to the liquidation of the Imperial family.[31]

In the third place, he has a strong anti-Marxist bias but with little understanding of Marxism. Thus, for instance, he declares that Lenin was inherently anti-democratic and opposed to the Soviets. He argues that Lenin's concept of the dictatorship of the proletariat in State and Revolution argues for a strong and repressive party-state. He contrasts his view with that of E.H. Carr, whom he views as seeing 'Western democratic state as inherently authoritarian and the Soviet regime as inherently democratic'.[32] He is not just anti-Leninist but anti-Marxist because it was Marx who used the term, the dictatorship of the proletariat, and Marx, like Lenin, did mean the suppression of the rights of the bourgeoisie in this process, but neither Marx nor Lenin conceived of the process as one in which the proletariat was also disenfranchised. The fact that Lenin, unlike Trotsky, distrusted the Soviets in October 1917, was a tactical not a political viewpoint. It is inherent in Marxism that the population should be enabled to rule themselves at every level.

Figes, therefore, appears as an opponent of Carr and so brings into stark relief Carr's very strengths. Carr did not fictionalize or trivialize. He was not a monarchist; and he understood the Marxist concept of emancipation. Figes' pedestrian analysis cannot catch the real meaning of the revolution. This is where Carr comes in. His works on the Russian Revolution have become twinned with those of Isaac Deutscher as having a profound influence on the post-war generation. Deutscher had the theoretical categories of Marxism and the understanding of the final goal, whereas Carr provided more of the fine detail required for students to understand that reality. Their combined influence cannot be underestimated. For many, Deutscher's books have been an introduction to Marxism, but with his concentration on the Russian Revolution, Carr is inevitably, the next port of call.

Conclusion

In conclusion, therefore, Carr played a complex role in a complex society. He provided a respectability for left-wing scholars engaged in the study of the Russian Revolution and the Soviet Union. He played a particular role in the Cold War, as a result. On the one hand, his more favourable view of the Soviet Union gave some support to Stalinism,

160 *Hillel Ticktin*

while on the other, his earlier and more historical work undermined Stalinism in so far as it showed the disparity between the original goals of the revolution and the reality under Stalinism. So on the one hand he stood with the Stalinists against the Cold Warriors, while on the other he helped, however unconsciously, together with Deutscher, to challenge Stalinism and so helped undermine the Cold War itself.

Notes

1 Jonathan Haslam, *Vices of Integrity: E.H. Carr, 1892–1982* (London: Verso, 1999).
2 The more offensive attacks on Carr more recently have been made by Daniel Johnson, 'Cold-blooded Colossus', *Daily Telegraph*, 31 July 1999, Noel Malcolm, 'History Served Chilled', *The Sunday Telegraph*, 1 August 1999, Norman Stone, 'Horrible History Man', *The Spectator*, 4 September 1999, Richard Pipes, 'A Very Cold Fish', *Times Literary Supplement*, 10 September 1999.
3 Tamara Deutscher, 'E.H. Carr – A Personal Memoir', *New Left Review*, No. 137 (January–February 1983), p. 84.
4 See Isaac Deutscher's comments quoted in Haslam, *Vices of Integrity*, p. 205.
5 For my analysis of the former USSR see Hillel Ticktin, *Origins of the Crisis in the USSR* (Armonk: Myron Sharpe, 1992).
6 See M. Cox, 'The Cold War as a System', *Critique*, No. 17, 1986, pp. 17–82.
7 Isaac Deutscher, *The Great Contest* (Oxford: Oxford University Press, 1960).
8 E.H. Carr, 'Stalin Victorious', in F. Mount, ed., *Communism* (London: Harvill, 1992) pp. 83–92.
9 Alec Nove put the point in a rather cruder form in defending Carr against Labedz: 'It is simply preposterous to assert that Carr and Deutscher shared a common interpretation of Soviet history or to regard Carr as marxist-inspired.' Quoted in Mount, *Communism*, p. 217.
10 E.H. Carr, *What is History?*, second edition (Harmondsworth: Penguin, 1987).
11 Norman Stone, 'Grim Eminence', *London Review of Books*, 20 January 1983, pp. 3–8. What made Stone's critique particularly unpleasant was its personal attack on E.H. Carr after his death. Moreover, by making it personal, the argument about Carr being too uncritical of the Soviet Union was lost.
12 Mount, *Communism*, pp. 217, 210–11 and 216–17.
13 E.H. Carr, *Bolshevik Revolution, Vol. 2* (London: Penguin, 1966), pp. 284–6.
14 R. Pipes, *Russia under the Bolshevik Regime, 199–1924* (London: Harper Collins, 1994), p. 410, footnote.
15 *Ibid.*
16 *Soviet Studies* Vol. 1, No. 1. The first issue of *Soviet Studies* in June 1949 declared in its editorial that it would neither attack nor defend the USSR (p. 2). The contributors were all well known for their past or present association with the Communist Party – with the exception of E.H. Carr – and included Rudolf Schlesinger, Jack and Molly Miller, and Maurice Dobb. The essay by E.H. Carr, in that issue, follows the line of the editorial on Soviet Foreign Policy and thereby produces a continuity between Lenin and Stalin. Four years later, the editorial is written by E.H. Carr on the death of Stalin.

While it is nuanced, it is undoubtedly pro-Stalin. He concludes that 'it is perhaps in the role of Peter the Great that history will best remember him. Paradoxically, posterity may yet learn to speak of Stalin as the great westernizer' *Soviet Studies*, July 1953, p. 7.

17   L. Labedz quoted in Mount, *Communism*, pp. 189–209 (*TLS*, 10 June, 1983)
18   *Ibid.*, p. 196.
19   *Ibid.*, p. 198.
20   L. Schapiro, 'Totalitarianism in the Doghouse', in Leonard Schapiro, ed., *Political Opposition in One Party States* (London: Macmillan, 1972), p. 276.
21   E.H. Carr, *Michael Bakunin* (London: Macmillan, 1937), p. 440.
22   E. Hobsbawn quoted in Mount, *Communism*. According to Hobsbawm: 'The history of Marxism among intellectuals is therefore largely a history of their relationship with the Communist Parties . . .'. p. 114.
23   Mount, *Communism*, pp. 124–6.
24   *Ibid.*
25   He discusses the concept of abstract labour but in a wholly muddled way. See Mount, *Communism*, p. 124.
26   R.W. Davies, From E.H. Carr's files: Notes towards a second edition, of *What is History?*, pp. 177–82.
27   According to Carr, 'Bakunin is one of the completest embodiments in history of the spirit of liberty.' *Michael Bakunin*, p. 440.
28   See my 'Soviet Studies and the Collapse of the USSR: In Defence of Marxism', in Michael Cox *Rethinking the Soviet Collapse: Sovietology, the Death of Communism and the New Russia* (London: Cassell, 1998), pp. 73–94.
29   See for instance the work of T. Cliff (Yigael Gluckstein) and Max Shachtman and their followers.
30   O. Figes, *A People's Tragedy, The Russian Revolution 1891–1924* (London: Jonathan Cape, 1996), pp. 802–3.
31   'E.H. Carr, for example, gave it no more than a single sentence in a three-volume history of the revolution. This is to miss the deeper significance of the murder. It was a declaration of the Terror. It was a statement that from now on individuals would count for nothing in the civil war.' Figes, p. 641.
32   *Ibid.*, p. 465 He says: 'It is interesting how many Marxists of Deutscher's generation (E.H. Carr comes immediately to mind) were inclined to see the Western democratic system as inherently authoritarian and the Soviet regime as inherently democratic. . . .'

III
International Relations

8
Carr and his Early Critics: Responses to *The Twenty Years' Crisis*, 1939–46

Peter Wilson

It is an interesting but little known fact that although E.H. Carr's *The Twenty Years' Crisis* is generally regarded to have had a devastating impact on the 'utopian' thinking of the inter-war period, the utopians themselves, or at any rate those so labelled by Carr, did not feel particularly devastated by it. Norman Angell and Alfred Zimmern, two of Carr's chief 'utopian' targets, wrote highly critical reviews of the book, and although he did not, to my knowledge, publish his thoughts on the subject, Arnold Toynbee, Carr's other major living target, agreed whole heartedly with what his utopian fellow travellers had to say. In addition, a number of thinkers not specifically indicted by Carr felt sufficiently wounded by his remarks to write lengthy replies. Among them can be counted a distinguished moral philosopher, Susan Stebbing, and a fellow man of the Left who shared many of Carr's ideas about the 'New Society', the Fabian and Bloomsburyite, Leonard Woolf. Other less than convinced respondents included the historian, R.W. Seton-Watson and, writing under a pseudonym, Richard Crossman, future government minister and political diarist, then a Labour local councillor and a journalist on the *New Statesman*.

The argument I want to make in this chapter is that although none of Carr's early critics produced a systematic and comprehensive critique of *The Twenty Years' Crisis* – such a critique is perhaps impossible given the tremendous complexity and range of the work – many of their objections and observations are valid. To this extent, it is regrettable that their views have been largely neglected in the secondary literature on Carr, and the broader literature on the history of international theory: this in spite of the fact that one of the great luminaries of the discipline, Martin Wight, recommended that Carr's 'brilliant, provocative and unsatisfying book' should not be read without Leonard Woolf's 'deadly reply' in *The War for Peace*.[1]

This neglect has led, I think, to an unbalanced and largely uncritical reading of this, perhaps the most influential of Carr's texts. Many students and teachers of the subject have been dazzled by Carr's rhetorical brilliance and have failed to recognize the deep flaws in his argument. They would not, I feel, have been quite so dazzled had they read Carr alongside his critics rather than in isolation from them. This is not to say that the 'utopians' were right and Carr wrong. To the present-day reader, far removed from the emotional intensity and sense of impending doom of the early war years, Woolf's book, for instance, does not read as anything like as deadly as Wight deemed it to be in the 1940s. It is to say, however, that a fuller and more rounded appreciation of Carr's remarkable text can be gained by taking into account the lively debate it provoked.

First, a few words on the scope of this chapter. Although fascinating, I will not examine the broader historiography of the book, from Morgenthau through Johnston and Bull to W.T.R. Fox and Michael Joseph Smith: this would require an article, at least, in itself. Nor will I say anything about the reception of the second edition of the book in 1946. My concern here is with the immediate reaction to the first edition – from those explicitly accused of utopianism, from those who felt they had been found guilty by association, and from those who felt they had escaped the charge but none the less had serious misgivings about the analysis.

Practical Impact

A consistently expressed fear of Carr's early critics was that the book would have – or had the potential to have – a damaging effect on Britain's ability to effectively prosecute the war against Nazi Germany. Angell wrote to Zimmern that 'the net influence of the book in so far as it has influence, is mischievous, since it is an attempt to justify a do-nothing-ism and over-caution on the part of those who have offended from these tendencies.' The general impression Carr gave was one of 'moral nihilism'. This was worrying in itself, but particularly so given Carr's recent appointment as Director of the Foreign Division of the Ministry of Information.[2] In a letter to Philip Noel-Baker, Angell went further, describing the book as 'completely mischievous a piece of sophisticated moral nihilism'.[3] In his published article on *The Twenty Years' Crisis*, he even suggested that Carr's theory that law, order and peace were not general interests but merely the particular interests of the rich and the powerful – and that 'collective security' and 'resistance to aggression' were merely slogans designed to help them maintain their privileged position – gave 'aid and comfort in about equal degree to the followers of Marx and the followers of Hitler'. Moreover, if it were true (fortunately it was not) it provided a 'veritable gold mine' for Dr Goebbels.[4]

Zimmern agreed with Angell that because of its moral nihilism the book would not have a good influence. It was more than a little peculiar, he felt, 'that the man who wrote the second sentence on p. 289 should be in charge of our foreign publicity'.[5] But Zimmern was not quite so alarmed as Angell. He did not think it inconceivable that 'the poacher can function as game keeper somehow'. Moreover, Carr's 'vogue' would not last long: there was 'not enough substance to him'. It was true that from the angle of his Foreign Office experience, Carr had something worthwhile to say, and he could have written a 'useful critical essay'. 'But some devil at his elbow persuaded him to write something that resembled a small treatise and to deck it out with a sociological theory, drawn apparently from Mannheim' – though it could be doubted whether 'the latter would acknowledge his child'. The result was 'a confusion beneath a surface of *fausse clarté*'.[6]

But these words did little to soothe Angell's nerves, and a few months later, as promised in letters to Zimmern and Toynbee, he published a book, significantly under the title *Why Freedom Matters*, in which he enlarged on many of the points he had made earlier. The thrust of the book was that the moral indifference peddled by Carr and his ilk, their disparagement of reason, their contempt for liberty and liberalism, was a disaster for the democracies and a boon for Hitler.

Angell began by noting the growth in recent years of 'a whole literature expressive of pessimism, defeatism, moral nihilism':

> The intellectual liberties for which Voltaire in France, and Locke and Mill in Britain fought so insistently as the very foundations of the good life, the guarantee of the moral values of a free society, have been systematically belittled by certain modern writers who have laboriously used reason to prove that reason cannot be trusted; and have maintained campaigns against liberty and liberalism, campaigns that would have not been possible but for the liberty and liberalism they would destroy.

Into the service of this doctrine of the unimportance of reason were pressed 'new readings of the old Calvinistic Predestination'.[7] Such thinking attuned men's minds 'to cruelties, ferocities, horrors, as something imposed by fate and nature, something for which man has no moral responsibility, which he cannot prevent'. Indeed, the doctrine of pre-ordained fate has hardened in much modern writing into an almost oriental fatalism, the sense that man cannot use his intelligence and the power of his mind to make his world decent and tolerable; cannot do appreciably better than he has done, cannot bring about, without recurrent killings, ferocities, hatreds, cruelties, and abominations, the changes which every living society must make. The possibility of peaceful change seems to be rejected as naive Utopianism by the 'realists' who insist that man is the helpless puppet of forces beyond his control.

Moreover, quite a number of those who were 'at this moment actually in charge of the task of informing the public mind about the purposes of the war' had expressed in public their conviction that 'the ideals for which we are supposed to be fighting are irrealisable ideals, shams and pretences.' This, Angell forlornly concluded, 'hardly seems a happy augury for making our next victory less barren of the things it aims at than the last proved to be'.[8]

Such thinly veiled attacks soon gave way to a more direct approach. Carr's book, Angell exclaimed in a chapter belligerently entitled 'Hitler's Intellectual Allies in Britain', showed just how far the 'fashionable disparagement of the principle of liberty and its allied principle of law' had gone. Toynbee's view, for example, that 'international law and order were in the true interests of the whole of mankind, whereas the desire to perpetuate the reign of violence in international affairs was an anti-social desire which was not even in the ultimate interests of the citizens of the handful of states that officially professed this benighted and anachronistic creed', was condemned by Carr as 'compounded of platitude and falsehood in about equal parts'. It was a 'familiar tactic of the privileged', Carr said, 'to throw moral discredit on the under-privileged by depicting them as disturbers of the peace'; and throughout the book he repeated the view that being in favour of peace merely meant that 'you want to keep that you've got'. Thus:

Just as the ruling class in a community prays for domestic peace which guarantees its own security and predominance and denounces class war which might threaten them, so international peace becomes a special vested interest of the predominant Powers.

And:

There can be no such thing as a common or collective resistance to aggression, nor is it any more moral to resist aggression than to commit it, for readiness to fight to prevent change is just as unmoral as readiness to fight to enforce it.

All the high-falutin' talk about fighting for peace and the interests of mankind was, therefore, so much bunk. The 'privileged' democracies were fighting for their own interests as against the interests of the 'under-privileged' totalitarian states. There were no interests of mankind. No general interests. Talk of such interests was revealed, on analysis, 'as the transparent disguise of selfish vested interest'. The supposedly absolute and universal principles of President Wilson, M. Briand, Mr Eden, and their utopian followers, were not principles at all, but merely 'the unconscious reflexions of national policy based on a particular interpretation of national interest at a particular time'.[9]

It was no coincidence, Angell continued, that Carr was 'as sceptical of the possibility, or the desirability, of liberty of opinion' as he was of 'the possibility of an international order ensuring peace'.

> Opinion [Carr claimed], like trade and industry, should according to the old liberal conception be allowed to flow in its own natural channels without artificial regulation. This conception has broken down on the hard fact that in modern conditions opinion, like trade, is not and cannot be exempt from artificial controls.

Not only was public opinion 'wrong-headed', but Carr strongly implied that it could not be otherwise.

All this added up to profound pessimism about the very purposes for which Britain was supposed to be fighting the war: 'future security and peace by means of the co-operation of many states making common cause against aggression'. It may turn out that Carr was right, that co-operation of this kind was 'foolish Utopianism':

> But if the public as a whole shared his view we should lose this war, for we should be fighting for a cause in which we did not believe against an enemy with a cause, an evil cause, in which that enemy did believe – believed passionately, and so believing is prepared to fight fiercely, as men have so often fought with passionate conviction and heroic self-sacrifice for causes that are mistaken and evil.

In addition, was it right, Angell asked, to appoint a man of such views to direct the presentation of Britain's case to the outside world? This act involved a great deal more than the making of an inappropriate appointment. It implied, taken in conjunction with several other appointments of a similar kind, that those in positions of authority did 'not attach importance to intellectual conviction of the rightness of the cause for which we fight'; did not perhaps 'regard convictions, ideas, opinions as of much consequence in relation to war'.

The state of mind of the so-called realist was, therefore, extremely defeatist. But this defeatism was not rooted in a recognition of material deficiencies, for it was plain that the material resources of the victims of aggression were, at least potentially, far superior to those of the aggressors. On the contrary, the defeatism of the realists was rooted in the conviction that 'the intellectual and the moral resources of the Allies are insufficient for combining, assembling, and mobilising the power they possess'. The pessimism of the realists was, thus, an extreme kind which said: 'Obviously, the thing could be done if men would will it, but they won't will it.'

It was precisely this defeatist attitude, Angell contended, which created the very absence of will that was invoked as justification for the initial pessimism. An example given by William James, in his famous defence of pragmatism, was instructive:

> I am climbing in the mountains and work myself into such a position that I cannot get back, and can only save myself by jumping a chasm. Can I do it? If I decide that I can, the decision gives me confidence, I make proper preparation, succeed, and my success is scientific proof, that of the event, that my decision was correct. But if I had decided the contrary, that I could not do it, had launched myself in desperation without preparation, and failed, my death would have been proof by the event that my decision was justified. The difference between success and failure depended upon the degree of faith and so, of will.

Sceptics would proclaim, of course, that if the chasm had been much wider, faith and will could have made no difference: the climber would have been confronted with a material fact that no amount of such resources could overcome. But this was not, Angell insisted, the situation facing the Allies. Given their overwhelming material superiority, the whole problem was a moral one:

> Have we the wisdom and intellectual capacity to combine and co-operate? Are we capable of rationalism sufficient to direct and dominate the nationalist impulses and instincts which stand in the way of

several states combining for defence? Can we overcome such obstacles to a defensive confederation?

The problem was purely one of will. This was why the views propagated by Professor Carr and his ilk were so damaging.[10]

All this fashionable 'realism' was thus, to cite the title of another of
Angell's chapters, 'The Way of Defeat'. For what did the realist say? He
said that man will always be guided by his instincts and passions. To
think otherwise, to think that man could be guided by reason, was sheer
utopianism. Reason, he asserted, was merely the process by which
actions prompted by instincts were justified. Law and morality were
merely rationalizations of selfish interests.

This was the thrust of so much recent political thinking: the 'revolt
against reason', 'anti-rationalism', 'realism'. And such thinking was not
confined to the ivory towers of philosophers. What such writers said
learnedly, and with academic distinction, the popular press shouted
loudly, without distinction, the result being xenophobia, nationalism,
jingoism, isolationism and a profound disbelief in the possibility or
desirability of international co-operation.

This was exactly what Hitler wanted. He knew that as long as the lesser
states remained incapable of combination against him, triumph would
be his. He knew, moreover, that

> so long as the old irrational tribalism dominates the relationship of
> European states they *will* remain disunited, and that he will be able to
> dominate them; that the fierce nationalism which serves the purpose
> of Germany will so disunite his enemies as to enable him to destroy
> them in detail; that if, in other words, irrationalism must dominate
> rationality in international politics, the future is his. . . . [11]

Prescriptive Value

Allied to the damaging effect they feared it would have on the current
political situation, Carr's critics also felt that his book had limited prescriptive value: it provided little guidance as to the kind of world it was
desirable, and feasible, to create or to the kind of policies that could be
employed to best bring it about.

In Zimmern's view, Carr's concluding chapter on 'The Prospects of a
New International Order' provided no more than a 'dim outline' adding
little to what he had said in the main body of the book. Moreover, what
he did say was undermined by his 'thorough-going relativism'. The

strength of the attack on absolute values, Zimmern continued, had always, from Aristotle onwards, resided in demonstrating that values 'drawn from a deeper realm' had been misapplied, *not* in denying their existence. But if it was true that no such values existed – 'if justice and liberty, courage and self-sacrifice, mercy and decency, right and wrong [were] only matters of ephemeral convention' – then the student of international relations was left in a state of 'blank frustration'. How could he find the requisite courage and determination to build something that was 'no more than a temporarily plausible conclusion'? The values required to promote the good life as it could be lived under twentieth century conditions could not be evoked, he insisted,

> by running away from the notion of good because it is liable to misuse by the ignorant, the muddle-headed and the ill-intentioned or by refusing to admit that one foreign policy or one national tradition or one political cause can be 'better' than another.[12]

Toynbee agreed. Carr, he said, was 'a consummate debunker', and if debunking were all that one needed his book would have been a 'very important contribution to the study of recent international affairs'. But debunking, however necessary and salutary, was only the preface to the real job, not the job itself. Carr left one 'in a moral vacuum and at a political dead point'. Debunking was barren unless it lead 'to a clearer view of what is morally right and wrong and what is politically destructive or disastrous'.[13]

R.W. Seton-Watson went further. It was, he said, 'incredible' that in Carr's 'long and brilliantly reasoned' chapter on international morality, the Church and the issue of religion did not arise once. To discuss morality in international politics without any consideration of Christian ethics or the Christian faith was, indeed, 'simply farcical'. Carr's assertion, in particular, that whatever the moral issue, the clash between the satisfied and the dissatisfied Powers was one in which power politics were equally predominant on both sides, amounted to an attitude of 'pagan negation'. It was just this negative attitude, coupled with his rejection of permanent values, which dominated the whole book. Unsurprisingly, when it came to putting forward a 'constructive programme', Carr had no foundations on which to build. World federation and 'a more perfect League of Nations' were dismissed as 'elegant superstructures'. The idea of an international union of democracies was dismissed in a single sentence. The cause of small states was implicitly abandoned as hopeless. And Carr offered little in their place but vague assertions about 'digging foundations', 'economic reconstruction', and 'the frank acceptance of [the subordination of] economic advantage to social ends'.[14]

Seton-Watson was not the only commentator to find Carr's 'constructive programme' disappointing. Norman Angell, while applauding the positive role Carr gave to utopianism in such statements as 'every political situation contains mutually incompatible elements of Utopia and Reality, of morality and power', commented:

> But we are left in the dark as to the manner in which, and the proportions in which, we are to mix our utopianism and realism in order to escape the strictures so freely levelled in this book.[15]

Even one of Carr's most enthusiastic reviewers found his general balancing act between power and morality, which lay at the heart of his conception of peaceful change, less than entirely helpful in the absence of more precise guidance as to the point at which 'concessions to new pretensions to power must be resisted lest the positions of the strong and the one-time weak should be reversed'.[16]

Yet in the opinion of nearly all of Carr's critics the final proof of the inadequacy of his outlook was the support he gave for a policy which had been entirely discredited by the time the book was published: appeasement. For Toynbee, the strangest thing about the book was the fact that 'the debunker himself had been decisively debunked by the outbreak of war'. Hitler's method of 'bluffing his way along by threats backed by armaments – which Carr held up as 'a normal part of the process of peaceful change' – had not resulted in peace but war. One of two conclusions flowed from this. Either this method was not, after all, 'calculated to produce peaceful change . . . but was heading for war as the Utopians foretold'. Or that:

> Munich, Prague, and the invasion of Poland ought not to have led to a general war between the Great Powers and that the present disaster is not Hitler's fault, but Mr Chamberlain's for abandoning Hitler's and Carr's principles and inexcusably turning Utopian.[17]

Toynbee took more than a little pleasure in pointing out that the second conclusion corresponded precisely to the line that Goebbels had been taking ever since the war broke out: i.e. that the Western Powers had foolishly converted a colonial war – a war of conquest against weak, backward, unimportant Eastern European states – into a European war.

Even those who welcomed much of what Carr had to say found his support for appeasement difficult to accept. Richard Crossman strongly commended Carr's exposure of the liberal fallacy of the sovereignty of law, morality and the popular will, and their 'airy neglect of the significance of power'. He similarly praised Carr's account of the enervating effect of utopian ideology on the will of the victorious Powers, who instead of using their power in defence of the *status quo*, or for the accomplishment of peaceful change, engaged in 'unilateral psychological disarmament'. But *The Twenty Years' Crisis*, as with that other masterpiece of power analysis, *The Leviathan*, led to practical conclusions that were already out of date by the time they were made. Carr's exposure of utopianism had led him to 'whole-hearted' support of appeasement, and the 'realistic' admission that since the balance of power had shifted, way must be made for Hitler. But this was to assume that Nazi Germany and Soviet Russia were nation-states on the nineteenth-century model, and that Hitler was simply a 'modern Bismarck'. Such an assumption, however, was an 'illusion as profound as that of Professors Zimmern and Toynbee'. In Crossman's view, the paramount fact of the age was the transformation, not only of nineteenth-century ideologies, but of nineteenth-century power. Nazi Germany and Soviet Russia were not simply new versions of the old model, but 'new forms of political and economic organisation which threaten to supersede the old order of national sovereignty'.

> We are witnessing [he concluded] the birth-pangs of a new world, and in order to take part in its shaping we must get rid not only of our old Utopias but of our old realism. Professor Carr has shown the entire inadequacy of Professors Zimmern and Toynbee. Who will demonstrate the entire inadequacy of Professor Carr?[18]

Errors of Interpretation

As to be expected, a number of Carr's early critics strongly disagreed with his interpretation of various episodes and events, and also with his interpretation of certain ideas and opinions that they, and others, supposedly held. Angell objected to Carr's assertion, on which rested a large part of his theoretical apparatus, that supporters of the League of Nations tried 'to apply to Twentieth Century conditions the principles of the Nineteenth Century *laissez-faire* philosophy'. *Laissez-faire*, Angell pointed out, was the absence of government in economic affairs: 'the assumption that individual economic relationships will work out to the common good if left to themselves without control, rules, authority.' To say, however, that a similar belief applied to the political relations between states was the idea which inspired the authors of the Covenant of the League was 'to turn the truth upside down'. The Covenant, Angell contended, was created precisely because its authors believed that political *laissez-faire* in the relations between states would no longer work, and that collective action was needed 'to ensure at least the basis of organised society namely, the defence, security, self preservation of its constituent members'. The League was not based on *laissez-faire* but, on the contrary, represented a movement away from it in the direction of 'government, rules of the road, collectivism'. Nor, since it recognized the need for cooperative action against violators of the rules, did it assume the existence of a 'natural' harmony of interests. Yet this was the belief that Carr repeatedly attributed to the League's supporters.[19]

Similarly, Carr asserted that the utopians were guilty of 'facile optimism' in assuming that there were no fundamental conflicts between states, and that peace could be maintained 'without sacrifice', 'without assuming onerous obligations or risks', 'by quite minor day-to-day adjustments', and by 'the maintenance of a friendly atmosphere'. The realists, on the other hand, fully recognized the 'gulf in outlook, moral values, interest, and philosophy' which separated the democratic, *status quo*, Powers from the totalitarian, revisionist, Powers. They faced head-on the inadequacy of mere day-to-day diplomatic adjustment and accepted the need for sacrifice, obligations, and risk as the unavoidable price of peace.[20]

Yet when applied to actual, day-to-day, politics these abstractions resulted in a curious reading of events. Carr's utopians were Robert Cecil, Gilbert Murray, W. Arnold-Foster and other prominent members of the League of Nations Union (LNU). His realists were Chamberlain and the 'appeasers' in his Cabinet. On this matter Carr had been explicit: before its radical shift (towards collective security) in March 1939, Chamberlain's policy, Carr said, 'represented a reaction of realism against utopianism'. But it had been the 'utopians' not the 'realists' who from 1932 onwards had insisted that the gulf between the totalitarian states and the democracies was vast; that the former were challenging 'a principle of international life indispensable to our own security'; that if action was not taken to defend this, the democracies themselves would sooner or later 'become the victim of its violation'; and 'that it would be better to take the risks of defending it in the early stages of the challenge... than be compelled to defend it when the risks might have become so very much greater.' By contrast it was the 'realists' not the 'utopians' who maintained, even as late as ten days before the invasion of Czechoslovakia, that the nation 'could now... settle down to a long period of peace'; who berated the LNU as 'fanatical war mongers' and 'jitterbugs'; who proposed to give to the Government powers 'to curb those newspapers and writers who wilfully disturbed the public's peace of mind by professing to see the likelihood of war'. For Angell, clearly, it was the 'utopians', not the 'realists', who were the real realists – even in terms of Carr's own definitions.

Angell also felt that Carr's core claim that law, order, peace, collective security, free trade, etc., were not universal interests but the special interests of the dominant powers, was not borne out by the course of events. It was when Britain was in a position of weakness and peril, not strength and predominance, that she turned, in March 1939, away from nationalism and appeasement and towards internationalism and collective security. Russia had joined the League when she felt threatened by Japan; only after she had added immensely to her power did she leave it to pursue a 'career of conquest'. America's isolationism and rejection of collective security was a function not of her insecurity but of her security. As soon as she felt threatened she would turn away from the former towards the latter – as she had done in 1917. These facts suggested that there was little correlation between the 'Haves' and collective security on the one hand, and the 'Have Nots' and nationalism and isolationism on the other.[21]

In the same vein, Leonard Woolf took exception to the implication of Carr's analysis that there was something intrinsic to states and their relations that gave their power and conflicting interests a peculiar reality over and above their cooperation and common interests. The doctrine that certain national interests possessed a peculiar reality was one of a number of recent doctrines in which

> interests are treated just as natural rights were regarded in the eighteenth century, as fixed and immutable 'natural' elements in society, hard facts or realities, like climate or navigable rivers or the sun and planets, and therefore causes whose effects upon history are naturally inevitable and outside human control.[22]

But in Woolf's view, interests, in general, were not natural and immutable, but unstable and fluid. They could change as a result of broader changes in society. In a significant passage, Carr had asserted that:

To internationalise government in any real sense means to internationalise power; and since independent power is the basis of the
nation-state, the internationalisation of power is really a contradiction in terms.

This assertion was identical to one made in the mid-nineteenth century against socialism. Socialism was utopian, it was said, because
society was based on private property; in abolishing private property,
socialism would only succeed in undermining society, and thereby
itself. Socialism and society were therefore incompatible: the interests
of private property were immutable: the idea that society could be based
on socialism was a contradiction in terms.

But the appeal of this assertion waned as the nineteenth century
progressed. By the beginning of the twentieth century a whole range
of ideas previously regarded as utopian – public education, municipal
control of utilities, extension of the franchise to non-property owners,
state provision of old age pensions – had become widely accepted as
sensible and correct. Private property had not been abolished, but the
view that the state had an essential role to play in the social and
economic life of the nation, had become normal. This inevitably
entailed the limitation if not the abolition of property rights.

This example clearly demonstrated, in Woolf's view, that interests
were not natural and unchanging. It followed that

one must hesitate to accept sweeping statements about interests,
conflicts of interests, and power being such immutable social or
political 'realities' that they inevitably determine the structure of
society and make any attempt to alter it . . . utopian.[23]

A Science of IR?

Carr claimed that the purpose of his book was to lay down the foundations for a 'science' of international relations. Few of his critics felt he
had been successful. Woolf argued that Carr's primary concepts were
ambiguous, and that no enquiry could be considered scientific if it
rested on such insecure conceptual foundations. Carr's whole argument
rested on the distinction between 'utopia' and 'reality'. But he failed to
make the distinction clear. In particular, he consistently used the term
'Utopia' in two very different senses. On the one hand, he used it in
opposition to 'realism', i.e. to describe a hope or an ideal or a policy
'incapable of fulfilment'. On the other hand, he used it in opposition to

'reality', i.e. to describe ideas and beliefs that were 'unreal' or 'false'. Thus, when Carr described the liberals of the nineteenth century and the supporters of the League of Nations as utopian, it was not clear whether he meant that their beliefs were false, or that their policies were impossible of attainment. Carr had a good deal to say about the falseness of their beliefs but, in Woolf's opinion, 'he never clearly demonstrat[ed] . . . why their objectives and policies were impossible of attainment'.[24]

In particular, Carr often implied that the failure of the League to maintain peace was 'inevitable' simply because it had failed. 'The first and most obvious tragedy of this utopia,' Carr said, 'was its ignominious collapse.' Woolf angrily denounced this view as 'vulgar' and 'false'. Failure was not *ipso facto* ignominious. Nor was it true that just because the League failed, it was bound to fail. There was a striking inconsistency in Carr's logic. Chamberlain's policy of appeasement had failed but this did not lead Carr to the conclusion that it was utopian; nor indeed that its failure was 'ignominious'. Similarly, Hitler's policy of creating a new European order based on German supremacy would fail, but neither did Carr view this as utopian.

The picture painted by Carr was thus a highly confusing one. It was true that the League had aimed at the unattained objective of preventing war. But Hitler and Chamberlain had aimed at the unattained objectives of, respectively, 'German hegemony based on force and conflict', and 'peace in our time'. If the criterion of Utopia was attainability, the policies of Chamberlain and Hitler should have been deemed no less utopian than the policy of the League. But, aided by selective use of evidence, Carr had come to the opposite view. The fact of the matter was, Woolf concluded, that Chamberlain was a realist because Carr approved of his policy and regarded it as 'capable of fulfilment' (but without explaining why); and Hitler was a realist because he accepted the 'reality' of force, conflict, and power (but without explaining why 'power, violence, and conflict are more "real" elements in society than . . . beliefs, law, and co-operation for a common end and common interests').[25]

The most trenchant critic of Carr's scientific pretensions was University of London philosopher, Susan Stebbing. Like Woolf (and, it should be added, drawing heavily from him, without acknowledgement),[26] Stebbing took particular issue with Carr's use of terms such as 'ideal', 'idealist', 'visionary', 'utopian', 'real', 'realism' and 'reality'. It was not difficult to see what Carr meant by 'utopian'; he meant 'an entirely unpractical, not to say foolish, visionary'. The utopian takes no note of facts, or realities, or the connection between cause and effect. His energies are wholly taken up with 'ideal aims, principles, and moral ends; he is interested in political problems but not in their conditions'.[27]

Carr's model idealist was Woodrow Wilson. President Wilson 'excelled in the exposition of fundamentals', basing his appeal on 'broad and simple principles, avoiding commitment upon specific measures'. With this insistence on general principles Wilson represented the 'characteristic intellectual approach to politics'.[28]

Stebbing found Carr's conception of an idealist, and his derision of Woodrow Wilson as such, disturbing. The implication was that a politician 'in touch with realities' could not be guided by 'fundamental principles'. But what did this mean? Did it mean that realist politicians had no aims or ideals which they sought to secure? And what were the 'realities' which the realist politician was exclusively in touch with? Carr usually spoke as if power and conflicting interests were the only realities. But in the latter part of the book he seemed to admit that there were, after all, some common, international, interests. It was all very confusing.

What Carr understood by 'realism' was more difficult to discern. He referred to Machiavelli as 'the first important political realist'. According to Carr, '[t]he three essential tenets implicit in Machiavelli's doctrine are the foundation-stones of the realist philosophy.' First, 'history is a sequence of cause and effect, whose course can be analyzed and understood by intellectual effort, but not (as the utopians believe) directed by "imagination".' Second, 'theory does not (as the utopians assume) create practice, but practice theory.' Third, 'politics are not (as utopians pretend) a function of ethics, but ethics of politics.' There can be no effective morality in the absence of effective authority. 'Morality is the product of power.'[29]

Stebbing took issue with three aspects of this formulation. First, she pointed out the rhetorical nature of Carr's words. Thus the 'tenets' (and one might add the 'foundation-stones') of realism were contrasted with what the utopians 'believe', 'assume' or 'pretend'. Second, she expressed puzzlement over the meaning of 'history being directed by imagination'. Did this mean that history was directed by the 'construction of imaginary utopias'? Presumably it did, but it was far from clear. Third, what was meant by 'theory creates practice'? Presumably it meant that action was a product of beliefs and principles. It was certainly true that Woodrow Wilson acted on the basis of his beliefs and principles. But was not the same true of Hitler? And what about Bismarck? If anyone was a realist, Bismarck was. Yet he clearly acted on beliefs, ideals, or aims. He even made moral judgements: one such judgement being that the unification of Germany under Prussia was necessary and desirable.[30]

The popular distinction between those who held that a worthwhile end justified any means, even though these means may be judged evil, and those who held that judgement of the means is relevant to the judgement of the end, was relevant in this respect. Carr seemed to be saying that the former was the realist position. But the implication of this – of equating 'the ends justify the means' with 'realism' – was that only an unscrupulous policy could be a successful one. Realism became, *ipso facto*, a doctrine of ruthlessness.

It was also apparent that such a stance was not consistent with the assertion that 'ethics is a function of politics'. The realist made the practical judgement that in order to obtain his ends he sometimes has to adopt evil means. But in this formulation it was important to note that the *ethical* judgement regarding means was not one based upon political expediency: 'on the contrary, political expediency is urged as an excuse for the adoption of means antecedently judged to be evil.'

To be fair, Carr did not speak of good and evil means. His preferred word was 'morality'. But even here, as with other fundamental terms in his vocabulary, Carr failed to precisely denote his meaning. Morality was sharply opposed to power. Pairs of opposites were utilized throughout the text as corresponding synonyms of morality and power: conscience, coercion; goodwill, enmity; self-subordination, self-assertion; altruism, self-seeking; utopia, reality. Perhaps more than anything else these pairs of opposites revealed the nature of the confusion into which Carr had fallen. Morality sometimes meant 'a system of moral rules', sometimes 'conscience', sometimes 'altruism', sometimes 'benevolence'. But it was never given a definite meaning. Furthermore, by equating morality, conscience, goodwill, *etc.*, with utopia, and power, coercion, enmity, *etc.*, with reality, Carr created the impression that whereas the latter were significantly 'real' the former were importantly 'unreal'.

This was manifestly incorrect. Power was not the only reality. Men's ideas and ideals were also factors in determining social change. Indeed, Carr recognised this in the latter part of his book. He claimed, *inter alia*, that morality and power, utopia and reality, altruism and self-seeking, were 'dual elements present in every political society':

> The state is built up out of these two conflicting aspects of human nature. Utopia and reality, the ideal and the institution, morality and power, are from the outset inextricably blended in it . . . . The utopian who dreams that it is possible to eliminate self-assertion from politics and to base a political system on morality alone is just as wide of the mark as the realist who believes that altruism is an illusion and that

all political action is based on self-seeking .... The attempt to keep
God and Caesar in water-tight compartments runs too much athwart
the deep-seated desire of the human mind to reduce its view of the
world to some sort of moral order. We are not in the long run satisfied
to believe that what is politically good is morally bad; and since we
can neither moralize power nor expel power from politics, we are
faced with a dilemma that cannot be completely resolved. The planes
of Utopia and reality never coincide. The ideal cannot be institutionalized, nor the institution idealized.[31]

For Stebbing this was an extraordinary conclusion to what was offered
as a 'scientific' analysis. Since Carr presented power and morality as
contradictions it followed that power could no more be moralized, nor
morality made powerful, than black whitened or white blackened. This
was no 'iron necessity' of history, or the nature of states, but a direct
consequence of the way Carr used his words. The statement 'the ideal
cannot be institutionalized' was a parallel truism. Since 'ideal' was equated with 'Utopia', and 'Utopia' meant 'imaginary, impracticable, ideal',
it followed that the ideal could not be institutionalised *by definition*. The
assertion concerning the utopian 'dream' of a political system based on
'morality alone' was problematic for the same reason. It was, moreover,
difficult to believe that any scientifically minded professor could deliberately use 'morality' and 'imaginary ideals' as synonyms.[32]

Moral Implications

It was, indeed, this aspect of Carr's analysis – what he said and implied
about the nature and content of morality – that provoked the strongest
reaction. The extreme moral relativism and the uncompromisingly
materialist sociology of knowledge that Carr seemed to be purveying
certainly came as a big shock to those who liked their morality, and their
knowledge, unambiguous and neatly packaged. Angell, as we have seen,
construed the book as an attack on reason, on political and intellectual
liberty, on the rule of law, on free will, on the very foundations of a free
society. It contradicted everything that Britain was fighting for in the
last war and in this. The failure to detect any fundamental moral difference between the totalitarian way of life and the democratic, in particular, represented a serious threat, at a time of great crisis, to the unity
and morale of the nation.

Zimmern, Toynbee and Seton-Watson were more concerned about
the longer-term implications of Carr's stance. His thorough-going

moral relativism left one in a moral and political vacuum, without starting-point or sense of direction. It left one, in other words, without the finite goal, the emotional appeal, the right of moral judgement, and the ground for action, which Carr himself posited as the 'essential ingredients of all effective political thinking'.[33]

Woolf and Stebbing felt that the main problem resided in the way Carr used his principal words. He created the impression that power, violence, and conflicting interests were 'more real' than cooperation, peace and common interests. By making success the criterion for realism, as he seemed to do in his comments on the League, on appeasement, and on the tactics and policy of Hitler, he strongly implied that nothing could ever happen except in the way it did. For Woolf, this amounted to a rationalization of nationalism and violence. For Stebbing it amounted to the empirically incorrect view that only a policy of ruthlessness could be successful.

One man who shared many of these fears, and who expressed them with a combination of moral passion and intellectual precision for which he latter became famous, was Friedrich Hayek. Carr was one of Hayek's 'totalitarians in our midst': benign and well-intentioned on the outside, but on the inside, totalitarian to the core. More than anyone else in Hayek's view, Carr illustrated the extent to which the disparagement of the individual and the ideal of liberty – in the name of 'maximum efficiency', the 'big state', the 'national plan' and 'scientific organization' – had gone 'in formerly liberal England'. Following the German 'historical school' of realists, Carr asserted that morality was a function of politics, that the only standard of value was that of fact, that the individualist faith in human conscience as the final court of appeal was utopian, and that the 'old morality' of abstract general principles must 'disappear' because 'the empiricist treats the concrete case on its individual merits'. In Carr's world nothing but expediency mattered. Even the rule *pacta sunt servanda*, we were told, was not a moral principle. That without abstract general principles, merit became a matter of arbitrary opinion, and without a rule making them morally binding, treaties became meaningless, did not seem to worry Carr.

Indeed, Professor Carr sometimes gave the impression that Britain fought the last war on the wrong side. 'Anyone who re-reads the statements of British war aims twenty-five years ago and compares them with Professor Carr's present views,' Hayek declared, 'will readily see that what were then believed to be the German views are now those of Professor Carr who would presumably argue that the different views then professed in this country were merely a product of British hypocrisy.' And how little the difference Carr was able to see between the ideals held in Britain and those practised in present-day Germany was illustrated by his assertion that

> [i]t is true that when a prominent National Socialist asserts that 'anything that benefits the German people is right, anything that harms them is wrong' he is merely propounding the same identification of national interest with universal right which has already been established for English-speaking countries by [President] Wilson, Professor Toynbee, Lord Cecil, and many others.

Did Carr realize, Hayek asked, that his assertion that 'we can no longer find much meaning in the distinction familiar to nineteenth century thought between "society" and "state"', was precisely the doctrine of Carl Schmitt, the leading Nazi theoretician of totalitarianism, and the essence of the definition of that term that Schmitt himself had invented? Similarly, did he realize that the view that 'the mass production of opinion is the corollary of the mass-production of goods', and that 'the prejudice which the word propaganda still exerts in many minds to-day is closely parallel to the prejudice against control of industry and trade', was really 'an apology for a regimentation of opinion of the kind practised by the Nazis'?

Furthermore, how curious it was to observe that

> those who pose as hard-boiled realists, and who lose no opportunity of casting ridicule on the 'utopianism' of those who believe in the possibility of an international political order, yet regard as more practicable the much more intimate and irresponsible interference with the lives of the different peoples which [international] economic planning involves; and believe that, once hitherto undreamed-of power is given to an international government, which has just been represented as not capable of enforcing a simple Rule of Law, this greater power will be used in so unselfish and so obviously just a manner as to command general consent.[34]

Assessing the Assessors

The preceding account gives some indication of the range and tone of the responses to a book that the emerging field of IR was soon to revere as one of its founding texts. Some of these responses were measured and thoughtful (Stebbing); others were angry and polemical (Woolf). Some sought to play down the significance of the book (Zimmern); others embarked on a full-frontal attack with no holds barred (Angell).

It would take a small book to do justice to the full range of views, the twists and turns of argument, the insights and distortions, the truths and half-truths, which the publication of Carr's famous tract so effectively provoked; and readers will have their own views, based on their own reading of *The Twenty Years' Crisis*, of the merit and veracity of the various arguments and opinions presented here. In the space remaining, however, it may be of some interest to briefly record some of my own.

First, it is true that the chief policy prescription of *The Twenty Years' Crisis* is appeasement; that appeasement failed to stop Hitler and prevent war; and that to that extent it was 'unrealistic'. Angell and Toynbee *et al.* had much fun pointing this out: that the chief prescription of the realists was something so abjectly unrealistic as appeasement. And history has been kind to them. Appeasement is associated in the national psyche with Munich, with the ineffectual and unworldly Edwardian statesmanship of Chamberlain, with failure. It is seen not as realistic but as the idealistic stratagem of foreign policy *par excellence*. 'Britain', in the words of one recent statesman, not known for her lack of resolve in such matters, 'does not appease dictators'.

But it would be wrong to identify *in toto* Carr's support for *a* policy of appeasement with *the* policy of appeasement pursued by Chamberlain and Halifax between March 1936 and March 1939. Carr did lend his support to the latter. He described Munich, notoriously, as 'the nearest approach in recent years to the settlement of a major international issue by a procedure of peaceful change'. Though he omitted many of the more insensitive and apologetic passages concerning Munich and appeasement from the second edition of the book,[35] it is significant, as W.T.R. Fox has pointed out, that such passages were not omitted from the first edition. The book was written in 1938 and 1939 and went to press in July 1939, reaching page proof in September. Chamberlain abandoned appeasement, and its dramatic fall from public grace began, after Hitler's seizure of rump-Czechoslovakia in March 1939. It may have been a typical act of courage on the part of Carr to stick to his intellectual guns – to the general line of policy suggested by his theoretical analysis – many months after the most striking attempt at such a policy had been officially abandoned and repudiated by an increasingly disillusioned public. But Carr may have felt, even as late as September 1939, that such a policy could yet succeed in avoiding the carnage of another world war. The fact that Mussolini had not yet formally fallen into the arms of Hitler was cited by Carr, in a smaller book published more or less simultaneously with *The Twenty Years' Crisis*, as proof that the policy had thus far succeeded with respect to Italy.[36]

The most important point, however, is the wider one. Carr conceived his policy of appeasement broadly. It was the international expression of the process of give-and-take between 'haves' and 'have-nots' which he saw as a necessary condition of all stable and orderly social life. Though there is a large degree of indeterminacy as to who is to count, at any given moment, as a 'have' and who as a 'have-not' – such categories defy objective definition, and Carr (not unproblematically)[37] accepted as 'have-nots' those who simply said they were – it is clear that Carr envisaged the process as a continuous one. Moreover, it was one which, as far as the international events of the 'twenty years' crisis' were concerned, should have began as early as the early 1920s, not left until the 1930s when a shift in the balance of power against the Western powers produced circumstances far less conducive to a favourable outcome.[38] Chamberlainite appeasement, Carr seemed to be saying, was a step in the right direction, and even at so late an hour, one which might just save the day. But it would have been so much better to have started the policy a decade earlier.

This leads to my second point. *The Twenty Years' Crisis* had a long gestation period. It was a product not only of Aberystwyth but of Paris, Riga and London. The framework for the book may have occurred to Carr in 1937. But many of its substantive contentions and opinions had been conceived and formed much earlier. Indeed, in a very real sense the book had been in the making ever since Versailles, the proceedings and conclusions of which appalled Carr as much as they had appalled that other great writer on the Peace, J.M. Keynes.

The long gestation period of the book, and the fact that its foundations, at least in part, were laid at a conference held twenty years before its publication, account for two important shortcomings. First, it is true, as several of his critics observed, that his interpretation of various things, theories, and persons (to use Woolf's phrase) was strangely out of date by the time the book was published. To portray Angell as a believer in a natural harmony of interests may have been valid before 1910, when his *Great Illusion* was first published, but it certainly was not valid by the early 1930s. By that time, war, revolution, and economic depression had ensured that Angell's liberalism, as with so many others, now took a sociological and interventionist form far removed from the elegant but easy assumptions of nineteenth-century *laissez-faire*. Indeed, in this respect Angell's position was not very far removed from the Carr of the final chapter *The Twenty Years' Crisis* and of *Conditions of Peace*.[39]

Harmony could no longer be assumed, but with increased social and scientific knowledge it might be possible to *create* it. In his faith in man's ability to manufacture some kind of technocratic New Jerusalem, Carr was just as idealistic as the 'utopians' he criticized.[40] Similarly, his interpretation of the League as a bulwark of the *status quo* may have had validity during its early years, the years, in particular, of French retrenchment. But to depict it as such in general, and to depict its supporters in the League of Nations Union (LNU) and elsewhere as sharing this view, would be a travesty of the truth. Numerous attempts were made to revise the Covenant of the League, and unlike its successor institution, several of them were successful.[41] Many of the most prominent members of the LNU – Angell, Zimmern and Woolf included – conceived it as a dynamic, not a defensive, institution, a force for change, not *stasis*. Indeed, the general view that emerged in the wake of the falterings of the 1920s and the failures of the 1930s was that the League was in many ways a flawed institution, but one which could still serve, with the requisite political will, as the focal point for a new, working, system of internationalism. In any case, as one of its most sophisticated observers pointed out, the League, *pace* Carr, was not one thing but lots of things. The League was what states made of it.[42]

The second shortcoming concerns the legacy of Versailles. The inconsistencies and the hypocrisy, as Carr saw it, of the Allied powers, and the iniquity of their treatment of Germany, inflamed in Carr a contempt for the former and provoked a sympathy for the latter that coloured virtually everything he subsequently had to say on the subject. This explains why his most stinging remarks were reserved for such relatively benign figures as Lord Cecil and Professor Toynbee, whereas 'Herr Hitler,'[43] the most frequently cited figure in *The Twenty Years' Crisis* along with Marx, escapes almost entirely unscathed.[44] It also explains why Carr was so prepared, remarkably with hindsight, to take the dictators at their word.[45]

This leads, third, to the complex issue of Carr's moral stance: to the cluster of assertions about (i) law, order and peace not being general interests but merely the particular interests of the rich and the powerful, about (ii) the democratic states being just as much to blame for the war as the totalitarian states, about (iii) the struggle being not one between 'welfare states' and 'warfare states' but one in which power was equally predominant on both sides. With regard to (i), the important point to note is that Carr's argument is a structural one inspired by Marx's concept of ideology and Mannheim's sociology of knowledge. He was not saying, as Zimmern chose to interpret him, that values were 'only matters of ephemeral convention' and that, consequently, 'one foreign policy or one national tradition or one political cause' was just as good (or bad) as any other. Rather, he was saying that values have a history, and that the values that we, as individuals, as a society, as a nation, hold are a product of a complicated process of social evolution. At any given time, the allocation of values is broadly determined by the structure of society. Those occupying a position of privilege – those who benefit from any given social order – put a higher premium on those values – order, security, peace – which sustain it than those who occupy a position of disadvantage (who put a higher premium on those values – equality, justice – which challenge it). And the process, Carr stressed, by which these values are allocated is an almost entirely subconscious one. He was not saying, therefore, that values were merely convenient tools of policy, or rhetoric, ways of justifying interests which could, in accordance with the needs of the situation, be solemnly invoked one day and cynically discarded the next. But, rather, that there was a complex sense in which all values were a manifestation of underlying interests; and that those who spoke the language of universal justice were often unaware of the fact that their language might be merely a clever disguise for the pursuit of narrow self-interest. Carr was not 'running away from the notion of good' so much as pointing out that 'good' was a good deal more complicated than many made it out to be.

It should also be noted that, on closer inspection, the relativist position Carr takes on values is not as uncompromising as it first appears. Already in his 'Realist Critique' Carr had suggested that the supremacy within a community of the privileged group could be, and often is, so overwhelming that its interests are, indeed, those of the community 'since its well-being necessarily carries with it some measure of well-being for other members of the community, and its collapse would entail the collapse of the community as a whole.' In the nineteenth century, for example, British statesman, 'having discovered that free trade promoted British prosperity, were sincerely convinced that, in doing so, it also promoted the prosperity of the world as a whole'; and the predominance of Britain in world trade was at that time so overwhelming that there was indeed a sense in which it did: 'British prosperity flowed over into other countries and a British economic collapse would have meant world-wide ruin.' Similarly, if Britain and France went to war with Germany and Italy, the sympathies of most countries would 'instinctively be ranged on the Franco-British side' since the defeat of Britain and France by Germany and Italy 'would produce a far more tremendous upheaval throughout the world' than the defeat of Germany and Italy by Britain and France.[46]

So long as the supremacy of the dominant group was sufficiently great, therefore, an identity of interests could exist between the dominant group and society as a whole. Consequently, there was a sense in which the values of that group were also the values of society as a whole. Both had a stake in stability, order and peace.

Thus far, the dent in Carr's relativism is not big. Values are still determined by interests even though there may be circumstances in which interests are common. But the dent gets bigger as the book goes on. 'There is a sense,' he says, 'in which peace and co-operation between nations or classes or individuals is a common and universal end irrespective of conflicting interests and politics.'[47] But he does not stipulate this sense. He alludes to the 'widespread assumption of the existence of a world-wide community' and 'the almost universal recognition of an international morality involving a sense of obligation to an international community'. But he refrains from saying that such an assumption, such recognition, such a morality, and such a sense of obligation might 'in reality' be little more than 'products of circumstance', 'tools of vested interests', or 'convenient weapons for belabouring those who assail the *status quo*'.[48] He asserts that the moral distinction between wars of aggression and wars of defence is misguided since 'if a change is necessary and desirable, the use or threatened use of force to maintain the *status quo* may be morally more culpable than the use or threatened use of force to alter it.'[49] But he fails to stipulate the grounds on which 'necessity' or 'desirability' can be calculated. He says that our view of justice 'is likely to be coloured' by our own interest, and that power 'plays a part' in determining our moral outlook – a clear derogation from his earlier, more robustly 'realist', stance.[50] He contends that 'a new international order and a new international harmony can be built up only on the basis of an ascendancy which is generally accepted as tolerant and unoppressive'; that 'the most effective moral argument' in favour of a British or American, as opposed to a German or Japanese, hegemony is that the former countries 'by a long tradition and by some hard lessons' had learned more successfully than the latter 'the capital importance of this task'; and that belief in the desirability of seeking the consent of the governed, and belief in the use of conciliation, had in fact played a larger part in British and American colonial and foreign policy than in German and Japanese. Here, arguably, we see a preference for liberty, democracy and peace not reducible to self-interest. By such

means, to paraphrase de Madariaga, does Carr smuggle ethical foundations into his store of spiritual thinking.[51]

Assertions (ii) and (iii) can be dealt with more briefly. In several places
in *The Twenty Years' Crisis*, Carr appears less than enthusiastic about the
virtues of democracy: indeed, his attitude towards democracy, certainly
bourgeois democracy, *vis-à-vis* totalitarianism often seems one of indifference.[52] This indifference was partly genuine: a reflection of his growing commitment to central planning and large-scale social and political
organization; and partly affected: a conscious ploy to counteract the
'sentimental and dishonest platitudinizing' of the satisfied Powers
which so irritated him. Along with his profound disappointment at
the missed opportunities for genuine political rapprochement with Germany in the 1920s, this indifference goes a long way to explain his
extraordinary claim that the democracies probably bore 'as large a
share of responsibility for the disaster' as the dictatorships. It is significant that in the second edition of the book Carr toned down this claim,
cannily substituting 'their' for 'as large a'.[53]

For the same reasons Carr unduly equated the democracies with the
totalitarian states with respect to the importance they attached to
power. He rightly, and with typical acuity, exposed the shallowness of
the distinction between 'welfare states' and 'warfare states'.[54] But in
doing so he overlooked the key distinction between desiring power as
a means to an end and desiring power as an end in itself: the democratic
states being far less guilty of the latter than the totalitarian states. For
many of Carr's critics this was, rightly, a sizeable error of omission.[55]

Fourth, Carr's critics, Woolf and Stebbing in particular, were also right
to argue that there is something conveniently elastic about the way Carr
used his principal terms. This can be illustrated by looking at one or two
cases. One of Carr's main examples of utopian doctrine is classical
political economy and, in particular, free trade. With respect to this he
makes three observations: (i) that classical political economy was
founded upon the 'negation' of existing, mercantilist, reality; (ii) that
it was predicated on 'certain artificial and unverified generalizations
about the behaviour of a hypothetical economic man'; and (iii) that
universal free trade – 'the normal postulate of economic science' – was
an 'imaginary condition which has never existed'. Just as no one had
ever lived in Plato's republic or in a Fourierian phalanstery, no one had
ever lived in a world of universal free trade.[56]

Carr's three observations correspond to three different meanings of
the term utopian. A utopian doctrine may be one that: (i) rejects an
existing state of affairs in preference for a more desirable, but not yet

existent, other; (ii) is based on unverified and artificial (meaning 'concocted'? 'abstract'? 'false'?) generalizations; and (iii) postulates as an economic, political or moral bench-mark a condition that has no historical precedent. The extent to which Carr was aware of the fact that he used not one, but three concepts of utopia, and that a good deal of slippage took place between them, is a moot point. The example shows, however, that Carr's critics were right to contend that his use of the term was, at best, rather suspect.

Further confirmation of this can be found at the beginning of his final chapter. Here, in the space of three pages, Carr uses the term 'Utopia' as a synonym and/or descriptive label for six significantly different things: (i) the peaceful and harmonious world order of the nineteenth century; (ii) the attempt to recreate this order; (iii) *any* liberal international order; (iv) *any* peaceful and harmonious world order; (v) *any* code of international morality; (vi) 'visionary hopes'.[57]

Allied with the sheer range of things that Carr denounced as utopian – from world government to 'all-in arbitration', from a 'United States of Europe' to a 'more perfect League of Nations', from the 'indivisibility of peace' to the 'futility of war' – the general looseness with which he employs the term suggests that, far from being a carefully defined scientific concept, it is little more than a convenient rhetorical device.

Ample confirmation of this fact can be found in the range of statesmen, politicians and thinkers whom Carr condemns as utopian. In addition to those already mentioned, Carr explicitly condemns Robert Cecil, John Dewey, Nicholas Murray Butler, and the international lawyers, Leon Duguit and Hersch Lauterpact. This is a small list. The list of those he *implicitly* condemns, however, is much bigger. It includes Presidents Taft and Roosevelt, and Secretaries of State Stimson and Hull (for believing that public opinion will always prevail and can be trusted to come down on the right side); David Lloyd George (for believing the same with respect to disarmament); Anthony Eden (for echoing the Mazzinian doctrine of a pre-ordained division of a labour between nations, each with its special contribution to make to the welfare of humanity); Winston Churchill (for failing to recognize the interested character of his denunciations of, first, the Bolsheviks and, later, the Nazis); *The Times*, Cecil Rhodes, Presidents McKinley and Theodore Roosevelt (for assuming that the national interests of their countries were synonymous with the universal good); Bernard Bosanquet (for separating politics from economics); Frederick Schuman (for doing the same); Karl Marx (usually quoted approvingly for his realism but in one instance criticized for being dominated by the nineteenth-century presupposition that economics and politics were separate domains); Gilbert Murray (for harbouring the 'illusion' that certain disputes are *ipso facto* justiciable and others *ipso facto* non-justiciable); Hans Kelsen (for entertaining the 'dream' of a tribunal 'exercising not only the judicial function of interpreting the rights of states, but the legislative function of changing them'); and Lord Davies (for entertaining the same). The diversity of this list is startling, and it demonstrates, perhaps better than anything else, the convenient elasticity of one of Carr's key terms. Alfred Zimmern encapsulated this nicely when he ironically asked: 'Who are these blind leaders of the blind against whom [Carr's] attack is directed?' Answering:

> The flash of Professor Carr's sabre is so dazzling that it is not very easy to distinguish them. At one moment it is 'the Left' in general, at another the Pacifists, at another the international lawyers, at another the Free Traders, at another the supporters of the League of Nations, at another the defenders of the *status quo* in the relations between the Great Powers, at another the exponents of ethical or spiritual values.[58]

But it would be wrong to conclude that Carr alone was guilty of rhetorical use of words and conceptual fancy footwork. A number of his critics – Angell and Woolf especially – were equally guilty of such crimes and misdemeanours, though they committed them with far less dexterity and flair.

In Angell's polemic – to call it a 'critical essay' would be too generous – the realist recognition of the irrational element in politics soon becomes equated with a whole range of less salubrious (and in many important ways different) things: that 'men never use their reason', that they 'think with their blood', act by instinct, are guided by their passions, by nationalism, by jingoism, that they never use 'thought', or the 'intellect', that they are 'irredeemably foolish'. Realism, at the end of this long and windy process, is reduced to such simple (and ideologically convenient) formulations as: 'Man is a fool, and therefore Hitler's enemies will always quarrel among themselves, and finally give victory to him'; or 'we are bound to go on making the same old errors; human folly can never be lessened or modified by any effort of the human mind'.

> The case for intellectual freedom [he says], *as against the case of the 'realists'* . . . is that the degree of reason or rationality shown in policy

will depend upon the extent to which the habit of weighing pros and cons has been developed; and the development of that habit will depend upon the degree of intellectual freedom we preserve, and that in turn upon the value we attach to it.[59]

Few men of wisdom, realist or non-realist, would disagree with this – except of course for the first two clauses which imply, wholly unfairly, that realists are against intellectual freedom. Carr, for one, not once, as far as I am aware, repudiated this principle. What he did do was suggest that in practice, due to the socially constructed nature of values and belief, it was a far more complicated principle than conventionally understood – especially by simple-minded liberals such as Angell.

Realism, in Angell, also becomes the belief that

> we can never achieve a degree of international co-operation suffi-cient to enable Europe to restrain violent minded gangsters who threaten the world's peace ... [and that] the whole conception of a defensive grouping of states to resist a common menace of aggres-sion is Utopian, impracticable, mischievous, and (in the view of a good many) immoral, unpatriotic; that the degree of political rationality which alone could make it successful is impossible of achievement.[60]

But it is absurd to suggest that realists are sceptical about the possibi-lity of *all* forms of international co-operation. They were, and are, sceptical about certain kinds of co-operation, permanent arrangements for collective security in particular, because such arrangements are based, they contend, on the flawed assumption of the indivisibility of peace. States, they say, have some interests in common and some in conflict; they will co-operate when their interests coincide; but they are unlikely to cooperate if there exists any margin of doubt about such coincidence – especially when the stakes, human and material, are high, as they are in 'collective resistance to aggression' 'coming to the aid of victims of aggression', and 'enforcing peace' (whose proper name, they add, is war). War in one part of the world does not necessarily threaten the interests of states in another; war, wherever it occurs, never effects all states equally. Some wars threaten a state's vital interests, others do not. Hence the highest form of co-operation that can be achieved (inevitably temporary as all history shows) is the political and military alliance against a concrete, common enemy (*vis-à-vis* an abstract enemy such as 'any other state' or 'war itself').

What Angell suggests, in effect, is that because of their emphasis on the importance – to put it relatively neutrally – of nationalist passions and unreason, realists maintain that all forms of combination between states are impossible. He is assisted in this effort by using a whole range of terms to describe 'what needs to be done to stop Hitler and prevent the recurrence of war', without any attempt to distinguish them. Examples include: 'common action by Europe in facing concertedly a common danger'; 'combination for defence'; 'a defensive grouping of states to resist the common menace of aggression'; 'a new, internationalist, conception of national duty'; 'a policy of international co-operation'; a 'Grand Alliance'; 'democratic internationalism'; 'common action and co-ordination of power'; 'some permanent association of nations by which the security of each shall be made to rest upon the strength of the whole'. By lumping these things together he makes Carr, and the realists, look not only absurd, but mischievous, irrational, dangerous. He makes them opponents of all forms of co-operation. This, of course, suits his propagandist purpose. But it severely misrepresents the realist case: a case which, among other things, rests on a sharp, indeed fundamental, distinction between collective security, on the one hand, and military alliances, on the other. Angell is right to say that Carr disparaged and undermined the one; but emphatically wrong to say that he disparaged and undermined the other.

Such disingenuousness is also apparent in Woolf. In his analysis of Carr's assault on President Wilson and the characteristics of the 'utopian' *vis-à-vis* 'realist' statesman, for example, he cunningly equates 'intellectual' with 'intellect', and 'intellect' with 'reason'. In so doing, he twists Carr's characterization of Woodrow Wilson as 'the most perfect modern example of the intellectual in politics' into 'a good example of a man who uses reason in politics'. If such an attribute, the use of reason in politics, is 'utopian', its opposite, the use of 'emotion', or 'passion', or 'instinct', becomes 'realism'. By doing this, Woolf is able to easily ridicule Carr's analysis. On the one hand, realism becomes an empirically dubious doctrine: Bismarck, that most impeccable of nineteenth century 'realists', certainly did not ignore reason; neither, for that matter, does Hitler. If these two men are not 'realists', then who are? Realism becomes (to paraphrase Carr) an imaginary doctrine which has never existed. On the other hand, because of its disparagement of reason, realism becomes an insane doctrine, a doctrine of madmen: after all, isn't the conventional definition of a madman someone who doesn't use, or haphazardly uses, his reason?[61]

Notes

1   'The Realist's Utopia', review of E.H. Carr, *Twenty Years' Crisis*, second edition, *Observer*, 21 July 1946, p. 3.
2   Angell to Zimmern, October 1939. Bodleian Library, Zimmern MS, p. 45.
3   Angell to Noel-Baker, 12 December 1939. Ball State University, Angell MS, Correspondence.
4   Angell, 'Who are the Utopians? And who the Realists?', *Headway*, January 1940, p. 5.
5   The sentence reads: 'It is a moot point whether the politicians and publicists of the satisfied Powers, who have attempted to identify international morality with security, law and order and other time-honoured slogans of privileged groups, do not bear as large a share of responsibility for the disaster as the politicians and publicists of the dissatisfied Powers, who brutally denied the validity of the international morality so constituted.'
6   Zimmern to Angell, 20 January 1940. Angell MS, Correspondence.
7   A clear reference to the writings of Niebuhr; but also to F.A. Voigt, a well-known BBC commentator on foreign affairs, whose *Unto Caesar* had just been published.
8   N. Angell, *Why Freedom Matters* (Harmondsworth: Penguin Books), pp. 35–6.
9   *Ibid.*, p. 44; E.H. Carr, *The Twenty Years' Crisis: An Introduction to the Study of International Relations* (London: Macmillan, 1939), pp. 102–12.
10 Angell, *Why Freedom Matters*, pp. 37–49.
11 *Ibid.*, pp. 50–6.
12 Zimmern, 'A Realist in Search of Utopia', *Spectator*, 24 November 1939, p. 750.
13 Toynbee to Angell, 23 January 1940. Angell MS, Correspondence.
14 R.W. Seton-Watson, 'Politics and Power', *Listener*, 7 December 1939, Supplement, p. 48.
15 Angell, 'Who are the Utopians?', p. 4.
16 W.P. Maddox, review of Carr, *Twenty Years' Crisis*, *American Political Science Review*, Vol. 34, No. 3 1940, pp. 587–8.
17 Toynbee to Angell, 23 January 1940. Angell MS, Correspondence.
18 R. Coventry, 'The Illusions of Power', *New Statesman*, Vol. 28, No. 457 25 November 1939, pp. 761–2 (reprinted in R.H.S. Crossman, *The Charm of Politics and Other Essays in Political Criticism* (London: Hamish Hamilton, 1958), pp. 91–4).
19 Angell, 'Who are the Utopians?', p. 4.
20 The phrase 'facile optimism' belongs to Carr, the others to Angell.
21 Angell, 'Who are the Utopians?', pp. 4–5. Similarly, Maddox had doubts about Carr's distinction between 'power' (or 'warfare') and 'welfare' states. The latter, Carr contended, were simply states which, 'already enjoying a preponderance of power, are not primarily concerned to increase it'. But what about Scandinavia?
22 L. Woolf, *The War for Peace* (London: Routledge, 1940), p. 129.
23 *Ibid.*, p. 142.
24 L. Woolf, 'Utopia and Reality', *Political Quarterly*, Vol. 11, No. 2 April–June 1940, p. 172.

25 Ibid., pp. 171–6; Woolf, *The War for Peace*, pp. 54–63, 114–42, 175–83.

26 Stebbing's discussion can be seen as a carefully reasoned version of Woolf's polemic. It is curious that so meticulous a scholar did not acknowledge her debt. The similarities are too substantial for the influence to have been unconscious.

27 L. Susan Stebbing, *Ideals and Illusions* (London: Watts and Co., 1941), pp. 6–7.

28 Stebbing quoting Carr. Stebbing, *Ideals and Illusions*, pp. 7–8; Carr, *Twenty Years' Crisis*, 20.

29 Stebbing quoting Carr. Stebbing, *Ideals and Illusions*, pp. 9–10; Carr, *Twenty Years' Crisis*, p. 82.

30 Stebbing, *Ideals and Illusions*, pp. 8–11. In a later passage, Stebbing, again echoing Woolf, argues that in pursuing ends regarded as worthwhile ('ideals'), and in using reason to achieve them (taking note of 'facts', making use of 'experience'), there was no essential difference between Bismarck and Woodrow Wilson, or indeed between a businessman and Madame Currie, or even Al Capone and Mahatma Ghandi. The distinction between them resided not in the fact that they had ends and used reason to attain them, but: (i) in the *nature* of their ends; (ii) in their acceptance or rejection of certain methods of attaining them; and (iii) in the quality of their reasoning. Stebbing, *Ideals and Illusions*, pp. 16–18. Woolf's frustration with this aspect of Carr's analysis is well summed by his statement: 'According to Professor Carr, we should have to say that Hitler is utopian in so far as he has ethical ends and a realist in so far as he uses power to attain them, and that the means, even though they attain the ends, are incompatible with the ends. There must be something very wrong with a theory and a definition which lead to such conclusions.' Woolf, *The War for Peace*, p. 119.

31 Stebbing, *Ideals and Illusions*, pp. 12–15; Carr, *The Twenty Years' Crisis*, pp. 124–5, 129–30.

32 Stebbing, *Ideals and Illusions*, pp. 14–16.

33 Carr, *The Twenty Years' Crisis*, p. 113.

34 F.A. Hayek, *The Road to Serfdom* (London: Ark Paperbacks, 1986 [1944]), pp. 138–41, 169–72. It is, indeed, curious that whereas Carr regarded a supranational political authority as utopian but an international economic authority as realistic, Hayek regarded an international economic authority as utopian but a supranational political authority as realistic. I comment on this further in my 'The New Europe Debate in Wartime Britain', in Philomena Murray and Paul Rich, eds, *Visions of European Unity* (Boulder: Westview Press, 1996), pp. 39–62.

35 Notably: 'If the power relations of Europe in 1938 made it inevitable that Czecho-Slovakia should lose part of her territory, and eventually her independence, it was preferable (quite apart from any question of justice or injustice) that this should come about as the result of discussion round a table at Munich rather than as a result either of a war between the Great Powers or of a local war between Germany and Czecho-Slovakia.' Carr, *The Twenty Years' Crisis*, p. 278. See also pp. 282–3.

36 W.T.R. Fox, 'E.H. Carr and Political Realism: Vision and Revision', *Review of International Studies*, Vol. 11, No. 1 1985, pp. 1–16; E.H. Carr, *Britain: A Study of Foreign Policy from the Versailles Treaty to the Outbreak of War* (London:

Longmans, 1939). The Berlin–Rome 'Pact of Steel' was signed on 22 May 1939; but the Tripartite Pact, the basic document of collaboration between Berlin, Rome and Tokyo, not until September 1940.

37   On the surface, Carr promises a structural theory capable of explaining actor behaviour without reference to methodologically troublesome factors such as individual preferences and perceptions. Actor behaviour becomes a function of two independent variables: (i) the distribution of power in the system; (ii) their position in the system. Accordingly, those who benefit from the system defend it until doing so risks a major, system-destabilizing, confrontation, at which point they make concessions; those who do not benefit from the system increase their power and challenge the system until they win such concessions as to put them in the position of the benefactors, at which point they defend it. 'Aggression' is the pejorative term of the 'haves' for the challenges to the system, justifiable or not, by the 'have-nots'. It is an effect of (i) 'have-not'-ness and (ii) adequate capability. But if 'have-not'-ness cannot be defined objectively, if it is a matter of subjective perception, the whole theory becomes shaky. Rather than an *effect*, aggression becomes *evidence* of 'have-not'-ness, and 'have-not'-ness becomes a rationalization of aggression. Was Italy, a victor in the First World War and in Abyssinia, a 'have-not' power because *Il Duce* said it was? Was Germany, a victor in all the major diplomatic quarrels of the late 1930s, still a 'have-not' power because the Fuhrer said it was? It was precisely Carr's willingness to take Mussolini and Hitler at their word, and to rest so much of his theoretical edifice upon the outcome, that so alarmed the 'utopians'. Was enquiry into the legitimacy of their demands *entirely* irrelevant? Did not the parallel between, on the one hand, the *status quo* powers and the revisionist powers and, on the other hand, capital and labour, somewhat flatter them?

38   Carr, *The Twenty Years' Crisis*, pp. 280–2.

39   See also the revealing passages in Carr, *Twenty Years' Crisis*, pp. 65–7, 103.

40   I have commented on this further in my 'The New Europe Debate in Wartime Britain', pp. 39–62.

41   See F.S. Northedge, *The League of Nations: Its Life and Times 1920–1946* (Leicester: Leicester University Press, 1986), pp. 46–69, 317–27.

42   A. Zimmern, *The League of Nations and the Rule of Law* (London: Macmillan, 1935), pp. 277–85.

43   The 'Herr' was dropped for the second edition.

44   His most critical words come in one of the paragraphs omitted from the second edition. After praising Munich as 'the nearest approach in recent years to the settlement of a major international issue by a procedure of peaceful change' and 'one which corresponded both to a change in the European equilibrium of forces and to accepted canons of international morality', he adds several words of caution. Hitler 'seemed morbidly eager to emphasise the element of force and to minimise that of peaceful negotiation'. 'The principle of self-determination, once accepted, was applied with a ruthlessness which left to Germany the benefit of every doubt and paid a minimum of attention to every Czecho-Slovak susceptibility.' Moreover, there was 'a complete lack of any German readiness to make the smallest sacrifice for the sake of conciliation.' These qualifications show that Carr's endorsement of Munich was not quite as complete, nor as cold-hearted, as

some critics (including Fox) have suggested. But they also show that Carr's representation of Munich as a good example of peaceful change is, at best, rather curious. Carr, *The Twenty Years' Crisis*, pp. 282–3.

45 See, above, note 37.
46 Carr, *The Twenty Years' Crisis*, pp. 102–5.
47 *Ibid.*, p. 111.
48 *Ibid.*, pp. 87, 187, 206, 211.
49 *Ibid.*, pp. 264–5.
50 *Ibid.*, pp. 278–9.
51 *Ibid.*, pp. 206, 302–3.
52 See, for example, Carr, *The Twenty Years' Crisis*, pp. 169–70, 172, 211–12.
53 And inserting 'as well' between 'disaster' and 'as'. See note 5 above; Carr, *The Twenty Years' Crisis*, second edition, (London, Macmillan, 1946), p. 225.
54 Carr, *The Twenty Years' Crisis*, pp. 152–4.
55 It should be noted in this connection that in the Preface to the second edition Carr confessed that the book had been written 'with the deliberate aim of counteracting the glaring and dangerous defect of nearly all thinking, both academic and popular, about international politics in English-speaking countries from 1919 to 1939 – the almost total neglect of the factor of power'; and that some passages stated their argument with a 'one-sided emphasis which no longer seems as necessary or appropriate to-day as it did in 1939'.
56 Carr, *The Twenty Years' Crisis*, pp. 8–11.
57 *Ibid.*, pp. 287–9.
58 Zimmern, 'A Realist in Search of Utopia', p. 750.
59 Angell, *Why Freedom Matters*, pp. 55–8. Emphasis is mine.
60 *Ibid.*, p. 55.
61 Woolf, *The War for Peace*, pp. 56–97.

9

E.H. Carr and the Quest for Moral Revolution in International Relations

Paul Rich

E.H. Carr has generally been viewed by analysts of International Relations to be a pioneer of the 'scientific' study of the discipline as well as an important theorist of state-centric 'realism'. His book *The Twenty Years' Crisis* has traditionally been considered one of the major texts that helped shape post-war realism, especially in the United States.[1] However, the significance of this text in the broader development of Carr's thinking on International Relations has been seriously neglected by analysts, who have tended to conclude that Carr was an advocate of *raison d'état* in which ethics was largely a product of power.[2] This view has also been reinforced by the sharp distinction Carr made in *The Twenty Years' Crisis* between the school of state-centric realism and that of utopian idealism, which was accused of having little understanding of the role of power in international politics and of confusing prescription with description.[3]

This simplistic reading of Carr has begun to be re-evaluated as a number of scholars have pointed to areas of common concern of both 'idealists' and 'realists'. A recent collection of essays *Thinkers of The Twenty Years' Crisis* points out, for instance, that a number of the inter-war writers whom Carr castigated as idealist did recognize the importance of power in international relations and were by no means so 'utopian' as might be supposed. Indeed, the 'idealist' school emerges as a complex body of opinion ranging from unreconstructed utopians such as H.G. Wells and Clarence Streit who passionately believed in the idea of a world state as a means to end war and more pragmatically inclined thinkers such as David Mitrany and Alfred Zimmern who were concerned to work within state structures and seek a gradualist evolution in norms of interstate behaviour and conduct.[4]

In this respect, a close reading of Carr's work indicates that his own goals were not so very different. The drift of his thought in both *The Twenty Years' Crisis* and his later study published in 1942 the *Conditions of Peace* suggests that his project for a 'science' of international relations was linked to a longer-term goal of educating idealist and opinion on the left into the dynamics of inter-state power politics. Carr considered that it was only the left that could think out 'principles of political action and evolves ideals for statesmen to aim at' and that the political right was largely bereft of original political ideas.[5] The problem with idealist 'utopianism' was that it was bankrupt intellectually since it was incapable of providing 'any absolute and disinterested standard for the conduct of international affairs'.[6] What was needed, Carr concluded, was a political science of international affairs that was 'based on a recognition of the interdependence of theory and practice, which can be attained only through a combination of utopia and reality'.[7]

Carr's approach was thus far from being a simple defence of an amoral Machiavellianism in international relations. He attacked the realist approach for being severely limited by its lack of any finite goal in politics as well as any emotional appeal, right of moral judgement or suitable ground for political action.[8] The absence of all four of these crucial aspects of political thought rendered it almost impossible for any supposedly 'realist' theorist to be completely consistent in practice. There was always going to be some form of continuous engagement even by the most hardened of realists with some aspects of what might otherwise be termed 'idealist' thought.

When read together, *The Twenty Years' Crisis* and *The Conditions of Peace* represent an attempt by Carr to shift the central axis of debate within IR towards a more professional concern with the examination and assessment of state interests and policy goals and objectives rather than to affirm the basic tenets of either realism or idealism as such. Carr was basically concerned during the early 1940s with shifting the central paradigm in IR away from what he considered to be the outmoded assumptions at the heart of the idealist vision with the nature and role of the state. Idealism, he considered, represented a continuation of nineteenth-century *laissez-faire* liberalism. Carr's defence of realism, on the other hand, was part of a wider intellectual enterprise to moralise the idea of both national and international planning and the rational re-ordering of modern bureaucracy on an international plane.

By the middle 1940s, many of Carr's aspirations became institutional-ized as the assumptions of national planning developed at the national level in the US of the New Deal or war-time Britain. The onset of the

Cold War however led to Carr being marginalized from the new post-war consensus. His departure from Aberystwyth in 1947 signalled a new orientation in his academic research as he effectively abandoned the terrain of IR as the intellectual space it had offered since the late 1930s to mount an attack on liberal notions of statehood now appeared more or less closed.

This chapter will thus argue that Carr's involvement in IR in the late 1930s and early 1940s needs to be seen in terms of an intellectual quest – lasting somewhat less than a decade – to foment a moral revolution within the discipline. It is divided into two main parts. The first part will discuss Carr's notions of idealism and realism before turning in the second part to his idea of moral revolution through state-led planning. The concluding section will assess Carr's continuing relevance for contemporary debate in IR theory.

The Debate with Idealism

Carr approached IR in the late 1930s from a background rooted in the optimism of late Victorian and Edwardian England. He was educated at Merchant Taylors School and Trinity College, Cambridge, where he took a double first in classics in 1916. His childhood at Highgate in London was shaped by the precepts of Victorian liberalism and it was only after the Russian Revolution of 1917 that he began to become acquainted with Marxist thought. He became part of a three-man team that examined Russian affairs in the Foreign Office before serving between 1925 and 1929 as a Second Secretary of the British legation in Riga.[9]

Monitoring the progress of the Bolshevik revolution in Russia encouraged Carr to start re-examining western models of social and economic organization. Russia had traditionally been viewed by observers in the West as a backward if not savage society, which continually posed a threat to the security of Western Europe. The employment of Marxist-Leninist ideology by the Soviet regime as part of a strategy of rapid economic and social modernization was a major challenge to western liberal intellectuals in the inter-war years. The Soviet model appeared by the 1930s to represent the only way forward from an apparently bankrupt liberalism that was incapable of resolving major problems of economic recession.[10] Some of these intellectuals would in time be known as 'fellow travellers' as they imported Marxist precepts in order to buttress a rationalist intellectual framework in which they no longer felt much confidence.[11] Carr displayed similar tendencies as he wrote of the centrality of Marx's thought in the intellectual development of the twentieth century. Marx was, he wrote in a biographical study published in 1934, the 'first important thinker for three centuries who did not deign to pay lip service to the fetish of individual liberty'.[12] Marxist thought was of central importance in freeing intellectuals from the stranglehold of humanism, though the price that was to be paid for this was Marxist 'fanaticism' once the moral limits on political conduct had been removed. The 'world of the twentieth century', Carr wrote, could be summed up as 'the world of mass production, mass dictatorship and Marx'.[13]

Marx, however, was not the only major intellectual influence on Carr at this time. In 1936 he left the Foreign Office to become Professor of International Relations at Aberystwyth where the Principal, Ivor Evans, was anxious to appoint someone of sufficient intellectual calibre who was not closely associated with liberal idealism.[14] At Aberystwyth Carr became acquainted with the work of the German sociologist Karl Mannheim. Mannheim arrived the same year from Nazi Germany and soon became a notable participant in social science debate in Britain.[15] Unlike many refugees from fascism at this time, Mannheim maintained a strong commitment to the rational reconstruction of western societies. Mannheim argued that rational elites should guide and mould mass opinion and steer it away from the irrationalism of totalitarian dictatorship.[16] He was also a pioneer in the sociology of knowledge and culture. In his book *Ideology and Utopia*, first published in English in 1936, he developed two Weberian ideal-types of ideological or established political thought: one which he argued reflected the thinking of ruling groups, and the other – utopian or revolutionary thought – that reflected the thought of excluded groups. In the book Mannheim also championed the idea of a free-floating intelligentsia that could stand to a considerable degree apart from the increasingly ideological politics of the mass societies of Europe and America. Mannheim envisaged this intelligentsia being able to perform a critical role in diffusing collective structures of thought as a means of steering industrial societies forward on more rational and technocratic lines.[17]

The impact of Mannheim's book can be felt obliquely in *The Twenty Years' Crisis*. Carr's study was concerned with the way ideas are generated collectively; he focused in particular on one major example of utopian thought in the form of liberal humanitarianism and the impact this had had on the conduct of Anglo-American foreign policy after the First World War. Carr's treatment of Mannheim was determined by two dominant intellectual and political objectives: of defending the basic trajectory of British foreign policy in the 1930s anchored around appeasement, and winning over the policy-making elite in Britain to an expanded foreign policy agenda that encompassed the social and economic reconstruction of western capitalist economies along the lines of planning. As Charles Jones has perceptively pointed out, he threw up a number of intellectual smokescreens in this enterprise and twisted Mannheim's sociological distinction in *Ideology and Utopia* between a dominant 'ideology' and a challenging 'utopia' almost out of recognition. The ruling elite's 'ideology' now became one of 'utopianism' centred on a rationalisation of a free market liberal ideology that was linked to Wilsonian internationalism and the League. Likewise the countervailing body of ideology that Mannheim had termed 'utopia' was not renamed 'realism' by Carr who preferred to confine this term to what Mannheim had called the 'sociology of knowledge'. There was as yet for Carr no coherent alternative ideology to the dominating 'utopianism' of the policy-making elites or the alternative 'realism' of the exponents of power politics in the tradition of Hobbes and Machiavelli. The only real ideological alternative to these two dominant positions for Carr was promised in the form of the growing appeal for socialist planning and the Soviet economic model. By obfuscating this ideological divide, Carr was able to present himself as the exponent of a rational middle of the road position between two basically unworkable extremes.[18]

The Twenty Years' Crisis needs therefore to be interpreted in a dialectical fashion reflecting a division in Carr's thought between the short and medium to longer term. As far as short-term political goals are concerned, the book ends up reflecting the disdain within the British official mind for the various efforts by intellectuals to influence the course of policy. Carr pointed out, for instance, that if intellectuals do succeed in achieving a high degree of neutrality they are continually at risk of being deprived of a secure base in politics. 'Even where the illusion of their leadership is strongest', he wrote, 'modern intellectuals have often found themselves in the position of officers whose troops were ready enough to follow in quiet times, but could be relied to desert in any serious engagement.'[19]

Carr considered that this was well exemplified by the role of intellectuals in the United States in mobilizing support for the League of Nations at the end of the First World War. Here, Carr argued, idealist intellectuals did much to secure US public opinion behind the League but were unable to maintain its support once the public realized the costs involved. This view has not been substantiated by more detailed historical reassessment. It may be true that at a general intellectual level many inter-war liberal idealists were victims of a political mythology surrounding the concept of collective security, which helped but-tress Wilsonian liberal internationalist ideology in the face of the Bol-shevik challenge.[20] However, in more specific political terms the influence of the Wilsonian liberal idealists was sporadic and condi-tional. Selig Adler, for instance, has pointed out that Woodrow Wilson's position ended up being undermined by many of his initial supporters. After initially mobilizing idealistically inclined liberal opinion behind the venture of the League Wilson then lost it when some leading liberals such as Oswald Garrison Villard and Herbert Croly (editor of the influential *The New Republic*) considered Wilson had abandoned his liberal promises by compromising with the European imperialist powers.[21]

Mannheim's idea of a free-floating intelligentsia also appeared to Carr to challenge the conventional role of the civil service in the area of British foreign policy. It had been utopian liberal idealists, he charged, who had been behind the Union of Democratic Control during the First World War and its claims for more democratic control over foreign policy. In contrast to what he called the 'missionary zeal' of the intellectuals, Carr wrote glowingly of the 'fundamentally empirical approach' of the civil service bureaucracy which was based on 'practice' and not 'theory'. 'The bureaucrat tends to make politics an end in themselves,' he argued. 'It is worth remarking that both Machiavelli and Bacon were bureaucrats.'[22]

Carr's arguments thus reflected in a short-term sense a broad section of Foreign Office opinion at a time when the policy of appeasement towards Germany was coming under increasing political attack. In August of 1939 – the same year that the first edition of *The Twenty Years' Crisis* was published – Carr also published *Britain: A Study of Foreign Policy From the Versailles Treaty to the Outbreak of War* with a warm preface by Lord Halifax, Foreign Secretary in the government of Neville Chamber-lain. The book represents a defence of the conduct of foreign policy by a professional political elite free from extraneous influences from the intelligentsia. Carr argued that this elite needed to stand back and adjudicate between competing political influences before it could resolve what the 'national interest' really was. Such an approach though had little to do with ideology. 'The foreign policy of a democracy,' Carr argued, 'must be based not only on prudent calculation of its interests, but on "principle", or an attitude of mind, and that attitude of mind will reflect what we can call the "sense of values" for which the country stands.'[23] As Hedley Bull pointed out, when stated in this way, Carr's ostensibly 'realist' conception of the national interest bore considerable similarity with idealism. This was because it presumed that national leaders who put their own nation's interests first are better able to recognise the interests of other states than those that see themselves as the custodians of mankind.[24]

It was evident by the time Carr published both *The Twenty Years' Crisis* and *Britain: A Study of Foreign Policy* that many of the assumptions behind what might be termed the enlightened bureaucratic approach to foreign policy-making were being undermined by international events. Carr defended the Chamberlain government's appeasement policy, which he considered came in the wake of a vacillating period of policy between 1933 and 1937. This phase was ended by the arrival of Chamberlain whom Carr considered realized more than any other political leader at this time that British foreign policy declarations were not matched by a 'willingness or capacity to act'.[25] He did not defend appeasement in terms of isolationist arguments or hopes for some form of closer imperial defence alignment. Carr recognized that the ability of Britain to fight a major war with a 'first-class power' depended on an alliance with the United States. Appeasement for Carr was really part of a longer-term strategy of managing Britain's decline as an independent great power and stabilizing it as part of an Anglo-American alliance that could secure global security together very possibly with the British Dominions.[26]

Such arguments though were fundamentally flawed. As Martin Wight argued in *Power Politics*, they failed to understand the essential nature of Naziism in Europe. They also misjudged the balance of power, which had frequently operated in European history to safeguard the independence of small powers rather than allow for their annexation. Most importantly of all, they represented a profound misjudgement about the nature of morality in international politics. Even though appeasement was in some respects a continuation of the older Concert of Europe, its operation by the late 1930s rested upon the suspension of the Covenant of the League and its replacement by an argument for peace at all costs. The word thus acquired its infamy because, as Wight pointed out, 'it acquired the sense of seeking to buy off an expansionist great power by the sacrifice of small allies whom there was a pledge to defend'.[27] The dubious morality behind appeasement to a considerable degree rubbed off on Carr's efforts to seek a new morality in international affairs through planning. His dismissal of the rights of small states and his elevation of the interests of great powers ultimately ensured that he failed to develop a convincing new set of international ethics by the end of the Second World War.

The Twenty Years' Crisis indeed, for all its Hegelian play of argument and counter-argument, can ultimately be read as a simple polemic concerned with securing in the medium to longer term a new political dialogue between the idealist Left, whom Carr saw as the major source of new ideas, and official policy-making. From the time of his appointment at Aberystwyth, Carr envisaged the study of International Relations being an applied science which was concerned with producing a body of informed public opinion. He was a champion of the steady professionalization of IR. If this did not occur, he warned that the study of international conflict would remain dominated by two main bodies of opinion. The first were deterministic theorists who saw war as a natural phenomenon over which there could be no real political control. The second were the groups of idealist intellectuals who were continually prone to misunderstanding the actual realities of international politics.[28] In contrast to these two bodies of opinion, Carr envisaged a new professionalized terrain of academic International Relations being able to provide a major forum for debate on international politics that was not linked to any narrow political agenda. To this extent, he saw it including a rather wider range of intellectuals and researchers than the more narrowly focused discussions in Chatham House. Moreover, it would also embrace a wider agenda than the high politics of diplomatic relations with other great powers. In this respect the book began to point to a wider agenda in IR debate than had been developed hitherto. This led Carr to a rather more profound challenge to the contemporary international order over the course of the next decade.

Moral Revolution through Planning

Despite a passionate attack on the limitations of utopian idealism, Carr began a discussion in the latter part of *The Twenty Years' Crisis* on the feasibility of an alternative international order. Carr considered that idealism was more or less played out as a force for a new international morality since its intellectual roots still lay in nineteenth-century Darwinian ideas of natural selection and *laissez-faire* economics. The prospects for an early transformation of the international system seemed grim and Carr castigated advocates on the Left of world revolution since they were 'largely blind to the lessons of history'.[29] Instead he suggested that in time a new international order could be forged through the extension from the national to the international plane of models of planning which progressively phased out the profit motive.[30] He hinted at the creation of regional blocs such as the idea of *Mitteleuropa* in

Central Europe suggested by Friedrich Naumann in a widely influential book published in 1916. Such blocs would in many cases reflect the needs of modern industry for closer economic integration and the creation of wider regional markets. This would not eliminate future political conflict as was presumed in the functionalist approach of David Mitrany in which regional and global integration occurs under the guiding hand of largely apolitical committees and groups of experts and technocrats. 'It is profitless,' Carr wrote rather sarcastically, 'to imagine a hypothetical world in which men no longer organise themselves in groups for purposes of conflict; and the conflict cannot once more be transferred to a wider and more comprehensive field... the international community cannot be organised against Mars.'[31]

Carr's approach to the issue of international economic reconstruction was stimulated by a transatlantic debate in the 1930s on state-led planning. He drew, for instance, on the work of the Austrian émigré economist Peter Drucker, whose book *The End of Economic Man* (1939) pointed to a changing awareness in the aftermath of the First World War of the anarchy of *laissez-faire* economics. Drucker stressed the uniqueness of modern totalitarianism, which he argued had suspended the workings of the market economy and created a 'non-economic society'. It was on the basis of such a model that Drucker envisaged a new non-fascist society being constructed in order to secure full employment.[32]

Many liberal intellectuals as well as those on the Left blamed the anarchy of the free market for helping create the conditions for war in Europe in 1914. This discussion was developed in rather greater depth in Carr's next book *The Conditions of Peace* in 1942. Here there is a notable change in note as the outbreak of the Second World War appeared to confirm the apparent bankruptcy of pre-war liberal idealism. There was now a twentieth-century rather than a twenty years' crisis, though Carr warned against any simplistic Marxist theory that rooted this in a mere struggle of labour against capital. He drew instead on Drucker's *The End of Economic Man* by pointing to the capacity of advanced capitalist states to incorporate organised labour into a corporatist system of joint control over the political machinery of the state.[33]

The Second World War represented for Carr the culmination of a revolution in world politics over the previous twenty years against three dominant concepts in international relations of liberal democracy, national self-determination and *laissez-faire*. Carr envisaged all these being swept away in a new revolutionary impetus which would usher in a new world order based upon a renewed definition of democracy that would extend economic and social rights as well as political ones; an end to the fissuring of the international order by ever smaller nations claiming the right of self-determination and the extension of international planning to end economic *laissez-faire*. The fact that the three concepts were in crisis was a reflection, Carr argued, of a deeper moral crisis in international politics brought on by the collapse of the nineteenth century utilitarian attempt to reconcile reason and morality through the doctrine of a harmony of interests.[34]

At the heart of *The Conditions of Peace* lay a plea for a rethinking of the moral purpose of international politics. Carr suggested that this rethinking needed to embrace a new faith that could define political goals in positive terms rather than the negative suppression of evil. It also needed to restore communal goals and solve the basic economic problems on a basis of an egalitarian ethic and an ethic of responsibility as much as individual rights. He failed to explain, though, exactly what this morality would consist of since he did not root it in either Christianity or communism. There seemed indeed to be limits to the role of intellectuals in the new revolutionary era ushered in by the war. 'There is all the difference in the world', he wrote:

> between an examination of the conditions which a new faith and a new moral purpose must fulfil and an assurance that this faith and this purpose will come to birth. They cannot be generated by an intellectual process, which can do no more than demonstrate the need for them if civilisation is to be saved.

Carr confronted what he considered to be a profound moral crisis at the heart of western civilization and then retreated from it. The *Conditions of Peace* revealed a loss of intellectual nerve which can be best explained by his failure to theorize the concept of a 'moral revolution' in world politics more robustly. Most of the texts that Carr employed to exemplify moral crisis were really concerned with social control. In the case, for instance, of describing the 'moral dilemma' at the heart of the contemporary epoch, Carr cited the work *The Folklore of Capitalism* by the American writer T.W. Arnold. Carr quoted Arnold as saying that 'the process of building up new abstractions to justify filling new needs is always troublesome in any society, and may be violent'.[35] Arnold's argument was really directed at social engineers concerned with devising a new social philosophy that could stabilize modern industrial societies. 'In the area of social control,' he continued, 'we are now going through a world shaking struggle, which threatens to be long, complicated, and pathetically ludicrous, to build up a set of abstractions or a social philosophy which will permit us to satisfy the practical needs of society.'[36]

The confusion in the *Conditions of Peace* over the meaning of moral revolution in international relations was largely due to Carr's uncertainty over the sort of role that both Britain and the United States would perform in the post-war international order. The book appeared at a very fluid political moment in world politics and it was almost impossible for anyone to predict with confidence the outcome of military conflict – at the Teheran conference in 1943, for instance, Franklin Roosevelt admitted to Stalin that he did not foresee the maintenance of US troops in Europe after the war.[37] Carr still thought it highly likely that policy-makers in the United States would wait for a British lead on issues of US cooperation with Britain and the Dominions.[38] So the book can be read as another contribution to the myth of an Anglo-American 'special relationship'. Carr hoped, though, that this would lead to a long-term Anglo-American military commitment to European regional security involving regional integration via a continental planning authority.[39]

By the middle of the Second World War some of the intellectual allies that Carr had sought to mobilize behind his vision of a new globally planned economic order were moving in a different direction. Peter Drucker, for instance, argued in *The Future of Industrial Man* that the Nazi experiment in Germany was a failed attempt to secure a functioning industrial society. The reconstruction of the post-war industrial societies by no means necessitated the build up of a draconian state structure. Drucker examined the institution of the modern industrial corporation that, like the state in the contract theory of John Locke, was nominally subordinated to the sovereignty of the stockholders. The corporation was an institution that could check the power of the all-embracing state as well as having a considerable fund of managerial talent to secure social and economic reconstruction.[40] This represented a significant departure from his earlier faith in large-scale planning. 'Total planning,' he now argued, was 'actually total improvisation. It is the renunciation of the deliberate and conscious attempt to work out our problem, in favour of a gamble on the guesses of a technician.'[41]

These arguments against total social and economic reconstruction would gain greater clarity after the publication in 1944 of the essay *The Road to Serfdom* by the Austrian émigré Friedrich Hayek. This was a passionate denunciation of state planning which Hayek argued would inevitably undermine democracy and lead society on a road to political 'serfdom'. Significantly, the book also contained a strong attack on Karl Mannheim's vision of industrial reconstruction by a rational, sociologically informed intelligentsia and was a powerful plea for the resurrection of the market economy as the basis for a free society.[42]

Carr did not treat such criticisms especially seriously. He argued that there was an irresistible tendency in western industrialized societies towards greater state planning in order to control economic forces. He dismissed what would now be termed neoliberal arguments for an expansion of the free market (for example, Walter Lippmann's *The Good Society*) as a feeble attempt to resist what appeared to be an inexorable tide towards ever greater state planning.[43] To some extent the *Conditions of Peace* was much in tune with the mood of the times and marked a strong attack on the more conservative sections of officialdom such as Alexander Cadogan, Permanent Under-Secretary at the Foreign Office between 1938 and 1946 who loathed anything to do with 'planning'.[44]

Carr's thinking drifted increasingly apart from the establishment consensus emerging in the West after 1946 and 1947. He found himself the subject of complaints by the Foreign Office when he urged in *The Times* closer relations with the Soviet Union – even if this was at the expense of the rights of peoples in Eastern Europe.[45] In a series of lectures published in 1946 as *The Soviet Impact on the Western World* he argued that the Woodrow Wilson's missionary role in defining Allied war aims during the First World War had been effectively taken over by Stalin by the time of the Potsdam Declaration of 1945.[46] He saw the Soviet Union now acting as a vanguard nation in the debate on post-war planning since the Soviet model was not simply an instrument of national power and aggrandisement but part of a wider project for social and economic reconstruction. This led him scornfully to rebuke managerial theorists of planning in the West such as James Burnham in *The Managerial Revolution*.[47] The Soviet economic model of state planning, he maintained, had now become the most significant model of economic reconstruction on offer.[48] There was no reference in Carr's discussion of the problems facing the Soviet economic system, nor any reference to the wild and largely unobtainable targets laid down by Stalinist planners.[49] Carr preferred to portray the Soviet planning experience in rather naively simplistic terms whereby it had 'most successfully combined the national and social aspects of planning into a single policy'. The relevance of the Soviet economic model was also underlined by the fact that the dominant ideology of the USSR had been 'framed in response to the new conditions of mass civilisation, and . . . it has arisen in a country where a sense of community has always been more active than the sense of individual rights'.[50]

These themes would eventually be examined in greater scholarly detail in *The Bolshevik Revolution*.[51] At one level Carr's lectures can be interpreted as a strong apology for Soviet policy. This was a reading academic colleagues tended to make in the increasingly bitter years of the Cold War with severe consequences for his career – he failed in 1945 to be elected to the Chair of Russian History at the School of Slavonic and East European Studies and the University of Oxford refused to elect him to the chair in International Relations. After he left Aberystwyth in 1947 he was without an academic post until 1955 when he became a fellow at Trinity College, Cambridge.[52] Carr's work at this time though was also predominantly concerned with the ideological challenge to western interests in Soviet policy in strategically vital areas such as the Balkans and the Middle East. He urged western policy-makers to pay more attention to the close relationship in contemporary foreign policy between economic and military power as well as the growing ideological cleavage between the Soviet and western conceptions of democracy.[53]

What was beginning to emerge as the Cold War was thus, for Carr, a rivalry between different political systems with their own modes of government, economic and social organization and dominant belief systems.[54] He appealed to western leaders to re-examine the ideological bases of their policy and mobilized to buttress his case the former Marxist philosopher Nicholas Berdyaev, who converted to the Russian Orthodox Church. Carr drew on Berdyaev's book *The End of Our Time* (1933), which was a pessimistic rumination (in a manner similar to the later work of Alexander Solzhenitsyn) on the inadequacies of western humanism to withstand the ideological challenges of Soviet Marxism. This humanism drew man away from his essentially spiritual state and left him an isolated and atomised unit which ultimately perished in the 'superhuman individualism' of Nietzsche.[55] Western democracy therefore was left with no ultimate ethical purpose as it became subordinated to a 'complete relativism' and a 'negation of all absolutes'.[56]

The centrality of ideology in Carr's examination of Soviet–Western relations indicated that there had been a change of emphasis from the state-centric realism of *The Twenty Years' Crisis*. In the period before the Second World War Carr was largely defending what he saw as the dominant tradition of European realism from idealist attack. In this earlier perspective, ideological factors in international politics had been largely subordinated to state interests. By the end of the war, however, he increasingly emphasized how political elites were at the mercy of the transnational ideological forces that made up their respective systems. Such a configuration failed to see how the Cold War international order became stabilized around two rival superpower hegemons in which there would be a high degree of congruence between power and purpose defined in terms of universal goals.[57]

Carr, moreover, failed to understand the drift of post-war opinion in both the United States and Western Europe. While there was a limited role for 'planning', it was largely centred on consolidating capitalist market economies rather than transcending them. The pumping of dollars by the US into Western Europe via the Marshall Plan after 1948 was more in accordance with the Keynesian model of pumping of western economies in order to reflate them out of recession. In all of the major western economies that did not fall into the Soviet sphere of influence the market survived even if there was an increased role for the state in regulating a series of mixed economies. The era of post-war reconstruction in Western Europe proved to be far less Soviet inspired than he imagined and ended up being dominated by figures such as Jean Monnet, who succeeded in post-war France in marginalizing socialist models of state planning in favour of a far less ambitious model of indicative planning through the *Commissariat Général du Plan* (CGP) involving relatively few civil servants.[58]

The creation of large regional blocs did not occur on Soviet lines either. In the case of Europe regional integration was largely secured as a result of what Alan Milward has termed the rescue of the nation state as the leading actors in Western Europe entered into a series of intergovernmental bargains to pool sovereignty, first around the European Coal and Steel Community in 1951, and later the European Economic Community after the Treaty of Rome in 1957.[59] Carr largely misunderstood this rejuvenation of the western capitalist economies and was still seeking to apply the rather more pessimistic prognoses of the European left from the 1930s.

After his departure from Aberystwyth in 1947, Carr largely sidestepped IR debate for the more specialized multi-volume study of the Bolshevik Revolution. One essay from 1949, however, indicated that he remained preoccupied with issues of power and morality. He showed considerable scepticism of the durability of the institutional structure of the post-war order, especially the United Nations, and pointed to the need to rethink the moral foundations or world order. This should, he suggested, be conceived in terms of the extension of 'doctrine of the common man' from the national to the international plane. Despite the hardening of the Cold War, he still held the hope that there would be the development of economic planning at the international level leading eventually towards a pooling of economic resources and the creation of supranational blocs.[60]

How Relevant is Carr for Contemporary IR Debate?

Carr's conceptualization of the debate between realism and idealism has maintained a remarkable durability in international theory, despite the fact that it was clearly a product of a particular set of historical circumstances in the late 1930s and early 1940s. As this chapter has sought to show, Carr's central imperative was an ethical one. While he acknowledged that ethical considerations in IR were clearly subordinate to issues of power and state interest he was concerned to show how a new ethical conception of power was entering international politics as a result of the long-term ideological impact of the Soviet revolution. He refused, though, to align himself formally with Marxism and remained for most of his career an intellectual fellow traveller content to draw on many of the moral challenges presented by Marxism to western liberalism.

The infusion of Marxism and class analysis into Carr's thought led him to present what seemed to be a rather more radical and wide-ranging critique of the world order in the late 1930s and 1940s than that of the idealist tradition. The group of scholars and intellectuals that Carr termed idealists were also preoccupied in the inter-war period with ethical issues and what Alfred Zimmern lamented as the 'decline in international standards'.[61] Much of this debate appeared nostalgic and backward-looking as it hankered after the apparent golden age of the nineteenth century and the heyday of the *Pax Britannica*. Carr's moral critique by contrast was infused with a more wide ranging social and economic imperatives derived from the Soviet experience with planning. This increasingly led Carr into becoming a champion of the Soviet model and Marxist ethics at a time when those of western humanist liberalism seemed ethically bankrupt and incapable of resolving the inter-war economic crisis of the western economic system.

Within ten years of the publication of *The Twenty Years' Crisis* the beginnings of European reconstruction made much of this seem outdated. Carr seriously misread the drift of post-war international politics and failed to detect the intellectual rejuvenation in western liberalism in the years after Hayek published *The Road to Serfdom* in 1944. The resurrection of a reformed liberalism from the late 1940s onwards undermined the charge that the western liberal tradition was bankrupt. Free market arguments of the Hayekian kind became progressively incorporated into the realist credo as it was pointed out that the collectivist assumption that war between states would disappear in a system of planned economies was really another form of idealist utopianism that failed to account for the survival of national identities.[62] Such arguments became increasingly cogent as a split became increasingly visible between the Soviet Union and China in the late 1950s.

If there had been what Hermann Rauschnigg had termed a 'revolution of nihilism' it had largely occurred as a result of the destructive impact of National Socialism on the insecure liberal fabric of Weimar Germany.[63] Elsewhere in the West, liberalism in the course of the late 1930s and 1940s made a series of accommodations with the demands for state-led planning though not on the scale that Carr thought essential to restabilize the international order. Carr exhibited a multiple series of intellectual identities throughout his career and was not only apologist for the Soviet model but also a strong believer in the essential beneficence of British governing power. Like many of his generation, he failed to see how British imperial hegemony would be so quickly replaced after 1945 by that of US global hegemony. Finally, he failed in particular to see how the apparently discredited leadership of Woodrow Wilson and his vision of a new world order, centred on the expansion of the free market and the rights of small states to national self determination, would be resurrected at the end of the Cold War.

Notes

1 K.W. Thompson, *Political Realism and the Crisis of World Politics* (New York: John Wiley, 1960), p. 25; Martin Wight, 'Western Values in International Relations', in M. Wight et al., eds, *Diplomatic Investigations* (London: Allen and Unwin, 1966), p. 121.

2 See, for instance, Justin Rosenberg, *The Empire of Civil Society* (London: Verso 1994), pp. 10–15; Scott Burchill, 'Realism and Neo Realism', in Scott Burchill and Andrew Linklater, eds, *Theories of International Relations* (Basingstoke: Macmillan Press, 1996), pp. 67–73.

3 E.H. Carr, *The Twenty Years' Crisis* (London: Macmillan, 1966).

4 D. Long and P. Wilson, eds, *Thinkers of The Twenty Years' Crisis* (Oxford: The Clarendon Press, 1996).

5 Carr, *The Twenty Years' Crisis*, p. 20.

6 *Ibid.*, p. 88.

7 *Ibid.*, p. 13.

8 *Ibid.*, p. 89.

9 For details of Carr's career see R.W. Davies, 'Edward Hallett Carr', *Proceedings of the British Academy*, Vol. LX1X 1983, pp. 473–511.

10 A good example of this outlook from a member of the 'Auden generation' in 1930s England is Stephen Spender's *Forward from Liberalism* (London: Gollancz, 1937).

11 D. Caute, *The Fellow Travellers* (London: Weidenfeld and Nicolson, 1973), pp. 5–6.

12 E.H. Carr, *Karl Marx: A Study in Fanaticism* (London: Dent, 1934), p. 302.

13 *Ibid.*, p. 303.

14 K. Martin, *Father Figures* (Harmondsworth: Penguin Books, 1966), p. 190.

15 For details of Mannheim's influence in England see Wolf Lepenies, *Between Literature and Science: the Rise of Sociology* (Cambridge: Cambridge University Press, 1988), pp. 328–33.

16 K. Mannheim, *Ideology and Utopia* (London: Kegan Paul 1940). 'the masses', Mannheim wrote in *Man and Society in an Age of Reconstruction*, 1940, 'always take the form which the creative minorities controlling societies choose to give them'. Karl Mannheim, *Man and Society in an Age of Reconstruction* (London: Kegan Paul, 1940), p. 75.

17 H.S. Hughes, *Consciousness and Society* (London: Paladin, 1974), pp. 418–27.

18 C. Jones, 'Carr, Mannheim and a Post-Positivist Science of International Relations', *Political Studies*, Vol. XLV 1997, esp. pp. 236–8.

19 Carr, *The Twenty Years' Crisis*, p. 15.

20 G.W. Egerton, 'Collective Security as a Political Myth: Liberal Internationalism and the League of Nations in Politics and History', *The International History Review*, Vol. V, No. 4, November 1983, pp. 496–524.

21 S. Adler, *The Isolationist Impulse* (New York: Collier Books, 1961), pp. 55–62. Adler also pointed out that Woodrow Wilson basically failed to make explicit the relationship of American security to the global balance of power. S. Adler, *The Uncertain Giant 1921–1941* (London: Collier Books, 1965), p. 5.

22 Carr, *The Twenty Years' Crisis*, p. 16.

23 E.H. Carr, *Britain: A Study of Foreign Policy from the Versailles Treaty to the Outbreak of War* (London: Longman, Green and Co., 1939), p. 16.

24 H. Bull, 'The Theory of International Politics, 1919–1969' in B. Porter, ed., *The Aberystwyth Papers* (London, 1972), p. 37.

25 *Ibid.*, p. 166.

26 *Ibid.*, p. 46; Carr, *The Twenty Years' Crisis*, p. 232.

27 M. Wight, *Power Politics* (Harmondsworth: Penguin Books, 1986), p. 214.

28 See in particular Carr's inaugural lecture at Aberystwyth reprinted as E.H. Carr, 'Public Opinion as a Safeguard of Peace', *International Affairs*, XV, 6 (November–December 1936), pp. 846–62.

29 Carr, *The Twenty Years' Crisis*, p. 226.

30 *Ibid.*, pp. 238–9.

31 *Ibid.*, p. 231. For a discussion of Mitrany's ideas see 'Functionalism: the Approach of David Mitrany', in A.J.R. Groom and P. Taylor, eds, *Frameworks for International Cooperation* (London: Pinter, 1990), pp. 125–36; C. Navari, 'David Mitrany and International Functionalism', in Long and Wilson, *Thinkers of The Twenty Years' Crisis*, pp. 214–38.

32 P. Drucker, *The End of Economic Man* (London: Heinemann, 1939); Carr, *The Twenty Years' Crisis*, p. 224.

33 E.H. Carr, *The Conditions of Peace* (London: Macmillan, 1942), pp. 24–5.

34 *Ibid.*, p. 102.

35 T.W. Arnold, *The Folklore of Capitalism* (Garden City: Blue Ribbon Books, 1941), p. 378, cited in Carr, *The Conditions of Peace*, p. 107.
36 Arnold, *The Folklore of Capitalism*, p. 379.
37 H. Thomas, *Armed Truce: The Beginnings of the Cold War, 1945–46* (London: Sceptre, 1988), p. 260.
38 Carr, *The Conditions of Peace*, p. 186.
39 *Ibid.*, p. 253.
40 P. Drucker *The Future of Industrial Man* (London: Heinemann, 1943), p. 53.
41 *Ibid.*, p. 198.
42 F.A. Hayek, *The Road to Serfdom* (Routledge, 1944), p. 16. For a recent assessment of the book's intellectual impact, see A. Gamble, *Hayek* (London: Polity Press, 1996), pp. 16–21.
43 Carr, *The Conditions of Peace*, p. xiv.
44 Thomas, *Armed Truce*, p. 302.
45 *Ibid.*, pp. 320–1. Carr tended to dominate the policy of *The Times* during the war, Davies, 'Edward Hallett Carr', p. 487.
46 E.H. Carr, *The Soviet Impact on the Western World* (London: Macmillan, 1946), pp. 2–3.
47 *Ibid.*, p. 27.
48 *Ibid.*, p. 34.
49 R.V. Daniels, *The End of the Communist Revolution* (London and New York: Routledge, 1993), p. 90.
50 Carr, *The Soviet Impact*, p. 103.
51 On the foundation of the Soviet model of planning see E.H. Carr, *The Bolshevik Revolution, Volume 2* (London: Macmillan, 1952), chapter 20. In the late 1960s Carr appears to have considered that many of the utopian ideals at the heart of the original Bolshevik project still had relevance in contemporary Soviet policy. 'No society entirely devoid of utopian aspirations will escape stagnation', he wrote ' Soviet society has not stagnated. In the long struggle over de-Stalinization in the 1950s and 1960s, the old clash between passionate idealists and cautious administrators is again apparent'. E.H. Carr, 'Editor's Introduction' in N. Bukharin and E. Preobrazhensky, *The ABC of Communism* (Harmondsworth: Penguin Books, 1969), p. 51.
52 Davies, 'Edward Hallett Carr', p. 491.
53 Carr, *The Soviet Impact*, pp. 77–8.
54 For a view of the Cold War as a clash of rival systems see F. Halliday, *Rethinking International Relations* (London: I.B. Tauris, 1994)
55 N. Berdayev, *The End of Our Time* (London: Sheed and Ward, 1933), p. 39. Berdayev had an influence on a number of Christian thinkers in the West in the 1930s and 1940s. See, for example, R.C. Mowat, *Climax of History* (London: Blandford Press, 1951), p. 153.
56 *Ibid.*, p. 175, cited in Carr, *The Soviet Impact on the Western World*, p. 15.
57 Z. Laidi, *Power and Purpose After the Cold War* (Oxford: Berg, 1994).
58 For details of Monnet's influence see F. Duchene, *Jean Monnet* (New York: Norton, 1994), pp. 147–80.
59 A. Milward, *The European Rescue of the Nation State* (London: Routledge, 1992).
60 E.H. Carr, 'Moral', in E.L. Woodward et al., eds, *Foundations of World Order* (Denver: University of Denver Press, 1949), pp. 55–75.

61 A. Zimmern, 'The Decline of International Standards', *International Affairs*, Vol. XV11 January–February 1938 pp. 3–31.
62 See, for instance, J.H. Herz, 'Idealist Internationalism and the Security Dilemma', *World Politics*, July 1950, pp. 176–7.
63 H. Rauschnigg, *The Revolution of Nihilism* (New York, 1933).

10
Theories as Weapons: E.H. Carr and International Relations

Tim Dunne

E.H. Carr would have been more comfortable with the self-description 'intellectual activist' rather than 'international theorist'. His interest in international relations was motivated by his desire to influence policy, whether it related to the response of the West to the Soviet Union or the economic imperative of reconstructing post-war British economy and society. This concern to shape the course of history in the early 1940s led to something of a collision between his two worlds of academe and policy-making when it came to the attention of the Woodrow Wilson board that their Professor was more engaged in the politics of *The Times* than the Department of International Politics at Aberystwyth. Compared to the controversies within the English-speaking academic world that his writings on International Relations and Soviet history were to generate, this fall-out at Aberystwyth was no more than a little 'local' difficulty.

In the discipline of International Relations, Carr's reputation stands or falls largely according to competing interpretations of *The Twenty Years' Crisis*. During the years of the 'first great debate', Carr found himself in the unfortunate position of being caught in the crossfire between different sides, neither wanting to claim him (or his work) for their own. Predictably, liberal idealists in the late 1930s and 1940s saw Carr as something of a menace.[1] But what is surprising is that the highest opprobrium was uttered by the so called 'high-priest' of American realism, Hans J. Morgenthau.[2] In contrast to his reputation in the early post-war period, Carr's stock has risen dramatically in recent years. In an influential piece written in the mid-1980s, Robert Gilpin identified Carr as one of the all-time 'three great realist writers'.[3] At the radical end of the discipline, participants in the post-realist debate such as Ken Booth, Robert Cox and Andrew Linklater, all appropriate from Carr key building blocks for the construction of a new stage in international relations theory.[4] Postmodernists have not dwelt long on *The Twenty Years' Crisis*, which is surprising given Carr's twin attractions to power and pragmatism.[5] None of this is to suggest that Carr's work does not continue to provoke criticism from all political sides, as important recent critiques testify.[6]

E.H. Carr's involvement with academic International Relations ended after the war. His voyage into the history of the Soviet Union enabled him to revisit his love of Russian literature and politics. Through this monumental study, Carr was able to engage deeply in academic inquiry, as well as influencing Western opinion on the Soviet Union. Just as he sought, in *The Twenty Years' Crisis*, to 'counteract the glaring defects' of state leaders in the 1930s, his representation of the Soviet Union similarly aimed to balance the 'propaganda' about the regime which was disseminated by the West during the Cold War. Here Carr was entering deeply troubled political waters, provoking vituperative attacks from the Conservative Right shortly after his death, and relative alienation from all but the Marxist Left during his life.

The focus for this chapter is not to enter the fray about whether or not Carr's analysis of the USSR was flawed, or whether his works in International Relations are contradictory. It will, however, draw on the interrelated spheres of Carr's biography, ideology and his place in the academy, in order to address the following themes. First, the question, what did Carr mean by 'realism' and 'utopianism'? It will be argued that the realism of *The Twenty Years' Crisis* is not a theoretical construct but a critical weapon which Carr turned against 'utopianism'. Crucially, he was dissatisfied with a non-utopian realism, privileging in the final analysis a complex relationship between the two constructs. This tension has been lost in the orthodox interpretation of the work as a founding text in the realist canon. The point here is not to deny that there are realist arguments in *The Twenty Years' Crisis*, but rather, the aim is to reveal the ambiguities inherent in the unstable relationship between 'realism' and 'utopianism'. The second theme to be addressed concerns the extent to which Carr was a moral relativist. How did Carr seek to ground his ideas about a new global order after the Second World War: in reason? or in power (as his critics suggest)? Here the focus will shift to Carr's idea, outlined in *What Is History?*, of achieving progress through 'the widening horizon'.

Carr and International Relations: 'Political Thought is a Form of Political Action'

Carr's education in international politics flourished whilst he was a diplomat in Riga, from 1925 to 1929, where his interest in Russian culture and history first took hold. Being somewhat of a loner, he opted out of the opera circuit beloved of charmed diplomatic circles, preferring to read nineteenth-century Russian literature. There was also a political dimension to these works. Carr saw in these writers a powerful critique of bourgeois capitalist society. In addition to his work as a diplomat and biographer, Carr developed a third vocation, that of a commentator and essayist. In some respects, it is in this last capacity that Carr was at his most brilliant, combining an agile discursive style with an impressive breadth of historical learning.[7]

Between 1930 and 1933 Carr acted as a Foreign Office advisor on League of Nations Affairs. In a critical review of *The Twenty Years' Crisis* Sir Alfred Zimmern admitted that Carr had 'sat in the Foreign Office with an observing eye'.[8] A good example of his dual role of diplomat and commentator is recounted in *The Twenty Years' Crisis* where Carr notes how he was profoundly influenced by a statement made by the Yugoslav foreign minister who criticized the 'things-will-right-themselves' school of economists, who failed to see that 'free' markets operated 'at the expense of the weakest.[9] This critique of the liberal doctrine of the 'harmony of interests' became the starting point for Carr's construction of 'political realism'. More broadly, it signified Carr's increasing disenchantment with liberalism's twin foundations of capitalism and democracy. This opened the door to what Carr saw as the main attraction of Marxism, its ability to 'debunk' the moralistic claims of liberal democracy.

Upon Carr's acceptance of the Professorship at Aberystwyth in 1936 he soon undermined the idea of liberal internationalism associated with the former US President in whose name the chair was created.[10] For David Davies, the realism that Carr brought to the position was the final nail in his idealist coffin. He bitterly regretted the way in which the department 'has worked consistently against the programme I have spent most of my time and money advocating; namely, the development of the League with a real international authority'.[11] Endowing chairs, Davies was forced to conclude, 'is a very dangerous experiment'.[12]

When viewing Carr's tenure as Wilson Professor, we should not be too swayed by Davies' fanaticism for the League and his concomitant rejection of reasoned criticism of idealism. As the historian of the University College of Wales put it colourfully, 'hell hath no fury like an idealist disillusioned'.[13] In many ways, Carr's years at Aberystwyth were remarkably productive. Within three years he had published three major works in addition to his war-time service at the Ministry of Information as director of foreign publicity.[14] After a dispute with the new minister, Sir John Reith, Carr increasingly devoted himself to writing editorials for

The Times although continuing to publish books and pamphlets, mainly on the challenges of constructing the coming peace.[15] Carr's involvement with *The Times* caused some conflict with his responsibilities at the University College Wales. Carr resigned from the Chair at Aberystwyth in 1947.[16] After his 'resignation' from the Wilson Professorship, Carr was passed up for a number of academic positions for which he was well qualified.[17] The most obvious explanation for his exile from the academy is that Carr's sympathy for the Soviet experiment had become a professional liability with the onset of the Cold War. As Haslam put it, 'Britain, too, had its equivalent of McCarthyism'.[18]

Why did Carr become a disenchanted liberal? In his short autobiographical notes, Carr recalled how at the peace conference 'my Liberal principles were still intact'.[19] By the early 1930s, his views were thoroughly pro-Soviet. Carr was not alone in holding these views. He was part of a generation of disenchanted liberals, who saw capitalism failing and the promise of democracy faltering. In the preface to *Britain: a Study of Foreign Policy From the Versailles Treaty to the Outbreak of War* Carr noted that 'there are now few thinking men who will dismiss with confidence the Marxian assumption that capitalism, developed to its highest point, inevitably encompasses its own destruction'.[20] International Relations scholars are fond of pointing out that Soviet foreign policy makers rapidly shed their revolutionary clothes and become diplomats. In the case of E.H. Carr, the diplomat became a revolutionary.

Theories as Weapons: Realism in *The Twenty Years' Crisis*

The Twenty Years' Crisis was published at the end of 1939, just after Britain officially declared war against Nazi Germany. To date the book has run to two editions – the second edition alone has sold over 30,000 copies.[21] It is interesting to note that by the end of the war Carr dismissed the work as 'a study of the period' which 'must be treated on its merits as such'.[22] Judging by the importance of the work in the historiography of academic International Relations, it is fair to say that Carr's assessment of the book is not shared widely within the discipline. Not only is it one of the first books students read, it is a book which more mature scholars often return to. More graphically, it might be one of the few books in the field 'which leaves us nowhere to hide'.[23] It is the only book written by a British International Relations theorist to have been adopted as a key realist text in the American academy. Stanley Hoffmann called it 'the first "scientific" treatment of modern world politics'.[24] More recently, Michael Joseph Smith argued that 'from its first appearance *The Twenty Years' Crisis* was treated as a challenge to the predominant intellectual approach to international relations, and it is still read today as a classic statement of realism'.[25] Not only has the text travelled well in the English-speaking International Relations world, its significance has been reified by the elevation of the work as the winner of the so-called first 'great debate' between realism and idealism.[26]

The analysis of *The Twenty Years' Crisis* offered below endorses Ken Booth's view that it is a 'brilliant' but 'flawed' work which has been 'misunderstood' by those who view it through a realist's eye view. The 'brilliance' lies in its use of realist theory as a weapon to undermine specious claims to universal truth and morality. 'Flawed' because the arguments, or 'evidence' on which he bases his critique does not stand up to close scrutiny. Carr's use and abuse of history is not the reason why most writers have criticised *The Twenty Years' Crisis*, citing instead Carr's subordination of morality to power, and utopianism to realism. It is in this sense that the work has been 'misunderstood', since it fails to recognize the genuine (if ambiguous) goal of utopianism, and moreover, wrongly construes the charge of 'relativism' so frequently laid at Carr's door (discussed in Part Three of the chapter). Where the analysis departs from that offered by Booth concerns the rejection of his charge that *The Twenty Years' Crisis* has been an 'unhelpful influence on the development of the subject'.[27] Arguably, it contains within it the possibility of an immanent critique of a number of core claims made by contemporary defenders of the international society project. For example, Carr's application of the sociology of knowledge to diplomacy enables us to penetrate the consciousness of actors in order to reveal the material forces and social structures which are shaping their actions, and crucially, distorting their self-definitions and explanations for their own actions. Furthermore, Carr's critique of the inequality of power in the international system poses deeply problematic questions for later writers in British IR theory such as Hedley Bull who invested in great powers a special role in maintaining international order. In this sense, inequality was a necessary condition for developing an order which benefitted *all* states.

E.H. Carr's motives in writing the book were both realist and utopian. Looking to the future, *The Twenty Years' Crisis* was dedicated to 'the makers of the coming peace', who would one day face the responsibility of building a new post-war utopia. Looking in the opposite direction, the book was written, in Carr's words, with the 'deliberate aim' of countenancing the 'almost total neglect of the factor of power' which had beset Anglo-American thinking in the interwar period.[28] The label Carr allocated to these 'children of lightness' was, of course, 'utopians'.

But *who* were the 'utopians', *how* were they responsible for the 'underlying' rather than 'immediate' cause of the breakdown in international order? What false diagnosis did they prescribe? And how could the malaise they identified be removed and the theory and practice of international politics be reinvented?

The first and most obvious point to make about Carr's treatment of the 'utopians' is the pejorative way in which he uses the term, particularly in the early stages of the text. To be a utopian is to be immature, infantile; to prefer wishing rather than thinking. In Orwellian language, utopians are the humans (two legs bad), realists the pigs (four legs good). His initial referent for utopianism is the discipline itself, which is evolving out of its 'primitive' phase – an evolutionary form which he attributes to all 'sciences'. One of the defining characteristics of this phase is the privileging of the 'end' over the 'means', a tendency embodied in Woodrow Wilson's famous quote about the League, 'if it won't work, it must be made to work'.[29] Notice here the shift in the referent for 'utopianism' from the discipline to particular state leaders. Utopians tend to privilege general principles, or 'absolute standards', rather than practical questions about how principles are to be applied in practice. From utopian state leaders, the referent then shifts to the terrain of the political 'Left', who tend to advocate ideas in preference to problem-solving approaches. Moving from the political to the philosophical, we discover that utopianism is as old as the Enlightenment tradition; the epistemology of utopianism is 'rationalism', the belief that reason can deliver unvarnished truth.[30]

Carr's expansive remarks on utopianism, make way in Part Two of the text to a more analytical consideration of the ways in which utopian thinking contributed to 'the international crises'. Faith in human reason articulated in philosophical sketches by Bentham and Kant began in the early part of the twentieth century to shape world-views of state leaders and western publics, who increasingly came to hold the opinion that reason could ground democracy, and democracy conquer anarchy. The referent for utopianism has now become 'democratic rationalism'.[31] Projected onto the international realm, rationalism was codified in the League of Nations covenants, with its universal standards for maintaining peace through collective security. Because these standards were self-evident, and applicable across time and space, any deviation from what is rational is designated as pathological. Hence, as Carr points out, the characteristic of utopian thinkers from 1931 onwards to describe the actions of revisionist states (and the lack of response to them) with adjectives like 'wicked', 'egotistic', 'cowardly'.

What is evident from the detour into utopianism is the generality (and inconsistency) with which Carr assigns the category to a multitude of referents, from individual thinkers and particular texts, to different disciplines and finally to domestic and international political orders (blurring its ontological status as 'principle' or 'action' in the process).[32] The next move in *The Twenty Years' Crisis* is to show *how* a theory of utopianism has *caused* a breakdown in the inter-war order. Here we come across the central explanatory theme which is said to unite all strands of utopianism across different disciplines, namely, the belief in a 'harmony of interests'. In philosophy, utilitarianism holds out the promise that self-interest promotes the general good; neoclassical economics brings together the interests of the individual with the efficient functioning of the market; and finally, liberal internationalism argues that there are no essential conflicts of interest between nation-states. The slow recognition, from the turn of the century onwards, that interests collided in international relations (between great powers and small states, for example) just as they conflict in the domestic labour market, is revealing the hollow nature of the hegemonic liberal conception of morality that has dominated political thought 'for a century and a half'. This leads Carr to conclude: 'The inner meaning of the modern international crises is the collapse of the whole structure of utopianism based on the concept of the harmony of interests.'[33]

The analysis of the breakdown in the inter-war system presented in *The Twenty Years' Crisis* is open to a number of objections. Even if 'the harmony of interests' pervaded thinking in France, Britain and the League as a whole between 1919 and 1939 (itself a contestable claim), it was clearly not part of the vocabulary of post-revolutionary Russia and the other revisionist states in the 1920s like Italy and Japan, who rejected liberal economic and political principles long before the descent into war. Similarly, how does the natural liberal harmony explain America's decision to remain outside of the League structure, an event which would appear to signal a clear disconnect between the national and international interest. A useful way to illustrate the weakness in the analysis provided in *The Twenty Years' Crisis* is counterfactually: even if state leaders in the 'satisfied' powers had recognized the reflection of their own national interests in the mirror of international principles, it is highly unlikely that this would have prevented the outbreak of general war. National forces and social movements beyond the control of western states were the primary cause of the Second World War, not illusions of perpetual peace harboured in liberal states.

Realism is the term Carr uses to describe the critique of utopianism. As will become clear below, it is of paramount importance to make a formal distinction between 'realism' as a theory of international politics, and Carr's version of realism as an epistemic 'tool' or 'weapon'. Using an analysis familiar to Marxists, Carr refutes the harmony of interests doctrine, reducing it to 'the ideology of the ruling group concerned to maintain its predominance by asserting the identity of its interests with those of the community as a whole'.[34] For example, Britain's arguments in the nineteenth century for universal free trade reflected Britain's particular advantages in securing such an outcome. Similarly, the Treaty of Versailles represented the interests of the satisfied victor powers, and not those of all humankind.[35] The utopian assumption that there is an international invisible hand which can masterfully co-ordinate a world common good out of the pursuit of a plurality of separate national interests is an illusion. Conflicts of interest are, Carr argued, '*real* and *inevitable*'.[36]

The purpose for realism is, therefore, to relativize all claims to a universal good in order to reveal the partial interests which underlie those claims. The 'absolute standard' which Carr was fighting was the law and the morality of the satisfied powers:

> What matters is that these supposedly absolute and universal principles were not principles at all, but the *unconscious* reflections of *national interest* at a particular time.[37]

Applying this lesson to international relations, he concludes that there can be no international order outside the interests of the dominant powers.[38] Clearly this was a devastating critique of the idealist movement to institutionalize a legal and moral order in the international realm. It is also a critical weapon that could be turned against Carr's successors such as Martin Wight, Hedley Bull and R.J. Vincent, who rejected Idealism but nevertheless believed it possible to defend international order on the grounds that it benefited all states.

As the following section will consider in greater detail, the relativism of realism is the issue which Carr's critics are united in condemning. For Carr it is precisely this relativism which represents the apotheosis of realist thought:

> The weapon of the relativity of thought must be used to demolish the utopian concept of a fixed and absolute standard by which policies and actions can be judged.[39]

Where does Carr derive this formula of realism-as-relativism from? Probably the most important source for the argument in *The Twenty Years' Crisis* was the Hungarian sociologist, Karl Mannheim. Carr acknowledges his debt to Mannheim in the Preface to the work, but the extent of his influence is more apparent in a later essay by Carr published in the *Times Literary Supplement* in 1953. Mannheim's principal academic innovation, Carr argues, was to systematize a body of ideas known as the 'sociology of knowledge'. The core claim here is the embedded nature of political thought in the social order, in other words, the sociology of knowledge is the appropriation of Marx's argument that ideas (superstructure) are a reflection of material circumstances (base), whilst denying a specifically economic character to the base. The intellectual impact of Mannheim's ideas on Carr is given prominence by Charles Jones. 'Mannheim deserves consideration by students of international relations', Jones argues, 'chiefly because he provided Carr with the dialectical structure of *The Twenty Years' Crisis* and a distinctively post-positivist social scientific methodology that would mark him off from the dominant positivism of the Anglo-Saxon world of his day'.[40]

Carr's exegesis on Mannheim is at the same time a vindication of his own method. As Carr said of Mannheim, 'he struggled hard against the imputation of 'relativism'. His one criticism of Mannheim suggests Carr's struggle against relativism was even greater. Carr resisted the idea, propounded by his mentor, that intellectuals could be quasi-autonomous. In a typically adroit comment, Carr wrote: 'The question is not where we are to find the standard-bearers, but where we are to find the standard.'[41]

Bringing Utopianism Back In

In his article '*The Twenty Years' Crisis* Thirty Years On', Hedley Bull argues that Carr's work is an exercise in critique which fails to excavate a new theoretical structure on top of the ruins of the old. The same claim is forcefully made by less sympathetic critics. In Morgenthau's words, Carr surrenders 'to the immanence of power'.[42] Leonard Woolf dismisses Carr as a realist with no sense of morality reducing the complexity of the text to the crude formulae: 'Power is a reality; force is a reality; war is inevitable; peace is utopian'.[43] Whittle Johnson asks how Carr is able to prevent his argument being 'washed over the rapids into a normless relativism?'[44]

These convergent representations of *The Twenty Years' Crisis*, and Carr's work in general, commits three related errors (each of which is considered below): first, they do not adequately consider the specific recommendations made by Carr in order to facilitate peaceful change in international politics; second, the antinomical relationship between realism and utopianism is fundamentally misunderstood; third, they understate the extent to which Carr was aware of the need to provide moral foundations By rethinking Carr's philosophy of history, it is evident that he provided (albeit cautiously) a grounding for reason in history (thereby overcoming relativism).

These commentaries on Carr's work uncritically accept a logocentric understanding of the relationship between realism and idealism; in other words, the power of realism displaces the wishful thinking of idealism. This is never endorsed by Carr in an unqualified form. Even in the opening chapter of *The Twenty Years' Crisis* Carr admits that realism is a 'corrective' that must itself be counteracted by 'utopianism'.[45] A revisionist understanding of the relationship between these 'two poles' highlights the movement of history and science through dialectical stages where the line between truth and falsehood is blurred rather than sharply defined opposites according to conventional logic. The case for a revisionist account is not helped by the fact that Carr 'slides' from a dialectical understanding to one in which realism and utopianism coexist in space rather than evolving through time.[46] The important point is not to try to unravel the precise relationship between 'realism' and 'utopianism', but to recognize the interpenetration of the two elements. This is precisely what was lost in the sound and fury of the so-called 'great debate'. T.L. Knutsen neatly articulates this argument:

> whereas Carr in the late 1930s had emphasized the dynamic interaction between utopianism and realism, scholars of the late 1940s often saw the two in static opposition. Post-war students, unaccustomed to Carr's dialectics, simply considered utopianism a naive alternative to realism; they treated it as a straw man which they could knock over in order to better portray the mature wisdom of the realist alternative.[47]

As a consequence of the colonisation of *The Twenty Years' Crisis* by realism, little attention has been paid to the way in which Carr uses the term 'utopianism' in a constructive sense. After the realist weapon has penetrated the mask of national interests, Carr recognized the need to build a new Utopia. What was *his* idea of a Utopia? At this juncture it is useful to draw on the distinction between 'end-point Utopias' and 'process Utopias'.[48] Carr's target, as discussed earlier, was the theorists and practitioners who signed up to an 'end-point Utopia', such as total disarmament or the renunciation of the use of forces, as though the conditions for its realisation were already in existence. But nowhere in *The Twenty Years' Crisis* does Carr dismiss the reformist steps of process utopianism. Indeed, in a later work, Carr describes utopianism as moving towards a goal 'even if this goal is never fully attained or attainable'.[49]

The problem of how to 'effect necessary and desirable changes' without war[50] was a prevalent utopian theme in international relations literature in the 1930s.[51] For Carr, British appeasement of Germany embodied the two sufficient conditions for peaceful change, the element of power and the element of morality.[52] But Carr does not address how we are to judge the synthesis of these two planes. For example, how many borders should Hitler have been allowed to change before the element of force was required to counteract the ethical accommodation of Germany's revisionist demands? The strength of Carr's dialectic for change is that it allows for the interplay of *both* elements of morality and power. But the weakness in the argument, like the difficulty with the balance between the background theories of realism and utopianism, is that Carr does not explain *how* it is possible to have both elements. 'All one can do,' as one critic put it, 'is see-saw between them.'[53]

Hedley Bull argued that Carr's defence of appeasement highlighted the moral bankruptcy of relativism, which 'denied all independent validity to moral argument'.[54] Yet this reading of his work does not take into account that Carr was clearly aware of the bankruptcy of political programmes which were devoid of ethical content. As Carr argued in a contribution to a volume entitled *Foundations for World Order*, although morality cannot be separated from the influence of power 'we must believe – in an absolute good that it is independent of power'.[55] Not entirely confident that morality could provide any firm 'foundations', he nevertheless provided important prescriptions for international reform, including an end to discrimination between 'individuals on grounds of race, colour or national allegiance', striving to find 'commonly accepted ground on which to meet and discuss differences' between states, and the provision of basic needs for all of humanity.[56]

These sketches of utopian thought in Carr's work serve to undermine the simplistic dismissal of Carr as a slave to power politics. They do not, however, amount to a theoretical escape from the relativism he encounters as a result of signing up to the sociology of knowledge. In *What Is History?* we find Carr's attempted escape route, although it would be premature to argue that this traces the path leading to Utopia on the outside, rather than merely another point inside the walls of the realist prison. When dealing with the vexed question about grounding moral judgements, Carr once again reiterates that there are no ahistorical standards by which actions can be judged. But in the final lecture in the George Macauley Trevelyan series, Carr opens up an ethical space which he refers to as 'the widening horizon'. In this space, Carr recalls romantically the age of the great nineteenth-century liberal historian, Lord Acton. His age, argued Carr, 'possessed two things both of which are badly in need of today: a sense of change as a progressive factor in history, and belief in reason as our guide for the understanding of its complexities'.[57] Here we see how 'reason' and 'progress', the two utopian scourges which Carr sought to banish in the early chapters of *The Twenty Years' Crisis*, are returning to provide the foundations for a new and more inclusive social order.[58]

Conclusion

E.H. Carr believed the realist-relativist critique to be the great strength of realism. For his critics, it was the Achilles' heel of *The Twenty Years' Crisis* and Carr's work in general. In this respect, the critics tried to debunk the great debunker. But were they successful? One response to Carr's critics is to contend that their argument against Carr relies on a misreading of his theory of realism as though it represented an unalloyed victory over utopianism. In place of this one dimensional reading of the text, the chapter has brought to the surface what Derrida calls the 'not-seen'.[59] This technique reveals alternative readings of the relationship between the contesting forces of signification: realism and utopianism as a dualism (opposites), duality (interpenetration) and dialectic (successive moments in the resolution of opposites). By locating the issue in the body of his thinking, particularly his philosophy of history, there are good reasons for thinking that realism and utopianism form the two components of a dialectic. The key phrase is Carr's recognition that 'we still need to build a new utopia of our own, which will one day fall to the same weapons'.[60] The only problem with this 'critical' reading is that it obscures the fact that utopianism remains an unstable category, one which is never adequately grounded despite Carr's hope that reason might open a 'wide horizon' for a social democratic politics to occupy. Given this instability, perhaps a more appropriate label for this position is postmodern realism. This term picks up on the (admittedly fragmentary) pragmatist epistemology found in Carr's work[61] and moreover, the deeply held belief that universal moral principles cannot escape the constant instrusion of power politics.

In the final analysis, any attempt to 'fix' a meaning or representation onto the central categories of thought in *The Twenty Years' Crisis* is bound to fail. We should, therefore, emancipate Carr from the meta-narratives – realism, Marxism, statism – which have framed our understanding of him. Instead, we should take from Carr's *The Twenty Years' Crisis* the clear rejection of positivism evident in his claim that there are no facts, only interpretations.[62] We should also carry with us into the next 80 years of International Relations his metaphor of realism as a 'weapon'. Given the fact of cultural diversity in world politics, claims to universalism are deeply problematic; forcing ourselves to confront the weapon of the relativity of thought opens up a space for thinking critically about the foundations – and the interests – which undergird knowledge claims.

Not only did Carr reject the idea that there could be any genuinely *common* values between states in a hierarchically ordered international political system, he believed that International Relations itself was part of the problem of inequality and not part of the solution. On this point it is significant that Carr turned the realist weapon back on the International Relations academy with the following indictment: 'The study of international relations in English speaking countries is simply the study of the best way to run the world from positions of strength.'[63] Ultimately it is this despair with the discipline which consigns Carr to being something of a dissident. He was in International Relations but International Relations was not in him.[64]

Notes

1 For a comprehensive overview of the idealists' reaction to the book, see P. Wilson in this volume.

2 H. Morgenthau, 'The Surrender to the Immanence of Power: E.H. Carr', *Dilemmas of Politics* (Chicago: Chicago University Press, 1962), pp. 350–7.

3 R. Gilpin, 'The Richness of the Tradition of Political Realism', in R. Keohane, ed., *Neorealism and its Critics* (New York: Columbia University Press, 1986), p. 306.

4 See K. Booth, 'Security in Anarchy: Utopian Realism in Theory and Practice', *International Affairs*, Vol. 67, 1991, pp. 527–45; A. Linklater, 'The Transformation of Political Community: E.H. Carr, Critical Theory and International Relations', *Review of International Studies*, Vol. 23, 1997, pp. 321–38.

5 Even if Carr does not elaborate a full-blown pragmatist epistemology, the anti-empiricism evident in *What is History?* sets him apart from the dominant strand of positivism in International Relations. The idea that there is a family

resemblance between Carr and postmodernism is challenged by Keith Jenkins, who argues that 'whilst Carr may well have learnt the late-modernist
notion of perspectivism, he hardly seems to have been ready for the post-
modernist lesson that perspectivism "goes all the way down"; that it includes
everything and everybody – including himself'. See K. Jenkins, *On 'What is
History?': From Carr and Elton to Rorty and White* (London: Routledge, 1995),
p. 62. For a survey of pragmatism, see S. Smith, 'Positivism and Beyond', in
S. Smith, K. Booth and M. Zalewski, eds., *International Theory: Positivism and
Beyond* (Cambridge: Cambridge University Press, 1996), pp. 11–46.

6 J. Rosenberg, *The Empire of Civil Society: A Critique of the Realist Theory of
International Relations* (London: Verso, 1994).

7 See, for example, E.H. Carr *From Napoleon to Stalin and Other Essays* (London:
Macmillan, 1980). This is a collection of extended essays written primarily
for the *Times Literary Supplement*.

8 Alfred Zimmern, quoted in M.J. Smith, *Realist Thought from Weber to Kissinger*
(Louisiana: Louisiana State University Press, 1986), p. 68.

9 Marinkovitch at the session of the Commission for European Union in
January 1931, quoted in Carr, *The Twenty Years' Crisis*, p. 57.

10 In November 1919, David Davies and his family contributed £20,000 as an
endowment of a Chair in Aberystwyth, for the study of those aspects of law,
politics, economics and ethics 'which are raised by the prospect of a League
of Nations and for the truer understanding of civilizations other than our
own'. Ieuan John, Moorhead Wright, and John Garnett, 'International Politics at Aberystwyth 1919–1969', in B. Porter, ed., *Aberystwyth Papers* (Oxford:
Oxford University Press, 1972), p. 86.

11 Quoted in E.L. Ellis, *The University College of Wales, Aberystwyth 1872–1972*
(Cardiff: University of Wales Press, 1972), p. 259.

12 Correspondence with Professor R.B. McCallum, Pembroke College, Oxford,
24 June, 1942. The purpose of the letter was to congratulate McCallum on a
damning review of Carr's *Conditions of Peace*, published in *The Oxford Magazine* 18 June 1942, pp. 372–3. I am grateful to Guto Thomas for bringing this
correspondence to my notice.

13 Ellis, *The University College*, p. 259.

14 In addition to *The Twenty Years' Crisis*, Carr published the following works:
International Relations since the Peace Treaties (London: Macmillan, 1937),
reissued as *International Relations Between the Two World Wars 1919–1939*
(London: Macmillan, 1947); *Britain: A Study of Foreign Policy From the Versailles Treaty to the Outbreak of War* (London: Longmans, 1939).

15 Many of these ideas can be found in Carr, *Conditions of Peace* (London:
Macmillan, 1943). For a comprehensive analysis of Carr's work at *The
Times*, see Charles Jones' contribution in this volume.

16 According to Norman Stone he was sacked. Stone 'Grim Eminence', *London
Review of Books*, 20 January–3 February 1983, p. 4. For a detailed examination
of Carr's years in Aberystwyth, see Brian Porter's chapter in this volume.

17 R.W. Davies lists the Chair of Russian History at the School of Slavonic and
East European Studies, the Chair of International Relations at Oxford, a
fellowship at St Antony's. Balliol even refused him a fellowship after two
years as a Lecturer in Politics. See R.W. Davies, 'Edward Hallet Carr', *Proceedings of the British Academy*, Vol. LXIX, (1982), p. 491.

18   See Jonathan Haslam's contribution to this volume.

19   Quoted in Davies, 'Edward Hallett Carr', p. 477.

20   Carr, *Britain: A Study of Foreign Policy*, p. v.

21   30,660 copies according to Tim Farmiloe at the Publishing Director at Macmillan. I am grateful to Tim for bringing this to my notice.

22   Carr, *The Twenty Years' Crisis*, preface to the second edition, 1946.

23   This imagery was presented in K. Booth: 'Human Wrongs and International Relations', *International Affairs*, Vol. 71, No. 1, 1995, p. 123.

24   S. Hoffmann, 'An American Social Science: International Relations', in Hoffmann, *Janus and Minerva: Essays in the Theory and Practice of International Politics* (Boulder, Col.: Westview Press, 1959, 1977), p. 5.

25   Smith, *Realist Thought from Weber to Kissinger*, p. 68. Christopher Hill also uses the term 'classic' to describe the work, in his, '1939: The Origins of Liberal Realism', *Review of International Studies*, Vol. 15, 1989, p. 324. Martin Griffiths believes the book 'is still rightly regarded as a "classic" in the discipline of International Relations, and rightly so'. *Realism, Idealism and International Politics: A Reinterpretation* (London: Routledge, 1992), p. 34.

26   W.C. Olson, 'The Growth of a Discipline', in Porter, *The Aberystwyth Papers*, p. 23. There is without doubt a consensus in the discipline that Carr's text is *the* symbolic representation of an hierarchical dualism between 'political realism' and 'utopianism' (in other words, a relationship which imputes power and dominance to the first term in the pairing). In *The Aberystwyth Papers*, the description of the part *The Twenty Years' Crisis* played in the epic inter-war paradigm shift is symptomatic: 'it sounded the death knell for all those writers who had focused their attention on the world as it ought to be rather than as it was'. I. John, M. Wright and J. Garnett, 'International Politics at Aberystwyth 1919–1969', *The Aberystwyth Papers*, p. 96. For a powerful critique of the tendency to view the historiography of the discipline through the prisms of 'great debates', see B. Schmidt, *The Political Discourse of Anarchy: A Disciplinary History of International Relations* (New York: SUNY Press, 1997).

27   Booth, 'Security in Anarchy', p. 530.

28   Carr, *The Twenty Years' Crisis*, preface to the second edition, 1946 (no page number in text). Emphasis added.

29   Carr, *The Twenty Years' Crisis*, p. 8.

30   *Ibid.*, p. 23, note 1.

31   *Ibid.*, p. 28.

32   As Cecelia Lynch puts it in an understated manner: 'He painted utopianism with a broad brush', 'E.H. Carr, International Relations Theory, and the Societal Origins of International Legal Norms', *Millennium*, Vol. 23, No. 3, 1994, p. 97.

33   Carr, *The Twenty Years' Crisis*, p. 62.

34   *Ibid.*, p. 44.

35   This argument of Carr's is contestable. As Lynch argues, 'the Great Powers have very often *not* been able to use global international organisation to further their interests'. Lynch, 'E.H. Carr, International Relations Theory', p. 617.

36   Carr, *The Twenty Years' Crisis*, p. 60. Emphasis added.

37   *Ibid.*, p. 83. Emphasis added.

38   Clearly this sensitivity for the use of theory shows how Carr was cognisant of the power of theory, an argument which is central to the critical theoretical 'turn' in International Relations theory. Robert Cox expresses the point well in the phrase, 'theory is always *for* someone and *for* some purpose'. See R. Cox, 'Social Forces, States and World Orders', in Robert Keohane, ed., *Neorealism and its Critics* (New York: Columbia University Press, 1986), p. 207.

39   Carr, *The Twenty Years' Crisis*, p. 75.

40   Jones, *E.H. Carr and International Relations*, chapter 6, p. 2.

41   Carr, *From Napoleon to Stalin*, p. 181.

42   Morgenthau, 'The Surrender to the Immanence of Power', p. 350.

43   L. Woolf, in Evans, 'E.H. Carr and International Relations', p. 88.

44   W. Johnson, 'E.H. Carr's Theory of International Relations: A Critique', *Journal of Politics*, 39, 1967, p. 863.

45   Carr, *The Twenty Years' Crisis*, p. 10.

46   As Carr put it: 'The state is built up out of these two conflicting aspects of human nature. Utopia and reality, the ideal and the institution, morality and power, are from the outset inextricably blended in it'. *The Twenty Years' Crisis*, p. 96. At other times, he also flatly contradicts this antinomical reading, for example, in his argument that 'Politics are made up of two elements – utopian and reality – belonging to two different planes which can never meet'. *The Twenty Years' Crisis*, p. 93.

47   Knutsen, *A History of International Relations Theory*, p. 224.

48   Booth, quoting Joe Nye, in 'Security in Anarchy', p. 536.

49   Carr, 'Foundations for World Order', p. 72.

50   Carr, *The Twenty Years' Crisis*, p. 209.

51   For example, A.J. Toynbee article 'Peaceful Change or War? The Next Stage in the International Crisis', *International Affairs*, 15, 1936, pp. 26–36.

52   Carr's discussion of the Munich agreement has variously been described as 'a brilliant argument in favour of appeasement' (A.J.P. Taylor, *The Origins of the Second World War* (London: Book Club Associates, 1972), p. 288); and a less fortunate argument for 'accommodation with Hitler' (Stone, 'Grim Eminence', p. 3), depending on which Oxford historian one reads. The level of opprobrium was fuelled by the author's editing-out of part of the argument from the second edition published in 1946, admitting in the *Preface* only to removing 'two or three passages relating to current controversies which have been eclipsed or put in a different perspective by the lapse of time'. Carr, *The Twenty Years' Crisis*, Preface, second edition.

53   Griffiths, *Realism, Idealism and International Politics*, p. 34.

54   Bull, '*The Twenty Years' Crisis* Thirty Years On', p. 629.

55   It is important to note that Carr qualified this comment with the following words: 'it is none the less difficult to pretend that human beings have more than a fitful and faltering knowledge of this absolute good'. Carr, 'Foundations for a World Order', p. 66.

56   Carr, 'Foundations', pp. 71, 74, 75.

57   Carr, *What is History*, pp. 152–3.

58   Linklater, 'The Transformation'.

59   J. Derrida, *Of Grammatology*, translated by Gayatri Chakravorty Spivak (Baltimore: Johns Hopkins University Press, 1976), p. 164.

60   Carr, *The Twenty Years' Crisis*, p. 93.

61 Evident, for example, in Carr's comment that realism is able to reveal 'the relative and pragmatic character of thought itself'. Carr, *The Twenty Years' Crisis*, p. 87. On pragmatism, See Smith, 'Epistemology' in Smith, Booth and Zalewski, *Positivism and Beyond*.

62 Carr was aware that in the social sciences, there can be no simple break between the subject and the object of investigation – as Carr put it, 'in the process of analysing the facts, Marx changed them'. Carr, *The Twenty Years' Crisis*, p. 4.

63 Letter from E.H. Carr to Stanley Hoffmann, in Davies, 'Edward Hallett Carr', p. 488.

64 I am indebted to Ken Booth for this formulation.

11
E.H. Carr, Nationalism and the Future of the Sovereign State

Andrew Linklater

The belief that Carr was an unqualified realist has been contested in the recent literature, but the question of how his position should be characterized lacks an established answer. Carr's writings have provoked very different readings. Some regard his work as exemplifying a utopian or critical realist approach to world affairs;[1] Others have suggested that his writings contribute to the development of a radicalised rationalism.[2] A third approach highlights various parallels between Carr's writings and critical theory in the Marxian or post-Marxist vein.[3] Other interpretations reaffirm the conventional reading of Carr which emphasises his part in creating a distinctively British variant on state-centric realism.

The affinities between Carr's writings on international relations and recent critical-theoretical approaches are the chief concern of this chapter. The key argument is that Carr was one of the first writers in the field to develop a vision of the triple transformation of political community.[4] Despite his reputation for realism, Carr envisaged new forms of political community, which would be more universalistic than their predecessors, considerably more sensitive to cultural differences and more deeply committed to reducing material inequalities. Carr's support for these three dimensions of the reconfiguration of political community is the essence of his legacy to the field.

There are three sections to the following discussion. The first analyses Carr's critique of the modern territorial concentrations of power and his bold vision of post-national forms of political organization. It notes his specific opposition to the idea of national self-determination, and to the fusion of nation and state, which had brought such devastation to the modern world. It highlights his belief that lasting solutions to mass unemployment and poverty could be found only in post-national

arrangements, which broke down invidious distinctions between citizens and aliens while respecting the cultural aspirations of minority
nations. The second section considers the question of whether Carr's
vision of new forms of political association was free from the utopianism
that he condemned in liberal internationalist thought. The answer to
this question pinpoints certain affinities between his approach to
the modern state and the method of immanent critique developed by
Marx and refined by western Marxists including the members of the
Frankfurt School. But although parallels with Marxist thought and with
realism are evident in Carr's writings, he rejected both perspectives. His
work may be read as an analysis of the prospects for international
political change, which sought to give expression to a critical approach
to world politics that escaped the limitations of realism and Marxism.
The final section assesses Carr's work for contemporary critical international theory. Various limitations in his writings are noted, including his
expectation that new international economic planning arrangements
would provide the solution to the crisis of European international
society and might, in time, prevail across the world as a whole. But
despite such problems, Carr's account of the transformation of political
community explored issues which lie at the heart of contemporary
critical approaches to international relations. In these respects, his
thought lends unexpected shape and direction to the modern critical-
theoretical project with its commitment to post-national forms of political organization.

E.H. Carr and the Post-National State

In an engaging preface to the second edition of *The Twenty Years' Crisis*,
Carr maintained that the first edition had been wrong to assume that
the nation-state would remain the basic 'unit of international society'.[5]
Subsequent events had demonstrated to the unbiased observer that the
small independent political community was outmoded and that 'no
workable international organisation' could be built on a 'multiplicity
of nation-states'.[6] The interested reader was invited to consult *Nationalism and After* for Carr's current views on this central subject.

In fact, one of the themes that *Nationalism and After* considered at
length had already been introduced in the last few sections of *The
Twenty Years' Crisis*. In those final paragraphs, Carr argued that British
policy might have to grant the population of Dusseldorf, Lille and Lodz
many of the rights which the people of Jarrow or Oldham already
possessed.[7] When making this comment, Carr assumed that the great

powers would continue to shape world politics, but they might yet become the 'Great Responsibles', to use Sir Alfred Zimmern's influential phrase.[8] In *The Future of Nations*, which had appeared in 1941, Carr maintained that the Great Powers ought to shoulder responsibilities for the military and economic security of other nations which they had frequently avoided in the past.[9] New international obligations in Britain's case would require it to link its defence with that of other European countries in a new system of transnational security. If Britain was to play the role of the great responsible, 'the principle of a common economic policy', which respected the interests of 'French, Belgian and German industry or of Danish and Dutch agriculture as well as of British industry or agriculture', would also have to feature prominently in the decision-making process.[10] Duties to promote collective economic security would be as necessary as obligations to develop common military security in a radically improved European order.

These movements towards transnational economic and physical security might seem incompatible with the principle of state sovereignty, but at no point did Carr assume that sovereignty should disappear entirely. 'What we are required to surrender,' Carr wrote in *The Future of Nations*, 'is not a mythical attribute called sovereignty, but the habit of framing our military and economic policy without regard for the needs and interests of other countries.'[11] Cautious optimism that this stale custom might soon disappear was expressed in *The Twenty Years' Crisis*. In the future, Carr suggested, 'the concept of sovereignty is likely to become . . . even more blurred and indistinct than it is at present'.[12] 'It is unlikely,' he added, 'that the future units of power will take much account of formal sovereignty. There is no reason why each unit should not consist of groups of several formally sovereign states so long as the effective (but not necessarily the nominal) authority is exercised from a single centre. The effective group unit of the future will in all probability not be the unit formally recognised as such by international law.'[13] The evolution of common military and economic policy would involve a radical break with the moral parochialism of the nation-state rather than the end of state sovereignty.

Carr's argument for the transformation of political community was centrally concerned with the scourge of unemployment and the absence of adequate material resources and meaningful opportunities for large numbers of Europe's population.[14] Nation-states had wrestled with these problems in the inter-war period, and many had looked to national economic planning for a solution. The consequences for international relations had been catastrophic. The elevation of the idea of national self-determination as a principle of international society, and the fusion of nation and state, had proved destructive in an age of mass unemployment and economic depression. Modern forms of nationalism had upset the balance between national sentiments and international loyalties which underpinned the European political order for much of the previous century. Carr's solution to this problem was to support a form of 'Continental Keynesian' in which international economic planning would safeguard human freedom, defined in Berdyaev's words as the 'opportunity for creative activity'.[15] International planning would be the main vehicle for promoting not the freedom and equality of nations, but the freedom and equality of individual men and women across Europe as a whole.[16] Welfare internationalism was necessary to promote the economic and physical security of individuals which the nation-state had once been expected to provide.[17]

Carr was confident that the small sovereign nation-state could no longer be taken seriously as the main instrument for promoting welfare and security, and sure that the enlargement of the boundaries of political association would be one of the dominant and possibly irreversible trends in post-war Europe. He was also acutely aware that international planning agencies would have equally undesirable consequences if they rode roughshod over allegiances to states and minority nations. 'The recrudescence of disintegrating tendencies' could prove to be the main consequence of efforts to build a new European political community.[18] In any case, the struggle between centripetal and centrifugal political forces would probably be 'more decisive' than any other issue for 'the course of world history in the next few generations'.[19] The tension between the pressures to expand and contract the boundaries of political community would continue until European societies had restored the balance between national identity and cosmopolitan loyalty.

Carr's enthusiasm for international planning agencies and functional authorities was linked with support for an equivalent to the principle of subsidiarity. It was necessary to create larger military and economic units in Europe for some purposes but also to retain 'existing or smaller units for other purposes'.[20] This emphasis on units which are smaller than the nation-state reflected his belief that wider post-national political allegiances had to coexist with loyalties to minority nations. Carr was optimistic that these latter solidarities could be integrated within more inclusive forms of political community. There was ample evidence that 'considerable numbers of Welshmen, Catalans and Uzbeks have quite satisfactorily solved the problem of regarding themselves as good Welshmen, Catalans and Uzbeks for some purposes and good British,

Spanish and Soviet citizens for others'.[21] Those nations or cultural groupings revealed how new modes of political association could develop which would not fuse state and nation. An 'extension of this system of divided but not incompatible loyalties' was the only means of balancing the need for post-national military and economic organisation with the powerful human desire 'to form groups based on common tradition, language and usage'.[22] In *The Future of Nations* he argued that the separation of state and nation would mean that people 'should be allowed and encouraged to exercise self-determination for some purposes but not for others'.[23] A willingness to 'determine themselves into different groups for different purposes' was 'the only tolerable solution' to the problems caused by organizing international society in accordance with the principle of national self-determination.[24]

These sentiments revealed that Carr was hostile to the ethic of national self-determination which had become a constitutive principle of international society at the end of the First World War. The devastation which had been caused by that decision made it necessary to 'discard the nineteenth-century assumption that nation and state should normally coincide'.[25] Carr understood that political communities will not command much popular loyalty if they resist demands for the public recognition of cultural differences, but claims for national sovereignty on the part of small nations had to be opposed. A 'group of individuals living in the middle of Great Britain or Germany cannot claim, in virtue of the principle of self-determination, an inherent right to establish an independent self-governing unit.'[26] By this principle, 'it would be difficult to claim for Wales, Catalonia and Uzbekistan, an absolute and inherent right to independence, even if a majority of their inhabitants should desire it; such a claim to exercise self-determination would have to be weighed in the light of the interests, reasonably interpreted, of Great Britain, Spain and Soviet Russia.'[27] This objection to those nations which might seek sovereignty within the society of states was 'also applicable to units which already enjoy an independent existence'.[28] Neither the subordinate nations which aspired to full sovereignty nor the established states which had their constitutional independence endorsed by international law should enjoy the right to take decisions without regard for the interests of outsiders. New forms of political community would recognize that the differences between citizens and aliens had lost much of their moral relevance, but they would support the popular desire to preserve cultural differences and they would do so in the course of developing international solutions to the inequalities of social and political power.

As noted earlier, Carr was aware that international planning arrangements might activate disintegrating tendencies. He envisaged a world in which nations would remain important elements in the new structures of international cooperation, but they would no longer have an automatic entitlement to constitute themselves as sovereign states. If novel systems of transnational cooperation were to survive, they would have to 'admit something of the same multiplicity of authorities and diversity of loyalties' as the multicultural societies.[29] Carr argued for 'the largest measure of devolution' and for much greater regard for the multiple loyalties and allegiances which enrich social life: new forms of international cooperation would recognize national loyalties rather than attempt to destroy them and, in so doing, emulate the more successful multinational states.[30] This way of balancing the nation and the wider world would mark 'the beginning of the end of the destructive phase of nationalism'.[31]

Beyond Realism and Marxism?

Everyone will recall the enthusiasm with which Carr despatched the utopians, and on that basis he earned his considerable reputation as the founder of British realism, but it is improbable that Carr would have revelled in this reputation.[32] *The Twenty Years' Crisis* was as much a protest against realism as a critique of idealism, even though it was this second attribute which was often stressed in subsequent interpretations of his work. The fact is that Carr mounted a brilliant critique of realism from the Left. All too often, he argued, the belief that certain conditions are unalterable is the product of a dismal lack of interest in social and political change. This malady was only too apparent in realism. Judged in this context, no one could seriously doubt the 'intellectual superiority of the Left' which stood alone in thinking out the principles and ideals which political leaders should seek to realize.[33] Of course, Carr did accept the realists' point that utopian thinkers ignored the realities of power, and it is true that at times he shared their conviction that reality and utopia are two horizons that never meet.[34] But from what has already been said about his critique of national self-determination and his vision of new forms of political community, it will be clear that Carr did not adopt a realist standpoint which assumed that the basic structure of international society is unchangeable and concluded that grand normative projects have no relevance for international politics. Indeed, Carr developed his own political vision, which he conceded was utopian, although he was quick to add that it had the redeeming feature of standing 'more directly in the line of recent advance than visions of a world federation or blue-prints of a more perfect League of Nations'.[35]

Carr did not analyse the possible alternative to the sterility and barrenness of realism and the naivety and exuberance of idealism in great detail.[36] Ken Booth has coined the phrase, 'utopian realism', and Richard Falk has introduced the neologism 'critical realism' to describe Carr's dissenting position.[37] Carr's remark 'that no political utopia will achieve even the most limited success unless it grows out of political reality' supports their interpretation,[38] as does his later observation that 'no valuable political activity can be carried on without that knowledge of conditions and possibilities which history affords'.[39] There are parallels here with Marx's critique of utopian socialism, but no ringing endorsement of scientific socialism. Carr came closest to Marx and the humanistic, or Hegelian, wing of Marxism when he argued that his vision was not hopelessly utopian but immanent within the line of the most recent advance. This emphasis on the respects in which a realizable Utopia was inherent within, though not guaranteed to emerge from, the existing order of things runs through Marx's early writings and post-Marxist approaches such as the Frankfurt School.

Carr's alternative to realism and utopianism accepted the Marxian theme that there is no Platonic realm of moral universals which stands above the world and reveals its terrible shortcomings. He shared the Marxian belief that pure reason could not penetrate the world of fleeting appearances to encounter a system of permanent and universal truths. Carr's third path accepted Marx's point that these appeals to the realm of absolute truths are ideological attempts to provide transcendental foundations for historically-specific and contested political standpoints and interests. But it did not issue grandiose Marxist claims about the meaning and direction of the whole of human history.[40] Reflecting Marx's observation that all that ideas might change are other ideas, Carr posed the troubling question of how any vision of an improved form of life could be embodied in concrete social practices. His answer contains more than a few traces of Marx's influence. Along with Marx, he believed that ideals with real transformative power take shape in the cauldron of social conflict and emerge in the womb of decaying social structures. From this vantage-point, radical or utopian thinking amounts to little unless it is linked with a sociological account of historical transformation which identifies the likely agents of social change. This method of immanent critique, which Marx employed in his analysis of the contradictions of capitalism and in his account of the social forces which felt those tensions most painfully and formed the vanguard of political change, best characterizes Carr's position on the prospects for moving beyond the nationalistic sovereign state.

As noted, there are dangers in pressing these parallels too far. Although Carr often worked in the spirit of Marxism, his thought was at odds with historical materialism which held that capitalism was the source of the most pernicious and destructive contradictions in society, while socialism was the universal panacea for the modern social problem and the proletariat was the key to political change. Carr denied that the antithesis between capital and labour was the central factor in political life.[41] Unemployment, poverty and inequality figured prominently on Carr's list of the deepest shortcomings of modern society but to assume, as Marxism had done, that socialism would rid the world of these problems was to underestimate the extent to which the merger of state and nation had been responsible for the crisis of modern politics. Marx's writings seriously misunderstood the importance of nationalism.[42] His belief in the centrality of class politics meant that he failed to wrestle deeply with the problem of the nation-state or to reflect on the forms of political community which might supersede it. These were the central elements in Carr's thinking but in Marx's thought they had been eclipsed by allegedly more fundamental questions about the transition from capitalist to socialist modes of production.

Any attempt to assess Carr's debt to Marxism must take account of the literature on imperialism which appeared in the aftermath of the First World War. Colonialism, international rivalries which culminated in violence and the collapse of the international socialist movement forced Marxists to reconsider the importance of nationalism, the state and war in modern history. These developments compelled them to reflect on the reasons for the growth of state power, the nationalization of communities which had been thought certain to fragment along class lines, and deepening estrangement between societies. Lenin and Bukharin attempted to explain the reasons for the emergence of these totalising communities in the early part of the century.[43] The same ambition pervades the first part of the argument of *Nationalism and After*, but the similarities extend only so far. Lenin and Bukharin believed that the emergence of state monopoly capitalism was the main factor behind the creation of totalizing communities, and they assumed that the revival of class warfare would sweep nationalism and inter-state violence aside. Carr developed a more complex explanation of totalizing forces in the first part of the century along with a more sophisticated understanding of how political community had to be reconfigured if similar outbreaks of large-scale violence were to be prevented in future.

The three stages in the development of the modern idea of the nation was Carr's central theme. In its first phase, nationalism was aristocratic since the dominant landed classes were alone in identifying with the nation. The distinguishing feature of the second phase was the 'democratization' of the nation as the middle classes won the right to vote and came to identify with the nation. A third phase was the 'socialization' of the nation, which occurred as the industrial proletariat acquired the right of political participation and harnessed nationalism in support of its social and economic ambitions. At the beginning of the third phase, labour organizations used their industrial and political strength to press their respective governments to protect them against the tyranny of market forces. The nationalization of economic policy which occurred alongside the socialization of the nation destroyed the liberal era of free trade and brought large-scale migration to an end. The 'geographical extension' of nationalist ideology combined with those forces to upset the comfortable balance between nationalism and internationalism which had existed for much of the nineteenth century. Many of the new states which appeared as a consequence of unification or secession were hard to absorb peacefully within the liberal international order. Some could not be accommodated at all.[44]

Various measures which had been designed to include the systematically excluded within inclusive national communities created new forms of social closure with disastrous consequences for international order. Economic nationalism created pressures to end immigration, and all major states began to close their frontiers after 1919.[45] After a lull of 125 years, Europe again witnessed the practice of deporting peoples to tidy up the frontiers.[46] Nationalism from the First World War onward encouraged total war, and popular hatred of the enemy blurred the distinction between military and civilian targets. The First World War was the first international conflict to embroil whole nations, and the first to collapse into total war.[47] The main reason for the crisis in European international relations was not the monopoly stage of capitalism, which might yet be destroyed by class revolution, but the fusion of state and nation, which resulted in totalizing conceptions of political community.

Judged in this light, the first part of the century was the climax of the totalizing project and the era in which its destructive potential was tragically revealed. It was the period in which states increased their ability to administer social and economic life within their respective boundaries, became ever more inclined to employ protectionist strategies, and enlarged the areas which they desperately wanted to control because vital interests were thought to be at stake. Totalizing logics became more central to political life than at any other time in recent history. 'In no previous period of modern history,' Carr argued, 'have frontiers been so rigidly demarcated, or their character as barriers so ruthlessly enforced, as to-day; and in no period . . . has it been apparently so impossible to organise and maintain any international form of power. Modern technique, military and economic, seems to have indissolubly welded together power and territory.'[48] Marxist theories of imperialism understood that these totalising processes were unprecedented in modern history, and they were right to condemn them, but they failed to uncover their root cause. The merger of territory and nation rested on much more than the temporary alliances between the bourgeois and the proletariat which duplicitous elites had recently forged.

Marx believed that the conflict between what Carr called 'the haves' and 'the have-nots' was essentially a struggle between the dominant social classes.[49] Marxist theories of imperialism argued that the struggle between nation-states had temporarily displaced class conflict but the struggle between social classes would soon become the motor of history once again. Capitalism which inevitably generated social conflict could not be reproduced indefinitely, and new forms of life would develop out of its internal contradictions. Carr argued that the conflict between 'have' and 'have not' nation-states was more profound than class struggle. This was the reason for his claim that Marxism had been wrong to regard the conflict between capital and labour as the decisive form of human struggle, and wrong to think that universalizing forces would weaken, even eradicate, nationalism. What Marx had maintained about capitalism, namely that it could not be reproduced indefinitely, was true of a world divided into sovereign nation-states, and there was no reason to suppose that a world consisting of socialist states would represent significant progress beyond a world made up of capitalist societies. As we shall see at a later stage, Carr supported new forms of social organization which would preserve the strengths of liberal democratic and socialist societies but cancel their profound structural and ideological weaknesses.

The contradictions within a world of socialised nations created the possibility of a fourth phase in the development of modern nationalism.[50] What had been created to protect individuals from 'the devastating consequences of unfettered economic individualism' turned out to be a threat to their 'security and well-being'; and just like all the forms of political association that preceded it, the socialised nation encountered 'a new challenge and new process of change'.[51] Carr argued that inter-nationalism must now become social, by which he meant that it must be concerned with the welfare needs of individual human beings rather than with inventing new legal covenants and charters for tying the hands of nation-states.[52] The corollary was that welfare politics would have to become international because of the crises caused by socialized nations. Citizens and aliens would need to come together as equals in a new form of international political community which would promote their security and welfare. They would have to create more universalistic modes of political organization if they were to address the problem of social inequality, and they would have to do so without effacing cultural differences. The fourth phase in the development of the nation would involve new forms of political organization which were aware that 'the exclusive solution' to the problem of community, which allowed 'white men, landowners, propertied classes and so forth' to monopolise valu-able opportunities and resources, was 'no longer acceptable'.[53]

Carr offered an account of immanent developments within the modern society of states which avoided complacent realism and naive utopianism. Some similarities with Marxist analysis are evident in the form of Carr's writings as well as in his more detailed critique of free market capitalism as a cause of poverty and inequality. But at no stage did Carr single out capitalism as the source of all social wrongs or privilege the working class as the revolutionary force which is destined to create the socialist utopia. Those who regard Carr as a realist, albeit of the critical or utopian variety, are correct to argue that what sets him apart from the Marxists is his emphasis on the centrality of the nation-state. Carr's realism is also evident in his belief that visions of alternative forms of world political organisation have to thread their way through the nation-state system. However, this is a form of realism which is at odds with those, such as Waltz, who believe that international politics can be understood in isolation from broader movements within society and the economy. Carr's larger perspective on the interplay between politics and economics is evident in his account of the contraction and closure of political community in the first part of the century. It is equally evident in his analysis of how the tensions within and between socialized nations in the inter-war period created the need for a new combination of state structures.

Carr emphasized these tensions in his claim that his own utopia was an extension of existing historical tendencies. Functional organizations had made significant progress within the League of Nations system, and the value of national and international planning had become ever more transparent during the Second World War.[54] Violent conflict had demonstrated the bankruptcy of nationalism, thereby creating the possibility that political institutions would downplay the moral relevance of the differences between citizens and aliens while publicly recognizing their multiple loyalties and allegiances. Commitments to freedom and equality pervaded modern political cultures with the consequence that unjust systems of exclusion could not escape contestation. This was the context in which the transition to a fourth phase in the development of the modern nation could occur.

Carr's writings are a reminder that the modern state has enjoyed unprecedented forms of territorialized power and has generated levels of violence which earlier forms of political organisation could not have begun to emulate. His writings also maintained that the modern state has been the site for progressive developments which question domination and exclusion in their multitudinous forms. Carr rejected the view that these were the conditions under which sovereignty was destined to disappear, shortly to be replaced by powerful international organizations. But this was the context in which new state structures could emerge to continue the struggle against unemployment and poverty without insisting on the retention of all their monopoly powers or subordinating diverse human loyalties to some totalising conception of community; this was the condition in which post-national polities could develop which would not purchase the autonomy of citizens by imposing heteronomy on other societies, or foster national identity through invidious comparisons with outsiders.[55] In form, Carr's account of latent possibilities in the post-war world was more Marxist than realist; in content it was often more realist than Marxist, not least because it stressed the tenacity of the nation and the enduring power of the state. But by arguing that the more progressive state structures could extend the moral and political boundaries of community, Carr began to develop an approach which moved beyond realism and Marxism into the realms of critical international theory. For the reasons outlined, the vision which was proffered in this context was far removed from the utopianism which Carr criticized in *The Twenty Years' Crisis*.

E.H. Carr and Critical International Theory Today

The question inevitably arises of whether Carr's writings, which were so clearly concerned with nationalism, totalitarianism and war in the first half of this century, have any significance for contemporary critical international theory. To answer this question, it is necessary to comment, first, on the normative vision which is developed in his writings; second, on his sociological account of international political change; and third on his remarks about the most likely agents of global reform. One preliminary point has to be made at this stage. What is true of any political thinker is necessarily true of Carr: much of his detailed analysis had little relevance beyond his own time. But what holds true of all major thinkers, namely that they articulate profound ideas of lasting significance, applies to Carr. It is his analysis of new forms of political community which will eradicate the most unjust systems of exclusion which is most significant and enduring.[56]

There are at least four respects in which Carr's normative vision was outdated or limited and in need of further development. First, Carr's enthusiasm for economic planning and public ownership inevitably seems dated in societies which have become accustomed to deregulation and privatization, and which are keen to make their own citizens assume greater responsibility for their long-term welfare and care.[57] Liberal and neo-conservative critiques of the threat that state power poses to individual freedom, which work in tandem with doubts about the state's capacity to deliver social services, have eroded the Left's commitment to public ownership and central planning.[58] What is more, Carr's bold claim that no one expects that private firms and investment will promote the development of Africa and Asia now seems odd not only to economic liberals but to many writers on the Left.[59] Suffice it to note that Carr's faith in centralised economic planning has few counterparts in at least mainstream contemporary political thought.

This is tied up with a second weakness in his thought, namely his belief that the future lay with new forms of social and political organization which would take the best from Western capitalism and state socialism. Capitalist societies had obviously failed to solve the problem of social injustice.[60] Freedom had been defined too narrowly to mean protection under the law and the entitlement to representation in politics. But liberty had little appeal if it meant 'liberty to starve', and to be 'effective' in the modern world, freedom had to be redefined to include 'maximum social and economic opportunity'.[61] In this respect, the initiative clearly rested with the dissatisfied powers which had been the first to turn to economic planning.[62] The Soviet conception of democracy which stressed economic and social rights rather than bourgeois freedoms posed the most significant challenge to the West.[63] But if the West had much to learn from the Soviet Union about the importance of duties to society, the Soviet Union had much to learn in turn about the obligations that society had to the individual.[64] Carr defended a vision of international social democracy or democratic socialism which would represent a third path between state socialism and western capitalism.[65] There is still much to admire in this normative vision in an age in which powerful forces are urging states to reduce their welfare functions, but his belief that some amalgam of western capitalism and state socialism was sure to triumph has surely had its day.

Third, although Carr defended the multicultural state and the rights of minority nations, his commitment to small nations was not unambiguous. Concerning the Baltics, he argued that the older generations in Latvia, Lithuania and Estonia had opposed the absorption of their countries within the Soviet Union, but the younger generation keenly anticipated the benefits which would result from amalgamation with the larger unit.[66] Parallels with Lenin's comments about economies of scale spring to mind. In *The Soviet Impact on the Western World*, Carr maintained that the smaller nations could no longer stand apart from international affairs but would sooner or later be drawn into the orbit of one or other of the great powers.[67] Carr's enthusiasm for some of the great powers has troubled several analysts of his work. Kaufman describes Carr's views that Nazi Germany was not just another revisionist power as an 'appalling statement' in which his sympathies for revisionist, planning states led him to ignore their moral depravity.[68] Yet Carr's observations about these matters need to be placed in a much wider context.[69]

Fourth, Carr's remark about 'the impossible task of creating an international community out of units so fantastically disparate... as China and Albania, Norway and Brazil' prompts one final critical comment about his normative vision, which is that it was almost exclusively concerned with the future of Europe.[70] Carr believed that welfare internationalism could be practised on a global scale, as his remark about 'putting... the individual Albanian on an equal footing, in respect of personal rights and opportunities, with the individual Chinese or the individual Brazilian' reveals.[71] But different levels of population growth across the world prevented global approaches to this objective – hence his belief that 'no single issue reveals more starkly the underlying lack of homogeneity which blocks the way to realisation of the ideal of world unity and imposes division and diversity of policy in the pursuit even of aims recognised as common to mankind'.[72] Apart from a few observations about possible directions for Africa and Asia, Carr had little to say about global policies and directions, and some of his observations about the possible decline of nationalism in Asia after the Second World War have turned out to be well wide of the mark.[73] Carr was concerned with regional solutions to an essentially European crisis, and it is as a theorist of the modern industrial state that he is best remembered.

In this respect, there is much in Carr's thought which is relevant to current thinking about the future of European international society. Here, it is important to return to his vision of the triple transformation of political community in which citizens and aliens would overcome their national hostilities in forms of international cooperation which would promote social equality and respect cultural differences. At the heart of this vision, as already noted, was a powerful commitment to reducing unemployment and poverty amongst the dispossessed. Current approaches take a rather different tack because they are more inclined to stress how the reconfiguration of political community can safeguard the *legal* and *political* rights of individuals and national minorities. These approaches argue that the citizens of national democracies are less able to shape the future development of their national societies because of the modern phase of globalisation. Visions of cosmopolitan democracy argue for advances in political autonomy which national democracies cannot guarantee. Various images of the European Union support greater universality in the form of new conceptions of European citizenship. They endorse greater devolution in the form of subsidiarity and strong regions, and they often defend a form of 'Continental Keynesianism' based on a commitment to welfare internationalism. There are clear links between these visions of new forms of community and citizenship and the image of a reconstructed, post-national Europe which can be found in the writings of Carr. These remain inspirational in this regard.[74]

Turning to the sociological dimensions of his thought, there are several respects in which its principal themes were concerned with immediate possibilities for change. Writing in the early 1940s, Carr pinned his hopes on the continuation of the war-time alliance.[75] Military cooperation between the great powers would continue, conceivably through the development of 'some standing international forces', and each might enjoy military bases on the other's soil with the consequence that frontiers would 'lose their military significance' and 'a ready escape from the dilemma of self-determination' would be provided.[76] As noted earlier, these efforts to create 'a system of pooled security' would have to be accompanied by a common economic policy if a workable international order was to survive.[77]

Carr's hope that a concert of great powers committed to welfare internationalism would develop in the post-war world raised questions about order and justice in international relations which have been central to modern Grotians, and many of his formulations would not look out of place in their more recent analyses of the transition from a European to a universal society of states.[78] Carr observed that the survival of any political community is likely to be in doubt if members are denied fair access to its material and other resources.[79] Exactly the same point applied to international relations: any international order which revolved exclusively around the self-interest of the great powers would fail to command widespread popular support. It was the powerful who were obliged to promote a 'higher ideal than orderly stagnation' and to pursue 'common purposes, worthy to command the assent and loyalty of men and women throughout the world'.[80] Upon them fell the duties to make amends: 'Those who profit most by that order can in the long run only hope to maintain it by making sufficient concessions to make it tolerable to those who profit by it least; and the responsibility for seeing that these changes take place as far as possible in an orderly way rests as much on the defenders as the challengers.'[81] Real sacrifices would have to be made to bridge the gulf between 'the haves' and 'the have-nots', but it was by no means certain, Carr argued in a formulation which brings Bull's writings about the revolt against the West immediately to mind, that the request for small sacrifices would inevitably fail.[82]

The move beyond orderly stagnation would be propelled by the more advanced moral ideas of the time: 'The driving force behind any future international order must be a belief, however expressed, in the value of individual human beings irrespective of national affinities or allegiance and in a common and mutual obligation to promote their well-being.'[83] Following Lauterpacht, he argued that widening human conceptions of the relevant moral community was one of the markers of 'the growth of civilisation'.[84] Quoting Zimmern, he believed that modern citizens had to realise that 'the *public affairs* of the twentieth century are *world affairs*' (italics in original).[85] Simply put, the meaning of this injunction was that 'the principle of self-sacrifice, which is commonly supposed to stop short at the national frontier, should be extended beyond it'.[86] If the 'ordinary man' was to respond to such an appeal, it was because of a growing recognition of the moral irrelevance of many of the divisions between human beings and because of a growing desire to sweep them aside.[87] Particular powers would lead the way. The Soviet Union had been especially concerned with eliminating discrimination based on the irrelevant distinctions of class, sex, colour and race.[88] In Carr's judgement, its practices compared favourably with those in the West, and they had already left their profound mark on the rest of the world.

The Grotian parallel can be pressed further by arguing that Carr was specifically interested in how new normative principles could be embedded within the society of states. It is perfectly true that in *The Twenty Years' Crisis* Carr wrote that the dominant morality of each epoch reflected the interests of the most powerful groups, and later interpretations of this work, including Bull's, criticized him for neglecting the extent to which states formed a society.[89] But Carr expressed rather different sentiments even in his most famous work on international relations which has long been regarded as quintessentially realist. He argued there that the 'fact that national propaganda everywhere so eagerly cloaks itself in ideologies of a professedly international character proves the existence of an international stock of ideas, however limited and however weakly held, to which appeal can be made, and of a belief that these common ideas stand somehow in the scale of values above national interests. This stock of common ideas is what we mean by international morality'.[90] As an earlier part of the discussion has shown, Carr's principal aim was not the relinquishment of sovereignty but the accumulation of international norms which would attract states to the wider moral point of view.[91] Quite how these norms become embedded within the society of states was not a subject which Carr considered in much detail, but several of his observations suggest that broad patterns of moral development make their impression on international society, not least when they have the support of one or more of the great powers. There are interesting affinities between Carr's sociology of international political change and more recent analyses of the impact of revolutionary states on world politics.[92]

Turning finally to the question of the agents of political change, Carr's references to the great responsibles illustrate his theme that '[e]very solution of the problem of political change, whether national or international, must be based on a compromise between morality and power'.[93] No Utopia, in his view, could lose sight of the truism that the ambitions of the great powers will usually prevail over the needs of smaller nations, that state managers are often unlikely to be at the forefront of radical change since most have a vested interest in resisting the rise of competing sites of power and authority, and that the modern state has been the site for unprecedented totalizing processes. History issued no guarantee that this would finally come to an end.[94] However, the realization of any normative vision was ultimately dependent upon great power altruism or enlightened self-interest which appreciated the need for concessions to the weak when the legitimacy of international arrangements was at issue. Anticipating the standpoint which Bull took in the 1970s and 1980s, Carr argued that the great powers benefit most from international order and it is therefore fitting that they should pay a disproportionate part of the cost of ensuring that it satisfies the needs of the majority of the world's peoples.[95] An additional consideration in his thinking was the extent to which their own domestic nature and ethical commitments required them to become great responsibles.

The character of his argument was set out in *The Twenty Years' Crisis* in an intriguing comparison between the United States and Britain, and Germany and Japan: 'Belief in the desirability of seeking the consent of the governed by methods other than those of coercion [has] . . . played a larger part in the British and American than in the German or Japanese administration of subject territories.'[96] The multi-ethnic composition of the great powers, including the Soviet Union, and their apparent success as melting points, appealed to him most. Herein lay the foundations of an alternative to the classical sovereign states-system.[97] Carr argued that forms of political organization which were 'based not on exclusiveness of nation or language but on shared ideals and aspirations of universal application' would represent a significant advance over communities based simply on the cult of the nation; and the rise of new multi-national centres of power would do much 'to encourage the spread of national toleration'.[98] When making this point, he suggested that states stood at the intersection between transnational patterns of social and cultural change and the principles of international society. The more enlightened great powers had an unequalled capacity and duty to convert progressive domestic moral commitments into the constitutive principles of the society of states. This emphasis may seem too statist for those who believe that states resemble 'gangsters' rather than 'guardians',[99] and it is certainly at some remove from those who insist that social movements rather than states have been the primary source of radical thought and action,[100] although it recognized the capacity of mass opinion and public pressure to influence national governments. Yet Carr was right that international political change cannot occur in the face of great power opposition and he was correct, as Hirst and Thompson have argued more recently, that states are the key to the development of new modes of governance at the sub-state and trans-national level.[101] Carr's account of the likely agents of global reform highlighted the great powers while warning that 'it is of the essence of power . . . that it can be abused'.[102] Carr needed no reminder that the great powers have a deeply ambiguous presence in international society.

Conclusions

Carr's writings have often been used to legitimate an approach to international relations which is cynical about projects of global reform, but
those who regard Carr as a critical or utopian realist do far more justice
to his thought, as do those who stress affinities with the English
School.[103] The approach taken here has suggested that there are broad
parallels between Carr's alternative to realism and utopianism and the
method of immanent critique associated with Marx and the Frankfurt
School. Claiming Carr for critical international theory may be conten-
tious, though far from absurd, and considering his writings in the light
of that perspective is instructive and illuminating. Carr was a superb
analyst of the crisis which led the first generation of the Frankfurt
School to doubt the possibility of future historical progress. Yet he
displayed a confidence in the immanent possibility of change which
was at odds with their pessimism without seeking the dubious comfort
of some unreconstructed Marxist vision of the socialist Utopia. He
argued that the industrial societies of his time had not yet exhausted
their potential for dismantling social arrangements anchored in morally
irrelevant differences between individuals, for recreating society given
that minority nations do not want to be incorporated within communities on exactly the same terms as everyone else and, not least, for
eradicating the scourge of poverty and unemployment through international action. This is why Carr was one of the leading theorists of the
triple transformation of political community.

His vision of new forms of political association anticipated the development of a fourth phase in the history of modern nationalism. This
phase would mark the end of totalizing conceptions of community in
which governments could destroy alternative sites of power and
authority, or create national communities which were deeply exclusionary
towards subaltern groups and aliens; it would represent an important
advance in the internationalization of national decision-making and in
the devolution of political power; it would involve the end of the era in
which national governments could simultaneously contract their sense
of the relevant moral community while enlarging the area thought vital
to national security with disastrous results. Such concerns are at the
heart of critical international theory today. The critical agenda has
been developed with little regard for Carr's thought. Now, more than
50 years after the appearance of his pathbreaking works on the future of
nationalism and the state, it is possible to understand just how much
they have in common.

Notes

1 K. Booth, 'Security in Anarchy: Utopian Realism in Theory and Practice', *International Affairs*, Vol. 67, 1991, pp. 527–45; P. Howe, 'The Utopian Realism of E.H. Carr', *Review of International Studies*, Vol. 20, 1994, pp. 277–97; R. Falk, 'The Critical Realist Tradition and the Demystification of State Power: E.H. Carr, Hedley Bull and Robert W. Cox', in S. Gill and J.H. Mittleman, eds, *Innovation and Transformation in International Studies* (Cambridge, Cambridge University Press, 1997).

2 T. Dunne, *Inventing International Society: A History of the English School* (London, Macmillan, 1998).

3 A. Linklater, 'The Transformation of Political Community: E.H. Carr, Critical Theory and International Relations', *Review of International Studies*, Vol. 23, No. 3, 1997, pp. 1–18.

4 A. Linklater, *The Transformation of Political Community: Ethical Foundations of the Post-Westphalian Era* (Cambridge, Cambridge University Press, 1998), chapter 5.

5 E.H. Carr, *The Twenty Years' Crisis: 1919–1939* (London, Macmillan, 1946), p. viii.

6 *Ibid.*

7 *Ibid.*, p. 239.

8 G. Evans, 'E.H. Carr and International Relations', *British Journal of International Studies*, 1, 1975, p. 92.

9 E.H. Carr, *The Future of Nations: Independence or Interdependence* (London, Macmillan, 1941), p. 55.

10 *Ibid.*

11 *Ibid.*, see p. 61.

12 Carr, *The Twenty Years' Crisis*, pp. 230–1.

13 *Ibid.*

14 See Carr, *Conditions of Peace* (London, Macmillan, 1942), p. 114. The following comments are also worth noting: 'Unemployment or fear of unemployment has been the most fertile cause of exclusion and discrimination in the modern world. It has sharpened and barbed every restrictive instrument of economic and financial policy; it has dammed and severely restricted the flow of migration from country to country; it has intensified discrimination against minorities, often raising it to the pitch of organised persecution; it has closed almost every door to refugees. Unemployment has been the specific social scourge of the contemporary western world and takes a high place among the ultimate causes of the second world war.' See Carr, *Nationalism and After* (London, Macmillan, 1945), p. 68.

15 E.H. Carr, *The New Society* (1951), p. 118. On Continental Keynesianism, see P. Hirst and G. Thompson, *Globalisation in Question* (Cambridge, Polity Press, 1996), pp. 163–4.

16 E.H. Carr, *Nationalism and After* (London, 1945), pp. 43–7, and Carr, *Conditions of Peace*, pp. 252–4. On the subject of Europe, Carr argued that it should 'not be interpreted with much attention to geographical precision' which 'may well prove both too inclusive and exclusive' but with regard to the area which 'participated, voluntarily or involuntarily, in the war and [had] been directly subject to its ravages'. See *Conditions of Peace*, 1942, p. 243.

17   For a discussion of welfare nationalism, see H. Suganami, *The Domestic Analogy and World Order Proposals* (Cambridge, Cambridge University Press, 1989), p. 13, footnote 34.

18   Carr, *The Twenty Years' Crisis*, p. 230.

19   *Ibid.*

20   Carr, *The Future of Nations*, p. 56.

21   *Ibid.*, p. 50.

22   *Ibid.* Parallels with Bull's thought come to mind. For further discussion, see A. Linklater, 'Citizenship and Sovereignty in the Post-Westphalian State', *European Journal of International Relations*, 2, 1996, pp. 77–103.

23   Carr, *The Future of Nations*, p. 49.

24   *Ibid.*, pp. 49–50.

25   *Ibid.*, p. 48.

26   *Ibid.*, p. 23.

27   *Ibid.*

28   *Ibid.*

29   Carr, *Nationalism and After*, p. 49.

30   Carr, *The Future of Nations*, p. 54.

31   Carr, *Nationalism and After*, p. 67.

32   Carr, *The Twenty Years' Crisis*, p. 36.

33   *Ibid.*, p. 20. See also p. 89.

34   *Ibid.*, p. 93.

35   *Ibid.*, p. 239.

36   *Ibid.*, p. 12.

37   K. Booth, 'Security in Anarchy: Utopian Realism in Theory and Practice', *International Affairs*, Vol. 67, No. 3, 1991, pp. 527–45; R. Falk, 'The Critical Realist Tradition and the Demystification of State Power: E.H. Carr, Hedley Bull and Robert W. Cox', in S. Gill and J.H. Mittleman, eds, *Innovation and Transformation in International Studies*, Cambridge, 1997. See also P. Howe, 'The Utopian Realism of E.H. Carr', *Review of International Studies*, Vol. 20, 1994, pp. 277–9.

38   Carr, *The Twenty Years' Crisis*, p. 10.

39   Carr, *The New Society*, p. 118.

40   The important point is that Marx (or later Marxists) did not take this critique of ideological thought far enough. Marx's argument that political visions have relative as opposed to transcendental importance, and his related claim that visions become ideological when they are loaded with suprahistorical significance, did not rule out totalising claims about the socialist future. Predictions about the end of history had an 'eschatological ring' about them which was more appropriate to theology than to history. See E.H. Carr, *What is History?* (Harmondsworth, Penguin, 1961), p. 115.

41   Carr, *Conditions of Peace*, (London, 1942), p. 24.

42   Carr, *The Twenty Years' Crisis*, p. 69.

43   This notion of totalising communities is derived from the 'totalising project' which Corrigan and Sayer use in their discussion of the development of the modern British state. See P. Corrigan and D. Sayer, *The Great Arch: English State Formation as Cultural Revolution* (Oxford, Blackwell, 1985), p. 4. They use this term to refer to the increased regulation of society, the creation of

homogeneous national communities and the exaggeration of differences between citizens and aliens to foster national solidarity.

44 See Carr, *Nationalism and After*, pp. 17–26 on the socialisation of the nation, the nationalisation of economic policy and the geographical extension of nationalism.

45 *Ibid.*, p. 22.

46 *Ibid.*, p. 33.

47 *Ibid.*, p. 26.

48 Carr, *The Twenty Years' Crisis*, p. 228.

49 On the 'haves and have-nots', see *ibid.*, chapter 13.

50 Carr, *Nationalism and After*, pp. 34–7.

51 *Ibid.*, p. 46.

52 *Ibid.*, p. 63.

53 *Ibid.*, p. 42.

54 *Ibid.*, p. 43; see also pp. 47–8.

55 See Carr, *The Twenty Years' Crisis*, pp. 70–1 for comments about how societies have cemented their national identity by wielding potent exclusionary symbols against some of their own members and against outsiders.

56 See Linklater, 'The Transformation of Political Community, pp. 321–38.

57 Falk, 'The Critical Realist Tradition and the Demystification of State Power', p. 48.

58 See Carr, *Conditions of Peace*, p. 140 for a defence of public ownership as opposed to state monopolies.

59 See Carr, *The New Society*, p. 96.

60 Social justice had three elements: equality of opportunity, freedom from want and full employment. See Carr, *Nationalism and After*, p. 64.

61 See E.H. Carr, 'The Future of International Government', *National Peace Council* (London, 1941), p. 3.

62 Carr, *Conditions of Peace*, p. xix.

63 See E.H. Carr, *The Soviet Impact on the Western World* (London, Macmillan, 1946), p. 116. See also Carr, *Conditions of Peace*, pp. 29–33.

64 Carr, *The Soviet Impact on the Western World*, pp. 103–4.

65 See Carr, *The New Society*, p. 79 where he writes approvingly of the Attlee Government's reforms. In Carr's view, Britain had done more than any other society over the past five years to set down new lines of social and political advance and to lay the foundations of an educated mass democracy.

66 Carr, *The Future of Nations*, p. 44.

67 Carr, *The Soviet Impact on the Western World*, pp. 84–5.

68 See R.G. Kaufman, 'E.H. Carr, Winston Churchill, Reinhold Neibuhr and Us: The Case for Principled, Prudential, Democratic Realism', *Security Studies*, 5, 1995, pp. 322–3.

69 See Evans, 'E.H. Carr and International Relations', pp. 77–97. Kaufman (see previous note) criticises Carr's endorsement of the policy of appeasement and acceptance of Germany's violation of Czechoslovakian sovereignty in the first edition of *The Twenty Year's Crisis*. See, however, Carr (*ibid.*, p. 59) on the illegitimacy of redrawing national frontiers on security grounds without popular consent.

70 Carr, *Nationalism and After*, p. 42.

71   Carr, *Nationalism and After*, p. 43.
72   *Ibid.*, p. 67.
73   See the following comments in Carr, *The Future of Nations*, p. 56: 'In Europe the present need is to build up larger military and economic units while retaining existing or smaller units for other purposes. In Africa and Asia it is to retain large inter-continental military and economic units (not necessarily the existing ones in every case), but to establish within these units a far greater measure of devolution and an immense variety of local administration rooted in local tradition, law and custom.'
74   See A. Linklater, 'Citizenship and Sovereignty in the Post-Westphalian State', *European Journal of International Relations*, 2, 1996, pp. 77–103, and Linklater, 'The Transformation of Political Community', pp. 321–38.
75   Carr, *The Future of Nations*, p. 58.
76   *Ibid.*, pp. 54, 58–9. Carr (*ibid.*, p. 58) referred to international military cooperation through leasing bases to the forces of other powers as 'far more promising than any formal attempts to create an international army'.
77   See Carr, *Nationalism and After*, p. 54.
78   See H. Bull, *The Anarchical Society: A Study of Order in World Politics* (London, 1977); H. Bull and A. Watson, eds, *The Expansion of International Society*, Oxford 1984, and T. Dunne, *Inventing International Society: A History of the English School*.
79   Carr, *The Twenty Years' Crisis*, p. 163.
80   Carr, *Nationalism and After*, p. 61.
81   See Carr, *The Twenty Years' Crisis*, p. 169; see also pp. 235–6.
82   *Ibid.*, p. 239. See Bull, *The Anarchical Society*, and H. Bull and A. Watson, eds, *The Expansion of International Society* (Oxford, 1984).
83   Carr, *Nationalism and After*, p. 44. See Carr (*ibid.*, p. 58) on the need for 'a solution which seeks to divorce international security and the power to maintain it from frontiers and the national sovereignty which they represent'.
84   Carr, *The Twenty Years' Crisis*, p. 212.
85   *Ibid.*, p. 169.
86   *Ibid.*
87   Carr, *The Soviet Impact on the Western World*, p. 101.
88   *Ibid.*, p. 45.
89   See Carr, *The Twenty Years' Crisis*, p. 79. See also H. Bull, 'The Twenty Years' Crisis: Thirty Years After', *International Journal*, 24, 1969, pp. 625–38.
90   Carr, *The Twenty Years' Crisis*, p. 145.
91   But some intrusions into the cherished sovereignty of the state should not be ruled out. Interestingly, Carr lamented the failure to establish fair war crimes trials at the end of the First World War. See E.H. Carr, *International Relations Between the Two World Wars: 1919–1939* (London, Macmillan, 1965), pp. 47–8.
92   See F. Halliday, *Rethinking International Relations* (London, Macmillan, 1994), chapter 6.
93   Carr, *The Twenty Years' Crisis*, p. 209.
94   See Carr, *Nationalism and After*, p. 62 on the 'dangers that threaten a world whose fortunes are inevitably dominated by a diminishing number of increasingly powerful units'. Moreover, 'there would be little cause for congratulation in a division of the world into a small number of large multi-

national units exercising effective control over vast territories and practising in competition and conflict with one another a new imperialism which would be simply the old nationalism writ large and would almost certainly pave the way for more titanic and devastating wars' (*ibid.*, p. 53).

95 Evans, 'E.H. Carr and International Relations', pp. 81–2.

96 Carr, *The Twenty Years' Crisis*, p. 236.

97 In *Nationalism and After* (p. 59) Carr refers to the 'system of overlapping and interlocking loyalties which is in the last resort the sole alternative to sheer totalitarianism'.

98 Carr, *ibid.*, 1945, p. 66. Carr (*ibid.*, p. 52) describes these multi-national centres of power as civilisations.

99 See N. Wheeler, 'Guardian Angels or Global Gangsters: A Review of the Ethical Claims of International Society, *Political Studies*, 44, 1996, pp. 123–35.

100 U. Beck, *The Reinvention of Politics: Rethinking Modernity in the Global Social Order* (Cambridge, Cambridge University Press, 1996).

101 Hirst and Thomson, *Globalisation in Question*, pp. 184–5.

102 See Carr, *Nationalism and After*, p. 60.

103 See Dunne, *Inventing International Society*.

12
Reason and Romance:
the Place of Revolution in the
Works of E.H. Carr

Fred Halliday

Revolution: Carr's *Leitmotif*

There could be no concept more central to the extended *oeuvre* of Carr than that of revolution. In a half-century of intellectual output Carr produced works of three broad kinds: in the early 1930s a set of four biographical studies – *Dostoevsky, Karl Marx, Michael Bakunin* and the *Romantic Exiles* – in the years after the Second World War a 14-volume study of the outcome of the Bolshevik Revolution spanning the years 1917 to 1932, accompanied by essays on the same theme, and, in the intervening decade a set of broad studies, historic and analytic, of international relations, among them *The Twenty Years' Crisis, International Relations Between the Wars, Nationalism and After* and *The Soviet Impact on the Western World*. His most famous work *What is History?*, though published in 1961, can be taken as part of the second period.

The first, and last, of these phases directly addressed issues in the study of revolution. Yet in the work of the central period, that which is in particular taken as most pertinent for the study of international relations, there are themes, and ideas, that also relate directly to the study of this theme. To chart this interlocking of ideas is not to presume consistency: it would be surprising, and tedious, if this were the case in the writings of Carr as of any other thinker. Carr's ideas changed, not least in response to world events, as he was the first, cheerfully, to admit.[1] Yet if one cannot step into the same Carr twice, one may none the less identify, and contrast, the manner in which his work as a whole relates to the issue of revolution, the better to understand that phenomenon as much as to penetrate the mind of this fascinating, at once dissatisfied and dissatisfying, thinker.

The subject of revolution has, in recent years, become a major pre-occupation in social science, and it may be relevant to point out the ways in which Carr's work does *not* engage with current concerns. In two respects, Carr does not appear to have been interested in what much preoccupies contemporary theorists and analysts of revolution, the definition of the term, or the causes of the revolution. In regard to the former, he offers no definition, assuming it is self-evident. In a usage of the term that most contemporary writers would reject he applies the term without qualification to the Nazis.[2] In regard to the issue of causation, he has almost as little to say: his theoretical interest in historical causation, evident in *What is History?* is not matched in his accounts of such upheavals. He is interested in two other aspects of the phenomenon, the aspirations of revolutionaries, often failed ones on the one hand, and the outcomes of revolution, within states and in international relations, on the other. In the preface to *The Bolshevik Revolution* he declares:

> My ambition has been to write the history not of the events of the revolution (these have already been chronicled by many hands), but of the political, social and economic order which emerged from it.[3]

As he was to say over and over, his concern was with the *achievement*, that is the aftermath within Russia and internationally, of 1917. Hence on causation he is almost silent. What he does do in his work, and in a variety of registers, is discuss themes which are central to any study of revolution and which are indeed given more prominence in his work than in many subsequent analyses. A discussion of these themes may cast his other work, on international relations, or nationalism, in a different light.

Realism and Revolution

What one sees in Carr's work is the interlocking of three different themes. One, that most familiar to later international relations readers of Carr, is a realist approach to politics in general, and to revolutions in particular. The critique of utopianism in the *Twenty Years' Crisis*, and of discourses of morality and aspiration detached from power, applies equally to the revolutionary movement. Equally, the critique of internationalism, as in effect a rhetoric of power masked as altruism, can be and has been directly applied to the internationalism of revolutionary states. We find here an echo of what others, Albert Sorel on France and Isaac Deutscher on Russia, had identified in the internationalism of revolutionary states.[4] Thus in *Twenty Years' Crisis* he writes:

> Just as pleas for 'national solidarity' in domestic politics always come from a dominant group which can use this solidarity to strengthen its own control over the nation as a whole, so pleas for international solidarity and world union come from those dominant nations which may hope to exercise control over a unified world... 'International order' and 'international solidarity' will always be slogans of those who feel strong enough to impose them on others.[5]

It is in terms of such a test of reality that Carr, in his life of Marx, criticises the latter's theory:

> Marx borrowed without hesitation from the preceding generation of socialists the splendid vision of a golden age in the past from which primeval man had emerged, and a golden age in the future to which socialist man would eventually return. Marxist mythology found room both for a Paradise Lost and for a Paradise Regained.[6]

Carr repeatedly criticizes Marx not only for his utopian view of progress, what he terms Marx's 'secular eschatology', and the implicit argument that history has an end,[7] but also for failing to see the growing power of nationalism, and the precedence it would achieve over internationalism or class loyalty in the late nineteenth and early twentieth centuries. There is in this theme a direct link between the trenchant critique of Marx in *Karl Marx: A Study in Fanaticism* of 1934 and the later, realist, critique in *Twenty Years' Crisis* of 1939.

Yet to equate Carr's analysis of politics, or revolutions, with such a realism is to simplify his thought. In one sense, Carr took his realism further than most theorists of international relations do: for their realism pertains to an assertion of the timeless anarchy, and competitiveness, of a world of states, a vision within which domestic change is irrelevant, whilst Carr not only sees history as progressive, but combines his analysis of international realism with an analysis of the domestic. In this, of course, he follows those who in earlier times had analysed both domestic and international politics through a pessimistic vein – Machiavelli and Hobbes amongst them. Recurring in Carr's work are a number of themes which, reflecting realist concerns, may be termed the elements of his *sociology* of politics. Unlike earlier realists this involved a belief in change and progress. Carr's central theme restated at the end of *What is History?* is that the world continues to change. This is very much a sociology of social change, not a political sociology in which actors, individual or collective, have a role. Indeed agency as an issue is largely absent from Carr – he is interested, as Namier was in his study of 1848, in failures: his history is one of largely impersonal social forces. Ultimately, it is an insistent, if illiberal, reason.[8]

Three of these sociological themes are familiar from the writings of the second period: the explanation of the First World War in terms of the nationalization of socialism, the incorporation of the masses into politics through a state-sponsored nationalism ('No welfare state without Sedan,' he approvingly quotes Bismarck); the longer-term transition from a politics, and ethics, based on the individual, characteristic of western European through from the sixteenth to the nineteenth centuries, to one based on collectivism and the industrial organization of society; and the gradual, but as yet unrealized, transcendence of the individual nation and nation-state by a set of broader civilizational groupings, based on power, which would one day provide the basis for a new, international, order.

In several respects these ideas are relevant to the study of revolutions. Carr's explanation of the late nineteenth century provides an incorporation of domestic change, and in particular the politics and social power of the workers' movement, into his explanation of 1914. He is clear that Marx had got it wrong, in arguing that class would transcend nation:[9] but he, equally, allows for that very discussion of international relations in socio-economic and political terms that orthodox international relations does not and which is a prerequisite for the study of revolutions. Indeed in two of his three explanations for this breakdown there is a distinct parallel with what others have argued in this field.[10] He relates the international crisis to the breakdown of a world order and the creation of national economies: this relation between world economy and parcellised sovereignty is one that later Marxists have made central to the analysis of international relations.[11] At the same time, Carr's argument on the multiplication of nations mirrors that early nineteenth-century impatience with nationalism that Marx himself exhibited, and that Carr elsewhere scorns. Indeed one might on the matter of nationalism, without too much injustice, summarize Carr's difference with Marx as being a matter of timing: neither liked nationalism, both despised smaller nations, and wished they would amalgamate with larger ones. Marx thought it was happening in the 1840s. Carr thought it was happening in the 1940s. Marx was just one century out.

Carr's belief in the shift from individualism to a socially planned collectivism is another *leitmotif* of his work.[12] It forms, in the first place, a central ethical theme: political, or individual rights, have become less important than economic or social ones.[13] His conclusion to *Karl Marx* spells out why and how Marx was right:

> In a sense, Marx is the protagonist and the forerunner of the whole twentieth century revolution of thought. The nineteenth century saw the end of the period of humanism which began with the Renaissance – the period which took as its ideal the highest development of the faculties and liberties of the individual . . . Marx understood that, in the new order, the individual would play a minor part. Individualism implies differentiation; everything that is undifferentiated does not count. The industrial revolution would place in power the undifferentiated mass. Not man but mass-man, not the individual but the class, not man the political animal, would be the unit of the coming dispensation. Not only industry, but the whole of civilization, would become a matter of mass-production.[14]

In *Karl Marx*, published in 1934, Carr did seek to go beyond this vision. In what some would take as an anticipation of the neo-liberalism of the 1980s and 1990s Carr foresaw the end of the Marxist period:

> Even if the near future produces an extension and an intensification of mass-rule, the inveterate tendency of man to individualize himself will ultimately reappear; and, unless all historical analogies are false, a new differentiation of the mass will lead to a new renaissance of humanism. Nobody will care to prophesy when and how this revolution will occur. But when it is consummated, the Marxist epoch of history will have come to an end.[15]

But this distancing of 1934 was not sustained: it contrasts with what Carr was later to write. In the conclusion of *The Soviet Impact on the Western World* published in 1946 Carr links the shift from individualism to collectivism to the Bolshevik Revolution itself and its broader international appeal. He singles out the Soviet success in planning, and in the use of propaganda, as well as its diplomatic style, one shorn of the hypocrisies Carr despised, as examples of how it has affected the world. The Soviet challenge was not a military one, but one based on economic and ideological performance.

The peaceful penetration of the western world by ideas emanating from the Soviet Union has been, and seems likely to remain, a far more important and conspicuous symptom of the new east–west movement. *Ex Oriente lux.*[16]

The belief in a new collectivist age is therefore a foundation stone of his view of the Bolshevik Revolution and of his favourable view of its achievements. Thus by the late 1960s, in his introduction to *The ABC of Communism*, he is praising the Soviet success in planning, and even entertaining the idea, put out by the Bolsheviks, that planning as a form of *social* control is an alternative to *state* control, and thus vindicates Lenin's views on the withering away of the state.[17] Carr argues that the sections of the *ABC* which deal with the expansion of production under communism are those which have best withstood the test of time. He cites figures for population increase, urbanization, literacy and, above all, the fact that the USSR had become the second industrial nation in the world:

It is sometimes argued that the industrial development of the USSR, which had begun before the revolution, had nothing to do with the communist régime. But this argument is difficult to reconcile with the fact that many procedures first preached by the Bolsheviks and emphatically repudiated elsewhere – the nationalization of major industries, planned economy, the rejection of the superior authority of finance, the integration of the trade unions into the control of economic policies – were later adopted, sometimes in covert and roundabout ways, in many western countries ... the USSR, thanks to the impetus of the revolution and to an ideology more amenable than the *laissez-faire* liberalism in which western capitalism was nurtured to the needs of modern technological development, has placed itself in the van of contemporary industrial progress.[18]

The sources of this collectivist, and to a large extent, determinist view of history in Carr's life and thought have been explored elsewhere. His views on power, on the dominance of great powers, in general, and his accommodation to appeasement in the first edition of *Twenty Years' Crisis* match his apparent respect, if not affection, for the Bolshevik Revolution. In one sense it was an elective affinity, the elitist Edwardian outlook shattered by 1914 and then by the crises of the late 1920s and early 1930s found, as it did for other anxious members of the British elite, a new point of reference and hope for social order in the collectivism of modern industry – if for some this took the form of Keynesianism, for others it involved affection, or at least, respect for the USSR; yet if this idea was already present in the early 1930s, as evidenced by his *Karl Marx*, it was to be amply reinforced by the Second World War and decisive Soviet role in the defeat of Nazi Germany. This coupled with the economic successes of Stalinism in the 1930s and again after the Second World War appeared to confirm the judgement. World history, the final arbiter, had spoken. Or so it seemed. For in another phrase that Carr liked, reason was to be more cunning than he realized.

These two broad themes in Carr's work would appear to confirm an approach to revolution, and to modern history more generally, that was deterministic and statist. There was little room for that side of revolutions which most revolutionaries, and students of revolution, have written about: the role of ideas, of leaders, of parties, the development of social movements, of consciousness, the role indeed of human will in shaping history. In this sense Carr, for all that he did not use the term 'structuralist', would appear to have anticipated the approach of writers such as Theda Skocpol: in her *States and Social Revolutions* she argues that 'revolutions are not made, they happen', and like Carr she focused most of her attention not on how the revolutionaries came to power, but on the state-building that followed. Skocpol only cites Carr once, but the downplaying of the subjective, and the emphasis on the post-revolutionary period, parallels his.[19]

The Romantic Moment

This determinist, anti-voluntarist note is, however, in marked contrast to another theme in Carr's writings, one most evident in the biographies of the early years but repeated, in defiant style, in the introduction to *The ABC of Communism*. This is Carr's romanticism, his belief not only in the importance of romance, utopia, dreaming in politics, but in its enduring importance.

There are two places in Carr's work where this general view of the romanticism of revolution is spelt out most clearly. What is remarkable about these two passage is that, on the one hand, these lines are penned by the same man who wrote *The Twenty Years' Crisis* and the statist history of the Bolshevik Revolution, and, on the other, that they come from two very different periods of his life – the early, biographical, phase, and the later phase of Soviet history. In the first passage, which opens the second chapter of *The Romantic Exiles*, Carr writes as follows:

The collocation of Romanticism and Revolution sounds forced and rather unreal to most English ears. In England, the Romantic movement remained (except for Byron and in part Shelley, who became, in virtue of his exception, spiritual outcasts) a movement for the worship of Nature and the liberation of literature from the dead hand of convention. In Europe, it was a movement for the worship of Human Nature and the liberation of the individual from the yoke of moral and political absolutism. It was not, in its first and most characteristic phase, a movement against religion and morality as such . . . Romanticism covered every phase of human thought. Its metaphysical counterpart was the Idealism of Fichte, Schelling and Hegel – 'Romanticism for the heart', as Herzen put it, 'and Idealism for the head'. Its supreme political expression was the French Revolution. The Romantic movement, from the seed sown by Rousseau, spread over Europe, flowered, decayed, and finally faded away (subject to sporadic revivals in later years) after the ineffective revolutions of 1848 and 1849.[20]

It was to the last, Russian, phase of this romanticism, which Carr studies in this book, and to the romantic, and in large measure self-destructive individuals, that he devotes such care and sympathy. It might be tempting to see this approach, epitomized in the first four biographical studies, as characteristic of an early, utopian or romantic, Carr. Certainly there is much in these figures that appears to match Carr's own view of life. It did not escape his attention that, for all their talk of revolution, they were both destructive and elitist. Nechaev, Bakunin, Herzen are celebrated for their passionate desire to destroy – therein lies the political dimension of their romanticism. They are the supreme angry and illiberal rebels. They are also elitist – Carr cites Herzen's discovery of the 'futility of universal suffrage' in the elections of December 1848 that brought Louis Napoleon to the Presidency.[21]

Surprising as it may be to find these sentiments in the Carr of the early 1930s it may be even more unexpected to encounter them, three and a half decades later in the historian of the Soviet achievement. Yet it is on this note, that which ended *The Romantic Exiles*, that Carr choses to commence his introduction to *The ABC of Communism*. The very first sentence of this introduction reads:

No movement that set out to change the world can do without its Utopia, its vision of a future which will reward the exertions, and outweigh the sufferings, of the present.[22]

Tracing the history of such thinking through the great religions, and the Enlightenment, he shows how, even within Marx and Engels' critique of utopian socialism in the *Communist Manifesto*, there is a utopian element, as there was in later socialism and liberalism. The Russian anarchists and *narodniks* were utopians, as was Tolstoy, and so too Carr asserts was Lenin: as he points out *What is to be done?*, the 1902 text of Lenin's that is normally read as the project for an elitist, vanguard, party, also contains a passage on 'the need to dream', illustrated by Lenin with a quote from the nihilist Dmitry Pisarev. Lenin himself laments the lack of dreamers in the socialist movement, and the excess of people who pride themselves on their sobriety.[23]

Nowhere is this commitment to romance more evident than in his *The Romantic Exiles*. This is a study of Russian exiles in western Europe, from the 1840s to the 1860s, of the intersection of their personal and political lives. From a distance, it might appear that they were a collection of no-hopers, with marginal influence on their own land, little on the politics of Europe as a whole, living off private incomes, and consumed with a heady mix of erotic obsession and internationalist delusions. In *What is History?* Carr was to cite, approvingly, the conclusion which Namier drew from his study of the failed revolutions of 1848, 'the hollowness of ideas in face of armed force'. Yet as is evident from the care and perception with which *The Romantic Exiles* is written, and the recapitulation of these themes in the other, contemporary, writings on Dostoevsky, and Bakunin, Carr is drawn to these tragic, utopian, figures in a way he is not drawn to Marx himself. Of all the figures whom he describes, perhaps the most sympathetic is Herzen, who through his journal *The Bell* and participation in internationalist activity in Europe was a forerunner of later Russian revolutionaries. Carr quotes from a letter of Herzen's in 1855:

> We do not build, we destroy; we do not proclaim a new truth, we abolish an old lie. Contemporary man only builds the bridge; another, the yet unknown man of the future, will walk across it. You perhaps will see it. Do not remain on this shore. Better to perish with the revolution than to be saved in holy reaction.
>
> The religion of revolution, of the great social transformation, is the only religion I bequeath to you. It is a religion without a paradise, without rewards, without consciousness of itself, without a conscience.[24]

In one sense, this was what Carr also held of Marx. In his biography he pours particular scorn on the illusory future Marx offers. Yet in discussing the romantic exiles, Carr is more sympathetic, even enamoured. Of Nechaev, he writes:

In any history of revolution the masterful figure of Sergi Nechaev must find a place. Nechaev was one of those who, by the sheer force of a dominant personality, impose themselves on their contemporaries and on posterity. In a meteoric career, which ended at the age of thirty-five, he achieved literally nothing... Nechaev believed in the overthrow of the existing order, not because he had, like Herzen, a romantic faith in democracy, or like Bakunin, a still more romantic faith in human nature. He believed in revolution as a tenet valid and sufficient in itself; and he believed in nothing else... He deceived everyone he met, and when he was no longer able to deceive, his power was gone. His audacity was unbounded; and he carried personal courage to the extreme limit of foolhardiness. He is an unparalleled and bewildering combination of fanatic, swashbuckler and cad.[25]

Anyone reading his life of Bakunin or *The Romantic Exiles* will be struck by his admiration for those, like Alexander Herzen, Mikhail Bakunin, even the anarchist adventurer Sergi Nechaev. This romanticism is also phrased by Carr in contrary terms, ones that recapitulate his view of the transition from individualism to collectivism, but in this context by relating it specifically to the question of revolution:

Marx was one of the few – perhaps the first since Luther – whose life has constituted a turning point in human thought. Marx was the prophet of the newly created, inarticulate, many-head proletariat which, emerging from the throes of the industrial revolution, dominates the present age. Marx perceived that this emergence heralded the end of the three-hundred-year period of history to which he gave the convenient, thought not entirely appropriate label of '*bourgeois* civilisation'.[26]

In saluting Bakunin as 'incomparably the greatest leader and agitator thrown up by the revolutionary movement of the nineteenth century', Carr argues that his time had passed, overtaken by the new generation epitomized in Marx:

The cause of revolution before Marx had been idealistic and romantic – a matter of intuitive and heroic impulse. Marx made it materialistic and scientific – a matter of deduction and cold reasoning. Marx substituted economics for metaphysics – the proletarian and the peasant for the philosopher and the poet. He brought to the theory of political evolution the same element of orderly inevitability which Darwin had introduced into biology.[27]

Carr signals his disapproval of this shift in his reference to 'the drab, respectably monotony of Marx's domestic existence' which he contrasts to the 'many-hued, incalculable diversity of the lives of the Romantic Exiles'. Not for Carr the 'grim, dogmatic, matter-of-fact characteristics of the late Victorian age'.[28] Moreover, while he acknowledged this importance of Marx he also in this earlier work rejected the consequences:

> if the quality of Marxist doctrine is to be summed up in a single word, that word should be 'fanaticism', for the essence of fanaticism is the denial to others of the right to think differently. The 'popular' dictatorships current in Europe at the present time are all based on the Marxist conception of mass-rule, substituting the uniformity of the mass-will for the diversity of individual caprice; and the only difference between the so-called 'dictatorship of the proletariat' and the dictatorships which prefer to hoist other flags is that the one proclaims its Marxist paternity and the others deny it. In *Capital*, Marx refers to the *régime* of *laissez-faire* capitalism as the world of 'liberty, equality, property and Jeremy Bentham'. It would be a fair parody to describe the world of the twentieth century as the world of mass-production, mass-dictatorship and Marx.[29]

What he wrote here of the 1930s would, of course, apply even more to the period after 1945.

How far Carr was able to reconcile this romanticism with his other work, how far he altered his views, would require another, more extensive study: suffice it to register here, in the face of the apparent collectivism and determinism of his more currently read works, *The Twenty Years' Crisis* and the history of the Bolshevik Revolution, that Carr also believed in the importance of the individual and that individual's utopian projects as one of the driving forces of life. This was not the least of the contradictions, or better creative tensions, within the historian, and the man.

Analytic Contribution

The three themes already discussed represent ideas that permeate Carr's work, informing his discussion of particular historical events, or processes. They are, in a loose sense, his theoretical approach, or philosophy. He does not claim to have resolved these issues, any more than he has that between power and morality in *The Twenty Years' Crisis*. They provide a set of ideas that should inform any study of revolution. They are, however, only part of what Carr himself contributed to the study of revolution, and to locating their place in the history of the modern world. 'So long as man is interested in exploring his past,' he wrote in 1967, 'nobody will doubt the credentials of the revolution of 1917 as one of the great turning points in history.'[30] For in addition to these broad theoretical indicators, there are in his work specific studies that point the way to a broader understanding of revolution. Five such themes merit attention here.

In the first place, Carr argues, throughout his work, for the importance of revolutions in the shaping of the modern world. This is most obviously the case in the time taken by his study of the consolidation of Bolshevik power, up to the 1930s, and the fact that this dominated the last 35 years of his life. He is aware, as are any revolutionaries, of the importance of previous revolutions: references to the English and French revolutions recur in his work, and he assumed a reader's familiarity with, and some sympathy for, these antecedent upheavals. It is, however, the importance of the Bolshevik Revolution, as the decisive moment of the twentieth century, that is the central premiss of his later work, and indeed of his earlier analysis of Marx. If, in the earlier work, prior to the Second World War, the importance of the Bolshevik Revolution lay in its pioneering of a new kind of industrial and social order, this secular sociological significance was reinforced by the Soviet defeat of Nazi Germany.

Within this overall emphasis on the centrality of the Bolshevik Revolution Carr provides a discussion of something too rarely distinguished in the study of international relations, the foreign policy of revolutionary states.[31] Carr was not naive about the idealism, or ideological purity, of revolutionary regimes, but he did analyse the foreign policy of Soviet state in terms distinct from those of conventional powers. Volume 3 of *The Bolshevik Revolution* is a detailed account of how the revolutionaries of Petrograd moved from their first outright rejection of 'bourgeois diplomacy' to a 'dual policy', combining diplomacy with revolutionary internationalism, and then to the later calculations of Lenin on consolidating the Soviet state in a hostile capitalist world. Here Carr was not dominated by what others might see as realist concerns: the concerns of state, military power and the amorality of calculation; these are there, but then so are the innovation of diplomatic style, and the continued commitment to the internationalist dimension of Soviet foreign policy. The thesis advanced in *Twenty Year's Crisis* – that power is also economic and ideological – is here put to practical effect. It is ironic that Carr, who in 1945 mocked 'the tragi-comedy of the Communist International',[32] should have chosen precisely this dimension to take his study of the Soviet Union furthest. In all four major parts of his study – *the Bolshevik Revolution, The Interregnum (1923–4), Socialism in One Country (1924–1926)* and *Foundations of Planned Economy (1926–1929)* – a substantial part of the study is devoted to foreign policy in general, and the Comintern in particular: his last two volumes were devoted to it – *The Twilight of the Comintern* and *The Comintern and the Spanish Civil War*. Thus if his internal work, on the planned economy, stops in the early 1930s: his study of foreign policy goes on.[33] In his earlier biographical work a similar attention is paid to what are, at the most, hare-brained and fantastical projects for international revolution.[34]

The study of the foreign policy of revolutionary states leads on to something Carr came to study particularly in the 1940s, namely the international impact of revolutions. Here he has little to say about what, for many writers, would be the decisive aspects of such an impact: military challenge and internationalist commitment. Rather, in the vein of the international sociological arguments he advances in many of his writings, he sees the Russian Revolution as having an impact because it was the harbinger of broader changes. This relates to his general insistence on the importance of propaganda in the contemporary world. This has the merit of correcting the bias often found in writings on social change, and reform, in the West, by which the external challenge is ignored as an explanatory factor. It mirrors to some degree what Hobsbawm has written on the impact of the Russian revolution on western capitalism. Yet by downplaying the element of challenge, of the rivalry between blocs, something Hobsbawm does not do, Carr rather excludes what many would see as the central dimension of the Bolshevik Revolution, namely the competition or rivalry between systems that that revolution occasioned. Carr's own prognosis on this matter fell into the field of what may be termed 'convergence', in victory for either side: 'the prospect is probably not an out-and-out victory either for the western or the Soviet ideology, but rather an attempt to find a compromise, a half-way house, a synthesis between conflicting ways of life.'[35]

The problem with this prognosis is not that it turned out to be wrong – many predictions do. The problem was rather that, by limiting the Soviet–western relationship to one of example, it misunderstood the very nature of the international impact of the Bolshevik Revolution *and* the manner in which the western capitalist world could, and did, react. This is evident in two different periods. One concerns the immediate post-revolutionary period and the League of Nations: Carr's critique of the League is clear enough, in both *The Twenty Years' Crisis* and *International Relations Between the Two World Wars*. It rests, famously, on a critique of the League's utopianism, and lack of realism. This is, however, the *opposite* to Lenin's critique, and it is debatable which is the more realist: for in Lenin's analysis the League, far from being a dreamy and ineffective body, was in fact a most effective, counter-revolutionary, organisation, a 'League of Robbers'. The Theses on the International Situation presented to the first Comintern Congress in March 1919 made clear the Bolshevik view:

> The 'League of Nations' is a delusive slogan by means of which the social-traitors, acting on behalf of international capital, split the forces of the proletariat and promote the imperialist counter-revolution.
>
> The revolutionary proletariat of all countries of the world must wage an irreconcilable struggle against the idea of the Wilsonian 'League of Nations' and protest against entry into this League of robbery, or exploitation, and of imperialist counter-revolution.[36]

A year later the Second Congress of the Comintern described the League as 'nothing but the insurance contract by which the victors in the war mutually guarantee each other's spoils'.[37] The League was designed both to promote counter-revolution against Russia and to inaugurate, through the trusteeship and other arrangements, a new era of imperialist control of the third world.[38] Ironically, Russia was to join the League in September 1934, just on the eve of the Abyssinia crisis when, in Carr's view, its final vacuity was to be demonstrated.

Carr's analysis equally, of course, misrepresented the long-term nature of the conflict between the Soviet and western systems in the post-war epoch. The accommodation of spheres of influence which Carr understood as the Cold War, legitimate to a considerable degree by concerns of strategic defence, would indeed have allowed for an indefinite coexistence and possible convergence. But there were two things wrong with this, longer-term processes that were excluded from Carr's view: one was the unregulated, and violent, rivalry of the two blocs in the Third World, the other was the erosion of the Soviet system itself from within *and* from the increasingly successful capitalist West, not least through that power over opinion that he saw as operating in the other direction. The years in which Carr was writing his volumes on the Soviet achievement were also those of the long capitalist boom: it was the latter, through peaceful, demonstrative, competition which was to undermine the former. Carr was in general terms perceptive about the impact of long-run social and economic change, as he was about the role of propaganda in the modern world. He did not envisage what this could, and would, do to the Soviet experiment itself. For all the accommodation of blocs, there was also a rivalry, in which one side had to prevail over the other.

Carr's contribution to the study of revolution may be held to contain a fourth element – one about which he himself was evidently uneasy, namely the role of ideas and ideology. Carr does not seem to have been impressed by arguments on historical agency or social consciousness. There could be no greater contrast between Carr's work on the Bolshevik Revolution and another English study of radical history which appeared in 1963 in the midst of Carr's publication, E.P. Thompson's *The Making of the English Working Class* a work as influential in a contrary manner as Carr's *What is History?* and published in the same year. Carr emphasizes production statistics and state plans, Thompson aspiration and organization of social groups: but in a way, each mirrors the weaknesses of the other. Yet as Carr's emphasis on romanticism and dreaming makes clear, and as his study of individuals and their ideas exemplifies, he continued to assert the importance of such ideas, within the constraints imposed by reality and power. Carr at one point says of Marx that the latter had nothing original to say about the issue of economic determinism and free will:[39] nor of course, does Carr. What he does do is insist, recurrently, and in different idioms, on the continued importance of ideas, be this in regard to the hopeless ventures of *The Romantic Exiles* in the 1850s and 1860s, or to the role played by Bolshevik ideology and vision in creating the Soviet state. In his introduction to *The ABC of Communism* Carr writes of the period of civil war in which *The ABC* was written:

> It was a period during which the energies of politicians and administrators were absorbed by the civil war and by problems of survival, and the mass of the population exposed to intolerable hardships and to constant calls for superhuman effort. Such periods commonly inspire, side by side with the harsh realism of current experience, and by way of compensation for it, far-ranging visions of a future social order to be attained through the present turmoil of exertion and suffering, visions embodying the ideals for which the struggle is

being waged. In such times of storm and stress the utopian elements inherent in any revolutionary doctrine are thrown into relief.[40]

This is a note strikingly absent from most studies of revolutions, and of their international dimensions. In nothing have otherwise different approaches to revolution – realist, liberal, structuralist – been so united as in their flight from the ideological and the subjective. Carr is saying that it is only possible to understand revolutions by studying what people said and thought. It is a lesson the all too flattened, objectified, study of revolution prevalent in the 1990s would do well to recall.[41]

The Cunning of Reason

Carr himself cannot, and would not have wanted to, escape the verdicts of history, on the events he analysed, and on the manner in which he chose to do so. No reader can doubt that, whatever his qualifications later in the book, he is broadly in sympathy with the view of historical judgement expounded in *The Twenty Years' Crisis*:

'World history', in the famous phrase which Hegel borrowed from Schiller, 'is the world court'. The popular paraphrase 'Might is Right' is misleading only if we attach too restricted a meaning to the word 'Might'. History creates rights, and is therefore right.[42]

It was this attitude, *die Weltgeschiche ist das Weltgericht*, which was to underlie his accommodation to Nazi Germany, it also inspired his view of Soviet Russia and the Bolshevik revolution. Its implications were to be spelt out in the introduction to the last of the volumes on the Russian revolution:

It is tempting to ask the hypothetical question whether the results could not have been achieved at a lesser cost, or – still more unrealistically – whether, if the costs had been foreseen, the results would have been achieved or attempted. But the very conception of a social or national balance-sheet of achievements and costs seems inappropriate and misleading. The main beneficiaries of an historical process are seldom or never those on whom the costs have fallen; and the model of the balance-sheet dissolves into an irreconcilable conflict of interests and purposes between different groups – a challenge to the illusion that every problem has a solution which will be free from ambiguity, free from suffering, free from injustice, free from tragedy.

The historian can only do his best to present the picture in all its aspects as a single whole, and, though well aware that the presentation will necessarily reflect his own provisional judgement, leave the ultimate verdict to the longer perspective of future generations.[43]

In his 1978 interview with *New Left Review* a similar, realist, view of history, and revolutions, is repeated.[44] Mention has already been made of one ethical position of Carr's – his endorsement of the displacement of political rights by socio-economic ones. This reinforces his more general reluctance to discuss the ethics of revolution itself.

Two problems, inevitable as they are unanswerable, pose themselves in regard to this approach. On the one hand, the moral stance taken towards revolutions raises, as does the realist approach to international relations, profound moral questions. No one can doubt that this is an underdeveloped area: if one takes three broad areas of modern political and collective activity, ones inexorably associated with discourses of right and wrong, it is striking that only in regard to one, namely war, has a remotely adequate moral compass been established. On the other two – nationalism and revolution – no such agreement is there, but rather a free fire zone of claim and counter-claim, tenuously related to concepts of justice and historical inevitability. Yet in nationalism and revolution it should be possible to ask the two kinds of moral questions classically asked of war – under what conditions is it legitimate to launch such an action, and what, assuming this is the case, is it morally permissible to do in pursuit of this aim. There is something too cold, too abstentionist, about Carr's approach to this issue. We have lost, in the 1990s, the historical underpinning that Carr, like Marx, used to substitute for a morality of revolution – a teleological vision of progress, within which revolutions, inevitable anyway, were further legitimated by their 'achievements' the latter assumed to be somehow permanent or irreversible. If the moral climate on nationalism has swung towards undue indulgence, casting a more favourable light on the reservations Carr had about nationalism, and the multiplication of states, the moral climate on revolutions has shifted in a different direction, and it casts a colder eye on Carr's analysis. In the light of the twentieth century it is more difficult to read with a neutral, let alone sympathetic eye, Herzen's praise of revolution as destruction.

If world history is the world court, then this must apply even more so to the final dénouement of the Bolshevik revolution itself. Carr's view of that event was shaped in the heat of World War II and he devoted his scholarly endeavours to the first twelve years of that regime. He died in

1982, ironically in the same year as Brezhnev: this was the year that marked the apogee of Soviet military power, and of its following in the Third World. It was, in retrospect, the year in which the retreat and collapse of the USSR began. Carr had maintained a long-run expectation of the survival and continued development of the Soviet system, as evidenced in his 1969 introduction to *The ABC of Communism* and, with rather more qualification, in his 1978 interview with *NLR*.[45] He cannot be exempted from the *Weltgericht* which passed its verdict in 1989–91. History moved faster and was *more* cunning than he had imagined.

To some degree the elements for an explanation of that event can be found in Carr's own work. The West prevailed over the East because of its economic and cultural power, its power over opinion. Carr's general sociology of change can, *if applied to communism not capitalism*, provide much of an explanation for the former's decline and collapse. At several points in his work he even adumbrated what was to be the decline of communism. As already noted, he concluded his biography of Marx by anticipating 'a renaissance of humanism', a revolution, as he termed it, that would bring the Marxist epoch of history to an end. In the final paragraph of *The Soviet Impact* he writes of England in terms that would, in the longer run, apply even more so to the USSR:

> The danger for the English-speaking world lies perhaps most of all in its relative lack of flexibility and in its tendency to rest on the laurels of past achievements. No human institution or order of society ever stands still.[46]

Even in his mistaken identification of the potential for a new utopianism in the USSR of the 1950s he uncannily adumbrated the very term that would mark the last years of Brezhnev, stagnation or *zastoi*:

> No society entirely devoid of utopian aspirations will escape stagnation. Soviet society has not stagnated. In the long struggle over de-Stalinization in the nineteenth-fifties and nineteen-sixties, the old clash between passionate idealists and cautious administrators is again apparent.[47]

That said, the collapse of Soviet communism in the late 1980s, and the refutation by the *Weltgericht* of the idea that any such post-capitalist order could be constructed in the contemporary epoch casts a critical light not only on Carr's view of the future, but on the very historical teleology that underlay his entire work on the USSR and on the ethical principles that inform his work. It will rapidly be said that it is too early definitely to answer this question, and that is so. But, in Carr's own vein, it has to be said that, from the vantage point of the 1990s the Bolshevik Revolution did not establish a political, economic or social system that endured, as the bourgeois French revolution had. Carr himself liked the phrase 'the test of time'. That is a test which his work on revolution has, to a considerable, degree, failed.

Conclusion

It is tempting, but probably fruitless, in an exploration of this kind to address the question of how far Carr's work can be read as a whole, how far there is consistency, or even continuity, between the different phases of his life and writing, or between the very different kinds of work he produced. Few modern intellectuals have had a range of output or a variety of contexts as diverse as he. His very commitment and range command respect. Who else has ranged from international theory and history, through social and economic history, to perceptive and judicious accounts of the love-life and dreams of nineteenth-century romantics? Part of the interest in reading Carr must be the tension between these two aspects of his life: awe at the range and development of his ideas, stimulation at the way in which, in diverse genres and historical contexts, the same ideas, reworked or not, recur. His ideas on revolution, like those on realism for which the international relations literature is most familiar, or his views on nationalism, may not form a unified whole: no intellectual *oeuvre* ever does. But there is a constant interaction, and counterpoint, that not only contributes to a wide variety of interests, but also serves to set the discussion of any particular topic in a more diverse light.

Carr is best known as, in international relations terms, a 'realist', and, as a historian, as that of the Soviet Union. In each of these, and in the combination of reflection and engagement they engendered, he bears comparison with others whose lives, and reactions to the events of the first half of the twentieth century, matched his. In the context of 'realism' and its implications for the study of the USSR, he bears comparison with George Kennan, a man who, like Carr, was born in the ordered world prior to the First World War, and who has tried, in academic and public engagement, to relate his theories to the international arena. Both are men nostalgic for a certain measured, elitist, world; both use their concern for power and the realities of world politics to attain some measured appreciation of the Soviet Union; neither, in a long life of writing and commitment, shows much interest in the world beyond Europe and North America. Carr had far greater philosophical, and historiographical, capacity than Kennan, but it was Kennan who, shaping his view of the USSR during his residence in Moscow in the 1940s, came to perceive more accurately than Carr the slow entropy of the Bolshevik system and the long-run vulnerability to the success of the West.[48]

The other person to whom Carr bears comparison was his friend Isaac Deutscher. Like Carr, Deutscher defined his philosophical position in contradistinction to a tradition from which he had emerged: in Carr's case Edwardian English liberalism, in Deutscher's orthodox Polish Judaism. Both devoted the bulk of their intellectual life to understanding the aftermath of the Bolshevik revolution. Both shared the belief, later to be confounded, that the revolutionary regime itself could be reform and could endure as a permanent rival to the West: the Second World War and the optimism of the Khrushchev period from 1956 to 1964 were the bases of this expectation.[49]

Yet unlike Carr, Deutscher was a committed Marxist, and, through his sympathy for the analyses of Trotsky, he devoted a far more critical eye to the nature of the Stalinist regime, its treatment of its own people, and its manipulation of foreign communists. Whereas in Carr biography and Soviet history were two separate domains, almost two contrasted sides of his own intellectual personality, in Deutscher they were fused, in the lives of Stalin and Trotsky and in the unfinished life of Lenin which he was writing when he died. We can learn much from what Carr wrote on revolutions and revolutionaries, as much for the light it casts on his broader theoretical writings, as for the ways in which it may help us to think about revolutions. That learning is, quite properly, tempered by two other perspectives, that of world history on the one hand, and that of the record of his contemporaries on the other. One suspects that Carr himself would have asked for no less.

Notes

1   E.H. Carr, *What is History?* (London: Penguin, 1961), p. 42.
2   E.H. Carr, *International Relations Between the Two World Wars 1919–1939* (London: Macmillan, 1947), chapter 10 'The Nazi Revolution'.
3   E.H. Carr, *The Bolshevik Revolution 1917–1923* (Harmondsworth: Pelican, 1966), Vol. 1, p. 5.
4   I. Deutscher, *Marxism, Wars and Revolutions* (London: Verso, 1989), chapter 4, 'Two Revolutions'.

5   Carr, *Twenty Years' Crisis*, pp. 86–7, see also pp. 106–7, 159, 226, 231. Significantly, Carr, in his examples of such self-interested internationalism does *not* include communism, or the USSR, but this may reflect a tactical reserve in the context of the Second World War. The relevance of his general point is evident.

6   E.H. Carr, *Karl Marx. A Study in Fanaticism* (London: J.M. Dent, 1934), p. 81.

7   Carr, *What is History?*, p. 116.

8   *Ibid.*, pp. 49–52, 137.

9   Carr, *Twenty Years' Crisis*, pp. 226–7, Carr, *Karl Marx*, pp. 77–8. For an exploration of the programme, and ambiguities, of Soviet thinking see his introduction to N. Bukharin and E. Preobrazhensky, *The ABC of Communism* (Harmondsworth: Penguin) pp. 47–9.

10 E.H. Carr, *Nationalism and After* (London: Macmillan, 1945) pp. 17–26.

11 J. Rosenberg, *The Empire of Civil Society* (London: Verso, 1994); Immanuel Wallerstein, *Historical Capitalism* (London: Verso, 1983).

12 Carr, *What is History?*, pp. 140–1.

13 Carr, *The ABC of Communismm*, pp. 38–43; Carr, *What is History?*, p. 124.

14 Carr, *Karl Marx*, p. 302.

15 *Ibid.*, p. 303.

16 Carr, *The Soviet Impact*, p. 112.

17 Carr, *ABC of Communism*, pp. 32–6.

18 *Ibid.*, pp. 35–6.

19 *States and Social Revolutions*, p. 226 on statistics for state employment.

20 E.H. Carr *The Romantic Exiles* (London, Serif, 1998) p. 25.

21 Thus Herzen is quoted as comparing French voters to orang-outangs and fulminating against the masses: 'Who that respects the truth would ask the opinion of the first man he meets? Suppose Columbus or Copernicus had put to the vote the existence of America or the movement of the earth?', Carr, *The Romantic Exiles*, p. 39.

22 Carr, *The ABC of Communism*, 'Editor's Introduction', p. 13.

23 *Ibid.*, p. 16. In the passage Carr refers to Lenin writes: ' "We should dream!" I wrote these words and became alarmed. I imagined myself sitting at a "unity conference" and opposite me were the *Rabocheye Dyelo* editors and contributors. Comrade Martynov rises and, turning to me, says sternly: "Permit me to ask you, has an autonomous editorial board the right to dream without first soliciting the opinion of the Party Committees?" He is followed by Comrade Krichevsky, who ... continues even more sternly: "I go further. I ask, has a Marxist any right at all to dream, knowing that according to Marx mankind always sets itself the tasks it can solve and that tactics is a process of the growth of Party tasks which grow together with the Party?" ' (Lenin in *What is to be Done?* in *Lenin Selected Works*, Moscow: Progress Publishers, 1970, Vol. 1, p. 255).

24 Carr, *The Romantic Exiles*, p. 134.

25 *Ibid.*, p. 255.

26 Carr, *Karl Marx*, p. 301.

27 Carr, *The Romantic Exiles*, p. 321.

28 *Ibid.*, p. 321.

29 Carr, *Karl Marx*, pp. 302–3.

30 'The Russian Revolution: Its Place in History' in *The October Revolution. Before and After* (New York: Alfred Knopf, 1969), p. 33.

31 There is a growing literature on the foreign policy of revolutionary states, notably David Armstrong, *Revolution and World Order* (Oxford: Clarendon Press, 1994). For my own reflections see chapter 6 of *Rethinking International Relations* (London: Macmillan, 1994) and my *Revolution and World Politics* (London: Macmillan, 1999).

32 Carr, *Nationalism and After*, p. 21.

33 The argument that he could take foreign policy further because the sources were available is rather thin.

34 E.H. Carr, *Michael Bakunin* (New York: Octagon Books, 1975) chapter 25, 'The League of Peace and Freedom'; chapter 26, 'The Birth of the Alliance'.

35 Carr, *The Soviet Impact on the Western World*, p. 116.

36 'Extracts from the Theses on the International Situation and the Policy of the Entente Adopted by the First Comintern Congress', 6 March 1919 in Jane Degras, ed. *The Communist International 1919–1943 Documents*, Vol. 1, 1919–1922 (London: Frank Cass, 1971), p. 33.

37 'Theses on the National and Colonial Question Adopted by the Second Comintern Congress', 28 July 1920 in Degras, *The Communist International*, p. 140.

38 The classic study is Arno Mayer, *Politics and Diplomacy of Peace-making: Containment and Counter-revolution at Versailles* (London: Weidenfeld and Nicolson, 1968).

39 Carr, *Karl Marx*, p. 79.

40 Carr, *The ABC of Communism*, p. 50.

41 I have gone into this in greater detail in my *Revolution and World Politics*.

42 Carr, *Twenty Years' Crisis*, p. 67.

43 E.H. Carr, *Foundations of Planned Economy 2 1926–1929* (Harmondsworth: Pelican, 1976), p. v.

44 E.H. Carr, 'The Russian Revolution and the West' *New Left Review*, No. 111, September–October 1978, pp. 25–6.

45 *New Left Review*, No. 111, p. 35 where he sees 1917 as an anti-imperialist not an anti-capitalist revolt.

46 Carr, *The Soviet Impact*, p. 116.

47 Carr, *The ABC of Communism*, p. 51.

48 G. Kennan, 'The Sources of Soviet Conduct' in *American Diplomacy 1900–1950* (New York, Mentor Book 1951) pp. 89–105.

49 For Carr's view of Deutscher see chapters 9 and 10 and the obituary of Deutscher in *The October Revolution. Before and After*. For Deutscher on Carr see *Ironies of History* (London: Oxford University Press, 1966), 'Between Past and Future'.

IV
What is History?

13
The Lessons of *What is History?*

Anders Stephanson

It is not for his monumental *A History of Soviet Russia* that E.H. Carr is best known today but for two less ambitious works. Thus no introductory course in international relations seems to be complete without *The Twenty Years' Crisis*, often included to represent, dubiously, something called 'classical realism'. Meanwhile, most historians in the Anglophone world and a substantial number elsewhere read *What is History?* (1961, henceforth *WIH*) as graduate students and probably go on to teach it to the next generation. Both works, in short, have become classics. The *Twenty Years' Crisis* is a canonical text within a field that takes such things quite seriously. *WIH*, by contrast, is seen as a handy way to open up some basic questions about a discipline which lacks a proper canon and whose boundaries are notoriously diffuse.[1]

How *WIH* achieved this status is not immediately obvious. As a series of lectures, the book was scarcely composed with classical longevity in mind and the early scholarly reaction did not indicate any such future glory.[2] The book was generally considered interesting, strongly argued and useful; but an instant classic it was not.[3] Moreover, Carr's book seems to fall somewhere between two genres of works on historiography. It has little of the didactic (or 'manualistic') flavour that attaches, for example, to that even older classic, Marc Bloch's *The Historian's Craft*.[4] Carr, to be sure, makes trenchant remarks about such problems as selectivity of facts in the constitution of historical evidence. But the nitty-gritty of method is not of much interest to him. It is not his subject-matter. What concerns him, to put it in a way he would have found congenial, are the conditions for producing histories that not only move along with history itself, but anticipate and facilitate its development in a desirable direction. The discussion of facts, objectivity, causation, generalization, and so on – standard problems of

283

method – is structured with that instrumental view firmly in mind. By the same token, Carr's book is not a 'timeless' treatise on the nature of history either. He prompts us to understand the coherent patterns of history so that we might accomplish useful things but eschews philosophical profundity. Just as epistemology is secondary to purpose, so it is with the deeper questions of what might govern history.

Instead Carr emphasizes (again and again) the 'situated' nature of the historian's practice; and these lectures are nothing if not situated in the intellectual politics of Britain in 1961. In an atmosphere he perceived to be defeatist and negative, Carr's lectures were meant to promote the idea of progressive action. Rarely if ever did he write in a 'writerly' way, as an aesthetic exercise in the sense of something purposefully purposeless. On the contrary, writing for him was a protopolitical (indeed *policy-making*) act, rather in the manner he had perfected in composing editorials for *The Times* during the Second World War. The tone here is sharp, not to say polemical. The targets are named. Arnold Toynbee, Karl Popper, Isaiah Berlin, Hugh Trevor-Roper, Oxford historians and philosophers, the Cambridge history faculty seated in front row of the lecture hall: all are taken to task in no uncertain terms. Indeed the attacks go beyond academic politics. Not for the first time, Carr is addressing, obliquely, the ruling strata of Britain, or at least its educated elite.

And yet, 'site-specific' though it is, the book turned out to be a marvellously vigorous introduction to history.[5] In the course of propounding the imperative of engagement, *WIH* manages to pose a whole range of large and interesting questions about 'the historiographical operation.'[6] Anyone can read *WIH* and most who do are moved to serious reflection in one way or another. If Carr has sarcastic things to say about the culture of common sense in Britain, his own style of reasoning falls solidly and to good effect within that tradition.[7] This is one reason it plays well among historians – an audience with limited tolerance for abstraction. Yet the simplicity is deceptive. Closer inspection reveals a layered and conflictual text, tensions that create the kind of depth befitting of a classic.

My own interest in this regard is, for lack of a better term, structuralist. Rather than following Carr's own, often cited behest to study the historian before studying the history, I shall be moving the opposite way (mostly) and ask what sort of author his text requires in order to be written as it is. The 'subject-position' from which this instrumental work is launched is thus the final problem here rather than the sundry problems of historiography as such. In order to arrive at the former, however, I must proceed from the inside out, following and reworking Carr's argument in its ascending order from facts through significance and generalization to the ultimately decisive question of historical direction. This movement, detrimentally in my view, is organized around the problem of objectivity and never really resolved; but the successive failures are of the greatest moment.

Empiricism and Subjectivism

The immediate source of inspiration is R.G. Collingwood, whom Carr famously and rightly calls the 'only British thinker in this century who has made a contribution to the philosophy of history'.[8] Collingwood allows him to set up an initial polarity about the status of facts. Carr's rhetorical strategy is often the time-honoured one of putting forth two unpalatable alternatives in order either to come down in some predetermined 'middle' or to disclaim them in the name of neither/nor-ism. However, the alternatives do not have to be equally unpalatable and in the case of Collingwood, Carr accepts more than he discards, at least in the Collingwood he chooses to deploy.

Thus we are first told that 'facts' are not, as the nineteenth century fervently believed, independent of the observer. They are not, in Carr's colourful but peculiar metaphor, 'fish on the fishmonger's slab'.[9] It is, he says, nothing less than a 'preposterous fallacy'[10] to think that subject and object can be radically separated and the consciousness of the historian erased from the production of facts. Historians interpret and their interpretations are as historically situated as they are themselves. Facts are created through a certain process of interaction between historian and source material, a process marked by what might be called interested selectivity.

After so dismissing common-sense empiricism (and by extension the philistine English rejection of theory), Carr goes on typically also to dismiss what he takes to be its polar opposite, Collingwood's subjectivism.[11] To say that historical knowledge is situated is not, Carr insists, to argue that all accounts are equally good. In making that sensible point, however, he suddenly reintroduces the existence of independent facts (or at least 'data', pre-facts). Consider, he suggests, a mountain. In observing it from different angles one gets different views, but 'it does not follow that . . . it has objectively either no shape at all or an infinity of shapes'.[12] The mountain is there, it has a definite shape and in theory one ought to be able to achieve some image of it that (presumably) corresponds quite closely to its form as an object. So there is some kind of objectivity of fact after all. Ultimately, the same holds true for the fish. Fishermen-historians choose 'the kind of fish' they want to get and the 'part of the ocean' where they want to find it, along with the method and means.[13] But the fish is really out there and when it is caught, it is what it is. To use another terminology, there are objective, ascertainable data, building blocks, 'raw material', that become facts when the historian deploys them to construct a totality, an analytical narrative. History, then, is the result of a continuous interaction with these 'bricks'.[14]

Carr wants, in short, to carve out a space between simple empiricism on the one hand and total anarchy on the other, between 'history as an objective compilation of facts' and 'history as subjective product of the mind'.[15] While 'situating' the production of facts and historical interpretation, he also has to avoid subjectivism and so he thinks it necessary to hang on to some notion of 'objectivity' – not reachable in practice perhaps but desirable. A pressing personal inducement to hold to this standard is the plethora of politically charged works in his own field of Soviet history, works based on the flimsiest empirical grounding. But Carr also wants to confirm the cumulative, progressive character of history itself. Truth does not simply vary with the times. History moves forward, if not in a straight line; and so does the level of historical interpretation. Generally speaking, we had a better idea of Bismarck in the 1920s than in the 1890s; and in the 1960s we have a better one still.

There are two serious problems here. The first has to do with the metaphorical use of physical objects as stand-ins for historical facts and accounts. Elsewhere Carr quotes approvingly Geoffrey Barraclough's dictum that in history we are really dealing with a 'series of accepted judgments';[16] but in that case we are also in a different realm from that of mountains and fish. Historians, professionally, do not view mountains. Nor do they catch fish. Historians interpret texts, that which has already been interpreted (I accept for the sake of the argument Carr's and Collingwood's hermeneutical frame). This points to a deeper problem, to what is today a central shortcoming of *WIH*. Carr has no account of language and representation – though in the early 1980s he planned to confront the issue in a revised edition. Language appears here only peripherally and is not fundamentally at issue. Historians are affected by their contemporary language: this is as far as he goes. One is inclined to think the question goes deeper than that. If language is no longer simply a means of description but structurally prior to any account of the world, then the world is not open, theoretically, to transparent 'viewing', nor can our histories or analyses come more or less close to some prelinguistic and suprahistorical standard of 'objectiv-ity' in Carr's sense here.

Second, the alternatives Carr poses form a false opposition. The altern-atives are not as limited as he indicates. One need not adhere to ontological ideas of some pristine reality subject to near-objective description in order to maintain differences in the quality of historical knowledge. The ensuing antinomies derive from the original subject–object distinction which governs his argument. Once the subject–object polarity is accepted, knowledge becomes a question of the procedures by which the subject can abstract inherent qualities from some externally given object with proper guarantees of certainty. But no grounds for certainty can ever be found which do not require other conditions of possibility. An infinite regress sets in. Carr, who dismisses any sharp separation between subject and object, nevertheless remains locked inside the polarity. Unable to find secure footing, he is forced into an argument that typically oscillates between the two poles.[17]

One might well say instead that whatever we want to analyse or describe is open to accounts whose validity vary according to spatio-temporal standards but which are 'better or worse' in how well they 'work', 'persuade' or 'explain'. This is not to fall into idealist 'constructiv-ism' pure and simple or to claim that historical writing is indistinguish-able from fiction. Nor is it to deny that there is a world out there or indeed that we 'know' more today than we did yesterday. It is, however, to remove the whole question of 'knowledge' from traditional epistem-ology to a historical plane more agreeable to Carr's own intentions. Indeed, elsewhere in the book he announces that 'the world of the historian, like that of the scientist, is not that of a photographic copy of the real world, but rather a working model that enables him more or less effectively to understand it and master it'.[18]

A pragmatic view is none the less unacceptable to Carr on the surpris-ing grounds that it is too instrumentalist. Pragmatists and Nietzscheans alike, according to him, subordinate the 'facts' of history entirely to present needs and thus their delineations tend to be inaccurate and distorted: the Sovietological syndrome once again. This is not a fair characterization of either school, but the objection to instrumentalism is of more immediate interest here. His own project, after all, seems to view history as a problem of present needs. For him, however, these needs are said to be historically derived, rooted not only in a sense of the past but also of future direction. What bothers him about the two other camps is not the instrumentalism as such, or even the epistemology, but the 'presentism'. They see history (he would say) in terms of the present while he sees the present in terms of the movement of history, from past to future. Carr's present, consequently, is *not itself a privileged space of interpretation*. It is, in a way, a mere moving instant whose real meaning is entirely determined by what comes before and what one thinks will come after.

Significance and Causation

This conception of the present is decisive for the manner in which, later on, he fundamentally reformulates the problem of objectivity in terms of significance. Facts only become facts, he argues, because historians invest them with significance and this procedure inevitably involves situated values. Hence there is an irreducible element of subjectivity involved and no absolute objectivity can be achieved. But objectivity, he now says, is not about 'facts' anyway, verifiable propositions such as dates and the like. Objectivity is about the quality of analysis and must begin with the frank recognition of subjectivity, the inevitable taint of subjectivity. Once historical variability and values have been clarified, historians can achieve objectivity to the extent that they are able to 'distinguish between the significant and the accidental' among the facts and relate this abstraction to the aim of the investigation.[19] All historians select from the past what they consider significant facts for their work; but the good (i.e. para-objective) historian is capable of choosing truly significant facts. The criterion of significance is 'relevance to the goal in view'. Such goals, in turn, are not 'static' but evolve along with history. Decent historians, then, get the facts (or pre-factual data) right; but great ones pick out 'the right facts' and apply 'the right standard of significance'.[20]

Significance and relevance of fact is thus Carr's initial criterion of this new, genuine objectivity. One is bound to ask then how the 'right standard' might be determined and by whom. To appreciate the 'objectivism' of Carr's answer, a word is necessary about the mediating level between facts and historical direction: causal ordering and generalisation.

The discussion of causation is analytically much the weakest in the book and can be dealt with briefly. After recognizing the horrendous difficulties involved, Carr simply goes on to talk about causation in the manner of 'everyday life'. Historians, as everyone else, must believe 'that human actions have causes which are in principle ascertainable'.[21] Causes in the mechanistic understanding of the nineteenth century might be wrong, but there has to be some notion of rational order for history to make sense. Differently put, history would be instrumentally useless if the ordinary sense of causality (as well as the instrumental relation between means and ends) were inoperative. Hence, as he argues in an earlier work, history must be understood 'as a coherent sequence in which one set of events or ideas leads on to another set of events or ideas and helps to influence and determine them'.[22] After establishing the hierarchy of significant facts, historians should thus establish the hierarchy of significant causes. Such causal ordering is accomplished by deciding what is 'amenable to rational explanation', more precisely the causal sequence which best fits the 'pattern of rational explanation and interpretation'[23] of the historian's choice. Relevant causal chains can so be determined, accidental ones thrown out.

Again, this begs the question of ultimate ground. Who is to decide what is accidental and what counts as rational explanation? If every historian is free to choose his or her scheme of rationality, one would be back in the morass of Collingwoodian subjectivism. To find secure land, therefore, Carr must situate his 'rationality' somewhere else. His solution to this pivotal problem is executed in two steps. The first has to do with 'generalization', while the second is a matter of whether the intended goal of the investigation has anything significant and relevant to do with the actual direction of history. The argument is not always clear but crucial.

Generalization

History, for Carr, is part of the overall scientific endeavour (understood in the German sense of *Wissenschaft*). Natural science, contrary to common perception, deals with events rather than static facts and is just as timebound as historiography. The aim for both is to determine causal connections between events and draw general conclusions which expand knowledge and lead to further research. History is more difficult to do because people act on the basis of experience and thus vary behaviour over time. Yet histories centring on the unique can teach no lesson other than Aristotle's that none is to be learned. The discipline is not, or should not be, about unique events in their glorious particularity. It has to be about extracting the universal from the particular, or, better put, seeing the general significance of the particular. The bridge between science and history, then, is the concept of 'generalization'.

This idea is an obfuscation. It subsumes two quite different kinds of inquiry under a misleading rubric. Natural sciences and a good number of the social sciences that ape them certainly 'generalize', if one understands that operation as the opposite of nominalism. Their standard model of investigation is repeated instantiation (or 'testing') of a nomothetic proposition, hypothesis or theory. In the social sciences, outside the controlled experiments of the laboratory, this way of understanding the scientific takes the quintessential form of the 'case study': a series of examples supposed to prove or disprove the given theory – or 'model' to use the preferred term. History as a discipline tends rightly to reject this procedure as inherently hostile to temporality.

The point of Carr's move, however, is not really to universalize any specific form of science, much less to argue that history should issue positivist 'laws' in the manner of the nineteenth century. What Carr is suggesting, more diffusely, is the articulation of hypotheses that will serve to advance the development of history in desirable directions. Such causal sequences 'are potentially applicable to other countries, other periods, and other conditions, lead to fruitful generalizations and lessons can be learned from them'.[24] This is a very different standard of generality from the nomothetic rules of natural science. Carr, incidentally, passes over hastily the embarrassing novelty of Heisenberg's indeterminacy principle in physics. For the most basic domain of natural science turns out paradoxically to be impervious to generalization. In order to maintain his everyday understanding of causality and the grounding criterion of generalization, Carr declares (without real argument) the indeterminacy principle inapplicable to historical events. The similarities between the two kinds of rational inquiry suddenly cease. But epistemological foundations and methods are always secondary problems for Carr. His overriding aim is to impress upon reluctant historians (and the British elite) the need for generalization and relevance.

What he is on about can best be seen in his illustrative fable about Jones and Robinson. Jones, driving drunk and with faulty brakes, comes to a corner with bad visibility where he hits and kills Robinson, who has popped out to buy cigarettes. The factual sequence of this 'event' can be established with reasonable certainty; but the important thing is the subsequent clarification of which facts and causes are significant. Whereas Oxonian philosophers might argue that the cause of Robinson's death was his smoking habit, historians (and sensible scholars in general) would look only for causes of wider relevance: driving under the influence, deficient braking systems or inadequate roads. These facts and causes are matters about which one can do something. Robinson's individual devotion to smoking, by contrast, is a unique, accidental feature which can have no historical consequences and is not subject to generalization.

History, like every other scholarly endeavour, should thus have general scope and palpable effects in the present. How the facts are ascertained is relatively uninteresting. Mere antiquarians can do it. Compilers of facts and subjective anarchists alike can accordingly be dismissed as philosophically unsound and lacking in proper engagement, incapable as they are of generalizing for instrumental use. Fascination with the past for its own sake or with the unique and accidental leads nowhere. Carr is symptomatically silent on Collingwood's most important contribution to historiographical theory, the idea of historical action as a response to an unrepeatable, unique situation, to a single question.

The marginal and accidental, then, has apparently no place in Carr's history. The historian's task is in fact to expunge it. To radical historians today, who think very differently about the marginal and accidental, this sounds altogether objectionable. But Carr is perhaps not as deaf to the marginal, or at least the losers, of history as one might think. His final standard is actually 'achievement', by which he means, positively, that which has an impact of sorts, and, negatively, that which is not trivial. Anything, indeed, that can be generalized in the form of lessons is admissible. Hence he might agree in principle that the 'truth' of any given epoch or event does not necessarily reside at the centre of political power – though there is no doubt that Carr himself is overwhelmingly concerned with winners as indeed he has to be.

Progress

Generalization, however, is only one aspect of writing purposeful histories. A genuine understanding of historical direction is also required. This is not easily achieved. Because historians are social products, part of the 'moving procession'[25] that constitutes history itself, their work is as mentioned earlier intrinsically perspectival (or 'subjective'). Yet – sociologically – 'relative objectivity' is possible because human beings (including historians) are neither totally determined by the outside, nor totally free from it. The outstanding historian manages to place himself closer to freedom than to determination. To write his 'durable' accounts he must be semi-detached and 'rise above the limited vision of his own situation in society and history'[26] and see further into the past and future. Only with such a 'sense of direction in history' can one 'order and interpret the events of the past' and project a reasonable[27] future that serves 'to liberate and organize human energies'. 'Good historians,' insists Carr, 'have the future in their bones.'[28]

One might detect a quiet ode here to some heroic historical spirit 'against the grain'. And doubtless Carr counted himself among the eminent class of detached historians, pointing to his self-chosen insularity from the dominant culture of the academy.[29] His foundationalist attachments seem ironically to lead him to 'subjectivize' history into a matter of individual clairvoyance. Yet such an image would run utterly counter to his strong emphasis on the irreducibly social nature of history and his criticism of the individualist approaches so agreeable to his English surroundings. His rather more appropriate point, I take it, is that to write wholly within the dominant culture is to write within what used to be called ideology, sheer ideology; and that only a properly dialectical way of thinking above the action and its conditions of possibility at the same time as one is thinking about the action itself will issue in any decent history, the whole process being understood of course in his forward-looking manner, for the present is always grasped as the not yet (to use Ernst Bloch's excellent term).

The direction of history itself is consequently Carr's ultimate answer to the question as to what will determine who is objective and durably relevant. His claim is not the trivial one that 'time will tell'. His claim is that only historians with a sense for long-term trajectories in both directions from the moving instant of the present have any hope of 'seeing' and attaining 'durability'. One might well agree, with the proviso that to call this 'objectivity' is to land oneself unnecessarily in deep trouble. 'Truth', in some Hegelian sense, would perhaps be a preferrable alternative, not as any ultimate ground but as a normative argument for a certain kind of historical way of being towards the world. Indeed, at one point Carr himself invokes this term when he says that 'historical truth' falls somewhere between 'the north pole of valueless facts and the south pole of value judgments'.[30] But this truth is still configured as 'objectivity', an objectivity doomed to indeterminate, perpetual movement within the polarity.

It must be said, then, that Carr's attempt to resituate the historiographical operation in terms of a modified notion of objectivity has so far been a signal failure. At no point during the ascension from facts to historical direction has he been able to find any solid guarantees. The word objectivity, he remarks elsewhere, 'is misleading and question-begging'.[31] Yet the argument, which has remained at the procedural level, now turns towards an account of the actual trajectory of history; and this substantial view will in turn illuminate and justify why Carr thinks objectivity is objectively possible, as it were. To anticipate, that move too will prove a failure but a valiant one. Carr, of course, had strong views on the direction of history, not to mention the kind of politics it would require. The moment has thus come to ask about directions.

It begins with a tactical concession to the 'pessimism and ultra-conservatism'[32] of the 1950s according to which progress, fundamental change, determinism and anything smacking of collective planning had become conceptually and morally tainted. 'I profess,' says Carr, 'no belief in the perfectibility of man, or in the future paradise on earth.'[33] One assumes that he does not want to be accused of that well-known abomination of the 1950s, a philosophy of history. He agrees, then, that the Poppers and the Berlins of this world have a point in attacking rigid schemes of history (but typically combines this retreat with a castigation of Popper's trite account of Hegel and Marx). No providential spirit governs history from the outside, nor is any single principle doing so from the inside. No telos or class subject, for example, carries it forward. History is open-ended, without clear beginning or end.[34]

Yet it is not one thing after another either. Carr rejects 'cynical' views according to which history has no meaning or is merely a bundle of entirely arbitrary meanings beyond adjudication. The process does have a pattern and a coherence which historians can reconstruct by means of rational investigation. In that sense, history has 'meaning'.[35] Causal connections and historical developments can be determined retrospect-ively. History is *intelligible*. On that premise, Carr nimbly revives what must be described as a modified version of the nineteenth-century view of progress. History, after all, is 'about' something. There is a 'meta-pattern' and it turns out to be the checkered rise of reason. 'The essence of man as a rational being,' Carr declares, 'is that he develops his potential capacities by accumulating the experience of past genera-tions'.[36] Perfectibility there may not be; but 'the possibility of unlimited progress'[37] will do well enough as a working hypothesis and goal. With-out such a notion of progress, in fact, there can be no history as Carr sees it. For 'real history' begins when people separate themselves from the natural order into societies and start to conceive themselves in a coher-ent progression from past to future. A process of interaction between mind and matter thus begins which is developmentally progressive, not in the linear fashion of the optimistic nineteenth-century imagination but unevenly progressive, correcting along the way various inevitable setbacks.[38]

Notably little, rational essence of man aside, is said here about the his-torical forces which presumably served to put reason into upward motion. No account of class, for instance, is offered.[39] There are materialist intimations of sorts, pronouncements that 'the structure of society at any given time and place, as well as the prevailing theories and beliefs about it, are largely governed by the way in which the material needs of the society are met';[40] but questions of structure, social forces and principles of change are largely ignored.[41] Carr's central argument is about historical directionality alone, and the crux of the story is about the emerging human mastery *over* history, mastery in an almost administrative sense.

Around 1900, he claims specifically, history took a decisive turn in the unfolding of humankind's struggle to control its conditions of existence. There was a critical reversal in the relation between the hitherto ruling material system and the order of thought. Development reached a stage where humankind (objectively) could master its own destiny through reason and will alone. The previous concept of autonomous developing 'laws' was replaced by a 'heightened consciousness of the power of man to improve the management of his social, economic, and political affairs'.[42] While humankind thus moved from 'the unconscious to the self-conscious',[43] there was also a transition from a competitive market system to a planned economy, marked by massive state interventionism. Society and its politicians and historians, at least the genuinely rational among them, were from then on objectively in a position to determine historical direction. In Carr's typical language: 'Man by his own action can be master of his economic destiny'.[44]

Thus the balance of power between humankind and nature undergoes a decisive shift at the turn of the century. Determination becomes freedom, its opposite. Rational transparency opens up the possibility of unlimited voluntarism. Humankind can even begin to reform its inner self (witness Freud). Historical patterns can be shaped. Like the mountain and the fish, mastery of history is really there for us to grasp and to exploit in the manner we might (rationally) desire. Unstoppable technological change, meanwhile, is deepening rationalization/reason socially in the West and spreading it spatially to new and rising continents such as Asia and Africa. Today (1961), virtually the whole world is thus entering real history. This, says Carr, is progress. Technology admittedly also gives rise to ways of manipulating opinion and, as he had put in an earlier work, the present political system is in fact far from democratic, consisting as it does of 'ill co-ordinated, highly stratified masses of people of whom a large majority are primarily occupied with the daily struggle for existence'.[45] Yet he thinks education might serve to transform mass society into a truly democratic order.

Assessing Carr

Such, in all brevity, is Carr's notion of history and historical direction. It is in many ways a remarkable view. What must first be noted in our present context is that the mastery of thought and will over circumstances forms the ultimate precondition in Carr's mind for the analogous possibility of historiographical objectivity. 'Historiography,' argues Carr, 'is a progressive science in the sense that it seeks to provide constantly expanding insights over a course of events which is itself progressive.'[46] To be 'objective' in history is to capture that always moving, changeable truth, a kind of mastering if you will. The omnipresent trope of 'mastery' and rational determination is expressive of the governing goal: control of our present and future conditions, as well as of ourselves. Carr, no doubt, envisaged the future as endless modernity with a comparably endless need of historical objectivity. Yet this seems to be a vision of post-history rather than history in any meaningful sense, Saint-Simonian administration of things rather than Marxian class struggle; and thus one wonders if the moment of post-historical transparency would not mean the end of historiography as well.

Carr turned out to be quite wrong, of course, about the trajectory from past to future. We know well enough what happened to rational planning. Planning is now apparently the exclusive property of global corporations which use it, no doubt rationally, to wrest from people any remaining control they might have over the conditions of their existence. So Carr failed his own criteria of objectivism – and rather spectacularly too. In that sense, the Nietzscheans (and, by extension, the Foucauldians) have a point: instead of distilling projections into the future from some relentlessly instrumentalized and continuous past experience, it might be better to think about the present as a situation which requires us to analyse why we came to regard the present as naturally continuous in the first place. One might then see the present as a potential rupture, as an opening for doing something radically different and discontinuous. Ironically, this would very much be in Carr's spirit. He was an electrifying demolisher of myth. And his 'continuism' was of course precisely an attempt to break the continuity of his times.

Evidently, Carr is 'a fideist of the Enlightenment'.[47] Critical though he often is of the nineteenth century, he cheerfully admits that he grew up amidst unbridled Victorian optimism.[48] Hence the exuberant faith, astonishing to our present eye, in reason, rationality and order. His strong conviction that historiography must serve as 'a guide to action'[49] is part and parcel of the same instrumentalist matrix. The phrase, however, also indicates figures closer to Carr's own field of expertise. For if John Stuart Mill is lurking somewhere in the background, so surely is Lenin. Is Carr's objectivity perhaps not a thinly veiled version of Lenin's? Let us say: 'the objective reading of historically changing situations on the basis of an objective conception of where things are going.'

Yet there is a very different way of looking at the act of mastering, namely, in terms of a certain mandarin 'technicism'. Carr was by training not a historian but a civil servant, and a civil servant in the British Foreign Office. The bold instrumentalism of *WIH* is certainly not that of a typical civil servant's brief. Indeed, Carr expresses contempt for the 'piecemeal engineering'[50] of civil servants, mere executors as they are of timid change when the true historic call is for fundamental, decisive action on a grand scale (if Britain, the old imperial power, wallowing about in the wake of the Suez fiasco, is to find its way in history).[51] Substitute policy-maker, however, for the (frustrated) civil servant and the imperative of producing knowledge to 'guide action' can readily be understood.[52] The auxiliary theme of Carr's 'mastery' is the need for 'adaptation' to the observable direction of history; and here it is not far-fetched to see the voice of a virtual policy-maker with a claim to clairvoyance. It is revealing that the upshot of his story about Jones and Robinson has to do with the question of what kind of policy one might extract from the accident. Robinson's smoking can have no possible effect in the domain of policy-making and is therefore insignificant, irrelevant. The whole analysis is overdetermined by the concept of policy, just as historical analysis of data to be turned into facts is over-determined by the functional object of building a house.

The controversial 'realism', the unflinching acceptance of history as necessity, can thus be grasped less as a form of quasi-Hegelianism than as expressive of the praxeological tradition of giving advice to the Prince, informing power how it must position itself if it is to survive and 'master' realities, realities that are historically produced and variable but nonetheless subject to rational analysis without reference to any providential or other extraneous forces. This is an analysis that must by nature be ahead of the present and project into the probable future. When Carr insists that politicians are called upon to 'consider not merely what is morally or theoretically desirable, but also the forces which exist in the world, and how they can be directed or manipulated to probably partial realizations of the ends in view',[53] he has also the historian in mind. The historian is the politician's double. Carr's utilitarian rejection of historical aestheticism, the kind of 'charm' of history for which Marc Bloch still had a certain appreciation, is predicated on this coupling to power. Historians that do not move (however critically) with power fail in the deepest possible manner because they fail to follow history. They become ahistorical.

Thus it becomes possible for him elsewhere to reduce Stalin's collectivisation to a problem of instrumental power, to classify it as the only way of extracting the surpluses necessary for industrialisation and consign its effects to the horrible cruelties of which history is very full indeed. 'Those who pay the cost,' states Carr laconically, 'are rarely those who reap the benefits.'[54] It is useless, he would write later, to think 'that every problem has a solution which will be free from ambiguity, free from suffering, free from injustice, free from tragedy'.[55] The historian's task, in short, is not to measure the past by any suprahistorical standards of morality but to situate 'the historically conditioned character of all values'.[56] There is no 'objectivity beyond history'[57] in the domain of beliefs and values. Carr's target here is the hypocrisy, as he sees it, of western historians who think nineteenth-century colonizations are historically progressive but find Soviet modernisation abnormal and abhorrent. This inconsistency is also what makes him suspicious of counterfactual history. Working in a politically sensitive and contemporary field, he is constantly faced with people who like to imagine that more 'agreeable things'[58] might have happened in 1917 'if only, etc. etc.'. For him, conversely, history had to happen the way it did.

One understands his predicament but need not agree with his stance. The instrumentalist notion of 'historical objectivity' – brutalities happened and must in some sense therefore have been 'objectively necessary' – and the hostility to counterfactuals lead eventually to accounts devoid of any moral principle at all. We can write history that is morally informed without falling into moralizing and simple condemnation.[59] Carr's opposition is once again a false one. In fact, if we are to take seriously Carr's thesis that all historians are inevitably 'subjective' in their values, it is hard to see how one could possibly write histories that are not on one level or another so 'informed'. From the perspective of a radical historicist, it is permissible and indeed crucial to universalize the values once considers 'right' without thereby grounding them in some absolute, supra-historical standards. In a similar vein, it is necessary, if nothing else for political reasons, to be able to imagine counterfactuals, the possibility within any given historical situation that things might have been otherwise, that the answer to the Collingwoodian question could have been different.[60]

Conclusion

WIH is an instrumental intervention calling for history as instrumental intervention. A final word is thus required about the aspect of contemporary politics. The most 'time-bound' of Carr's topics seems to be his chapter on 'society and the individual', though he also deals here with the question of accidents and contingency which is of greater contemporary interest. He wants to counter ingrained British views of history as the heroic individual struggle for liberty against systems, structures and groups, as well as the concomitant epistemological privilege accorded to accident (and 'free will') over determination. 'The individual,' asserts Carr rightly, is always social. After decades of withering attacks by structuralists and poststructuralists on 'man' and 'the subject', we are likely to read this chapter as old news from a fairly crude but politically friendly paper. After Thatcherism, the massive success of hoary myths of individual enterprise and the adjacent return of 'individual liberty' as a governing thematic in British historiography, we have perhaps cause to linger a little longer and pay better attention. Carr, at any rate, will have found this ideological development historically incomprehensible except as a sign of British (or English) decline. By the time he finished his 14 volumes on Soviet Russia in 1978, he still believed that capitalism was historically doomed, but he had lost faith, apparently, in the transformation of western 'mass civilization' into an egalitarian community of rational planners, putting his money instead on the revolutionary potential of the third world.[61] In 1961, however, he was reading his objects of derision symptomatically as signs of historical reaction. Cultural pessimism, loss of faith in progress and in the capacity of society to control its future, celebration of the accidental, attacks on planning and prediction as totalitarian, irrationalism and anti-scientism, the return of cyclical theories of history and the novel refusal to see any pattern or meaning whatever in history: all, together with the odes to the heroic individual, reflected the fact that Britain's moment in the sun was over. They were querulous, if powerful, expressions of ideological reaction at a time when the old was dead and the new not yet quite born.

Carr was bound to read it this way because he believed history was 'progressive' and the future of rational planning on a global scale already here. The shibboleths of English ideology could thus be nothing, 'objectively', but a superstructural reflection of a laggard imperial formation. *WIH* was in that sense an attempt within a particular political conjuncture to awaken the British elite from its historical slumber. In his preface to the never completed second edition, he deplores that the ensuing 'twenty years frustrated these hopes and this complacency' on his part. Writing in the early 1980s, when the triumphant resurgence of global capitalism in the name of nineteenth-century liberalism was yet to come, Carr still reads the contemporary expressions of doom and gloom as an irrational, elitist form of intellectual neurosis and a reflection of decline. 'Scepticism and despair,' he says, is the product of 'elite social groups' in 'elite countries' whose domination has been undermined, nowhere so conspicuously as in Britain. 'Pessimism' remains his *bête noire*. He himself, however, is now less optimistic. Modestly, he pleads for 'a saner and more balanced view outlook on the future'.[62]

We (a certain 'we' at any rate) are by contrast far from sure about the why, the whence and the whither of history. We are sceptical about progress. We find the language of 'mastery' unseemly. We incline towards Adorno's and Horkheimer's critical view of instrumental reason. Those of us who think theoretically about history and historiography find Carr's intervention deficient, lacking not only an account of language and temporality but also any probing of the existing continental and analytical traditions in the field. We are aware to the point of excess of the 'constructed' nature of sources and its 'facts'. Thus, after the advent of linguistic indeterminacy and the radical questioning of identity and subjectivity, after the discovery of the centrality of marginality, after the end of transparency and the beginning of narratology, it is easy to dismiss E.H. Carr as essentially passé, a hopelessly modern and modernizing figure whose misfortune it was to have written on the very eve of postmodernity, when contingency was to become the sign of the times and the very existence of the historical itself about to fade into a mere succession of instants.

Such a dismissal would be rash and improper for reasons I hope to have shown. In this moment of indecision and doubt, when history itself has become hard to think, when direction has become nigh-on unintelligible and the determinate negation seemingly absurd, it is well to recollect Carr's edict that we are always already in a certain historical flow which we can understand and act upon. And so we are moved to ask ourselves where our own interventions might now be made.

Acknowledgement

Thanks to R.W. Davies, Jonathan Haslam and Charles Jones, all of whom generously conveyed insights in conversation from their extensive work with, and on, E.H. Carr.

Notes

1   All page references in the text are to E.H. Carr *What is History?* (New York: Knopf, 1962). References to the second edition (R.W. Davies, ed., London: Penguin, 1987) appear in the notes only. The 14 volumes of *A History of Soviet Russia* was published over almost 30 years. *The Twenty Years' Crisis* appeared in 1939 and again (with a notorious preface) in 1946.

2   Carr composed much of the book travelling by ship to San Francisco. Because of their very synthetic quality, lecture books can however be unexpected successes. Another example, as it happens also 'realist', is George F. Kennan's short lecture book *American Diplomacy, 1900–1950* (Chicago: Chicago University Press, 1951), written at breakneck speed but endlessly reissued.

3   The reviewer in *American Historical Review*, Vol. 67, No. 3, p. 676, offers the most effusive praise, calling it 'the best recent book in English' on its subject but he had nothing much of interest to say about it. The *Mississippi Valley Historical Review* (predecessor of the *Journal of American History*), Vol. 49, No. 1, p. 173, merely noted its appearance with a single sentence to the effect that Carr was 'readable' on the subject-matter. *History and Theory*, Vol. 3, No. 1, p. 136, appropriately, published a fairly long piece on it by Jacob M. Price. He said it was 'unfortunately a personal and parochial book' and was generally critical – in part on good grounds. This journal, the preeminent Anglophone publication in the field, has devoted no special issues or articles since to Carr's work. The *English Historical Review*, No. 308, July 1963, pp. 587–8, argued that Carr 'showed robust common sense rather than profound thought' on issues such as causation and found the book lively in its attack on 'scientific history'. Andreas Hillgruber in *Historische Zeitschrift*, 1963 pp. 361–2, was favourable on the occasion of the German translation, noting the acidic, '*geistvoll-ironischer*' attack on liberal, conservative and positivist historians but otherwise kept his review to a straight condensation of the content. This is rather a haphazard survey but at least it indicates the mixed response.

4   Marc Bloch, *The Historian's Craft* (New York: Vintage, 1953 [written in the early 1940s]). Carr knew the text in the French original. Cf. E.H. Carr, *The New Society* (London: Macmillan, 1951), p. 8. Curiously, there is no reference to it in *WIH*.

5   This is my main dispute with Keith Jenkins's critique of *On 'What is History?'* (London: Routledge, 1995) which I read after completing this essay. Jenkins uncovers, perceptively, serious internal contradictions and outward limitations in Carr's work. However, Jenkins frames this critique in the language of an eradication campaign: Carr, 'naive', 'earnest', 'unreflexive', 'certaintist', 'out of date' and assorted other ills, simply should not, must not, 'be in a central/introductory place' any longer. He should not be 'taken seriously'. He is, we are informed, irrelevant, or at any rate he ought to be (see pp. 61, 63). I find this unhelpful. On what postmodern 'grounds', I wonder, is 'irrelevance' to be determined? A more dialectical analysis would ask what it is about Carr that works and continues to work.

6   I borrow the expression from Michel de Certeau, *The Writing of History* (New York: Columbia, 1988).

7   D.S. Mirsky, authority on Russian literature, says in a preface to Carr's first and seldom read work on Dostoevsky (1931) that it is an 'eminently readable', 'well written' and 'sensible' book with 'no nonsense'. 'Preface', E.H. Carr, *Dostoevsky* (London: Allen & Unwin, 1931). The verdict may well stand for Carr's ruminations on history three decades later. The feisty Mirsky also criticizes Carr for imagining that there is some essential Russian spirit.

8   *Ibid.*, p. 23.

9   *Ibid.*, p. 6.

10 *Ibid.*, p. 10.

11 Collingwood's idealism is both something less and something more than this. See Paul Hirst's criticism of Carr's appropriation, 'Collingwood, Relativism and the Purposes of History', in his *Marxism and Historical Writing* (London: Routledge, 1985).

12 *Ibid.*, pp. 30–1.

13 *Ibid.*, p. 26.

14 In Carr, *The New Society* (London, Macmillan, 1951) p. 10, he talks of what is commonly considered facts (dates and the like) as raw material, 'bricks or steel or concrete', that which will become part of a structured whole and thus made into facts, meaningful through their functionality. Even simple dating, however, is not a self-evident procedure, couched as it is, for one thing, in a system invented by a monk in the sixth century who wanted to date the birth of Christ, but probably got the 'actual' date wrong and in any case could not have imagined the secular manner in which his 'time' would one day rule the world.

15 Carr, *The New Society*, p. 34.

16 *Ibid.*, p. 14.

17 The epistemological way of thinking, with its constitutive subject–object distinction, is pre-eminently visual and Carr's string of specular metaphors is not accidental.

18 Carr, *The New Society*, p. 136.

19 *Ibid.*, p. 160.

20 *Ibid.*, p. 163.

21 *Ibid.*, p. 125.

22 E.H. Carr, *The Soviet Impact on the Western World* (London: Macmillan, 1947), p. vii.

23 *Ibid.*, p. 138.

24 *Ibid.*, p. 140.

25 *Ibid.*, p. 43.

26 *Ibid.*, p. 163.

27 *Ibid.*, pp. 163–4.

28 He is paraphrasing Sir Charles Snow describing Lord Rutherford. *Ibid.*, p. 143.

29 See E.H. Carr, 'The Russian Revolution and the West,' interview, *New Left Review*, 111, September–October 1978.

30 *Ibid.*, p. 175.

31 *Ibid.*, p. 158.

32 *Ibid.*, p. 185.

33 *Ibid.*, p. 158.

34 In *The New Society*, 1951, p. 5, he writes that history is a 'procession of events' that 'moves constantly on and never returns to the same place'. I should add

that Isaiah Berlin, his two concepts of liberty notwithstanding and always a bit of a social democrat, was not adverse to the ameliorist tenor of Carr's position.

35   He is not always clear on this point. In *The New Society* he seems to argue that pattern and meaning are merely imposed by the historian, thus implying that history has no pattern in itself. But this would contradict his admonitions against subjectivism and idealism, as well as his insistence elsewhere that history is causally intelligible.

36   Carr, *The New Society*, p. 150.

37   *Ibid.*, p. 158.

38   'These evils also carry with them their own corrective' p. 195. In *The New Society*, 1951, he had been less sanguine: 'Our problem is to discover why, between 1815 and 1914, men succeeded in conducting their political affairs with a reasonable show of decency and without large-scale destruction, and why, since 1914, hatred, intolerance, cruelty and mutual extermination have once more become the staple of political action over a large part of the world', p. 8.

39   Carr refers to class in a discussion of Marx and Lenin but in a subsidiary fashion. Carr, *The New Society*, p. 183.

40   *Ibid.*, p. 19.

41   Given aims and audience, this may have been intentional. His materialist conception of ideology is perhaps one reason *A History of Soviet Russia* was planned in each of its 'moments' to deal with the trinity of politics, economics and foreign relations but had no independent place for ideology (though incisive analyses of it appeared within).

42   Carr, *The New Society*, p. 190.

43   *Ibid.*, p. 188.

44   *Ibid.*

45   Carr, *The New Society*, p. 75.

46   *Ibid.*, p. 165.

47   I take the epithet from John Gray, who said this, as I recall, of Perry Anderson in the *London Review of Books* a few years ago.

48   Carr quotes Dampier, his tutor, who said that 'future ages will see no limit to the growth of man's power over the resources of nature and of his intelligent use of them for the welfare of his race', Carr, *The New Society*, p. 147. It is well to remember that Carr was already twenty years old in 1912. In the preface to the planned second edition he talks instead of 'the afterglow of the great Victorian faith and optimism', Carr, *The New Society*, p. 6.

49   *Ibid.*, p. 88.

50   *Ibid.*, p. 207.

51   I am extrapolating, perhaps unduly: Suez is not mentioned.

52   Kennan, another civil servant turned Soviet-Russian scholar came to mind again – though Carr, of course, had a period as expert on international relations in between. Both, incidentally, began their second career by writing biographies of literary Russian figures, the difference being that Carr published his book on Dostoevsky, while Kennan kept his manuscript on Chekhov forever hidden. The field of western 'sovietology,' with its premium on intelligence and 'expertise', features a good deal of traffic between academy and policymaking. Alec Nove was another example.

53   Carr, *The New Society*, pp. 170–1.

54 *Ibid.*, pp. 104–5.
55 E.H. Carr, *A History of Soviet Russia: Foundations of a Planned Economy, 1926–1929* (London: Macmillan, 1971) Vol. 2, p. ix.
56 *Ibid.*, p. 108.
57 *Ibid.*, p. 109.
58 *Ibid.*, p. 127.
59 This is Perry Anderson's salutary point in *Arguments Within British Marxism* (London: Verso, 1980), p. 86, about E.P Thompson's moralism. Anderson also makes an observation pertinent for other reasons: 'a monopoly of political power' is not to be confused with 'a mastery of historical process', p. 24; though he goes on, less persuasively but wholly in Carr's spirit, to say that among social formations only 'full socialist democracy is likely to generate accurate knowledge of its own deepest laws of motion', p. 25.
60 Without counterfactuals for heuristic purposes my own field, diplomatic history, would lose a great deal of its critical potential. If one cannot say that a policy, within the parameters of a particular kind of regime, could have been different, the remaining alternatives seem to be either to write uncritical records of dusty dealings or to denounce the whole regime and call for its abolition. The obverse problem with diplomatic history is the tendency to write entirely within the subject-position of 'power' and 'policy-making', to lose sight of the structural underpinnings of the process itself.
61 E.H. Carr, 'The Russian Revolution and the West', interview, *New Left Review* 111, September–October 1978. His friend Herbert Marcuse was a continuing influence on Carr's negative evaluation of the revolutionary potential of western workers. Cf. R.W. Davies' afterword to the second edition of *WIH*.
62 E.H. Carr, *WIH*, second edition, pp. 3–6. This preface, with its obsessive *ressentiment* against intellectuals, does not do justice to his work.

14

An English Myth? Rethinking the Contemporary Value of E.H. Carr's *What is History?*

Keith Jenkins

In 1991 Routledge published a short, polemical work which I had written called *Rethinking History*.[1] Meant as a very general introduction for advanced level students, it soon began to sell in large quantities in universities. As a result, Routledge asked me to write a second text developing some of the ideas essayed in *Rethinking History*, aimed this time directly at the undergraduate market. In *Rethinking History* I had taken a very general swipe at the kinds of ideas put forward in some of the most popular introductions to 'The Nature of History' (Marwick, Tosh, Stanford *et al.*)[2] in order to open up a gap for the insertion of postmodern approaches. The thinking behind my second book – *On 'What is History?' From Carr and Elton to Rorty and White*[3] – was thus part of my continuing project to make some space for the kinds of approaches to history I thought valuable, this time at the expense of 'getting rid of' that famous old duo E.H. Carr and Geoffrey Elton, and replacing them with postmodern thinking of the type advocated by Richard Rorty and Hayden White.

My reasons for choosing Carr and Elton as *the* two historians to replace was due to the dominant position that their two books[4] – *What is History?* and *The Practice of History* respectively – have held on 'introductory' reading lists for a generation. First published in 1961 (Carr) and 1967 (Elton), but drawing on ideas formed much earlier, it didn't seem sensible to me that, as history teachers, we should still be suggesting to our students that their first (and sometimes their only) port of call with regard to the question of 'what is history?' should be the Carr–Elton debate. Or at least, I argued, it should give us pause for thought. I mean, how many discourses introducing students to their *current* practices recommend as basic reading 30-year-old texts? And I thought this not least because over the last 30-odd years there has developed around and about this dominant academic discourse (which Carr and Elton represent) a range of theories (hermeneutics, phenomenology, structuralism, poststructuralism, feminism and post-feminism, deconstructionism, post-Marxism, neo-pragmatism, postmodernism, and so on) as articulated by a range of theorists (say, Ricoeur, Foucault, Barthes, Althusser, Derrida, Kristeva, Judith Butler, Laclau, Baudrillard, Lyotard, Fish...) which have reached levels of reflexive sophistication *vis-à-vis* the question of historical representation which one could not even hazard a guess at from a reading of Carr and Elton's vintage texts, or from their later thoughts on the subject come to that. From these discursive positions, Carr and Elton's theorising cannot help but appear *passé*, and so I suggested, as I have already indicated, that students ought to forget Carr and Elton (and their ubiquitous 'debate') and move on to theories and theorists of the type just mentioned – and in *On 'What is History?'* to Rorty and White – if 'we' are to gain a better understanding of how the discourses of history are being currently rendered.

My attitude towards all this was further hardened by Dominic La Capra's comment about just how ubiquitous the Carr–Elton debate had become. Drawing on a very different experience of introducing students to history from my own, La Capra points out that:

> A standard practice in historiography seminars is to begin by assigning Elton's *The Practice of History* and Carr's *What is History?*... as representing the alternatives in the self-understanding of the discipline. This practice is sure to generate heated debate among students, and it starts the course with a pleasant 'Steve Reeves meets Godzilla' scenario. The result is usually a more or less pragmatic and electric 'synthesis' of the two works that may serve as a tenuous consensus on which the seminar may proceed in its study of less 'theoretical' and 'methodological' assignments.[5]

But I had never really bought into the 'debate' idea – at least at the level of their having been a meaningful, ongoing engagement between Carr and Elton themselves; relative to their two most famous texts it had always seemed contrived to me and, in its effects, curiously distorting.[6] Thus, with regard to its contrivance, there is in fact only one reference in Carr's text to Geoffrey Elton, where he makes the approving remark that, 'as Mr Elton has neatly put it... "what distinguishes the historian from the collector of historical facts is generalisation"', while in Elton's *The Practice of History*, of the five comments he addresses to Carr only one, where he challenges Carr's idea that 'because the past cannot be re-enacted there is, by definition, no such thing as truth,' is really germane to the so-called debate.[7] And whilst this objection to Carr mustn't be ignored, the distortion which it has led to *vis-à-vis* the polarity occasioned by the 'debate' – the widespread idea that Carr is the great relativist, sceptic and constructionist whilst Elton is the passionate objectivist, truth-seeker and certaintist – is somewhat wide of the mark.[8] Yet, despite sometime qualifications, even such an acute commentator as Gregor McLennan pigeon-holes Carr as a 'sceptical relativist', while La Capra argues that if one wanted to rebut Elton's 'documentary objectivism' one might well be 'forced to line up with E.H. Carr and the relativists'.[9] Consequently, given such widely accepted comments, it is therefore no surprise that students (and others) are generally unaware that Carr's final answer to the question of 'what is history?' is neither sceptical nor relativist, but is expressed explicitly as a belief in objectivity, in 'real' historical progress, and in truth, while Elton goes out of his way to insist that 'our' attitude towards upper-case (metanarrative) histories in particular, but lower-case (professional/academic) histories too, should include a dose of healthy (if carefully targeted) scepticism.

Consequently, in my treatment of Carr and Elton I didn't concentrate on their 'debate' (save to mention, as here, its relative slightness and, as it became subsequently enlarged in the literature, its polarised over-simplification), but rather I posed to each of them separately (as I later posed to Hayden White) two questions: what, were their respective views on the question of 'what is history?' and what use were their answers to students coming to that question in 'our' arguably postmodern days. And, as might be expected by now, my answer, *vis-à-vis* both Carr and Elton was, 'not very much'. My previous readings of Carr had already indicated to me that I should have little trouble 'finding' Carr *passé*, and this my closer reading (you might cynically say 'but of course') confirmed.

Concentrating from now on on Carr, then, the comments I have already made must make it fairly clear that I had never thought much of Carr as a theorist of 'history'. But obviously many other people did.[10] And this perplexed me. Thus, for example, and going back briefly to McLennan and his extremely wide-ranging *Marxism and the Methodologies of History* (1981),[11] McLennan sees Carr as having produced perhaps 'the most sustained critique of British empiricist historiography' ever. Again, in 1991, John Tosh could still write (in his influential introduction to the 'pursuit of history') that 'the controversy between Carr...and Elton...is the best starting point for the debate about the standing of historical knowledge', adding that Carr's famous text is still 'probably the finest reflection by a historian on the nature of his subject in our time'.[12] And in 1992, in his introductory remarks to *Myths of the English*, Roy Porter was of the opinion that 'the questions of historical objectivity and historical method have never been better discussed than in E.H. Carr's *What is History?*'. Yet, this comment, in footnote 6 of Porter's introductory *Notes* (referring to the wider discussion of 'history today') is then followed, in footnotes 7 and 8, by references to some of the more recent and extended discussion of this area by Barthes, Baudrillard, Culler, Greenblatt et al., against which Carr's contribution seems to me to be banal. Consequently, I commented in my book that, given that this was the case, privileging Carr above such theorists *today* could only be a ritualistic nod, a knee-jerk reaction (for certainly Porter's comments could not be sustained), concluding that what Porter termed Carr's 'deserved prominence' was, maybe, just one more example of an 'English myth'.[13]

It is this 'negative' evaluation of Carr that I now want to try to substantiate. My approach has three parts. First, I want to argue that Carr's famous historical scepticism and relativism are not only slight but also extremely misleading, drawn as they are pretty much from the opening pages of Carr's text. Second, I want to argue that if you read on, Carr becomes an ideological truth-seeker and objectivist in ways far stronger than Elton ever was. And third, precisely because of his Marxist-Victorian attitudes, Carr's 'certaintism' is of little use either to forward today's key discussions on the 'nature of history', or to help undercut them. Carr may well have been interesting and variously influential in his own time, and his (much qualified) scepticism and relativism did help break down some of the old certaintist attitudes he ironically – in his own way – clung to. Similarly, the much contrived and much mythologised Carr-Elton debate has obviously had effects, its popularity has helped set much of the agenda for some if not all of the crucially important fixing, preliminary discussions about the question of what is history – though today maybe that's the problem! For my conclusion is that, notwithstanding all these things, Carr (and Elton) should no longer have a central/introductory place in our understandings of history. Let me now turn to each of these three areas before pulling them together in a short conclusion.

Carr begins *What is History?* by arguing that what passes for him as the 'common-sense' view of history – a view that fetishises both 'the facts' and the documents said to 'contain' them at the expense of the shaping powers of the historian – must be rejected:

The empirical theory of knowledge presupposes a complete separation between subject and objects. Facts, like sense-impressions,
impinge on the observer from outside and are independent of his
consciousness. The process of reception is passive: having received
the data, he then acts on it.... This is what may be called the
commonsense view of history. History consists of a corpus of ascertained facts.... First get your facts straight, then plunge at your peril
into the shifting sands of interpretation – that is the ultimate wisdom
of the [dominant] empirical, commonsense school of history.[14]

So, how does Carr attempt to refute this 'position'? He has three
arguments – one epistemological, two overtly ideological – and I want
to outline all of them. For in the literature this is rarely, if ever, done.
Normally only the epistemological refutation is given, this lapse being
largely responsible for the popular mythology of Carr as the unalloyed
relativist and sceptic. Consequently, this being very precisely a partial
reading, I shall outline the epistemological argument first to be followed
immediately by the crucially important ideological ones.

Carr's epistemological argument runs as follows. Common-sense historians fail to distinguish between the 'events of the past', the 'facts of
the past' and 'historical facts'. Carr isn't denying that the past occurred,
that events happened, nor that there are certain basic facts which form,
as he puts it, 'the backbone of history'. But he thinks that the insertion
of variously authenticated facts into a historical account and their sig-
nificance/meaning relative to other selected/dismissed facts, depends
not on something *intrinsic* to the facts 'in and for themselves', but on
the reading of events the historian *chooses* to give:

It used to be said that facts speak for themselves. This is, of course,
untrue. The facts only speak when the historian calls on them: it is he
who decides to which facts to give the floor, and in what order of
context.... The historian is necessarily selective. The belief in a hard
core of historical facts existing objectively and independently of the
historian is a preposterous fallacy, but one which it is very hard to
eradicate.[15]

Carr then offers several illustrations of this point, perhaps the most
famous being his discussion of the process by which an event/fact from
the past was transformed into a 'historical fact'. Thus, Carr tells us, at
Stalybridge Wakes in 1850, a gingerbread seller was killed by a mob; this
is a well-attested event/fact from the past. But for it to become a histor-

ical fact, to enter into historiography, it needed to be recognised by historians and given interpretive significance. As Carr puts it:

> Its status as a historical fact will turn on a question of interpretation. This element of interpretation enters into every fact of history.[16]

Now, the above remarks contain, in fact, the substance of Carr's (extremely slight) epistemological argument, which he nowhere 'deepens'. This is the 'position' which readers (and especially students) generally take from Carr (then to juxtapose against the 'objectivist' Elton), so that one hears them saying things like, 'Carr thinks that all history is interpretation and that there are no such things as facts' which, while it has an element of accuracy in it, is far from being the whole story. For if we stop the reading of Carr at this point, then not only are we left with the idea that Carr's view of the nature of history and the status of all historical knowledge is epistemologically relativist/ sceptical, but we are not in a good position to see why, only a few pages after the Stalybridge example, he rejects as 'too sceptical' the 'relativism' of Collingwood and why, a few pages after that, he begins to reinstate 'the facts' in unproblematicised, objectivist ways. We thus need to follow briefly Carr's two further, ideological arguments, the first of which is uncomplicated. Carr says that he is opposed to the 'fetishiza-tion of facts', etc., because of his views on the ways in which Rankean-ism, positivism and empiricism were yoked together under the auspices of nineteenth- and twentieth-century liberalism; in other words, because the resultant common-sense view of history was/is an ideolo-gical expression of liberalism.

Carr's second argument is this. The classic, liberal idea of progress was that, left to their own devices, individuals and, by extension, socio-economic, national and international spheres, would, in exercising their freedom in ways taking cognisance of the competing claims of others, somehow and without too much intervention, move towards a harmony of interests. Carr thinks this argument also applied to a sort of intellectual *laissez-faire* – that from the free competition of ideas there would emerge a harmonious acceptance of the best (true) argument for everyone – this general state of affairs including the study of history. For Carr, the fundamental idea underpinning liberal historiography was that historians all going about their work in different ways but appreci-ative of the work of others, would be able to collect 'the facts' and then, pretty much without their intervention, allow the free play of such facts (as though guided by their own 'hidden hand' the 'weight of the evidence') effectively to speak for themselves, thus ensuring that they were in harmony with the events of the past now 'truthfully' represented. As Carr put it:

> The nineteenth century was, for the intellectuals of western Europe, a comfortable period exuding confidence and optimism. The facts were on the whole satisfactory, and the inclination to ask and answer awkward questions about them was correspondingly weak... The liberal... view of history [therefore] had a close affinity with the economic doctrine of *laissez-faire*... Let everyone get on with their job, and the hidden hand would take care of universal harmony. The facts of history were themselves a demonstration of the supreme fact of a beneficent and apparently infinite progress towards higher things.[17]

Carr's argument is thus explicitly ideological. His point is that the idea of freedom of the facts to 'speak for themselves' arose from the happy coincidence that they just happened to speak liberal. But of course, Carr did not. Thus, knowing that in the history he wrote the facts had to be *made* to speak in a way other than liberal (i.e., in a Marxist kind of way) than his own experience of making 'the facts' *his* facts is universalised to become everyone's experience. *All* historians, including liberals, have to transform the indifferent 'facts from the past' into 'historical facts' by their positioned, interpretive practices. And so Carr's second argument is not epistemological at all but, as stated, ideological. And so is the third. But this argument is more complicated, it needs to be approached by way of a few preliminaries.

Now, in his first two critiques, Carr had argued that the facts (and obviously the documents wherein they were held to be inscribed) have no *intrinsic* value, no fixed, automatic significance within any historical account/narratives. Facts have only *relative* value, use value, they only speak when called upon to do so. However, as seen, liberals had not seen the shaping power of the historian because of the 'cult of the fact'. It thus seemed to Carr that historians generally subscribed to the idea that historians acted merely as a conduit through which 'the facts of the past for their own sake' were allowed self-expression.

So far so good. But then Carr switches his attention from the nineteenth century, to the 1950s and, in his Preface to the second edition of *What is History?* to the 1960s and 1970s. And here Carr writes that he senses that liberal and other expressions of a general optimism were being undermined by precisely the 'facts' of the 1960s and beyond.

These 'new' facts seemed dismal: the Cold War had intensified, unemployment had, as he put it, spread like a cancer throughout western society; things looked bleak. Carr wrote:

> In these conditions any expression of optimism has come to seem absurd. The prophets of woe have everything on their side .... Not for centuries has the once popular prediction of the end of the world seemed so apposite.[18]

Yet, Carr remained stubbornly optimistic. For two reasons. First, the pessimistic diagnoses of most of his fellow intellectuals, though purportedly resting on 'the facts' were, of course, just their wearied interpretations. Second, Carr saw other facts which gave him reason to be optimistic, other facts drawn not from 'the West' but from the rest of the world. Consequently, and drawing his own conclusions from these facts, Carr dismissed the pessimism of western intellectuals as the product of social groupings whose security and privileges were being eroded; these were purveyors of the ideas, as he put it, 'of the ruling social group which they served'. Accordingly, while Carr certainly considered himself an intellectual, the idea that he was that kind of intellectual was anathema to him, styling himself as an 'intellectual dissident' who could and would reaffirm his own faith in progress. For, as he put it, he was an intellectual who had grown up

> not in the high noon, but in the afterglow of the great Victorian age of faith and optimism, and it is difficult for me even today to think in terms of a world in permanent and irretrievable decline.[19]

Consequently, all this being the case, Carr has thus got this specific ideological reason (that he must not go along with the pessimists and their facts/interpretations and renounce progress) to add to his earlier opinion that one must not fetishise the facts. Accordingly,

> In the following pages I shall try to distance myself from the prevailing trends among Western intellectuals ... to show how and why I think they have gone astray and to stake out a claim, if not for an optimistic, at any rate a saner and more balanced outlook on the future.[20]

It is this very clearly flagged position which thus stands behind and gives much, if not all, of the *raison d'être* for Carr's writing of *What is*

History? For his text is profoundly misunderstood if it is seen as some kind of disinterested study of historical epistemology. Carr is himself clear that the impetus behind his text was the ideological necessity to rethink and rearticulate the idea of historical progress amidst the 'conditions' and the doubting Thomases of his own 'too sceptical' days.

But and this is the point of running this third argument – as his text unfolds, Carr's early epistemological relativism continually returns to trouble him. And you can easily see why. For despite his own epistemological scepticism, Carr still wants to find some *real* grounds for his own belief in progress. Given this, we can now see where such scepticism and his dismissal of 'the facts' and 'intrinsic' meaning has got him. Because if, as Carr says, the various diagnoses of hopelessness purportedly held by most of the intellectuals around him were not based on the facts in some entailed way but were simply their jaded opinions, and if the same goes for all those nineteenth-century liberals whose liberal optimism was based on similar selections of the facts to suit themselves; if, in other words, there are no factual grounds *per se* for either pessimism or optimism given that 'past facts' have to become 'historical facts' by the historian's selective desires, then Carr is hoisted with his own petard. For given that there is no fact – value entailment available for anybody, then Carr's own optimism cannot be incorrigibly supported by 'the facts', so that his opinion remains just 'his opinion', as equally without a basis as those held by old optimistic liberals and their contemporary, pessimistic counterparts. Consequently, the only logical conclusion to draw from all this is that of a general historical and moral relativism. But Carr – Victorian Marxist as he is – cannot accept this. What he will thus try to show is that there are some foundations which really do confirm his own position both in terms of what constitutes history as a discipline and in terms of the past conceived as history. That is, Carr will be driven back from the epistemological scepticism/relativism he has outlined in the first twenty pages of his book – and for which he is best known – precisely so that he can embrace a more *certaintist* position for overtly political reasons. To be sure Carr can't go all the way, the days of absolutes have gone. But, as his text unfolds, Carr will do his best to claw back his earlier agreements so to make them compatible with the task he has actually set out for himself so clearly: to underwrite his faith in progress.

This is my first (three part) general argument, then, that Carr's famous epistemological argument is not only slight but, if one thinks that this is his view on the status of historical knowledge, then one is being misled. I now turn to my second point, to recall, that for ideological purposes

Carr has to end up an old-fashioned objectivist and truth-seeker such that – and it is this (again to recall) which will lead me to my third point – Carr's 'modernist' views on history are arguably of little or no use in our own, postmodern days.

Carr's 'clawing back' has three parts to it: (1) a rejection of Collingwood's too sceptical 'idealism'; (2) a reinstatement of the facts in an attempt to fuse previously separated 'fact and value'; and (3) an attempt to link the past into a dialogue with not only the present and the past, but the future too, in ways reminiscent, if not identical to, nineteenth century teleologies, thereby trying to derive a sense of history that is objective and, maybe, even true.

With regard to Collingwood, Carr argues that Collingwood holds that the past is dead unless the historian can understand the thought processes of those in the past who infused it with life; hence, 'all history is the history of thought.... The re-enactment in the historian's mind of the thought whose history he is studying!'[21] This reconstruction is variously dependent on empirical evidence but is not in itself an empirical process and certainly cannot consist of a 'mere recital of facts'. On the contrary, the interpretive, reconstructive process governs the selection of facts and their 'given' significance.

From this potted resumé of Collingwood, Carr then draws three 'truths' congenial to his own position: (1) facts are always impure; they're always refracted through the 'mind' of the historian so that, in Carr's famous phrase, when we read a history 'our first concern should not be with the facts which it contains but with the historian who wrote it';[22] (2) that historical understanding requires some form of empathy; and (3) that the past is necessarily understood present-centredly. But, having thus reinforced his own first, epistemological argument, Carr's ideological agenda alerts him to Collingwoodian dangers. Pressed to its logical conclusion, Carr warns, Collingwood's emphasis on the 'creative' power of the historian rules out any objectivity at all; indeed says Carr, Collingwood comes close to saying that history is something spun out of human brains with as many histories as brains, thus raising the spectre of an 'infinity of meanings, none any more right than any other'.[23] But just because, argues Carr, interpretation plays a part in establishing historical facts, it doesn't follow that one interpretation is as good as another, or that 'the facts of history are in principle not amenable to objective interpretation' (adding immediately that he will go on at a later stage to consider what exactly is meant by 'objectivity in history')[24] ... and when he does we will follow him. But before going on, Carr sees an even bigger danger lying in Collingwood. For if all history is present-centred, and if the historian (ideologically) construes history for present/future purposes, then the awful prospect arises that the historian may 'fall into a purely pragmatic view of the facts, and maintain that the criteria of a right interpretation is its suitability to some present purpose'[25] . . . for which we might be forgiven for thinking thus far that this was precisely Carr's own purpose. But apparently not. For if this is the case Carr worries, then what is to stop might being right?; what if what passes for objective history (including his) is just what those with the power to define, define it as? Accordingly, Carr sees his task clearly. He must re-instate those very facts (his facts . . .) which will act in the quite conventional way of presenting 'anything goes'.[26] Carr is explicit about this: 'How, then, in the middle of the twentieth century, are we to define the obligation of the historian to his facts?'[27] Accordingly, it is here that he begins to develop a different 'epistemological stress to that originally forwarded and for which he is best known. It has three component parts.

First, says Carr, when 'making history' the historian begins with only a provisional selection of facts and a provisional interpretation. As the historian gains more information, so the facts/interpretation undergo subtle, interconnected changes. This 'reciprocal' action also involves a reciprocity between the present and the past so that Carr is quickly able to give a preliminary answer to the question of 'What is History?' History, he says, 'is a continuous process of interaction between the historian and his facts, an unending dialogue between the present and the past'.[28]

Second, now the facts and the historian have been joined in mutual dependency – and now that he needs the facts to objectively support his belief in progress – so Carr will have to try and unite, in *non-arbitrary* ways, facts and value. For if this cannot be achieved, if facts and value (significance) cannot be entailed then, as already suggested, any interpretation/meaning/significance Carr favours will be, in the end, just his personal taste. Carr's second argument thus attempts to solve the fact-value problem.

It cannot be said he succeeds. Nor can he. The fact-value problem, which has plagued mainstream western philosophy, remains problematic. But Carr's attempt is particularly inept. His method, after some preliminaries, is simply to go through a list of historians who have yoked together facts and value as if there wasn't any problem. As Carr casually comments: 'Let us see how a few historians, or writers about history, chosen more or less at random, have felt about this question.' And sure enough, those who appear on Carr's far from random list have all felt fine (Gibbon, Carlyle, Marx, Tawney, et al.). But it is obvious by the way Carr frames the problem that he doesn't understand what it is. Carr puts it thus:

> Let us now take another look at this alleged dichotomy between fact and value. Values cannot be derived from facts. This statement is partly true, partly false. You have only to examine the system of values prevailing in any period...to realise how much of it is moulded by the facts of the environment.... Or take the Christian church.... Contrast the values of primitive Christianity with those of the mediaeval papacy...These differences in values spring from differences of historical fact. Or consider the historical facts which...have caused slavery...to be generally regarded as immoral. The proposition that values cannot be derived from facts is to say the least, one-sided and misleading....[29]

But none of this is to the point. For the fact-value argument doesn't refuse for a moment to recognise that all of us, everyday, run facts and values together. Rather the argument hinges on whether or not it is logically demonstrable that one, and only one, value can be derived from one fact, or one set of facts, in terms of an incorrigible, absolute entailment. And as I say, I think all attempts at this have failed. Besides, if facts and values were conjoined in the everyday way Carr suggests (that is, you just do it and it's all right) then Carr wouldn't be able to argue – as he had done earlier in his text when it suited him – that those contemporaneous intellectuals who surrounded him and who drew the value of pessimism from the facts of the 1960s and 1970s were 'wrong' to do so. No, what we have here are all sorts of people drawing all kinds of values from the same (or same sort) of facts precisely because there is no 'single' entailment to stop them.... Carr hasn't refuted 'anything goes'. The circle that Carr is trying to square here is that, whilst he really 'knew' that all historiography is interpretive all the way down – and that the utterly promiscuous past will go with anybody – he still wanted his own interpretation to be somehow exempt. That in some way the 'history' which he interpreted as 'progressing' really was progressing in exactly the way his interpretation suggested, and would have been doing so whether he had spotted it or not: whether by luck or by judgement his interpretation had just happened to come out not as an interpretation at all, but the truth.

Well, it's a view, but it seems to have been a view Carr considers as really being 'the case'. Consequently, Carr will go on to argue that progress isn't in an evaluation of the past, but is in the past *per se*:

Progress in history is achieved through the interdependence and interaction of facts and values. The objective historian is the historian who penetrates most deeply into this reciprocal process.[30]

Third, then, Carr will now push this line right up to the end of his text. For in this direction lies precisely that sought for objectivity and truth. We can move quickly now as we move towards that end via several long quotes from Carr. Thus, as he commences to answer the question of 'what is history?' his position becomes obvious:

Somewhere between these two poles – the north pole of valueless facts and the south pole of value judgements still struggling to transform themselves into facts – lies the realm of historical truth. The historian . . . is balanced between fact and interpretation. He cannot separate them. It may be that, in a static world, you are obliged to pronounce a divorce between fact and value. But history is meaningless in a static world. History in its essence is change, movement, or – if you do not cavil at the old-fashioned word – progress.[31]

Accordingly, Carr adds:

History properly so-called can be written only [sic] by those who find and accept a sense of direction in history itself. The belief that we have come from somewhere is closely linked with the belief that we are going somewhere.[32]

Accordingly, Carr now enlarges his previous definition of what history is by adding the 'future' to the previously stated dialogue between the present and the past:

When . . . I spoke of history . . . as a dialogue between past and present, I should rather have called it a dialogue between the events of the past and progressively emerging future ends. The historian's interpretation of the past, his selection of the significant and the relevant, evolves with the progressive emergence of new goals.[33]

This is what Carr means by objectivity. Only the future

can provide the key to the interpretation of the past, and it is only in this sense that we can speak of an ultimate objectivity in history.[34]

What then, asks Carr, do we mean when we say a historian is object-ive? Or when we say one historian is more objective than another? He is clear. What makes one historian superior to another – what makes Carr a better historian than another – and what prevents any old history being equal to any other (for Carr is now no relativist) is whether or not the historian chooses the 'right facts'; it is whether he/she chooses the 'right standard of significance'. So that when we call an historian 'objective' we mean two things he says:

> First of all, we mean he has the capacity to rise above the limited vision of his own situation in society and history – a capacity... partly dependent on his capacity to recognise the extent of his invol-vement in that situation, to recognise... the impossibility of total objectivity. Secondly, we mean that he has the capacity to project his vision into the future... to give him a more profound and more lasting insight into the past than can be attained by those historians whose outlook is entirely bounded by their own immediate situation. No historian today will echo Acton's confidence in... 'ultimate his-tory'. But some historians write history which is more durable, and has more of this ultimate and objective character, than others, and these are the historians who have... a long-term vision over the past and over the future. The historian... can make an approach towards objectivity only as he approaches towards the understanding of the future.[35]

Such objectivity isn't absolute then. Absolute truth escapes. But in so far as historians – like Carr – can approximate objectivity and truth – *now the aim of the historian* – the touchstone by which to do so is the future. In this last quote from Carr, he just about says it all:

> The absolute in history is not something in the past from which we start; it is not something in the present, since all present thinking is necessarily relative. [pragmatic] It is something still incomplete and in the process of becoming – something in the future towards which we move, which begins to take shape only as we move towards it, and in the light of which... we gradually shape our interpretation of the past.... Our criterion is not an absolute in the static sense of some-thing that is the same yesterday, today, and for ever: such an absolute is incompatible with the nature of history. But it is absolute in respect to our interpretation of the past. It rejects the relativist view that one interpretation is as good as another, or that every interpretation is

true in its own time and place, and it provides the touchstone by which our interpretation of the past will ultimately be judged. It is this sense of direction in history which alone enables us to order and interpret the events of the past – the task of the historian – and to liberate and organise human energies in the present with a view to the future.... I now come back to my starting point by declaring my faith in the future of society and in the future of history.[36]

Well, it goes pretty much without saying that Carr's notions of objectivity and truth relative to a putative future is, of course, still, as one might put it (without committing a performative contradiction) absolutely relativist *vis-à-vis* other ways of putting the past 'under a description'... you can always get another description. For simply change what you think the future ought to be and you change the perspective from which you read the past; shift the end-point slightly and you change the criteria for significance. Carr may have liked to give the impression that he'd escaped relativism, but privately, as R.W. Davies tells us, 'the problem of objectivity in history evidently continued to trouble him long after he had completed *What is History?*'.[37] But on the reading I'm giving here, the point I want to make is not that Carr's 'solution' to scepticism and relativism failed, but that, *pace* most interpretations of Carr, what is central to his historical theorising is that he tried to be 'objectivist'; that he wanted to *find* the truth, and that (and this is important) what scepticism he had was reserved, ironically, for those historians who did not see history in the upper case way he certainly did. Here, then, lies Carr's weakness if we wish to use him today. This weakness is not that he didn't understand, say, the fact-value problem (though he didn't); or that his epistemiological scepticism is slight and platitudinous (though it is), but that he thought that objectivity and historical truth – no matter how well qualified – were still on the agenda. Carr's self-conscious decision to stick with his self-proclaimed Victorian optimism of a Marxist type is just too certaintist, too unreflexive and, in a way, too naive to be taken seriously today.[38]

The third and final point I want to make in this brief critique of Carr's text is therefore to underline the fact that, from a contemporary perspective, his book is of no, or very little, significance *vis-à-vis* the sorts of discussions constitutive of 'history today'. Nor is there anything in his Notes towards a new edition of *What is History?* to suggest he had picked up on all those postist-type discussions which were embryonic or indeed fully fledged well before his death and which could have indicated to him the 'end of modernist history', certaintist style. The briefest of examinations of the Index of the latest edition of Carr's text – which includes items from his Notes – shows few references to historiographical works of the 1950s, 1960s and 1970s, or to theories then being developed by intellectuals with an increasingly high public profile. Thus there are no references to, say, Barthes or Foucault or Derrida or Lyotard or Auerbach; no mention of feminism, hermeneutics, narratology or poststructuralism, while structuralism and existentialism are written off, generally in one-liners. Nor, within the broadly Marxist frameworks within which Carr works, is there really any mention of those sophisticated (often epistemiological) revisions within 'Western Marxism' which took place from the 1920s; certainly there is no analysis of them. Thus, Lukács gets only a sentence in the Notes, the Frankfurt School gets no mention. Adorno gets one entry in the Notes. Gramsci, Della Volpe, Benjamin, Althusser, Jameson, are missing. So is Cauldwell, E.P. Thompson, Christopher Hill, Raymond Williams, Victor Kiernan, Eric Hobsbawm...that whole raft of communist historians and critics Carr must have known of. Nor is there any reference to that whole gamut of intellectual movements drawn on by Hayden White in the 1950s and 1960s in the making of his *Metahistory* (1973)...and so on and so forth.

No, even in 1961 Carr's was an old book; old-fashioned and fashioned in old ways. What Carr draws on for his discussion of 'What is History?' are the authors and texts of his 'youth': Acton, Arnold, Bury, Barth, Bloch, Carlyle, Clark, Collingwood, Dilthey, Eliot, Fisher, Green, Grote; so one can run through Carr's reference points and emerge with a clear understanding of why Carr is so unhelpful today: he is just...out of date.

For whilst Carr may have learnt the late modernist lesson of perspectivism, he hardly seems to have been ready for the idea that it goes 'all the way down'; that it includes everybody – including him. Carr's faith in objectivity and progress and historical truth 'beyond the level of the statement or the chronicle' is just that, a faith. Hence that tension which runs throughout his text caused by him needing to be, on the one hand, sceptical and perspectival *vis-à-vis* his critique of Ranke, positivism and empirical commonsense, and on the other, non-sceptical, objectivist and non-relativist about his own position. And yet, it is maybe this tension, and this refusal to embrace scepticism and relativism as the best solution to the problem of historical ontology, epistemology and methods, that accounts for his 'central place' within an English historiography which in its mainstream realist, objectivist, empirical, documentarist, own-sakist formulations, sees Carr's famous toying with relativism as being just about as much as it can take. It is, perhaps ironically then, Carr's 'dangerous' (albeit somewhat mythological) flirting with relativism which has perhaps helped to sustain his 'radical' reputation amongst one of the most conservative discourses around: English historiography...and there's nothing mythological about a statement like that.[39]

Notes

1   K. Jenkins, *Rethinking History* (London: Routledge, 1991).
2   A. Marwick, *The Nature of History*, third edition (London: Macmillan, 1989); J. Tosh, *The Pursuit of History*, second edition (Longman, 1992); M. Stanford, *Companion to History* (Oxford: Blackwell, 1994).
3   K. Jenkins, *On 'What is History?' From Carr and Elton to Rorty and White* (London: Routledge, 1995).
4   E.H. Carr, *What is History?* (London: Macmillan, 1961), edition used here: second edition (London: Penguin, 1987 (1990)); G. Elton, *The Practice of History* (1967) (London: Fontana, 1969).
5   D. LaCapra, *History and Criticism* (London: Cornell University Press, 1985), p. 137.
6   Jenkins, *On 'What is History?'*, pp. 36–40.
7   Carr, *What is History?*, p. 64.
8   Elton, *The Practice of History*, pp. 75ff.
9   LaCapra, *History and Criticism*, p. 137; G. McLennan, *Marxism and the Methodologies of History* (London: Verso, 1981), p. 103.
10   Of course, some disliked Carr very much (Norman Stone for example), whilst Arthur Marwick has recently taken Carr to task: A. Marwick: 'A Fetishism of Documents?' The Salience of Source-Based History, in H. Kozicki, ed., *Developments in Modern Historiography* (New York: St. Martin's Press, 1993), pp. 107–38.
11   McLennan, *Marxism and the Methodologies of History*.
12   Tosh, *The Pursuit of History*, pp. 5, 29, 148, 236.
13   R. Porter, ed., *Myths of the English* (Oxford: Polity Press, 1992), p. 7.
14   Carr, *What is History?*, pp. 9–10.
15   *Ibid.*, pp. 11–12.
16   *Ibid.*, pp. 12–14.
17   *Ibid.*, pp. 19–20.
18   *Ibid.*, p. 4.
19   *Ibid.*, p. 6.
20   *Ibid.*
21   *Ibid.*, p. 22.
22   *Ibid.*
23   *Ibid.*, p. 26.
24   *Ibid.*, p. 27.
25   *Ibid.*
26   In conventional, lower-case history, the facts, to quote Hayden White, 'are taken to *be* the "meaning" of [events].... Facts are supposed to provide the

basis for arbitrating among the variety of different meanings that different groups *can* assign to an event.... But [actually] the facts are a *function* of the meaning assigned to events, not some primitive data that determine what meaning an event can have'. H. White, 'The Modernist Event' in V. Sobchack, ed., *The Persistence of History* (London: Routledge, 1996), pp. 17–38, p. 21.

27 Carr, *What is History?*, p. 27.
28 *Ibid.*, p. 30.
29 *Ibid.*, p. 130.
30 *Ibid.*, p. 131.
31 *Ibid.*, p. 132.
32 *Ibid.*
33 *Ibid.*, pp. 123–4.
34 *Ibid.*, p. 123.
35 *Ibid.*
36 *Ibid.*, pp. 121, 132.
37 *Ibid.*, p. 162.
38 The kind of comparisons I have in mind are: The difference between Carr's formulations and contemporary, postmodern ones, can be seen in the following where F.R. Ankersmit summarises 'what history is' postist-style:

> That narrative language has the ontological status of being an object that is opaque; that it is self-referential; that it is intentional and, hence, intrinsically aestheticist; that the narrative meaning of an (historical) text is undecidable in an important sense of that word and even bears the marks of self-contradiction; that narrative meaning can only be identified in the presence of *other* meaning (intertextuality); that as far as narrative is concerned the text refers but not to a reality outside itself; that criteria of truth and falsity do not apply to historiographical representations of the past; that we can only properly speak of causes and effects at the level of the statement; that narrative language is metaphysical (tropological) and as such embodies a proposal for how we should see the past; that the historical text is a substitute for the absent past; that narrative representations of the past have a tendency to disintegrate... all these postmodern claims so amazing and even repulsive to the modernist can be given a formal or even a 'modernist' justification if we are prepared to develop a philosophical logic suitable for dealing with the narrative substance.
> F.R. Ankersmit, 'Reply to Professor Zagorin', *History and Theory*, Vol. 29, No. 3, 1990, pp. 275–96, pp. 295–6.

39 That proper, professional, old-fashioned traditional historians (Roberts' own description of himself) still see Carr (and Elton) as being 'relevant', is outlined in Roberts' review of my On 'What is History?' .... Roberts argues that, *pace* my reading of Carr, he is best understood through theories of social action. I have found Roberts' review perceptive in various ways, but I see little in either Carr and Elton to support the social action interpretive position. G. Roberts, 'Review Essay, 'On What is History?' From Carr and Elton to Rorty and White', *History and Theory*, Vol. 36, No. 2, 1997, pp. 249–60.

15
E.H. Carr and the Historical Mode of Thought

Randall Germain

> The world of politics – and what is not political today? – is the world of history.
>
> E.H. Carr[1]

E.H. Carr occupies a most peculiar position among the handful of scholars whose intellectual legacies dominate the discipline of International Relations. He is first and foremost associated with the initial articulation of realism in the twentieth century, and his seminal text in this regard – *The Twenty Years' Crisis* – is read everywhere as one of the earliest and clearest expositions of a self-conscious realist discourse. For most International Relations scholars and teachers, therefore, he is intimately bound up with the origins of the discipline as a distinct field of inquiry. Yet, as a scholar Carr refused throughout his long working life to return to the themes marked out in *The Twenty Years' Crisis*, preferring instead to treat that part of his intellectual development as a closed book. Indeed, from 1944 until his death nearly 40 years later, his primary preoccupation – one might even call it a fixation – was either writing about history (in his case Soviet history in the 1920s) or reflecting about the nature of the historical enterprise.

It is precisely this movement from politics to history, however, which best explains the answer to the paradox of E.H. Carr the International Relations theorist.[2] His brand of realism was, in fact, powerfully informed by his view of history, and his reluctance to embrace the assumptions of twentieth-century political realism was primarily due to his insistence on the historical character of knowledge and what he called the historical approach.[3] In order to highlight the distinctive elements of this approach within the context of International Relations, I will associate Carr's work with what Robert Cox has characterized as the historical mode of thought.[4] Although the historical mode of thought is sensitive to the contexts of history, and to the need to use historical detail accurately in the course of analysis, its signal importance resides in the series of claims it makes regarding the construction of social experience and the form of knowledge appropriate for comprehending the social world. In Carr's case, these claims centre on how we are to understand the possibility of human agency (including the role of ideals and guiding myths in the making of history) and the nature of institutional change in the modern world.

This chapter will consider E.H. Carr the International Relations theorist in light of his work as an historian. It will argue that his use of the historical mode of thought provides a powerful way of understanding the changing role of the state within the structural context of international politics. This historical approach so changes Carr's brand of realism that it becomes disingenuous to identify him simply as a 'realist'.[5] While it might be impossible to overcome this label in terms of Carr's intellectual legacy, it should be possible to distance his work from that of more recent writers in this genre by adding a qualifying adjective to the term 'realist'. Two adjectives may be considered: critical or historical.[6] While the former stresses his affinity to today's critical theorists, I would argue that the latter term is perhaps closer to Carr's own intellectual concerns.

To identify Carr as a historical realist is to 'historicise' him, to place him in a long line of other so-called 'realists', including predecessors such as Friedrich Meinecke and Ludwig Dehio, writers contemporary with Carr himself such as Antonio Gramsci and Karl Polanyi, and modern-day descendants such as Robert Cox and Craig Murphy. Considered on these grounds, Carr's singular contribution to the discipline of International Relations lies not so much in his celebrated articulation of political realism, as important as that may be for some. Rather, his principal intellectual achievement in International Relations, and his enduring legacy, remains the way he infuses a concern with the historicity of knowledge into how both power and change are understood within the history of international politics. Ultimately, Carr's work helps to prepare the ground for the eventual meeting of a philosophically informed history with an historically informed international relations theory.

Why History?

Carr was convinced towards the end of his working life that 'the present age is the most historically-minded of all ages'.[7] By this he meant that we 'thought' historically, or in other words that we understood our-selves as intimately shaped by past events which we are able to compre-hend rationally. In this he stands in line with the Oxford philosopher and historian R.G. Collingwood, who asserted that to be historical was to 'know thyself': 'the value of history . . . is that it teaches us what man has done and thus what man is'.[8] People have not always been histor-ically conscious, and it is one of the great achievements of the modern period to have widened human horizons to the point of being able to think historically.

This notion of thinking historically is an integral aspect of the histor-ical mode of thought, and one which connects to wider debates within the social sciences. In the first place, following the eighteenth-century Neopolitan philosopher Giambattista Vico, the social sciences in the broadest sense only become possible when human beings recognize that they 'make' history, and because of this it is they alone who can understand it. Not only do human beings provide the standpoint or subject of knowledge, they also create it. All knowledge of human beings, in this sense, must be historical knowledge:

> For the first principle posited above is that this world of nations has certainly been made by men, and its guise must therefore be found within the modifications of our own human mind. And history cannot be more certain than when he who creates the things also narrates them.[9]

In the second place, the association of *res gestae* – the actions of human beings which have occurred in the past – with knowledge is meant to be inclusive, and it leads necessarily to the proposition that the various disciplinary elements of the social sciences are inevitably historical in character. Fernand Braudel has taken this notion of his-tory's inclusivity to its logical end by calling for history to be used as the meeting ground of the social sciences. Is not history, in his words, 'the most useful line to take toward a way of observing and thinking com-mon to all the social sciences'.[10] The cardinal hallmark of history, in Braudel's estimation, is its recognition of the multiplicity of time, which he construes as being comprised of the event, the conjuncture and the *longue durée*. By suggesting that the social sciences locate themselves and their various foci along a temporal axis, Braudel is arguing that know-ledge must not only take account of time, it must be also explicitly organized to address the specifically human problematic of time. In short, knowledge must contain a temporal dimension.

Carr's historical mode of thought resonates with these broad themes. At one level this is expressed in his work in terms of the relationship between past and present. Here Carr sides with Croce in his dictum that all history is contemporary history, albeit minus the teleological connotations which Croce's use of the term contains. For Carr, the 'historian undertakes a two-fold operation: to analyse the past in light of the present and the future which is growing out of it, and to cast the beam of the past over the issues which dominate the present and future'.[11] We seek understanding of the past in light of where we are now, and consider who and what we have become as a consequence of past practice. All history is contemporary history because our questions are informed by our present circumstances; and our knowledge of these questions is historical because they arise out of a consideration of *res gestae* and the modifications of our own human mind. Past and present thus frame the domain of human knowledge, leading Carr, as it led Collingwood and Braudel, to consider all knowledge of human affairs to be 'historical' knowledge. The importance of history reveals itself in this way as the proper method by which we gain understanding about human affairs. For Carr, knowledge about human affairs loses its meaning unless it takes an historical form.

At another level, Carr's historical mode of thought resonates with the debate over the standpoint of judgement used by the social sciences. If knowledge of human affairs is necessarily framed in terms of time and place, its objectivity can be called into question, and its validity undermined. Carr approached this question in line with the general tenets of historicist writers of the past, by arguing that there could be no extra-historical standard by which human actions could be judged once and for all. Such standards were moving standards, in terms both of explanation and ethical judgement.

Carr gave a novel twist to the meaning of objectivity in history, however, by linking it to what he called 'progressively emerging future ends'.[12] The standpoint of objectivity in history is bound up with the task of recognizing what the important developments of the future will be, and then using that standpoint to interpret the past. 'Only the future can provide the key to the interpretation of the past; and it is only in this sense that we can speak of an ultimate objectivity in history.'[13] What this objectivity does, for Carr, is to allow the historian to arrange, or judge, events and chains of causation in terms of their significance for our understanding of the future. It provides the historian with the tools to construct an interpretation of the past that is informed by the possibilities of future developments. It is on this basis that judgements are rendered regarding the decisions and accounts of past historical subjects. Considering past, present and future as the proper domain of knowledge about human affairs not only encourages history and the social sciences to meet, it also provides a standard against which judgements about human affairs can be framed.

The Mode of History: Change and Agency

When Carr first delivered the lectures eventually published as *The New Society* in 1951, he sought to analyse what he saw to be the most significant historical developments over the course of the previous 150 years. Many of the themes he addressed – mass democracy, the planned economy, the welfare state, the place of the individual within material civilisation, the role of reason in human affairs – were to be revisited a decade later in *What is History?* and throughout the course of his *History of Soviet Russia*. Here I focus on the foundations of what Carr called the mode of history, namely how we should understand change and human agency within history, and briefly outline their place in his historical mode of thought. It is these foundations which inform Carr's consideration of the changing nature of the state in today's world.

Change

In *The New Society*, Carr begins his outline of the historical approach by rejecting two claims. First, he dismisses as 'anti-historical' all those who would echo Thucydides' dictum that history is devoid of substantive change.[14] Rather, the starting point for a modern historical consciousness was the conviction that change was a central postulate of human affairs. At the same time, Carr is keen to cast doubt on those claims which understand the substantive changes of the last several hundred years to be somehow retrograde in character, having led humanity from a higher to a lower point of development. Instead, he is insistent that these changes should be viewed in progressive or developmental terms. Throughout the post-war period, for example, Carr insisted that the scepticism and despair which informed much of what passed for the scholarly analysis of contemporary history was fundamentally flawed. His understanding of change meant in the first instance restoring a 'saner and more balanced outlook on the future'.[15]

In this sense, change for Carr was not simply the repetition of familiar events and themes in different contexts, albeit with new *dramatis personae*. Real historical change had a direction that made it understandable in rational terms. Moreover, what made change rationally comprehensible was in part the different ways in which the historian could assemble or order explanations of change to take account of ascending hierarchies of causation, each of which incorporated other more narrowly focused accounts until the most appropriate explanation was reached in light of 'progressively emerging future ends'. That these ends are themselves 'progressive', or have a certain direction which the scholar can discern, allows Carr to make judgements about the significance of different kinds or classes of historical acts for understanding history. Thus Carr insists on the centrality for politics and international relations of the profound social transformations of the past 200 years. The starting point for understanding the 'new society', he maintains, is nothing less than a radical rethink of how human affairs in their broadest measure are organized.

In *Nationalism and After*, Carr provides some of the intellectual tools that might assist with this radical rethink. He begins by distinguishing four phases of nationalism, which he associates with the changing nature of economic and social organization within nations. It was not until nationalism became associated with the economy, and society itself thoroughly nationalized, that the catastrophe which consumed the various nationalist movements in Europe was unleashed.[16] To reorganize and indeed to rebuild international society in the face of the power of nationalism after World War II, however, required for Carr a move to a new unit of account – the individual: 'The driving force behind any future international order must be a belief, however expressed, in the value of individual human beings, irrespective of national affinities or allegiance and in a common and mutual obligation to promote their well-being.'[17]

Nevertheless, Carr's view of the individual was not the traditional liberal view of the free and autonomous individual making his or her own way in society, but the individual as embedded within what Carr termed the 'service state' (that is, what we understand today as the welfare state). The full institutionalization of the 'service state' was the only way in which the latent common ideal of social justice could be realised within the post-war international order. For Carr social justice must be predicated on the realisation of three constituent elements: equality of opportunity, freedom from want and full employment. But it is the latter factor which lends 'reality' to the first two elements.[18] Thus the international order which will help to realize the 'new society' is one predicated on full employment provided by the service state to individuals. A full 30 years before John Ruggie coined the term 'embedded liberalism',[19] Carr saw this as the only trajectory consistent with the progressively emerging future ends of the mid-twentieth century, namely the emergence of the planned economy and mass democracy. It was the impact on state structures of these emerging trends which mark out inter-state behaviour as entering a new phase in the post-war period.

It is worthwhile pausing here to consider briefly how realist and neorealist scholars conceptualise change in international relations, and its importance in explaining historical phenomena. To a classical realist such as Hans Morgenthau, the notion of change is linked directly to his understanding of human nature. The attempt to identify 'object-ive' laws in politics is only made possible by the existence of a distinct and unchanging human nature. This 'human nature' Morgenthau believed to be rooted in the elemental bio-psychological drives of indi-viduals through which society is in turn constructed.[20] In other words, despite the numerous forms taken by different societies throughout history, including a staggering array of social and institutional arrange-ments, Morgenthau believed that past, present and future were under-standable precisely because of their uniformity. The causal relations which shed light on one set of social experiences are able to do so for others as well, even though separated in time and across space. For Morgenthau, the point of analysis is not to discern what is new and novel in international politics, but to identify what is permanent and unchanging, and to base our understanding of international relations on these certain foundations.

Scholars such as Kenneth Waltz and Robert Gilpin, although arriving at similar conclusions, approach the question quite differently. For Waltz, the phenomena of importance in international politics revolve around the structural characteristics of the international system, and these have not changed in their principal dynamics over millennia. International politics remains driven by an anarchical system in which the distribution of capabilities across states produces their positional arrangements. Although these may alter over time, the dynamic itself does not change: in Waltz's words, we have transformations *in* the system rather than *of* the system.[21] Or as he has put it more recently: 'Despite changes that constantly take place in the relations of nations, the basic structure of international politics continues to be anarchic.'[22] Gilpin echoes this view of change as repetitive and cyclical (and thus static): 'Ultimately, international politics still can be characterised as it was by Thucydides: the interplay of impersonal forces and great leaders.'[23] These modes of analysis would be described by Carr as 'anti-historical' in so far as they detect some kind of permanent sub-stratum upon which the understanding of change is to be built, whether

Morgenthau's bio-psychological drives, Waltz's ordering principles or Gilpin's repetitive interplay of great leaders and impersonal forces.[24] They are diametrically opposed to the developmental and progressive understanding of history which Carr embraces.

Writing from the vantage point of the middle decades of the twentieth century, Carr could not but be struck by the ferocity and destructiveness of organised violence, and by the enthusiasm of states to unleash it. Neither could he easily answer the obvious question of why the nineteenth century was a less violent and more 'peaceful' era than the twentieth century. He refused to believe individual human beings were more war-like in one era than another, or that such a result was due entirely to a series of historical accidents (that is, that the temporal distribution of 'great leaders', for example, fortuitously favoured the nineteenth over the twentieth century). Instead, he focused his (rational) explanation on the changing nature of the state over this period and a deep-seated breakdown in the system of relations among states. The history of the twentieth century indicated that a profound change in the organisation of social life had occurred, and to explain the history of the period in any other way was to abandon an historical view of human development.

Agency

Carr's historical view clearly placed human agency at the centre of his analysis of change. He did this, however, by reaching for a balance between voluntarism and determinism which explicitly acknowledged the structural determinants of human agency. This balance inclined Carr to consider human agency in collective terms. He was, for example, scathing in his denunciation of what he termed variously as the 'Good Queen Bess' or 'Bad King John' vision of history, which viewed the direction of history as dependent upon the actions and accidents of individuals.[25] As important as individuals were to history (and he refused to eliminate them in his work), their actions were always embedded in two broader sets of social formations.

The first broad social formation was the immediate social context within which individuals acted. People were rarely free to act solely according to their whims; and even when they did have a fair degree of latitude in determining their actions, they always acted under the influence of their own past, their immediate social circles, and the limited number of opportunities genuinely achievable at any one time. Although Carr was no Marxist, he was very sympathetic to the historical materialist strand of Marxism, and often quoted the famous passage from Marx's *Eighteenth Brumaire of Louis Bonaparte*: 'Men make their own history, but they do not make it just as they please; they do not make it under circumstances chosen by themselves, but under circumstances directly found, given and transmitted from the past.'[26]

The second broader social formation that must be considered is the group. It is not individuals as such who 'make' history. Any genuinely meaningful notion of human agency must understand such agency in collective rather than individual terms. Here Carr uses his historical approach to investigate the institutionalized nature of social life, most importantly the way in which institutions channel collective action to certain ends. For example, it is the institutional dimension of monarchy rather than individual monarchs that demands our attention if we want to understand the transition from feudalism to modernity, just as it is the institution of the state rather than individual statesman that we must understand if we want to inquire into the breakdown of international order during the first half of the twentieth century. It is institutions which agglomerate and channel individual actions towards a collective impetus to change; thus it is the changing institutionalization of group behaviour in the contemporary period which warrants attention if the object of our inquiry is to understand the direction of change today.[27]

This concern with the institutionalization of group behaviour motivated Carr to argue that the shift from individualist to mass democracy is one of the most significant developments of modern history, one which demands nothing less than a rethink of how political institutions work in the contemporary period. He believed that the emerging practices of mass democracy imperilled the workability of those political institutions which had taken root during the seventeenth and eighteenth centuries. Democracy as it was conceived and practised from Locke and Rousseau to Jefferson and Lincoln was in danger of foundering on the inclusion of masses of the property-less into the lines of accountability which run from citizens through to government. For Carr, rational argument among equals over comparatively few questions had given way to complex bargaining among non-equals over the distribution of resources by a strong and bureaucratically organized state. Carr's main point here is not to bemoan the loss of the early modern sense of freedom or democracy, which in any case had outgrown its social origins. Rather, he was concerned that we no longer had a clear idea of what democracy meant because its key institutional features were completely new, the product mainly of the twentieth century.[28] New ways of understanding and accommodating collective agency in institutional terms had to be found if democracy was to be revitalized and made relevant to organized political life.[29]

Carr's concern with the modalities of human agency also extended to the motivations which drove people to 'make' their own history. In line with his collective use of human agency, however, he understood these motivations in terms of the ideals and myths which infused people at a general level, and which informed their conceptualisation of certain issues. The doctrine of the harmony of interests, for example, was treated by Carr as both a myth which helped to make sense of the nineteenth-century world order for the dominant bourgeois class, and as an ideology which helped to enlist support for the status quo in the twentieth century. As a myth it helped to explain how and why certain kinds of agency were necessary within a given structure of the world, while as an ideology it helped the powerful to co-opt the weak into their view of the world. In either case we can see how collective human agency is motivated by certain ideational features.[30] This use of ideals and myths as central motivational features of human agency is a recurrent and significant theme in much of Carr's work in international relations, specifically in his consideration of the conditions of peace during the Second World War,[31] the moral foundations of world order,[32] the prospects of internationalism in the post-war era,[33] and in the impact of the Soviet Union on world politics.[34]

Of course, Carr was careful to argue that the way in which motivations engendered collective action were complex and often times difficult to ascertain, not least by agents themselves.[35] But his point here is not that motivations are unimportant, but rather that we must understand them to consist of swirls of ideas which often lie 'behind the act', so to speak.[36] That is, we should look not to individual motivations in particular but generalized motivations as the key which unlocks a collective understanding of how individuals see themselves and their activities. Such a concern connects the individual to society across a number of key social relations, reinforcing Carr's claim to view agency in collective terms. While acknowledging that in history 'numbers count',[37] he also makes it clear that before they can make themselves felt they must be motivated to act.

The Historical Mode of Thought and Historical Realism

For the discipline of International Relations, much yet remains to be gained by engaging with the broader corpus of Carr's work. Indeed, I would argue that a wider reading of Carr helps to set *The Twenty Years'*

Crisis into its proper historical and intellectual context, much as it is imperative to read Machiavelli's *Discourses* alongside *The Prince* if we are to gain an appropriate insight into the meaning of the latter work. *The Twenty Years' Crisis* is Carr's polemical treatment of the burning issues of the day, and cannot be properly read apart from either *Nationalism and After*, where he explores the possibilities of the future in light of the disastrous consequences of the past, or *The New Society* and *What is History?*, where he explores in more detail the thematic and theoretical reasoning behind some of the suggestions he first made as the clouds of war gathered over Europe and the world in the late 1930s.

As this chapter has suggested, the proper intellectual context for considering Carr's work in International Relations is his embrace of what I have called the historical mode of thought. This way of thinking about the social world rejects outright any claim to stasis in history, and indeed is predicated on the notion that profound social transformations have undermined many of the institutions through which humanity is organized and the ideas which have provided them with their intellectual and moral legitimacy. Understanding change, moreover, requires us to examine the direction which change is taking, and to explain that direction in line with what Carr called 'progressively emerging future ends'. These future ends are shaped by collective human agency acting through institutions and informed by guiding myths and ideals. In contrast to mainstream realist and neorealist accounts of international politics, Carr does not rely on impersonal forces, ordering principles or elemental bio-psychological drives to explain historical developments. Rather, his approach is 'realist' in terms of its practical acceptance of the structural parameters of everyday life and historical in terms of his method; hence the term 'historical realist' to identify Carr's place within the pantheon of International Relations scholars.

As foundational as Carr's work is to the articulation of the historical mode of thought, however, it is not without problems. First, Carr nowhere explicitly considers the nature and meaning of time. Instead, he works with an unproblematized understanding of time in terms of its unity and homogeneity. Second, Carr's emphasis on 'general history' is clearly misplaced. The general history that Carr seems to prefer is not the only type of history that can be legitimately and profitably pursued; many interesting and important questions take us of necessity into more specialised branches of historical inquiry. And finally, although Carr is fully cognisant of the range of interpretative problems in history, he is strangely silent on the problem of representation in his work. Just who represents what for whom is an issue that is left open, with serious consequences for the integrity of some of his arguments.

Acknowledging these problems reinforces the point that Carr's work does not on its own constitute a cast-iron alternative to mainstream realism in International Relations theory today. Rather we should seek to place his work into a broader spectrum of historically informed theorizing about the nature of change and the complex role of human agency within history. When placed within such a spectrum the problematic aspects of Carr's work identified above can be attenuated. For example, if we consider Carr's concern with change to equate to a concern with time, we can supplement his notion of the relationship between past and future with Fernand Braudel's conceptualization of time as multi-dimensional, consisting of the *longue durée*, the conjuncture and the event.[38] This would strengthen the conceptual links Carr is at pains to highlight between motivations and human agency, and which help to embed collective actions within the structural constraints of their particular social context.

A more finely tuned appreciation of the multiple experience of time would also help to shift the emphasis of Carr's work beyond his single-minded determination to write general history. Simply put, different kinds of historical narratives are appropriate for the consideration of different historical time spans. Carr was clearly softening his preference for general history in his later years, when he was making the revisions to the second edition of *What is History?*. Here he indicated some dissatisfaction with what he termed the tedious study of social history, and a willingness to explore more thoroughly the place of literature and the arts in historical narrative.[39]

The problem of representation in Carr's work, however, is a more difficult one to address by using the broad currents of historicism that inform much of the historical mode of thought.[40] Here we can reach out to some of the most interesting work currently being done within the discipline of International Relations to connect Carr's concerns with those animating geographers, constructivists and others for whom the notion of identity is a central problematic.[41] The axis of connection here is the substantial agreement which exists between these critical theorists and Carr over the nature of the subject/object relationship within the social world. Although Carr famously labelled the emerging discipline of international politics a 'science', he also clearly identified the differences which exist between the natural sciences and the branch of knowledge associated with what we now call the social sciences.[42] In other words, he did not consider knowledge of human affairs in positivist terms. Nevertheless, Carr refused to consider that both knowledge in general and the knowing subject in particular were necessarily framed in terms of representation. He saw no need to account for the specific way in which the knowing subject creates knowledge in the first place, beyond recognising that ideology and false consciousness were difficulties to be worked through.[43] Supplementing his work with that which does problematise how the social world is represented to human agents will both strengthen the historical mode of thought and build bridges between critical theorists and those who seek to reason historically within the discipline of International Relations.

The enduring legacy of E.H. Carr for International Relations thus stems directly from his historical approach. This approach distinguishes his work from mainstream realist thought by devoting careful attention to the changing nature of social relations which underpins both the state and the international system of states. Despite his inclusion as a 'realist' in the pantheon of International Relations scholarship, therefore, perhaps it is more accurate to identify Carr as an 'historical realist', that is, a theorist of international relations who reasons historically in order to explore the changing social foundations of the state as one of the key forces shaping international politics today. In this Carr is much closer to today's critical theorists than he is to mainstream realists, and it is on this basis that we can say that he remains an International Relations theorist for our times.

Notes

1 E.H. Carr, *The New Society* (London: Macmillan, 1951), p. 118.
2 See Jonathan Haslam, *The Vices of Integrity, E.H. Carr: 1892–1982* (London, Verso, 1999).
3 Carr, *The New Society*, p. 1.
4 Robert W. Cox, with Timothy J. Sinclair, *Approaches to World Order* (Cambridge: Cambridge University Press, 1996), p. 91.
5 For an argument which stresses that realism should be understood less as a coherent intellectual position and more as a site of contested claims, see R.B.J. Walker, *Inside/Outside: International Relations as Political Theory* (Cambridge: Cambridge University Press, 1993), pp. 105–6.
6 Paul Howe has suggested the term 'utopian realist'. While I am sympathetic to Howe's argument, I believe that Carr's challenge to today's mainstream realism goes far beyond what Howe suggests. Paul Howe, 'The Utopian Realism of E.H. Carr', *Review of International Studies*, 20, 1994, pp. 277–97. Richard Falk has recently suggested the term 'critical realist' in order to link Carr to the work of Hedley Bull and Robert Cox. Richard Falk, 'The critical realist tradition

and the demystification of interstate power: E.H. Carr, H. Bull and R.W. Cox', in S. Gill and J. Mittelman, eds, *Innovation and Transformation in International Studies* (Cambridge: Cambridge University Press, 1997).

7 E.H. Carr, *What is History?* (London: Macmillan, 1961), p. 134; cf. *The New Society*, pp. 1–2.

8 R.G. Collingwood, *The Idea of History* (Oxford: Clarendon Press, 1946), p. 10.

9 G. Vico, *The New Science of Giambattista Vico*, translated by T.G. Bergin and M.H. Fisch (Ithaca: NY Cornell University Press, 1946/1984), para. 349.

10 F. Braudel, 'History and the Social Sciences: the Longue Durée' in *On History*, translated by S. Matthews (London: Weidenfeld and Nicolson, 1980), p. 50.

11 Carr, *The New Society*, pp. 17–18.

12 Carr, *What is History?*, p. 123.

13 *Ibid.*

14 Carr, *The New Society*, p. 1; cf. Carr, *What is History?*, pp. 109–10.

15 E.H. Carr, *What is History?*, second edition by R.W. Davies (Harmondsworth: Penguin Books, 1985), p. 6.

16 E.H. Carr, *Nationalism and After* (London: Macmillan, 1945), pp. 17–26.

17 *Ibid.*, p. 44.

18 *Ibid.*, p. 64.

19 J. Ruggie, 'International Regimes, Transactions, and Change: Embedded Liberalism in the Postwar Economic Order', *International Organization*, Vol. 36, No. 2, 1982, pp. 379–415.

20 H. Morgenthau, *Politics Among Nations*, third edition (New York: Alfred A. Knopf, 1965), pp. 4 and 33.

21 K. Waltz, *Theory of International Politics* (Reading, MA: Addison-Wesley, 1979), pp. 199–204. This dimension of stasis in Waltz's work has been noted by J. Ruggie, 'Continuity and Transformation in the World Polity: Towards a Neorealist Synthesis', *World Politics*, Vol. 35, No. 2, 1983, pp. 261–85, and R. Cox, *Approaches to World Order*, pp. 91–3.

22 K. Waltz, 'The Emerging Structure of International Politics', *International Security*, Vol. 18, No. 2, 1993, p. 59.

23 R. Gilpin, *War and Change in World Politics* (Cambridge: Cambridge University Press, 1981), p. 228.

24 Such an 'anti-historical' view is evident, for example, when Gilpin argues that 'The conclusion of one hegemonic war is the beginning of another cycle of growth, expansion, and eventual decline.... It has always been thus and always will be, until men either destroy themselves or learn to develop an effective mechanism of peaceful change'. *War and Change*, p. 210.

25 Carr, *What is History?*, pp. 45–53.

26 R.C. Tucker, ed., *The Marx-Engels Reader*, second edition (New York: W.W. Norton & Co., 1978), p. 595.

27 This focus on institutions might be one reason why Carr, although influenced by Marxist analysis, never accepted the centrality of class for his own work: the institutionalisation of classes has always been difficult to assess, while the institutionalisation of more focused group behaviour (based, for example, on ethnicity, state or firm) is at least easier to identify historically.

28 Carr, *The New Society*, pp. 75–9.

29 These conclusions are in line with one of Carr's contemporaries, the Italian marxist theorist Antonio Gramsci. Gramsci called for new forms of collective

agency to be realised if workers were to be mobilised against the power of existing historical blocs. This new form of agency was the mass political party, which he dubbed the Modern Prince. See A. Gramsci, *Selections from the Prison Notebooks*, ed. Quintin Hoare and Geoffrey Nowell Smith (New York: International Publishers, 1971), pp. 125–33 and 147–56; cf R.W. Cox, 'Gramsci's Thought and the Question of Civil Society in the Late Twentieth Century', paper delivered at the conference on 'Gramsci, Modernity and the 20th Century', Cagliari, Italy, April 1997.

30   E.H. Carr, *The Twenty Years Crisis*, second edition. (London: Macmillan, 1946), pp. 41–62 and 80–5.

31   E.H. Carr, *The Conditions of Peace* (London: Macmillan, 1942), chapter 5.

32   E.H. Carr, 'Moral Foundations of World Order', in Ernest L. Woodward et al., *Foundations of World Order* (Denver: University of Denver Press, 1949).

33   Carr, *Nationalism and After*, part II.

34   E.H. Carr, *The Soviet Impact on the Western World* (London: Macmillan, 1946), chapter 5.

35   Carr, *What is History?*, pp. 49–55.

36   *Ibid.*, p. 52.

37   *Ibid.*, p. 50.

38   Braudel's temporal framework has been used within the context of international political economy by R.D. Germain, 'The Worlds of Finance: a Braudelian Perspective on IPE', *The European Journal of International Relations*, Vol. 2, No. 2, 1996, pp. 201–30; and E. Helleiner, 'Braudelian Reflections on Economic Globalisation: the Historian as Pioneer', in Gill and Mittelman, eds, *Innovation and Transformation*.

39   Carr, *What is History?*, second edition, pp. 170–5.

40   One strand of historicism which does consider this problem, however unevenly, is inspired by the work of Gramsci. For an overview of this literature's contribution to International Relations, see R.D. Germain and M. Kenny, 'Engaging Gramsci: International Relations Theory and the New Gramscians', *Review of International Studies*, Vol. 24, No. 1, 1998, pp. 3–21.

41   Examples of such scholarship include J. Agnew and S. Corbridge, *Mastering Space* (London: Routledge, 1995); A. Wendt, 'Collective Identity Formation and the International State', *American Political Science Review*, Vol. 88, No. 2, 1994, pp. 384–96; and D. Campbell, *Writing Security* (Manchester, Manchester University Press, 1992).

42   Carr, *The Twenty Years' Crisis*, pp. 2–5.

43   As, for example, in his discussion of the distorting impact of the ideology of the harmony of interests, which he presumed could be eliminated with some clear thinking. This formed the basis of the realist critique outlined in *The Twenty Years' Crisis*.

Appendices

Appendix 1
E.H. Carr: Chronology of His Life and Work, 1892–1982

1892   Born 28 June in Upper Holloway, London, to what Carr later called a 'middle, middle class' family

1905   Wins scholarship to Merchant Taylor's School, London

1906   Awarded class prize, mathematics prize and a divinity prize

1910   Wins full scholarship to Trinity College, Cambridge

1911   Goes up to Trinity to study classics

1914   War breaks out

1916   Graduates with a First

1916   Unfit for military service, joins the Foreign Office

1917   Work for the Contraband Department organizing blockade of Bolshevik regime

1918   Transferred from Contraband Department to the Northern Department dealing with Russia

1919   Attends the Versailles Peace Conference and remains in Paris until 1922

1920   Awarded CBE in recognition of his work at the peace conference

1921   Appointed Third Secretary

1925   Marries Anne Rowe, a widow with three children – Rachel, Phillippa and Martin.

1925   Posted as Second Secretary to British Legation, Riga, Latvia

1925   Begins learning Russian

1926   Birth of son, John Carr

1927   Makes first visit to Moscow

1929   Publishes his first review 'The Jewish Raskolnikov' in *The Spectator*

1929   Publishes first academic article 'Turgenev and Dostoevsky' in *Slavonic and East European Review*

1929   Begins writing study of Dostoevsky. Later he confessed that what 'appealed' to him about nineteenth-century Russians like Dostoevsky and Bakunin 'was that ... they thought in an entirely different way from the very conventional world in which I had been brought up in'.

1930   Transfer to League of Nations section of the Foreign Office.

1930   Begins writing regularly for *Fortnightly Review* under name of John Hallett. In a September article 'England Adrift' he argues that the country needs 'a faith – or at any rate a passable fetish' to overcome its 'defeatism ... scepticism, of disbelief in itself'.

1931   Publication of *Dostoevsky: 1821–1881*

1933   Promoted to First Secretary

1933   Publication of study on Alexander Herzen and his circles in exile, *The Romantic Exiles* (reissued 1968 and 1998). In an epilogue, Carr talked of 'the many-hued, incalculable diversity of the lives of the Romantic Exiles. In them Romanticism found its last expression' before 'that typical Victorian *savant*, Karl Marx' entered the political scene.

1934   Publication of *Karl Marx: A Study in Fanaticism*. In the introduction he notes: 'The Marxist is a blind enthusiast; the pseudo-Marxist is muddle-headed; the anti-Marxist is merely wrong headed. I am neither of these'.

1935   Begins publishing with Macmillan, a small family firm

1935   Submits application for Woodrow Wilson Chair of International Politics, Aberystwyth, Wales

1936   Resigns from Foreign Office and takes up Wilson Chair. Carr writes to his publisher Harold Macmillan: 'the fact that the best of these chairs in the country is located in Wales, is of course due to Lord Davies; but fortunately the obligations of residence are extremely small'. On 14 October, Carr delivers his Inaugural lecture, 'Public Opinion as a Safeguard of Peace' – an attack on the Treaty of Versailles.

1937   Publication of *International Relations since the Peace Treaties* his first book with Macmillan and the only book of his translated into Welsh, under the title *Cydberthynas y Gwledydd Wedi'r Cyfamodau Heddwch*

1937   Begins broadcasting for the BBC

1937   Publication of fifth book and fourth biography: *Michael Bakunin* 'true child of the romantic age' according to Carr. In 1978 he admitted that 'the book never sold, yet in a way I'd almost say it was the best book I ever wrote'.

1937   Becomes active at Chatham House

1937   Visits Germany and the Soviet Union and in a lecture given at Chatham House 'Impressions of a Visit to Russia and Germany' (12 October) observes that while 'the German regime' is not 'more enlightened than the Russian regime...in Germany there is still surviving a tradition of freedom which the Nazi regime has not been able to break down entirely'

1939   Publishes *The Twenty Years Crisis, 1919–1939. An Introduction to the Study of International Relations*.

1939   Publishes *Britain: A Study of Foreign Policy from the Versailles Treaty to the Outbreak of War*

1939   Outbreak of War: Carr joins Ministry of Information

1940   Resigns from Ministry of Information. In a private memorandum to his close associate Barrington-Ward in August, he puts the case for social reform, but advises 'we should avoid like the plague all ready made schemes of political organization – League of Nations, Federal Union and so forth...Our approach must be not through the medium of ideas but through the concrete medium of planning'. In an address delivered at Chatham House in the same month he argues: 'We cannot define our war aims in altogether political terms...we shall need to resort to a certain extent to social terms. We shall have to talk, to a certain extent, in terms of social revolution rather than in terms of mere national victory'

1941   Appointed assistant editor of *The Times* under Barrington-Ward.

1941   Germany attacks the Soviet Union

1942   Publishes *Conditions of Peace* an influential critique of 'laissez-faire' economics and politics.

1944   Takes decision to write a history of the Soviet Union

1944   Winston Churchill attacks Carr lead article on Greece as being 'a very unhelpful contribution to the government in handling the Greek situation.'

1945   Foreign Office Permanent Under Secretary Cadogan confides that he hopes 'someone will tie Barrington-Ward and Ted Carr together and throw them into the Thames'. Carr is also attacked in a Foreign Office memo: 'The one weak patch in our position are the leader columns of *The Times* where Professor Carr, with persistence and impartiality, continues to sabotage the policy of the Labour Government and of its predecessors on all matters where Russia and her Eastern Bloc are concerned'

1945   Signs contract for a *History of Soviet Russia since the Revolution*

1945   Publication of Chatham House study *Nationalism and After*

1945   Fails to be appointed to a Chair in the School of Slavonic and East European Studies, London

1945   Separates from his first wife, Anne

1946   Ceases to work full time for *The Times*

1946   Publishes *The Soviet Impact on the Western World* – his most pro-Soviet book in which he argues: 'It was Marshall Stalin who consciously or unconsciously usurping Woodrow Wilson's role, once more placed democracy in the forefront of allied war aims'

1946   Reissues a Second Edition of *The Twenty Years Crisis* that was to be reprinted sixteen times between 1946 and 1984. In the preface to the 1946 edition Carr wrote that 'the condition now seems to impose itself on any unbiased observer that the small independent nation-state is obsolete or obsolescent and that no workable international organization can be built on a membership of a multiplicity of nation-states'

1946   Moves in with Joyce Forde

1947   Formally resigns Chair in Aberystwyth

1947   Meets Isaac and Tamara Deutscher

1947   Confides in a letter to Daniel Macmillan that 'the thing' which 'frightened' him most about his *History of Soviet Russia* was 'that the more I work on it, the more material I find'

1947   *International Relations since the Peace Treaties* is reissued under the new title *International Relations Between The Two World Wars, 1919–1939* and then reprinted sixteen times between 1948 and 1989

1950   Series of six broadcasts on 'The New Society' appear in *The Listener*

1950   Publication of *The Bolshevik Revolution 1917–1923 Volume 1*

1950   Publication of *Studies In Revolution*

1951   Publication of *The New Society*, possibly his most systematic attempt to outline a vision of a possible future 'destination' for humanity in which planning will play a central economic role.

1952   Publication of *The Bolshevik Revolution 1917–1923 Volume 2*

1952   Publication of *German – Soviet Relations Between the Two World Wars 1919–1939*

1953   *The Bolshevik Revolution 1917–1923 Volume 3*

1953   Carr appointed to a three year tutorship at Balliol College, Oxford

1954   Publication of *The Interregnum: 1923–1924*

1955   Appointed to a Senior Research Fellowship at Trinity College, Cambridge. In a letter to Deutscher he noted that 'the advantages are a) no teaching, b) no retirement age, c) it's my own place.'

1956   Elected to the British Academy

1956   Meets Bob Davies

1958   Publication of *Socialism In One Country, 1924–1926, Volume 1* Carr noted in the Preface; 'The years 1924–6 were a critical turning-point, and gave the revolutionary regime, for good or evil, its decisive direction'. And the regime that emerged was what he termed an 'amalgam' between 'two opposed principles of continuity and change'. He observed: 'Nothing in history that seems continuous is exempt from the subtle erosion of inner change; no change, however, abrupt and violent in appearance, wholly breaks the continuity between past and present'

1959   Publication of *Socialism In One Country, 1924–1926, Volume 2*

1959   Invited to give Trevelyan Lectures. In a private letter to Bob Davies, Carr says he has 'been looking for some time for an opportunity to deliver a broadside on history in general and on some of the nonsense which is talked about it by Popper and others'

1961   Delivers Trevelyan lectures – published as *What is History?* his most popular book (it went on to sell over 250,000 copies) and possibly most influential. Attacked amongst other things for its 'relativism', belief that history should move closer to the social sciences and notion of progress, it remains the most read book on the practice of history in the English language

1964   Publication of *Socialism In One Country, 1924–1926, Volume 3*

1966   Marries Betty Behrens

1967   Isaac Deutscher dies: Carr writes appreciation in *Cambridge Review*.

1969   Publication of *1917: Before and After*

1969   Publication (with Bob Davies) of *Foundations of a Planned Economy 1926–1929, Volume 1, parts 1 and 2.*

1971   Publication of *Foundations of a Planned Economy 1926–1929, Volume 2* Carr notes that whereas Volume 1 dealing with the economics was a 'study of achievements', Volume 2 dealing with the politics is a study of the 'costs' 'In action,' he notes, 'Stalin exploited the worker as mercilessly and as contemptuously as he exploited the peasant'. And he concluded: 'Seldom perhaps in history has so monstrous a price been paid for so monumental an achievement'

1976   Publication of *Foundations of a Planned Economy 1926–1929, Volume 3* Parts 1 and 2. Carr admits that 'the third volume has . . . swelled far beyond my original intention and expectation'

1978   Publication of *Foundations of a Planned Economy 1926–1929, Volume 3* Part 3. Carr writes upon completion of his work: 'My first impression on sitting down to write the preface to this final volume of the *History of the Soviet Russia*, is one of thankful relief that I have been able to finish the project on which I embarked thirty years ago. Had I realized at that time the formidable dimensions of the task, I might not have been rash enough to undertake it . . . I am not sure exactly what I envisaged when I began to research and write. But it was something far smaller and more restricted in scope than what has emerged'

1979   Publication of *The Russian Revolution from Lenin to Stalin, 1917–1929*
1980   Publication of *From Napoleon to Stalin and Other Essays*
1982   4 November, Carr dies
1982   Posthumous publication of *The Twilight Of the Comintern, 1930–1935*
1983   Posthumous publication of *The Comintern and the Spanish Civil War*
1987   Publication of second Penguin edition of *What is History* with a new
        introduction by Bob Davies

Appendix 2
Papers of E.H. Carr, 1892–1982

These papers were presented to the University of Birmingham in the 1980s and were acquired from several different sources, including John H. Carr (E.H. Carr's son), the late Tamara Deutscher, Brian Pearce, R.W. Davies and Jonathan Haslam (then a lecturer in the University's Department of Political Science and International Studies but now a Fellow of Corpus Christi, Cambridge). The deposit agreement included a time restriction on access to and the use of these papers, and consequently the collection was not made immediately available for research. The papers were initially housed in the Baykov Library in the University's Centre for Russian and East European Studies but have been subsequently transferred to Special Collections in the Main Library, and it was only in 1998 and 1999, following the appointment of an archivist, that substantial progress has been made in the work of sorting and cataloguing them. It is hoped that the brief description below will provide an introduction to the scope and content of the collection.

The papers document many aspects of Carr's long and varied life and include material relating to his schooling and employment as a civil servant and also to his multi-faceted career as a biographer, journalist, critic, essayist and historian. The papers relating to his education, for example, include some of his essays and the Latin oration which he gave as head monitor of Merchant Taylors School in London; letters relating to the award of scholarships at Trinity College, Cambridge; and printed copies of the Latin poem and epigram and Greek verse translation for which he won prizes while at Trinity. Although there is little material relating to the nature of his work as a civil servant, the official documents relating to his appointment as a temporary clerk in the Foreign Office in 1916 and his subsequent preferments, rising to the position of First Secretary in the Diplomatic Service in 1933, have survived.

The papers also include what appears to be a comprehensive collection of very many contributions of book reviews and short articles of comment published principally in the *Spectator*, *Fortnightly*, *Christian Science Monitor*, *Slavonic Review* and *The Times Literary Supplement* but also in *The Times* and *The Sunday Times*. They were written over a span of five decades from 1929 to 1978 and for the period 1929–51 are accompanied by chronological listings compiled by Carr himself. In 1939 alone, for example, Carr published in excess of 70 such reviews and notes. From 1945, Carr appears largely to have restricted his contributions to *The Times Literary Supplement*, and these included a series of front page articles published between 1950 and 1963. The subject matter of these reflect Carr's wide-ranging interests in and breadth of knowledge of Russian culture, European and Soviet history, and the politics and international relations of the twentieth century. These are largely preserved in the form of cuttings from 1936; prior to that they are an admixture of manuscripts and typescripts as well as cuttings.

Carr's papers also include scripts of some unpublished manuscripts, lectures and radio broadcasts which he gave from the late 1930s to the 1950s. These include scripts of papers delivered at meetings of the Royal Institute of International Affairs at Chatham House to which Carr was invited as Professor of International Relations at University College, Aberystwyth: 'Impressions of a visit to Russia and Germany' (1937), 'What are we fighting for?' (1940) and 'The post-war world: some pointers towards reconstruction' (1940). The broadcast scripts include a series of weekly political/news talks (some manuscript, some typescript), given between April and September 1940, and cuttings of various broadcast talks and discussions, as published in *The Listener* including a series of six on 'The New Society' (1951) and others on British foreign policy in 1946.

The most extensive material in the collection, however, relates to Carr's research and publications, but it should be emphasised that by no means all of his books and articles are represented. The raw research material includes typescript and manuscript notes and jottings, copies and transcripts of documents, copies of relevant published articles, drafts and reworkings of texts and correspondence with other scholars. There is a quantity of material relating, for example, to parts of his monumental 14-volume *A History of Soviet Russia* on which he was engaged for nearly 40 years; and to *The Twilight of Comintern 1930–1935* published in 1982. The papers relating to the latter include notes and correspondence of Tamara Deutscher, who worked as a researcher for Carr for many years and who posthumously published Carr's last manuscript, *The Comintern and the Spanish Civil War* in 1983. The material relating to *The Romantic Exiles* (first published in 1933) includes Carr's transcripts of more than 100 letters, written between 1848 and 1851, by Alexander Herzen (1812–70, Russian radical journalist) to George Herwegh (1817–75), German revolutionary and political poet) and Emma, his wife (the originals of which were made available to Carr by Max Herwegh, eldest son of the poet and are now deposited in the British Library). The collection also includes detailed notes made by Carr for a planned new edition of *What is History?* (first published in 1961); and a small amount of correspondence relating to his research for the biography of *Michael Bakunin* which was published in 1937.

There are also proofs and annotated published texts for some of his publications. These include bound corrected second proofs of *The Bolshevik Revolution. 1917–23, volumes 1–3* (1950–53); page proofs with corrections of *Foundations of a Planned Economy, 1926–29, volume 2* (1971); annotated copies of *Socialism in One Country, 1924–26 volume 3, parts 1 and 2* (1964), for a possible revision; and corrected proofs of *From Napoleon to Stalin* (1980). Also of interest is a typescript draft of chapters of another incomplete volume about the Comintern in the period 1935–38, which were not included in *The Comintern and the Spanish Civil War*.

Some research use has already been made of the papers, most notably by R.W. Davies (with whom Carr collaborated in the writing of *Foundations of a Planned Economy, 1926–29, volume 1* (1969) for the second edition of *What is History?* which was published in 1986, by Charles Jones in the research for his book, *Carr on International Relations* (Cambridge, 1998) and by Michael Cox for his research on *E.H. Carr: A Critical Appraisal* when working on this volume. Interest in the archive has also recently been expressed by other researchers relating, for example, to Carr's understanding of nationalism. It is hoped that a detailed catalogue will be made available soon and that, as a result, the collection will become much more accessible to scholars.

Index

The Aberystwyth Papers: International Politics 1919–1969 (1972)   64
Acton, Edward   7
Acton, Lord   228
Angell, Norman   7, 165–71, 174–6, 184, 185, 186, 191–3
and *The Great Illusion* (1910)   185
Aristotle   289
Arnold, T.W.   207
The Folklore of Capitalism (1941)   207–8
Arnold-Foster, W.   40, 41, 42, 43, 45, 55, 175
Astor, John   76

Bailey, Stanley   41
Barraclough, Geoffrey   41
Barrington-Ward, Robert   68, 72, 73, 76, 77, 83
Beaverbrook, Max (Lord)   74, 76
Behrens, Betty   27
Bentham, Jeremy   268
Berdyaev, Nicolas
The End of Our Time (1933)   210
Berlin, Isaiah (Sir)   3, 5, 7, 10, 28, 32, 132, 133, 146, 284, 293
Bevin, Ernest   68, 76, 80, 81, 82, 83
Bloch, Ernst   292
Bloch, Marc   287
The Historian's Craft (1953)   283
Boffa, Guiseppe   120
Booth, Ken   217, 221, 240
Bosanquet, Bernard   190
Bowes-Lyon, David   68
Bracken, Brendan   76
Braudel, Fernand   324, 325
Brogan, D.W.   5, 40
Bukharin, Nikolai   5, 6, 91, 241
Bull, Hedley   7, 203, 221, 224, 225, 227, 249, 250
Burnham, James
The Managerial Revolution (1941)   209
Butterfield, Herbert (Sir)   3, 5, 41, 42, 63
Butler, Nicholas Murray   190
Brzezinski, Zbigniew   4

Cadogan, Alexander (Lord)   209
Carr, E.H. (Chair of International Politics, Aberystwyth)   ix
Carr, Edward Hallett (1892–1982)
Aberystwyth (and The Woodrow Wilson Chair)   4, 13, 27, 36–67, 93, 129, 185, 200, 201, 211, 217, 220–1
appeasement   xviii–xix, 4, 51, 68–9, 91, 102, 184, 202, 204, 227, 263
'Autobiography' (1980)   xiii–xxii, 100, 102
The A.B.C. of Communism (Editor's Introduction, 1969)   263, 264, 265, 272–3, 275
Bolshevik Revolution   xv, 10–11, 22–3, 93, 94, 111, 114, 115, 118, 121, 149–50, 263, 269
Britain: A Study of Foreign Policy (1939)   52, 203, 204
British communists   110
British power   9–10, 33, 73–4, 77–8
Cold War   9–12, 14, 32, 76, 82–3, 104–5, 134–5, 145–61, 271–2
collapse of Soviet communism   11–12, 34, 106–7, 118–21, 140–2, 157–8, 275
The Comintern and the Spanish Civil War (1983)   11, 270
Conditions of Peace (1942)   xix, 7, 8, 28, 56, 70, 185, 199, 206–8
critics   4–5, 7–11, 30, 32, 75–7, 91, 137–40, 145, 166–77, 223–5
critical theory   12, 234–5, 323
democracy   189, 330
Dostoevsky, 1821–1881 (1931)   xvi–xvii, 4, 92, 258
family background   xiii–xiv, 13, 21–2, 93–4
Foreign Office   xv, xvi, 4–7, 22–7, 41, 80–1, 94, 127, 200, 203, 219, 296
free trade   xiv, xvii, 189, 224
The Future of Nations (1941)   236, 238
Germany   9, 23, 26–7, 94, 102–3, 247, 273

Carr, Edward Hallett – *continued*
  *German–Soviet Relations between the
    Two World Wars* (1952)   114
  history   5, 15–16, 33, 285–91, 319,
    322–36
  historian   29–32, 137, 283–303,
    304–21
  A History of Soviet Russia (1950–1978:
    14 vols)   2–3, 7, 29, 31, 33,
    61–2, 91, 103, 109–10, 111, 115,
    117, 118, 119, 120, 121, 129,
    132, 258, 259, 269, 270, 298,
    326
  international relations (IR)   14–15,
    177–81, 198–216, 217–33,
    245–51, 323–34
  *International Relations Since the Peace
    Treaties* (1937)   52
    reissued as *International Relations
    Between the Two World Wars
    1919–1939* (1947)   271
  Karl Marx: A Study of Fanaticism
    (1934)   xviii, 4, 258, 260, 262,
    264, 266, 267, 268, 272, 275
  liberalism   2, 4, 199, 200, 201,
    219, 220
  The Listener   7
Marx, Karl   xv, xvii–xviii, 6, 92, 94,
    100, 186, 190, 200–1, 261,
    262, 330
Marxism   xviii, xx, xxi, 6, 7, 10, 94,
    100, 110, 113–17, 120, 121, 139,
    142, 152–4, 201, 206, 219, 224,
    229, 234, 235, 239–45, 319
'Marxist'   2, 6, 24, 128, 140, 154,
    159, 244, 245, 254, 274, 277,
    310, 312, 318, 329
Michael Bakunin (1937)   xvii, 4, 6,
    28, 34, 52, 92, 135, 151, 155,
    258, 265, 267
Nationalism and After (1945)   xix, 8,
    70, 114, 235, 241, 258, 327
nationalism and self-determination
    (small nations)   9, 74–5, 193,
    234–57, 261, 274
New Economic Policy (NEP)   114–15
The New Left Review (interview
    1978)   8, 11, 61, 146,
    274, 275
The New Society (1951)   xxi, 7, 8,
    103, 326
planning   xviii, 12, 73–4, 103–4,
    189, 199–200, 202, 205–12, 246,
    262, 263, 295, 298, 328

political views   32, 105, 146,
    151–2, 155
post-WWII international order
    74–5, 74–83, 77–80, 104
progress   291–5, 309–11, 312
Public Opinion as a Safeguard for Peace
    (1937)   50–2
realism   92, 114, 187, 191–3, 198–9,
    220–5, 228–9, 235, 239–45,
    260–1, 276, 322, 331–4
'Red Professor at Printing House
    Square'   68
relativism   xiv, xvii, 187–8, 227–8,
    312, 320
revolution   15, 138, 258–79
Riga   xvi, 23–4, 94–5, 185, 200
The Romantic Exiles (1933)   xvi–xvii,
    4, 28, 258, 264, 265, 266,
    267–8, 272
*The Russian Revolution from Lenin to
    Stalin* (1979)   118
*The Soviet Impact on the Western
    World* (1946)   61, 104, 209–10,
    247, 262, 275
Soviet Union (USSR)   xviii–xx, 2,
    5–6, 9, 11, 13, 25–7, 34, 55, 73,
    74, 91–108, 136–7, 147–8, 200,
    209–10
Soviet writings on   109–24, 127
The Times   xix, 1, 6, 7, 28–9, 53, 55,
    57–8, 61, 68–87, 101, 126,
    209, 217
Trevelyan lectures (*What is
    History?*)   3
The Twenty Years' Crisis (1939)   xix,
    2, 14, 27, 52–3, 62, 69, 70, 82,
    110, 165–97, 198–9, 201, 202,
    217–18, 220–9, 235–6, 250, 251,
    258, 260, 263, 264, 268–9, 270,
    273, 283, 322
Twilight of the Comintern: 1930–1935
    (1982)   11, 31, 270
United States   9–10, 77, 78, 79
utopia (utopianism)   xix, 6, 28, 73,
    92, 127, 137, 181, 189–91,
    198–9, 221–3, 225–9, 240, 244,
    250, 252, 259, 264–8
visit to Soviet Russia (1937)   101
What is History? (1961)   xxi, 3–4, 8,
    14, 106, 110, 132, 153, 227–8,
    258, 259, 261, 266, 272,
    283–303, 304–21
world depression   24–5, 96
World War I   xiv–xv, 22

World War II xix–xx, 28–9, 53–61,
69–78

Carr, John ix

Cecil, Robert (Lord) 40, 55, 175, 183,
186, 190

Chamberlain, Neville 26, 55, 69, 70,
175, 178, 184, 203, 204

Chamberlin, W.H.
The Russian Revolution, 1917–1921
(1935) 98
*A False Utopia: Collectivism in Theory
and Practice* (1937) 102

Chatham House (Royal Institute of
International Affairs) 55, 102

Chernik, Violetta 114–18

Christian Science Monitor 93

Churchill, W. 7, 28, 68, 76, 82

C.I.A. (Central Intelligence
Agency) 141, 151

Cockatt, Richard 71

Cobban, Alfred 41

Cohen, Stephen 6, 119

Cold War xx, 5, 125–6, 128, 134, 135,
137, 147–8, 200, 210, 270–2

Cole, Robert 69

Collingwood, R.G. 30, 285–6, 289,
291, 297, 309, 313, 324, 325
The Idea of History (1946)

Colville, Jock 76

Cox, Michael 145

Cox, Robert 217, 322, 323

Critique 156

Croce, B. 325

Crossman, Richard 165, 174

Daily Express 70
Daily Herald 70
Daily Telegraph 70
Daily Worker 28, 68

Davies, David of Llandinam (Lord)
vii, 13, 36–47, 49, 55–62,
19, 219
see Aberystwyth
Force (1934) 53
The Problem of the Twentieth Century
(1938) 38

Davies, Gwendoline 37

Davies, Margaret 37

Davies, R.W. 4, 109, 110, 117,
153, 318
*Foundations of a Planned Economy
Vol. 1* (1969) 91, 120

Dawson, Geoffrey 70, 71

Dehio, Ludwig 323

Derrida, Jacques 228

Deutscher, Issac 3, 6, 10, 14, 31, 32,
125–44, 146, 148, 153, 156, 158,
159, 160, 260, 277
Stalin (1949) 128, 130–1
Soviet Trade Unions (1950) 130
The Prophet Armed (1954) 132
The Unfinished Revolution (1967)
128, 133, 140
Heretics and Renegades (1955;
1969) 133
Lenin's Childhood (1970) 133–4
Russia after Stalin (1953) 136
*Mr E.H. Carr as Historian of Soviet
Russia* (1955) 138
The Great Contest (1960) 148

Deutscher, Tamara 11, 23, 31, 125,
127, 130, 133

Dewey, John 190

Drucker, Peter
The End of Economic Man
(1939) 206

Duguit, Leon 190

Duke of Devonshire 68

Eden, Anthony 77

Elibanks, Lord 68

Ellis, E.L. 63

Elton, Geoffrey 3, 7, 304, 305,
306, 307
The Practice of History (1967) 305

Encounter 5, 150, 155

The English School 252

Evans, Ifor L. 39, 41–6, 53–4, 59–60,
62–3

Evans, Richard 12

Fainsod, Merle 11

Falk, Richard 240

Figes, Orlando 158–9

Forde, Daryll 62, 64

Forde, Joyce (Mrs) 62

Fortnightly Review 93

Foster, Alan 72

Fourth International 127

Fox, W.T.R. 184

Frank, Pierre 127

Frankfurt School 235, 252, 299, 319

Friedlander, Lilian (Mrs Vranek)
48–9, 53

Galbraith, J.K. 34

Geffler, Mikhail 112

Geller, Mikhail 120

Gilpin, Robert　217
Gorbachev, Mikhail　110
Graham, Ronald (Sir)　39
Gramsci, Antonio　323
Greene, Jerome　39, 41, 60
Greenwood, Sean　81

Halifax, Lord　70–1, 74, 184, 203
Hallett, John (pseud. E.H. Carr)　93
Haslam, Jonathan　135, 145, 220
Hayek, F.A　182–3, 208–9, 212
　The Road to Serfdom (1944)　103, 208
Healey, Denis　40, 63
Herbert, Sydney　39, 41, 48
Herodotus　xiv, 33
Herriot, Edward　99
Herzen, Alexander　xiv, xvi, 6, 265,
　266, 277
Hindus, Maurice　96–7, 98–9
　Red Bread (1931)　96
Hitler, Adolf　26, 70, 73, 74, 75, 102,
　171, 174, 178, 184, 191, 193
Hoare, Samuel (Sir)　71
Hobbes　260
　Leviathan　174
Hobsbawm, Eric　270
Hoffmann, Stanley　220
Housman, A.E.　xiv, 6, 30
Hughes, Howard　55

Ilin, M.
　Moscow has a Plan: a Soviet Primer
　　(1931)　97–8

John, Ieuan　61
Johnson, Whittle　225
Joll, James　1
Jones, Charles　202, 225
Jones, Thomas　60

Kant, Immanuel　222
Kaufman R.G.　247
Kennan, George F.　10, 24, 276–7
Keynes, John Maynard (Keynsianism)
　21, 113, 185, 237, 264
Knutsen, T.L.　226

La Capra, Dominic　305, 306
Labedz, L.　7, 134, 149, 150, 151, 154
　see Survey
Lauterpact, Hersch　190
Lawton, Lancelot
　Economic History of Soviet Russia
　　(1932)　98

League of Nations　13, 22–3, 37,
　46–7, 175, 178, 190, 200–1,
　271
League of Nations Union (L.N.U.)　39,
　47, 51, 175, 186, 271
Lenin, V.I.　xv, xviii, 10, 11, 22, 101,
　105, 128, 130, 133–4, 139, 159,
　241, 247, 266, 269, 296
Linklater, Andrew　217
Lippmann, Walter
　The Good Society　209
Lloyd George, David　xiv, xv, 24,
　37, 190
　The London Review of Books　7
Lyons, Eugene
　Assignment in Utopia (1937)　102

McCallum R.B.　56
McCarthyism　32
McClelland, Gregor
　*Marxism and the Methodologies of
　　History* (1981)　306
McDonald, Iverach　71
Macartney, C.A.　39, 41, 42
Machiavelli (Machiavellianism)　2,
　27, 62, 179, 199, 203, 204, 213,
　260, 332
Mannheim, Karl　27, 167, 186, 201–3,
　209, 225
　Ideology and Utopia (1936)　xviii,
　　27, 201
Manning, Charles　43, 45, 53, 61, 63
Martin, Kingsley　40
　Marxism Today　113
Marwick, Arthur　7
Maude, Aylmer
　Life of Tolstoy (1930)　96
Meinecke, Friedrich　323
Melman, Seymour　104
Mill, J.S.　296
Millar, Jack　150
　see Soviet Studies
Mirsky, Dmitri　92
Mitrany, David　39, 41, 198, 206
Morgenthau H.J.　40, 63, 114, 166,
　217, 225, 328–9
Moseley, Oswald　76
Murphy, Craig　323
Murray, Gilbert　40–3, 46, 58,
　175, 191

Namier, Lewis　23, 27, 146, 261
Nechaev, Sergei　265, 267
Neiman, Abram　112–14

Nenarokov, Al'bert 119–20
New Left 33
The New Republic 131
New Left Review 138
Nicholson, Harold 26
Niebuhr, Reinhold
   Moral Man and Immoral Society 27
Nitze, Paul 28
Noel-Baker, Philip 43, 51, 55, 166
Nove, Alec 3, 149, 150, 155, 156, 157

Olegina, Irina 111–12, 121
Orwell, George 137

Pipes, R. 10, 12, 30, 31, 120, 149–50, 154, 155
Pisarev, Dimitry 266
Polanyi, Karl 323
Popper, Karl (Sir) 3, 5, 113, 132, 284, 293
Porter, Roy
   Myths of the English (1992) 307
postmodernism (postmodernists) 305, 318, 319

Rhodes, Cecil 190
Roosevelt, Theodore 190
Rosdolsky, Roman 139–40
Ross, Graham 81
Routh, Dennis 53
Ruggie, John 327

Salter, Arthur (Sir) 40, 43, 55
Schmitt, Carl 183
Schapiro, Leonard 8, 11, 151
Schlesinger, Rudolph 150
   see *Soviet Studies*
Schuman, Frederick 190
Segal, Louis 99
Seton-Watson, Hugh 8, 53, 54, 61
   Eastern Europe Between the Wars, 1918–1941 (1945) 54
Seton-Watson, R.W. 165, 172–3, 181
Shaw, Bernard 99
Simmons, Ernest 137
Singer, Daniel 130
Skocpol, Theda
   States and Social Revolutions (1979) 264
Smith, Michael Joseph 220–1
Solzhenitsyn, Alexander 210
Sorel, Albert 260
Soviet Studies 138, 150

The Spectator 93
Stalin J.V. (Stalinism) 3, 5–6, 25, 27, 29, 77, 91, 101, 104, 105, 119, 134, 135, 136, 137, 139, 148, 151, 152, 153, 264, 277, 297
Stebbing, Susan 7, 165, 178–81, 182, 183, 189
Stone, Norman 3, 7–8, 12, 134, 149
Street, Clarence 198
Survey 150

Taylor, A.J.P. 1, 8, 91
Thatcher, Margaret 32
Thompson, E.P. 319
   The Making of the English Working Class (1963) 272
Thucydides 326, 328
Times Literary Supplement 30, 93, 130, 131, 132, 150, 155, 225
Tosh, John 306–7
Toynbee, Arnold 40, 165, 168, 172, 173–4, 181, 183, 184, 186, 284
Trevor-Roper, Hugh (Lord) 5, 284
Trotsky, L. 6, 10, 119, 127, 134, 139, 140, 155, 277
   My Life (1930) 96
   History of the Russian Revolution (1932–1933) 98
Trotskyism 127

United Nations Organization 80

Vansittart, Robert 26
Versailles Peace Treaty xix, 22–3, 74, 94, 185, 224
Vico, Giambattista 324
Vincent, R.J. 224
Vranek, Jiri 48

Wales 46–8, 60
Waltz, Ken 244, 328
Webb, Beatrice and Sydney 27
   Soviet Communism: a New Civilization? (1935) 99
Webster, Charles (Sir) 39, 41, 48, 50, 58, 59, 60
Wells, H.G. 198
White, Hayden 306, 319
Wight, Martin 53, 204, 224
Wiles, Peter 104
Wilson, Woodrow (Wilsonianism) 13, 174, 179, 183, 193, 203, 204, 213, 222

Wolfe, Bertram D.   31
Woolf, Leonard   7, 165, 176, 178,
    182, 183, 185, 186, 189, 191,
    193, 225

Zimmern, Alfred (Sir)   41, 43, 48, 60, 61,
    62, 165, 166, 167, 171–2, 181, 184,
    186, 187, 191, 198, 212, 219, 249
Zweig, Stefan   27